WOMAN OF TWO WORLDS

KAREN WILLS

Karen Wills

Printed Worldwide
First Printing 2024
First Edition 2024

ISBN: 979-8303236080

10 9 8 7 6 5 4 3 2 1

Interior Book Design by Walt's Book Design
www.waltsbookdesign.com

WOMAN OF TWO WORLDS

Dedication

To Jerry, my love and mainstay, and to my father Bernt Lloyd Wills who believed humanity could be, and should be a fellowship. He instilled that belief in me and generations of his students. I thank him.

Acknowledgements

Thank you to the helpers including my family. I'm also grateful to Janice Goodison, Bonnie Smith, Carla Mettling, Karen Feather, Cindy Mish, and to the staff of the George C. Ruhle Library at Glacier National Park Headquarters. As always, I thank my love, Jerry.

INTRODUCTION

The Twentieth Century's arrival brought change to the American West. The era of Indian Wars, open range, and homesteaders like Nora and Jim Li in this story passed into the romance of legend. Their children and grandchildren became citizens of a nation where tribes like the Blackfeet lived on reservations. For others, ranching or farming expanded to urban industry. Wealth for some increased along with appreciation of the arts, and the entire United States seemed to move at a faster pace. Concern for preserving the natural beauty of places like Glacier National Park fired visions leading to engineering feats that encouraged tourists to travel to the wonders of their own country.

The Great War in Europe led to turmoil in America as it destroyed lives in incomprehensible numbers. Citizens turned wary, ill at ease, and full of dissent. Most in the United States wanted to stay out of war. But an understanding that the nation had transformed into a global presence took hold. Americans accepted the responsibility to protect democracy even if it meant sacrifice.

This is what happened within one Montana family.

Chapter One

State of Montana

August 1906

Since early morning Dawn had ridden double on the gray gelding behind Michael, her arms clamped around his waist, Stiff-necked from looking to the side, she leaned back, tipping her head and staring into a white-blue sky, so bright it brought tears. She closed her eyes, leaned forward, and rolled her forehead against the hard muscles and knobby vertebrae of Michael's upper back. She fell into a reverie, trying to understand how life at home went awry to the point that they'd eloped.

At sixteen her form had the symmetry, curves, and planes of a girl on the cusp of true womanhood. Her hair and eyes shone like black onyx. Sweet Grass, Dawn's mother, had been a full-blood Blackfeet

Dawn grew up knowing only the North Fork of Montana's Flathead River with its dark, old-growth forests, lush meadows, pines pushing nearly to the sky before yielding to the granite spires of the Rockies. Dawn already missed the ranch. Its owners, Irish Nora and Chinese Jim Li had been happy to raise her at her father Beartracks request. After her mother Sweet Grass died Beartracks could not fill his natural role as father. Feckless and irresponsible, all Beartracks could do was wander the deep wilderness by himself.

Mama Nora often said that owning land meant being certain of a safe place in this world. With land, a free human was the equal of royalty. Dawn knew how hard her parents worked to build and keep the ranch. She shuddered at the thought that she and Michael, Nora's natural son, might never go back. Evening Star Ranch meant love and safety. Mama Nora and Papa Jim must be heartbroken that Michael, Dawn with him, rode off without even saying goodbye. It seemed heartless that Michael would just abandon them to the hard work that Evening Star Ranch demanded.

Dawn tended to be reticent, but Michael liked to talk. He was muscular with tawny hair that caught the sun and bleached in summer. An optimist, he could sometimes be rigid to the point of simplicity. He tended to see things as right or wrong. Capable of holding deep grudges. In spite of such flaws he could be funny. Strangers liked him, and he formed friendships with an ease that baffled Dawn. At times she feared he might not be ready to make sound decisions as required by the head of a family.

The unyielding wind blew hot and dry, rushing the earthy scent of prairie straight at the riders. Was the world on the Eastern Front always this harsh and arid?

The country altered as they rode east after Marias Pass, becoming more open, showing hints of prairie that would spread to a vastness she'd never seen. She yearned for the timber-bound wilderness of her childhood. But its familiar beauty had disappeared behind her.

Michael had decided to leave their family ranch four days ago, furious with his mother for lying to him about the real identity of the father he'd never known. He'd killed that vicious stranger when he found the man trying to kill Jim. Outrage that Michael himself had unknowingly killed his natural father consumed him. Dawn tried to persuade Michael that his mother only loved and wanted to protect him from hard truths. Michael, shocked and resentful, still wouldn't listen.

Would she ever see their folks at Evening Star again?

Despite her guilt at leaving Mama Nora and Papa Jim, she'd been in love with Michael since she was fourteen. She insisted he take her with him when he decided to ride off. She believed with all her sixteen-year-old heart that life without him would be impossible.

As the couple rode east the mountains took on a sun baked look, wind-scoured as if swept bare by a huge rough hand. Dawn's skin felt abraded and so did her heart. She flicked her tongue over cracked lips even though she knew doing that only made them worse. She kept on as she muttered, "This is an inferno."

As Michael and Dawn descended the Rockies' Eastern Front, water in dwindling ponds rippled and bumped against the knees of impassive moose. Unperturbed geese and ducks drifted on the same shining surfaces. Soon, thick colonies of aspen clattered protesting leaves as wind gusts raked them. Young pines struggled to grow upright.

After arduous hours, the couple emerged into vast swales of amber and yellowish-brown prairie with patches of olive green, golden orange and sulfuric white. Mountains, still prominent but hazed purple, rose for miles behind them and off to their left. Open prairie ahead promised nothing—no more water, no shelter, no cooling shade. Dawn's backside chafed against the saddle's leather skirt. Her thighs burned and stung, blistered from rubbing against the saddle skirts and the sweat-stained saddle blanket for four days.

Sighing, she gave up trying for a comfortable position, put her hands on Michael's shoulders, and pushed herself up to peer ahead, then to each side. She slumped against his straight back again. How she hoped love for Michael would overcome her anxiety and homesickness.

Michael guided the gray as it followed a road, really little more than an old buffalo trail, said to lead to the settlement of Midvale. Beyond Midvale lay Browning, the Indian agency town in the country of the Blackfeet. Michael hoped to find work on one of the ranches bordering the reservation. But he'd promised her they'd marry in Midvale first. She hoped this would mean the beginning of happiness.

She shifted again, tucking her wrinkled skirt between her legs and the saddle when Michael announced, "There it is! Midvale!" After a pause he added in a let-down tone, "Not much to it, is there? Just a little siding for the Great Northern Railroad."

She smoothed her skirt down and tightened her hold around him. They rode into a shallow draw that was puffed up and scratchy from wild roses, then through a ravine with a shallow creek trickling through it. They entered Midvale, and Dawn saw that Michael had been right. There wasn't much to see except a string of weathered wood structures.

But a small clapboard church sat a few hundred yards to the right of the railway tracks. Dawn recognized it from Mama Nora's endless recounting. This had to be the very Catholic Church where Mama and Papa Jim married.

Dawn nudged Michael and murmured, "The church."

Michael nodded and turned the gray toward it. The gelding picked his way across rails and ties. Dawn scrutinized the building as they moved closer. They'd lived far from any church. And Mama had described her Catholic God as so judgmental and commanding. How strange that He would live in such a small structure. Dawn wondered about the priests and nuns devoted to Him. What were they really like? Fierce and strict? Making people do things in order to be forgiven for past sins?

Papa Jim told of a more gentle approach to spirituality learned in his Taoist and Buddhist upbringing in China. How could religion be seen so differently between two good people? `Dawn once asked Mama whether Papa Jim would go to hell since he wasn't even a Christian. Mama replied that Jim was the best man she'd ever known, and she trusted God to see his goodness, too.

Dawn hoped someday she'd know what her Blackfeet relatives believed. Had they all converted? Some people called them heathens, but they must have ideas about how to worship. Her father Beartracks didn't claim any religious faith and refused to talk about anything sacred. He only said the Creator was vast and mysterious.

The church wore long-dulled brown paint. But bright Black-eyed-Susans, wild roses, and daisies splashed over straw-stiff prairie grass to line the stone path to the door. Michael brought the sweating gray to a stop, dismounted, and led the horse to a hitching post beside the church. Dawn swung a leg, painful enough for her not to care that she was being immodest, over the gelding's back, then reached for Michael to lift her down. She winced as she stood.

"All right?" He frowned in concern.

"Yes. Just sore from all that time riding such a broad-backed horse."

"I'm sorry. I'll make it up to you, I promise." He shoved his hat back.

Dawn looked into his worried face. She brushed aside the light, reddish-brown hair that fell across his forehead. "I'll be fine." She smoothed out her rumpled blue cotton skirt and tucked back strands that had escaped the long black braid hanging down her back. She tried to ignore the unnerving, empty prairie facing her and made an effort to sound enthusiastic as she said, "Let's go in."

"Yes." Michael offered his arm. She accepted it and he shot her that irresistible grin of his. She didn't have to force her answering smile. The wait to marry was finally over. As they approached the little frame building, Dawn's mouth felt dry from the sudden return of nervousness. She entered this small church with a sense of destiny. Nothing would ever be the same.

But what then would it be? How would her life be different? Things had taken such a turn and all so fast and unexpected.

Michael, having spent his first fifteen years in the mostly Irish mining town of Butte, Montana, would feel more at ease entering a Catholic church than she did. Dawn found peace among her own sacred places in the natural world surrounding Evening Star Ranch. For her, nature radiated its own divinity.

Mama Nora and Papa Jim had sheltered her, each having known harsh prejudice visited on unwanted immigrants and nonwhites in the greater world. Dawn's beauty, they warned, couldn't protect a mixed blood. She knew a few neighboring settlers like the Hogan's, who'd become like family. Michael sought out Nora after being orphaned for the second time in his life by the deaths of the Irish couple Nora had given him to on the night of his birth.

Dawn watched as Michael tested the church door. Finding it unlocked he stepped inside, and she followed. The walls were the white of snow and purity, the windows open to the sunny day. Dawn stayed close behind Michael. Each made the sign of the cross before they moved toward the altar, its crucifix frozen in a grimace of agony.

An old priest who resembled some gnome or leprechaun of a fable stepped from behind that altar. His skin had been burned to nearly as brown as the Blackfeet who might be among his parishioners. He moved with agility for a man advanced in age. He squinted at them, but his blue eyes and warm smile seemed joyous. They'd come into his church, and he welcomed them.

"Young people?" he asked, pushing thick round glasses higher up the bridge of his nose and peering down the center aisle. "What can I do for you, my children?"

"You can marry us, Father, if you would." Michael reached forward to shake the man's mottled hand.

"Well, come and sit with me and we'll see what's to be done. I'm Father John. And you are?" He pulled a nearby chair to sit in front of them in a front pew.

"I'm Michael Larkin. This is my fiancée, Dawn Benton. We've come from over by the North Fork of the Flathead River, hoping to start married life working for one of the ranches around Midvale."

The old priest leaned forward. "How old are you? Each of you."

Michael didn't hesitate. "Eighteen. We're both eighteen, Father. We're young, but we've known each other a few years. There could never be another for either Dawn or me."

Dawn tried not to show amazement or disapproval at Michael's lie. He was almost eighteen, but she had close to two years to wait. Did the law say she had to be eighteen? Was it a sin to lie to the old Father? Would the marriage be real? Would Mama's God punish Michael for lying right inside this Catholic Church? Perhaps this was the very Priest who'd married Mama and Papa Jim. Had Mama called him Father John when she told the wedding story? Dawn felt confused. A cloud seemed to dim the flood of sunlight coming through the windows.

But the two men had moved past the subject of age like horses flicking away flies with their tails. Dawn wondered if she should be concerned, or didn't the law matter?

"And your parents?" the Father asked.

Michael smiled. "They've known of our wish to marry for some time now. They expect us to and don't object."

Dawn swallowed hard, hoping the Priest didn't notice her slight flinch. In fact, Mama Nora and Papa Jim had insisted the sweethearts wait at least another year, but everything had changed in that terrible afternoon when Michael learned the truth about the man he shot.

"Then we shall marry you today." Father John spoke in a brisk manner. "And I suggest you go to the Flowers' Ranch, Dan and Eleanor Flowers' spread. They're hiring ranch hands and I happen to know that Eleanor is looking for a girl to replace her maid. That young woman had the temerity to marry and leave Flowers' employ to start her own life. It's good for dear Eleanor to have her plans upset now and then. God must have thought so, too."

Michael stood up. "Thank you, Father. I appreciate the help."

The old man rose with knee-popping effort. "I'll fetch my housekeeper for a witness. We must have one other. Blisters Coggin the grave digger has been at work in our little cemetery. He'll do well enough.

"It is well for us to have a marriage this week. Unfortunately, two of our congregation passed to the Lord recently. The Blackfeet in my congregation have been stricken with cases of tuberculosis. A terrible disease. As if those poor souls haven't suffered enough these last years of loss and starvation."

Dawn and Michael stood at the windows watching as the Father entered a small house behind the graveyard that sloped from the church. He came out with a plump woman who stooped to gather wildflowers into a bouquet as they approached. A gangly gray-haired man with ropey muscles showing below rolled-up sleeves joined them, leaving his shovel where he'd been using it to deepen a coffin-sized rectangle in the earth.

Father John introduced Dawn and Michael to their witnesses. Dawn accepted and held the fresh-picked bouquet of Black-eyed-Susans. Her nervousness vanished as the sprightly Father began speaking the words in his Irish brogue that reminded her of Mama's. Being married in the little church where Mama Nora and Papa Jim had been joined in matrimony made her feel as if they were here with her. Mama would like it that they had the wedding in the place where she'd been so happy to finally become Jim Li's legal wife. Someday Dawn would tell her. Someday Michael would find it in his outraged young heart to be forgiving. Then everything would be the same as it had always been at the Evening Star ranch.

After Father John declared Dawn and Michael married, they kissed. They kissed twice more. The Priest raised his eyebrows, but then smiled at such youthful passion. “May you be blessed with children,” he added to his other good wishes.

The Father entered the required information about them and the day’s date into the Parish Register. He told them he’d forward the information on for a marriage license when the formation of a county around Midvale became official. The county seat would likely be the town of Cut Bank to the east. He expected that change to be established within a year. For time being, the parish records would do to show proof of their marriage.

Dawn walked out of the church in a daze. Her life had altered so in just a few short days. She’d become Mrs. Michael Larkin, a name she’d written in the wet earth and sand of river and creek beds since they met.

Chapter Two

By the time the couple reached the Flowers' ranch five miles east of Midvale, Dawn's spirits plummeted. The infernal wind had wreaked havoc with her appearance. She smoothed her hair and skirt as they followed the long road toward the ranch house and outbuildings. She hoped sweat hadn't made obvious rings under her armpits.

Flowers' two-story house, with its long windows, veranda, and cedar shake roof looked as though created to stand before the backdrop of the distant Rockies. "They must spend half their time repairing that roof with this weather tearing at it all the time," Michael said.

Dawn noted the aspen, cottonwood, and poplars in the yard. Two eager-looking little blonde girls peered out from behind lace curtains at the windows. Michael dismounted and held the gray's reins while she joined him. They tied their horse to a rail and, without speaking, walked close together to the front door.

From the veranda, Dawn heard strains of music. Piano music. She'd never heard such a melody. It sounded slow, almost sad, but beautiful. Michael knocked and they stepped back a little in nervous unison.

The music stopped abruptly, and in seconds Eleanor Flowers answered the door herself. There could be no doubt that the tall, slim, elegant woman was Flowers' wife. From her bearing, Eleanor knew her place to be one of authority. An awkward pause followed.

Dawn thought of the words Papa Jim and Mama often told her. "Be proud of who you are." She amazed herself by holding out her hand. "Mrs. Flowers? I'm Dawn Larkin and this is Michael, my husband. The Father who married us this morning advised us to speak to you about finding possible work here."

Eleanor studied Dawn. With the barest hesitation, and a stiff smile, she took Dawn's hand in a quick grasp, dropped it, and turned to Michael. She offered him her hand without pausing to peruse him.

"Mr. Flowers is in the corral behind the barn, Michael. You can talk to him there. Dawn, is it? Why don't you come in, and we'll talk about what I'd expect of you."

Dawn followed Eleanor into a parlor. One end contained what Dawn surmised was a grand piano. All the furniture appeared heavy and stained dark to almost black, its upholstery a deep rose. The woman gestured for Dawn to sit on a chair and took a seat across from her.

Eleanor frowned at her little girls who'd turned from the window, their eyes fixed on Dawn.

"Are you a Blackfeet?" the taller of the sisters asked.

Eleanor raised a disapproving eyebrow in the child's direction but didn't speak. Dawn guessed the woman before her wanted to hear the answer. She swallowed and began, "Yes. My mother was. She passed away when I was born."

"Were you sent away to school?" Eleanor asked. "You are well spoken."

"No. My father, Beartracks Benton, settled me with two wonderful people on the North Fork of the Flathead. They raised me."

Eleanor fixed her eyes on her daughters. "Girls, go upstairs. I want to speak to Mrs. Larkin with no interruptions."

They went. Within an hour, Dawn had convinced Mrs. Flowers that she could clean, assist with preparing food in the big kitchen, do laundry, and help with the little girls. She admitted, "Only caring for children will be new to me, but I don't imagine they'll be troublesome. They appear to be polite children."

Eleanor's face relaxed into a smile. "They are, of course. But if you do have trouble with them, don't be afraid to bring your concerns to me. I don't coddle my girls."

Dawn noted that Eleanor wore her hair in a low knot just above her collar in back. She dressed in a simple style, but there were some elegant details in the dress—pleats and tucks—and it was of better quality than calico or gingham. That spoke of money.

Eleanor explained that Dawn and Michael could have a two-room bunkhouse for their private living quarters rent free. "You'll have to clean it, though. It's been standing empty since we built the bigger one. More land and cattle mean we've needed to add hands. Your husband came at an auspicious time. You as well."

Not wanting to prolong the first conversation into awkwardness, Dawn gratefully agreed to move in and start work in three days. Eleanor Flowers gave a smile just a little less reserved than the first she'd given the newlyweds. She also wrote a note so the couple could purchase paint and other necessary items at the general store on the ranch account. Dawn wondered what Mama Nora would think of proud Eleanor.

Dawn followed Eleanor's directions and walked to the bunkhouse that stood midway between the house and barn. Just a well-built shed, its walls were solid, and four windows let in good light. It had a wood burning stove. Off the second room, an attached lean-to contained a pump, as the ranch house kitchen did. Dawn looked around her. Cobwebs hung from the unfinished ceiling and both rooms needed scrubbing, but she could make this a cozy first home. A pang struck her with the thought that she couldn't show it to Mama and Papa.

She wandered to the corral and spotted Michael in its center, breaking a big appaloosa stallion. He stayed on as a ring of men, almost all young, shouted encouragement. A hawk-faced older man who had to be Dan Flowers appraised his newest hand's abilities with expert concentration. He practically swaggered merely standing with one foot on the lower rail. Dawn stayed a distance from him to avoid having to introduce herself. She'd summoned all the confidence she could for one day.

At first, eyes fixed on Michael, Dawn didn't pay attention to the stocky cowboy next to her. Then she realized how intent the fellow appeared as he stared at her. She made herself look back with a steady gaze.

His expression slithered into a leer. "Well, looky here. You the new hired gal? I didn't think Mrs. Flowers would bring a squaw into her house with the little girls there and all. You're a half-breed though, ain't you? More of you around all the time. You're a good-looking mixed- blood. That's a fact undeniable."

Dawn focused her attention back on Michael, not acknowledging the offensive speaker who couldn't have been much older than she was. She felt relief when Michael pulled the horse up in a whirl of dust and dismounted. He saw her, waved, but turned to Dan Flowers. The rancher spoke to him, and the two shook hands. Dawn sighed in relief. They'd both been hired. She walked over to Michael.

Flowers' foreman Oscar Sims, a thin old wrangler prone to lift his hat and massage his bald head, introduced Michael to the other men. Michael in turn introduced Dawn to each. The smirking cowhand who'd stood next to her was the only one who didn't lift his hat. He addressed Michael. "So, you're a squaw man, huh, Larkin?"

Michael didn't answer for a moment. Then, "I'll let this one pass, but my wife is a lady. If you speak of or to her in any disrespectful way again, I'll show you how I learned to fight in Butte."

Sims stepped forward. "Apologize to Mrs. Larkin, Bill Baskin. Now. Or else take your gear and move on."

The smirk disappeared. The youth called Bill muttered, "Didn't mean no disrespect. Sorry if it sounded that way."

Dawn thought Baskin didn't appear sorry. Nor was his tone apologetic, but she nodded her acceptance. She didn't want trouble when they'd just been hired.

Michael nodded. "Let's go, Dawn. We start in three days. That gives us time to ride back to Midvale and get what we need for fixing up our place."

Dawn showed him the bunkhouse, and they made a list of what it would take to settle in there. They rode out happy and amazed that they'd found work so soon. They felt a little scared, too, about their ability to do everything the Flowers' ranch might demand.

~ ~ ~

Not sure where to spend their wedding night, they rode back to Midvale and the church. They hoped Father John could direct them to a decent place. Another surprise waited. Three people, a white man, his weathered face scarred down one cheek, and two Blackfeet women stood in the churchyard speaking to the Father. The newlyweds dismounted and Michael took the gelding to the hitching post. He walked around the little group back to Dawn. Father John turned into the church again when his housekeeper called him.

One of the women, tall and appearing to be perhaps in her forties, had arresting black eyes that searched Dawn's face. The younger appeared to be about Dawn's age. At first, the girl stared at the ground as only the shyest people do. Both women had long black hair parted in the middle with the two sides braided, the ends tied in plain white strips of cloth. The man stood as tall as the handsome older woman. Despite the rifle that rested in the crook of his left arm, he kept a pleasant enough expression.

The older woman ignored Michael who'd begun to bristle at the trio staring at Dawn. But Michael seemed invisible to the three. They studied Dawn as though her appearance could reveal the answer to some life-or-death question.

The tall woman, head cocked to one side, mouth open in a slight smile, eyes gentle, intense, and unselfconscious, leaned toward Dawn. No one spoke at first, but in moments the woman made a little noise between a cry and an exhalation. The two women spoke to each other in their language. An evening breeze off the prairie entered the conversation, making it sound timeless.

"What is this about? Who are you?" Michael, his tone sharp, broke into their words.

The man stepped forward and offered his hand. "Virgil Caldwell," he said. "This is my wife, Molly, and stepdaughter Marissa."

Michael took Caldwell's hand in a firm shake. "Michael Larkin. No offense, Virgil, but what do you want with us? You seem most intrigued, all of you, with my wife Dawn." At the word 'wife' Michael's mouth twitched into a smile as though he couldn't help it.

"We were advised to come and ask the Father for his help in finding you."

"Who advised you to do that?" Michael asked, the smile replaced by a suspicious downturn at the corners of his mouth.

"An old friend of Molly's. The mountain man, Beartracks Benton. Well, more than a friend. Some years ago he took Molly's sister, Sweet Grass, off to the North Fork of the Flathead, then up to the Belly River Country in Alberta, and beyond that to British Columbia. From all we heard, he treated her well. It grieved us to learn of Sweet Grass passing some years ago."

Virgil continued to expound. "Then this very afternoon old Beartracks rides into Midvale. We'd brought the wagon in for supplies. Beartracks and Molly met up and talked like long lost kin. He explained how he'd followed you from the North Fork of the Flathead to here. He saw you young folks go to the church. Looking to be married and find work at some ranch, he figured. He doesn't want to bother you since you eloped and all, but told us you'll need family in these parts. Also, Beartracks says its high time Dawn here learned about her Blackfeet mother's people, how they live, who her grandmothers and grandfathers were."

Dawn studied the woman and girl. "You're my auntie and my cousin." This was all so new. Married for just hours and then meeting her Blackfeet kin. She took a hesitant step forward. "I've always known my mother had family here, but I never had the chance to come all the way over the pass. I'm glad to finally meet you."

Molly Caldwell took a step toward Dawn. She grasped Dawn's hands in her own darker ones, then released them and lifted hers to cup the air around Dawn's shoulders. Then she embraced her sister's daughter. Dawn caught a sweet scent of pine from Molly's hair. Had her mother's carried it as well?

"You look like my sister," Molly told her. "And like me, too. I have that dimple in my cheek the same as she did. So does Marissa. All of us have it, don't we?"

Marissa smiled, then ducked her head. Dawn had caught a glimpse of dimples in her cousin's round cheeks, though. Marissa also had a widow's peak like her own. Mama Nora always told Dawn it was a sign of beauty in Ireland and other countries, too.

"We have a cabin and lodge, some would call it a tipi, up on Square Top Mountain," Virgil said. "We'll prepare the lodge and a feast, too, for your wedding night. My women are housekeepers like no other, white or red." He grinned.

Dawn looked up at Michael. "I'd like to accept, Michael. Wouldn't you?"

Michael appeared to be calculating. He'd no doubt planned a different wedding night. Dawn cast him a pleading look. He had to understand what this meeting would mean to her. These people knew and could tell her about her Blackfeet mother and that side of her family. And the two of them had nowhere else to stay on a night that, with the long shadows of late afternoon reaching toward them, promised to be cold.

"Well, I hadn't counted on a wedding feast, but it's a kind offer," Michael answered her. "You've got a right to know your mother's people. I hope it works out better for you than it has for me."

Dawn looked away from him. His resentful words seemed unfair to Mama Nora and Papa Jim. But she wanted to know all she could about her newfound auntie and cousin. She'd never even seen how women clothed themselves on the reservation. These two wore long blue cotton dresses, and white wool shawls with bright stripes of red, yellow, and black made from blankets. Dawn had heard of Hudson Bay blankets, but never seen people wearing them cut into fringed shawls. The women also wore moccasins with just a little bead work on the tops.

Virgil Caldwell wore white man's clothes. But his jacket was of tanned elk hide. He, too, wore moccasins. He gave Dawn and Michael a smile, made crooked by his scar. "You won't be sorry. We have our wagon down by the livery. You can follow us home."

The others turned to walk to the livery. Michael mounted the gray and reached down for Dawn. His strong arm swung her up behind him with no visible effort. They followed the Caldwells through the Midvale business district's ramshackle set of stores, one doctor's office, a one-story hotel, the livery, and a telegraph office. Virgil stopped there long enough to confer with another employee.

Michael and Dawn followed the wagon on a narrow, rutted road. The Caldwells' home, a small log cabin with a row of windows facing the town, sat in a meadow, a tipi about forty yards away.

"That's the lodge," Marissa said, speaking at last, her shyness lessened once she'd arrived back home. "It's where you'll sleep. Just give me time to make it ready. Give me your packs and go on into the cabin."

Michael handed over their dusty possessions.

Dawn felt grateful to her relatives for providing privacy on her and Michael's wedding night. She was tired and travel-gritty, but the solid, cozy cabin beckoned. In an hour, Molly had heated water, and sent the men outside so Dawn could bathe.

Molly saw Dawn wince when she finished bathing and touched the towel to her blistered inner thighs. Her aunt reached to a high shelf and brought down a large jar. "Try this poultice." She handed it to Dawn. "It's women's sage. Pat it where your skin hurts. You'll feel better."

Dawn rubbed the salve into her skin. Relief washed over her. She looked to her auntie with grateful surprise. Molly only smiled.

Later, Molly and Marissa served a beef stew with potatoes, turnips, wild onions, and peas cooked on the cabin's wood stove. She'd also served a restorative herb tea that tasted wonderful.

Molly and Virgil spoke about how Sweet Grass had come to fall in love with the aristocratic English hunter and trapper known as Beartracks Benton. "He fell in love, too," Molly said. "He was a handsome man. He had that way of talking that we never heard before, not even Virgil ever heard it.

"Anyway, people here were falling sick. Breaking out in spots and dying. Beartracks asked our father if he could take Sweet Grass with him, and she would be his wife. He wanted to take her away from this place with so many people dead and dying. A horrible time. He promised our father he would never go back to England and leave her behind or abandon her to some other man."

Virgil set down his fork and picked up the story. "She was really young, but Molly's father wasn't well, and he wanted to know his youngest would be cared for, never be hungry or cold in the winter. The old man knew Beartracks was a good hunter and a fierce fighter from when he raided other tribes with the Blackfeet men. He fought well, side by side with his Blackfeet brothers. The girls' father gave his consent. It brought him peace to know Sweet Grass would be with Beartracks."

Molly also told stories of Sweet Grass in her childhood. "She liked to laugh," Molly said. "She could make us laugh, too."

They ended the meal with berries and more tea.

After they'd talked until they were tired, Virgil handed the couple a lantern and pointed them to the lodge. "You're worn out from your journey. Time for you to be alone," he said.

~ ~ ~

Although Molly and Marissa treated Dawn like a virginal bride, she and Michael had often made love at Evening Star and on the journey to Midvale. Both felt they'd always been married. The ceremony of that morning had been to create the aura of respectability they needed coming into the new community and looking for work, especially as Dawn was a mixed blood.

The tipi was painted in a design with circles on a black band at the top, animals dancing, and hill-like mounds on the bottom. When they entered, both noted how comfortable the interior felt. Marissa had started a low fire in the center, smoke drawn up and out the opening at the top. Hides and furs lay on both the floor and beds. Panels with designs and porcupine quill work hung around the sides of the lodge like tapestries.

The newlyweds undressed and lay under a buffalo robe on a low bed farthest from the door. Michael stroked Dawn, careful of the poultices on her thighs. "We'll wait for anything more," he murmured. "Let's just rest together now. I love you so much for coming with me. We have the rest of our lives to make love until our bones become brittle and we're just a pile of powder heaped up and mixed together."

Dawn nestled into him, her head on his chest. This was the gentle side of Michael that she loved. Michael was right. Being married meant having all the time in the world to make love.

"I didn't just gain a husband today," she murmured. "We married exactly where Mama and Papa did, most likely with the same priest to say the vows, and then we met my first mother's people. We met the past and stepped out into our future."

"And we know Beartracks followed us," Michael muttered. "That old scoundrel."

~ ~ ~

In the morning they awoke to shafts of sunlight pouring down on them in the still warm lodge. They lay surrounded by beautiful designs of glistening quill work and paint on the liners that kept the drafts from reaching them from outside. Dawn's soft inner thighs already seemed less chafed. She breathed a sigh of thanks to her kind aunt. She felt rested and ready for what the day would bring.

After adding sticks to the embers, they reached for each other and made love for the first time as husband and wife. Afterwards, spent and contented, Dawn held Michael's head against her breast.

She stroked his hair, and said with the confidence of youth, "Now we'll be together forever."

CHAPTER THREE

After morning greetings and breakfast Dawn expressed a desire to wash Michael's and her travel-soiled clothes. Molly and Marissa walked her down to the little creek that ran near the Caldwell's cabin. Dawn dunked her laundry in the clear water. She rubbed at stains with white clay and the homemade lye soap flakes Molly provided her from a jar. Then Dawn rinsed and wrung the clothes out. After that each woman disrobed and bathed in the creek, immersing to let the current push refreshing water through her hair. They dried themselves, dressed, and carried the laundry back in baskets to hang each piece on the line.

Michael had ridden off with Virgil. The women formed a triangle as they sat on an elk hide under bright sunshine. Drying clothes snapped back and forth on the wire line. Dawn visited with her aunt and cousin while they shared venison jerky and bread for lunch.

Molly made a face when Dawn expressed excitement about going to work for the Flowers. In answer to the other's puzzled look her aunt said, "You haven't been here enough time to know. That white man, Flowers, he started his ranch back when your parents were young. He could have helped us Blackfeet the way Grinnell—Manistokos, the Father of the People—did in the starving times. But like many whites, Flowers only cared about getting rich. He cut fences to graze his herds on our land. Ranchers like him, and one after another the crooked agents at Browning, held back food and other things we needed. They made bad times worse on our reservation."

Dawn bit her lower lip and shook her head. "I didn't know. Michael and I should avoid the Flowers' ranch. I won't work for them."

"No." Molly rested a hand on Dawn's arm. "You and Michael need work. Us Caldwells do all right because Virgil has a job at the telegraph office four days a week. Virgil hunts game with my brothers. Marissa and I keep a garden. But plenty here go hungry and cold. You don't want to be like them, skinny and hollow-eyed. We do the best we can for my relatives, but it is not enough." She paused and her voice shook when she said, "Starving is a bad death."

Dawn could only nod, realizing what deep pain lay behind Molly's words.

Molly continued, "That's right. My sister's daughter should have better. Sweet Grass would want you to have good food and clothes. You were raised by whites. You know how to talk to them. You'll manage all right with Flowers and his proud wife."

Marissa asked, "Did those folks who raised you send you to school?"

"No. Papa Jim came here from China." Dawn considered for a moment telling them that Beartracks had smuggled him into America from Canada. But she thought better of it. Papa Jim's illegal status was a family secret, almost never mentioned, certainly not outside Evening Star.

She ran her hand across the grass beside her and continued, "Papa Jim taught me as much as I could take in of what he knew. I can read and write and do sums. He taught me about countries all over the world, too. And history. Mama told me about Ireland where she came from, and Boston, in Massachusetts, and Helena right here in Montana.

"What about your schooling?" she asked Marissa.

Marissa's face darkened. Molly reached to pat her daughter's shoulder. "Virgil and I wouldn't send our daughter to that Indian boarding school, Willow Creek. Virgil being white, nobody made a fuss about it.

"Sweet Grass was gone away with Beartracks, and I was already married to Virgil when they opened up that place and made the children go there. Our little brothers and nephews had to go. They put that building up all wrong. They used green wood and it dried and let snow blow in during winter. Water stands in the basement all the time. They get dead mice and rotting vegetables floating around in it. It stinks. They can smell that clear up on the second floor.

"Children die there, and we fear many are beaten or worse. Even now they get sick from tuberculosis or even typhus like so many did awhile back. Sometimes the children get so sick that the teachers fetch a doctor who signs a paper so the kids can go home to recover. Those are the lucky ones.

"Sometimes they die in that place, but the parents don't learn about it right away. In some cases the children disappear like ghosts. Parents are told that no children by their name ever attended. Or that their child died fast and has been buried near the school."

Dawn gave Molly a shocked stare. "A school like that is still open? The law should shut it down!"

"The elders have asked, and made complaints, and demanded that. Doctor Jenkins, he keeps trying to get Superintendent Bathgate to close it because it's so bad for our children's health, but that Bathgate keeps putting us off. He gives us promises he can repair it or says the new school that's supposed to be about ready in Cut Bank will be better. They want our children away from their families. They take the children of other tribes away, too."

Dawn stood and stared down at the other two. "And the whites like Flowers do nothing?"

"They care about their own," Marissa said, ducking her head again. "Not our children."

When Michael came back, Dawn told him what she'd learned. He'd bathed in a creek, too, and as he changed into clean clothes, he told her Virgil had filled him in on the town and the country around it.

Michael looked serious as he said, "I hope I haven't brought you to a place you won't be happy in. Virgil says Flowers was a wild one in his youth. Heck, they nicknamed him Wild Flowers. He established his spread in 1884. Before that he served as a Union soldier, worked as a cowboy on the early trail drives, and was sometimes an Indian fighter. He married late in life. Apparently, his wife Eleanor sort of civilized him, made him a community leader. They have those two daughters. He treats his cowboys fair but expects a full day's labor every sunrise to sunset. We need the work, Dawn. We need to make some money."

She stood in the lodge, trying to decide what to do. But Michael looked so worried. She didn't want him to regret bringing her with him, so she put her arms around his neck and nuzzled the tanned skin above his freshly washed bandanna. He smelled like clean air and sunshine. She took a deep breath. "All right, I'll give them a chance if they'll give us one."

Michael smiled and kissed her. "I know you will. We'll try them out and see how it goes."

The next morning they visited with the Caldwells. Virgil and Molly loaned Dawn their young roan mare for an indefinite period. She and Michael wouldn't have to appear at Flowers' ranch again riding double on the gray. "That makes a sorry impression. You two ride in looking proud," Virgil said, shrugging in answer to their thanks while flashing his crooked grin.

Dawn appreciated how Virgil Caldwell didn't see just race, but also character in the people he met. She felt grateful to Beartracks for making sure they had people like the Caldwells to care about them. She knew he'd also reassure Nora and Jim about their situation.

They said their farewells and rode to town to buy paint and cleaning supplies, groceries, fabric for Dawn to make curtains for the bunkhouse, and two extra blankets. Before they'd left, they planned with Caldwells to meet at the church in Midvale on Sundays. Molly said she would take Dawn to the reservation to meet more of Sweet Grass's relatives. There would be elders among them, people who'd even known Dawn's grandparents. Dawn wanted to meet these Blackfeet, but wondered, too, what Mama and Papa Jim would think about this new life. They would always be the mother and father who'd taken care of her, sick or well. Would they feel slighted? Left behind? What were they doing now?

She sighed. She'd made her choice to be with Michael no matter what the necessary sacrifice. She would do the same again. She would never lose her certainty on that point.

~ ~ ~

The first days at Flowers' ranch proved hard for Dawn. Eleanor labored in her own way, sewing, gardening, teaching her girls, and planning menus. But she left all menial, unsavory tasks to Dawn: the scrubbing of floors, beating of rugs, scouring of pots and pans, washing of clothes and linens. They prepared some meals together, but Dawn felt alone. Eleanor wasn't unfriendly, but there was no question of their ever being friends. Or equals.

To her relief, Beartracks popped in to see their bunk house home during their first week. Dawn cried a little while they talked, telling him she felt homesick, but proud of being married. She felt comforted when he promised to come again and carry news back and forth between her and her family.

He advised her to become acquainted with all her cousins, and she brightened as she thanked him for making sure she met Molly, Virgil, and Marissa. That made for a comforting start.

~ ~ ~

In the weeks that followed Dawn caught Eleanor giving her puzzled looks. Once, after chastising one of the girls for telling a fib, their mother had muttered "Oh, what a tangled web we weave," only to have Dawn laugh and add, "When first we practice to deceive."

Eleanor's eyebrows flew up. She hadn't expected this beautiful mixed-blood hired girl to recognize her occasional quotes from Shakespeare or Keats. And Dawn did everything that was asked of her, including emptying chamber pots, without question or complaint.

Michael had a bent for working with horses. Flowers soon declared his newest cowboy a top hand.

On Sundays, their days off, the newlyweds usually rode into Midvale and went to Mass with the Caldwells. It became a habit that after Mass the five of them would ride out to Browning for late afternoon visits with their extended Blackfeet family.

Dawn loved the hours spent listening to elder storytellers. Michael and Virgil often rode away to hunt with the younger men. Dawn, Molly, and Marissa joined the women and sometimes the old men. Dawn gradually learned some history of her mother's people and of all that they'd lost after living so long in freedom. They'd been part of the grasslands and mountains. Nature provided them with plants for food and medicine, dyes for clothes, and meat: buffalo, elk, deer, bear, porcupine, beaver, and rabbit. Animals made it possible to have warm clothes, food, and tools created from bone and horn.

There were still such proud elders who remembered a time of freedom and abundance. Dawn read so much yearning in their faces and voices. This strong people had fought hard to keep their way of life, but the Army, the

United States government, and the unending numbers of settlers reduced the tribe in the end to poverty and sorrow.

The elders remembered a world of free life and ceremony before these terrible times. The Bureau of Indian Affairs and the reservation agent expected them to eke out a living by digging furrows in the earth, even in some instances with their hands. Very little of the land proved tillable and warriors of the plains knew nothing of farming. Successful agriculture demanded many tools, such as plows, harrows, and teams of work horses. The Indians had no money to buy these necessary items.

They could no longer make raids on their enemies for horses and women. The Christian whites threatened to forbid even the traditional Sun Dance ceremony, although for the present the tribe still held it in the time when the sun came closest to the earth. Worst of all, the conquerors removed Blackfeet children, taught in the old days to live good lives by imitating their mothers and fathers, from their homes to live in the squalid, punitive Willow Creek School. The government destroyed a culture and way of life that the Blackfoot had sustained for generations.

The quick result meant starvation and mounting deaths from the white man's diseases. The Blackfeet had no immunity to these new illnesses and died in devastating numbers. The size of the tribe shrank to less than half its original number.

Some things Dawn learned surprised her. One of her favorite old women, Anna Kills a Bear Woman, told them of being married when just a little girl of seven. Her listeners were seated in Anna's lodge when she recounted her early life. She'd built a small fire, and her eyes watched the low flame as she remembered her girlhood.

"I played with toys in my husband's lodge. I learned to be a housekeeper from my older sister, his first wife. When I became a woman I took on a woman's responsibilities. I was useful and happy. I bore my husband two sons. But they died of white man's sicknesses. When the whites made us settle on the reservation, that agent told my husband he could only have one wife. He argued, but in the end he kept my sister and sent me back to my mother and father's lodge. We were poor and struggled, but I married a young man my own age. I had two girls with him."

Dawn thought of Anna's calm recounting of her childhood and young adulthood. Hardship didn't begin to depict her life after she and the others surrendered and began life on the reservation.

~ ~ ~

One Sunday Dawn and Michael stayed at the Caldwells so Molly could teach Dawn how to prepare a deer hide for tanning. That day, as they rested after the lessons, Dawn learned how Molly's mother, her own grandparent, died. Molly told her the story as they sat outside watching golden aspen leaves shimmer against the pale September sky.

"Our family, our mother and father, Sweet Grass and I, were with Heavy Runner's band." She brushed a fly away from her face and cleared her throat. "He moved us to our winter camp on the Marias." She paused and looked toward the forest for long moments before starting to speak again. "This was thirty-six years ago. This was after the times of many deaths because of the scab disease whites call smallpox. The old medicines did not help. Death stalked everyone during that hungry time. Many families lost their best hunters.

"The disease had shown pity to our family and passed us by that winter when I was ten. With hunters bringing game home for us to eat, we found the energy to have some fun once more. Girls made sleds out of raw buffalo hides. Boys made theirs with runners out of rib bones. We played 'Hunting the Buffalo' on our sleds."

Molly fell silent. Dawn and Marissa exchanged wary sidelong looks but didn't speak. Dawn sensed she was about to hear something terrible. Something she might rather not know. After a long silence, Molly shuddered and rubbed her eyes as though waking from a nightmare. Her eyes glistened with unshed tears.

Marissa touched Molly's arm. "You stopped telling us your story," she said. "Will you tell us the rest now?"

Dawn knew that Marissa must have heard the story before and asked her to continue.

Molly collected herself with a visible effort. She shredded a few fallen aspen leaves, threw the pieces away, inhaled a shaky breath, and picked up the thread of her memories. "One night, I dreamed for the third time that owls sat on our lodges. When I woke, I heard the men, including our father, leave to go hunting. I went to the river for water. Mist came up all around me. That's when I heard shooting, screaming, and crying. Sweet Grass came running toward me and tumbled down the bank. I grabbed her and dug a shallow snow cave for us behind some tall dead grass. We were so afraid, and we were trying to hide from the blue coat killers.

"The soldiers came down to the edge of the bank where we crouched. They stood right above us laughing, and we tried not to breath. They moved around searching, but then they just cursed. They never found us. I heard the crackle of our lodges burning and smelled the smoke. I smelled burning bodies, too. The bodies of our families.

"For a long time, Sweetgrass and I held on to each other and shivered. When all had been quiet for a while I crept out with my poor little sister. We crawled up the bank.

"We saw Heavy Runner. He had been shot many times. He lay with his warrior spear in his right hand. He was dead. Other old men who had stayed in camp were also dead. Our mother was dead. Our friends, the little kids we played with, were dead. We saw with horror that the bodies of our tribe were stacked like firewood and fire consumed them.

"Horror and terror paralyzed us. We stood that way for a long time. Our sense of time deserted us. When thought returned we saw we had nothing left but ash and the embers of our lodges where our winter camp had been. We had no time to mourn as it grew colder.

"Of the women, old people and children—most were dead. A few who'd made it to the forest and hid crept out toward us. I took Sweet Grass by the hand and we followed the creek with those other survivors. Sometimes I carried my little sister. She never cried.

"Many around us were wounded. They, too, kept silent. No one felt able to speak. Even the birds kept quiet. Some of our people died on the trail without making any death sounds. That's a big part that I remember. The frozen earth joined with us and our dead in our silence.

"We found our way to the winter camp of the Lone Eaters, another Blackfeet band. It was a horrible time. It was weeks before anyone could allow themselves to grieve in the old ways. We stayed there with our wounded father who also survived that terrible day. We lived with those people for years until I married Virgil, and Sweet Grass went north with Beartracks."

Then Molly looked toward the earth and did not speak further. Dawn's tears mirrored those of her aunt and cousin.

~ ~ ~

Dawn repeated Molly's telling of the Marias River Massacre as she and Michael rode home. It seemed a piece of family history she would have known as a little girl had Sweet Grass lived.

Michael shook his head at the cruelty. He'd grown to like the Caldwells. He said, "The Indian Wars brought out the worst of both sides at times. Bad things were done. All kinds of horrible things were done. Horrible things have always been done by humans on every side of wars that I've heard of. Look what some tribes did to each other. Look what the English have done to the Irish. But I'm sorry for what happened to Molly and Sweet Grass and the others."

Dawn lay awake long after Michael fell asleep beside her in their little bunkhouse. She finally rose and went to gaze out the window at the stars wheeling their arcs across the night's otherwise empty, black void.

This was not what she'd expected, this privation her mother's people had to endure. And yet, she thought, they could still make jokes, tell stories, and want her to learn how life had been. They had a language and a religion, and they knew so much about the earth and the ways of birds and animals of water, land, and sky. Life continued amidst defeat on the reservation. This was a different world and she meant to fill a place among her Blackfeet relatives.

She might be barely out of her girlhood, some would say still in it, but in time she would find a way to help her Blackfeet mother's people. She made that silent vow to Sweet Grass and herself. She would do all she could to keep her mother's culture alive.

A shooting star made a sudden trajectory among the constellations, a messenger in the night sky. Maybe there were white constellations and Blackfeet constellations, Dawn thought. Maybe she could be that shooting star that soared across and unified them. A link like a shooting star. Born of two peoples, Dawn Larkin determined to find a way to keep her promise and help form a peace with understanding.

Chapter Four

August 1907

Dawn dropped a flour sack half-full of clothespins onto the clean, wet linens and clothing in the big basket. Grunting, she lifted and held it above her rounded belly while maneuvering past the large sink in Eleanor's narrow laundry room. Stepping out the back door into sunshine, Dawn noted the air's stillness. Meadowlarks singing on the wing or on posts or in the leafy branches of trees sounded sharp and clear.

She staggered a little on the uneven ground as she carried her burden to the wire clothesline. There she dropped the basket, which hit with a soft thud. Her back ached more than usual. She arched it and looked across the undulating grassy hills toward the Eastern Front. The mountains had the comforting effect of arms waiting to enfold and shelter her.

She hoped to see a familiar figure riding toward her with news of the North Fork. She'd expected Beartracks to arrive the day before. He'd sent a telegram to Virgil that he planned on coming then and asked him to let Dawn know. But her mountain man father had an untrammeled soul's predilection for ignoring the passing of hours or even days. When he did show up at Flowers' place, he usually brought precious letters from Mama Nora and Papa Jim. He carried Dawn's responses back to them. That correspondence remained the one secret she kept from Michael.

Squinting east as the sun climbed high and flooded the landscape, she searched for Beartracks. Dawn remembered when she'd turned ten and Mama and Papa Jim sat her down in the cabin at Evening Star. They explained they were her foster parents and why Beartracks, her natural father, only stopped in from time to time.

"Sure, and he came here as a remittance man, didn't he?" Mama had announced with a hint of sharpness in her tone, although she and Beartracks were great friends.

Dawn had looked up at her Irish Mama, so critical of English ways, and asked, "What does that mean?"

Then Papa Jim made a gentle explanation of how Beartracks had been an English lord's youngest and wildest son. At his exasperated father's insistence, Beartracks immigrated to North America. The lord kept his rogue son on a monthly retainer so long as Beartracks stayed far away and left his image-conscious relatives in peace. He established his traplines, hunting cabins, and occasional unlawful exploits like smuggling in foreigners among the North Fork of the Flathead River drainage, British Columbia, and Alberta's Belly River Country.

Mama added that Beartracks' older brother and heir to the family estate created a trust after their father died that didn't depend on Beartracks' behavior. Beartracks could have returned home and continued reaping the trust's benefits. But he had no wish to leave the freedom of his life in American and Canadian lands. Beartracks still explored, trapped, hunted, and guided wealthy adventurers. "And he loved your mother. He confided to me once his family would never have accepted her."

"Because she was a Blackfeet?" Dawn's eyes had widened.

"Not everyone could see what a dear girl she was," Mama answered, smiling at the memory of her friend. "After Sweet Grass died from illness after childbirth, your father asked us to raise you. He had no idea how to bring up a son or daughter… especially not a daughter. We agreed. Beartracks became what he is to you, more like a fond uncle than parent."

Dawn loved her avuncular father now more than ever. She felt a growing gratitude that he acted as her go-between with Mama and Papa Jim.

Dawn stretched again to straighten her back, and then finished fastening the wet garments to the line. She unhooked the faded cloth bag that held the wooden clothes pins, dropping it into her empty basket. She'd reached the eighth month of being in the family way. How hard it must be for Mama and Papa Jim, she thought, to know about her condition while Michael remained adamant, refusing all contact. He said he couldn't trust Nora about anything. Not when she'd lied to him about his parentage.

During her pregnancy Dawn pondered what values she wanted to instill in their child. She resolved that most of all, she wanted to teach the little one to cherish and nurture love. That had to include forgiveness when loved ones wronged us.

Dawn carried the basket in and went to the kitchen to start breakfast for the family. She frowned as she cracked eggs and set bacon frying. Michael seemed unreasonable and stubborn after all this time. His mother never intended to harm him, only wanted to spare her son harmful truth. His father had been a cruel man with serious vices who seduced Nora when she grieved the loss of her first husband. Dawn, growing in maturity, realized it could have happened to any woman left vulnerable in the West.

Her thoughts turned to the darker sides of human nature. Working at the Flowers' ranch, not to mention visiting her Blackfeet family on the reservation, Dawn learned how the world swings between generosity and greed, thoughtfulness and cruelty. The state of her mother's people showed her that not just relationships, but land and all that put down roots in it can be degraded and lost.

~ ~ ~

Hours later when Dawn stepped outside the house to carry in the dried clothes, she finally spotted Beartracks riding toward the house. He approached as sunlight slid into charcoal shadows reaching like long fingers across the prairie. Dawn often thought they seemed like the dark hands of Blackfeet spirits groping to recover what landowners like Flowers had wrested from them.

She'd spent a long day inside cleaning and helping Eleanor with preparations for a dinner party. Dawn had felt so disheartened at the thought of having to wait yet another day for Beartracks. She brightened when she saw him in his familiar buckskin clothes and moccasins. The big man never lost the habit of preferring old-time footgear with its deerskin, beaded tops, and rawhide soles. The elders sewed them with sinew in the old way that he favored. He kept several pair at a time made for him by tribal women.

Dawn shoved the basket inside the laundry room and rushed outside again and around the side of the house as fast as her condition allowed. The two usually met in Dawn and Michael's little bunkhouse, where they'd catch up on all the news. But today Beartracks dismounted and strode in his flatfooted way toward the Flowers' home, up their steps to knock on the heavy door.

Dawn hovered unnoticed, hidden behind a blooming lilac bush at the end of the veranda. What business could Beartracks want to conduct with her and Michael's employers before seeking her?

As usual Beartracks's timing wasn't the best. Eleanor had awakened keyed up that morning and stayed on edge all day. Important guests were traveling by train to Montana's scenic mountains. Specifically, the Great Northern would be carrying them toward the Flowers' ranch. Born to an elite New York family, Eleanor took her hostess role seriously.

She told Dawn all the details that afternoon while choosing her finest dinner dress and accessories for that evening. "The new president of the

Great Northern Railway, Louis B. Hill, will be with us in a matter of hours. Besides being James J. Hill's son, Louie is a landscape artist. He loves the West as we do. George Bird Grinnell, the publisher and editor of *Field and Stream*, will be with us, too," she added.

Dawn breathed the man's name. "George Bird Grinnell. My aunties have told me about him."

Eleanor smiled. "Well, they would know and talk about him. He's been a friend to Indian tribes from the Southwest to Montana. The Blackfeet love him. He's a great advocate of national parks, too."

"He's really coming here tonight?" Dawn asked. She became as nervous as Eleanor.

"Yes, of course. He's Louie's guest on that private rail car of his. Perhaps you can meet him after you serve at dinner."

Watching Beartracks' mysterious arrival from her hiding place behind the lilacs, Dawn wished he'd ridden in sooner. The Flowers had hired extra kitchen help, a Helena chef and two Blackfeet women experienced in domestic work, to make sure the evening went well. Dawn would soon be called on to change into clean and pressed clothes, to help Eleanor oversee final dinner preparations, and to serve dinner. Before all that, she would see that the girls had taken their meal in the kitchen and were settled in their room.

But now Dawn just had to find out what Beartracks wanted. Dan Flowers had come in from the range early and cleaned up so that when he answered the door he looked every inch the weathered, well-established rancher.

Breathing in the heavy, sweet scent of blossoms, Dawn eavesdropped while Beartracks introduced himself. Flowers ordered an approaching ranch hand to see to Beartracks' horse.

Dawn watched the tired, dust-covered boy take the horse without question. Dan Flowers was king on this ranch. He gestured to Beartracks to follow him into the house.

Beartracks didn't move. Dan Flowers turned to him and said, "I know you by your reputation as a man with an expert's knowledge of our mountains, sir. Please, come in. Join our little party for dinner. George Bird Grinnell is our guest along with Louie Hill."

Beartracks declined. "I came only with the purpose of seeing Dawn and Michael, not to dine with your eastern gentlemen. My time is limited, but I thought it overdue that I introduce myself so you'll know who I am when I'm on your ranch to see my daughter and her husband. I'll dine with none but them."

Dawn peered around the lilacs and saw Flowers's eyes tighten with anger. Not many men had likely spoken to the rancher with such assurance, at least not for many years. Michael said most of the hands were scared of him.

Flowers stared at Beartracks, then said, "Wait here. I'll be right back."

Dawn slipped along the veranda and joined Beartracks at the door. They exchanged raised eyebrows on hearing Dan call his wife to a room off the parlor. Eleanor, if her rising voice meant anything, became agitated during the brief conversation that followed. The two on the veranda couldn't help but overhear.

Eleanor said, "You want me to invite this half-breed hired girl and her ranch hand husband to dinner with Louie Hill? No one will be comfortable. I thought this Benton was a friend of Dawn's North Fork people."

Dan's voice rose in response. "Both those kids are well-spoken, Eleanor. I want this Beartracks for Grinnell, and I mean to have him. That mountain man knows the Rockies better than any other we'll ever meet. Hell, dinner will be a lot more interesting than I expected."

Their voices lowered. And then Dan reappeared in the doorway with Eleanor, her color high, standing at his side. Seeing Dawn beside Beartracks they invited both her and Michael to join the dinner party.

Beartracks relented. He excused himself to wash and put on a clean shirt in Dawn and Michael's bunkhouse.

~ ~ ~

The distinguished visitors arrived two hours later. They joined the others for dinner at the Flowers' table with its Wedgewood China and Waterford goblets. The dignified, slim-faced Grinnell's obvious delight in meeting Beartracks proved that inviting Dawn's father had been a wise decision. Grinnell questioned the mountain man with an outdoorsman's avid curiosity about the state of nearby wilderness. Beartracks in turn told stories including one about Nora Li, the Irish immigrant landowner, shooting a grizzly. Michael, Dawn noted, paid exaggerated attention to his steak as Beartracks praised Nora's courage.

Dawn found it hard to eat, so amazed to be in the company of these elevated people. She also felt miserable, whether from the physical discomfort of being so near her time or missing Nora and Jim she couldn't have said. It always felt wrong to be without them in a situation they would've found interesting. They could have contributed wilderness knowledge, too.

Grinnell turned to the subject of his life's dream. He envisioned a great national park even bigger than Yellowstone to the southeast, that place with devilish hot pools and geysers.

"And think where I believe such a new national park should be?" Hill eyed his listeners, his tone eager and forceful.

"Where, Louie?" Eleanor defused the aggression of his stare. "Don't make us guess."

The distinguished Grinnell couldn't hide the excitement in his voice and jumped in. "It would be one million acres, including Lake McDonald, the land east of the North Fork of the Flathead River near Canada, and the East Front of the Rocky Mountains. Theodore Roosevelt shares our interest in this great project."

While the others lifted their eyebrows, impressed at the size of the proposed park, Flowers barked a harsh laugh. "In our backyard?" he asked, looking like a man who craved something stronger than French wine. "I explored these mountains when it all still belonged to the Blackfeet, and now the government's going to tell me I can't hunt them?"

Dawn held her breath. Flowers took pride in his reputation for going where and doing what he pleased. Why wasn't what he owned ever enough? Why the greed for more power, more of everything? How could a man satisfy an appetite for more than everything? How could he live with such a load of greed?

Eleanor rested her hand on her husband's arm. "But you love these mountains, too, Dan. It will all be changed anyway if it's bought up and used by miners and loggers."

Her husband scowled. "That may well be, dear. I just hate like hell to admit it."

Beartracks spoke up. "I have a cabin at the foot of Lake McDonald. I built it myself as part of my trap line and lived there off and on for years. I filed my deed and all other requirements." He glared at the narrow-faced Grinnell, brushing off the other's prideful reference to being friends with the president. "What's Uncle Sam going to do? Try to steal it back?"

"There's a term for what you'd be," Grinnell answered, raising his goblet as if proposing a toast. "You'd be one of the inholders. That is, you'd be one of the landowners who keep title to land inside the Park boundaries because you owned it before the Park's creation."

"Can Beartracks sell his land, Mr. Grinnell?" Michael spoke for the first time.

"Yes. Inholders continue to own their property free and clear. You can do what you like with the homestead as far as keeping or selling or willing it to family. It stays private property for the next owners." Grinnell paused to cut into his braised carrots.

Dawn nudged Michael. As though reading her thoughts, he asked, "You say the park would extend only as far as the east side of the North Fork of the Flathead River?"

The other nodded. "It would."

"Michael and Dawn have family with a place on the west side. It wouldn't be affected?" Beartracks asked.

"No. Not at all. There will be limitations imposed on east bank landowners. Hunting, trapping, and logging restricted."

Louis Hill broke in. "Not everyone will be happy, but those who don't want to comply will probably sell out to the government or someone else and move."

Beartracks looked thoughtful. He turned to Michael and Dawn. "I'm glad your folks took my advice all those years back. My guess is those East side settlers will move on over to the west side of the North Fork."

Louis Hill nodded with enthusiasm. "Better for everyone. Simpler. The property they sell to the government will become part of the park lands. We'll make this area more attractive to tourists than the playgrounds of Europe. We'll call the Montana Rockies 'The American Alps.' The Blackfeet will be known as the 'Park Indians.' They'll add to the atmosphere of the lost Old West. They've already sold much of their mountains to the government, but still hold timber and hunting rights. I'll provide them with employment."

Amazed, Dawn gaped at Louis Hill. Her face heated. She'd learned from Molly and other relatives of the government's broken promises. Powerful men took advantage when they found it a means to making a profit. One of the grandmothers told her that greed stole such men's souls.

Beside her, Michael busied himself with mashed potatoes and gravy. After more talk over huckleberry pie and coffee the men adjourned to the long porch to take in fresh air between pulls on their pipes or cigars.

Dawn and Eleanor moved to the kitchen to oversee the washing up and putting away of dishes and leftovers. Once the two Blackfeet women who'd come in to help and the red-faced German chef finished setting the kitchen back in order, Eleanor paid them. They said their goodnights. The weary women would ride their ponies back to their homes near Browning while the chef slept in a room off the kitchen.

Dawn felt so fatigued as to be weak. Her backache had worsened. She turned to thank Eleanor for the rare evening at her dining table when a birth pain struck. She cried out and dropped a teacup she'd been holding. It bounced against the worktable and shattered on the floor. Breathing hard, Dawn sank into a kitchen chair.

Eleanor's urgent call for Michael brought him running. For the rest of that night, Eleanor Flowers paid no heed to her status. Either they'd miscalculated or the baby had decided to come early. Eleanor donned a heavy apron and assumed the role of midwife, able to handle it with the same level of competence she summoned to play a Chopin Etude or stitch up a cowboy's cut finger. She ordered the thunderstruck men who'd followed Michael into the kitchen to help her with such matters as hot water. Wearing stunned expressions, they obeyed.

~ ~ ~

Dawn presented Michael Larkin with their firstborn before light strengthened enough to cast shadows of antelope racing across the prairie or of Blackfeet emerging from cabins and lodges to greet their Sun God Creator.

Eleanor, looking confident to the point of smug, opened the guest room door to admit Michael. She said, "Well, your little wife certainly upstaged me at my own dinner party."

Michael took long strides to the bed. He kissed Dawn, then laughed with joy at the sight of his newborn son lying in her arms. The light brown baby had a tuft of fine, dark brown hair and long limbs that bespoke his Blackfeet heritage.

"We need to settle on a name for our little man." Michael lifted his baby into the crook of his arm and studied the puckered little face.

"My aunties told me about the starving time of 1883," Dawn said. "When the people were dying because the government agent couldn't or wouldn't give them food, Mr. Grinnell pitied them. He published pleas to his political friends and in his magazine. He wrote pieces in the *New York Times*. He helped make things better."

"I never heard about that," Michael said.

"Mr. Grinnell became a champion, a warrior. The Blackfeet adopted him into the tribe and made him a chief. To them he is 'Father of the People.'"

Michael sat down on the bed next to her and Dawn snuggled against him. "I never expected to meet that man," she said. "I couldn't even speak in his presence. Shall we name our son after George Bird Grinnell? Or should we name him after you?"

"No, not another Michael. How about naming him after Jim Li? He's the best man I ever knew. He wanted Mama to tell me the truth about my father right from the first night I stayed at Evening Star." Michael drew his thumb across the sleeping baby's hair.

Dawn wrinkled her nose, then brightened. "Bird. Like Mr. Grinnell's middle name. Jim Bird Larkin. Jim-Bird. We'll have the world's first Jim-Bird."

Michael grinned. "One of a kind, and that's a fact. But let's shorten it to Bird. Too many Jims otherwise. I grew up in a house with two Michaels. I won't put our little man through that." He stood. "I'll see you later, Bird, and your beautiful mother." He bent over them and kissed Dawn, then left his weary family to cuddle and drowse.

But Dawn lay awake. She realized and took joy in the fact that Michael had just spoken as though they would, indeed, return one day to Evening Star, to the sheltering family and mountains of the North Fork.

~ ~ ~

Michael didn't close the door to the hall when he left. Dawn listened to an exchange between him and Beartracks that took place outside her room.

"I plan on telling your mother and Jim about Bird," Beartracks spoke. Dawn sat up and peered at him. He carried a cut glass decanter in one hand and two shot glasses in the other.

Michael took one of the glasses and Beartracks poured whiskey into it. Michael drank, then shook his head. "No. They'd come, and I don't want to see her."

Beartracks stepped back from the doorway so Dawn couldn't see him, but she heard the anger in his voice. "Don't call Nora 'her.' If you're old enough to father a son, you're old enough to think like a grown man." He stepped forward again and Dawn could see his fierce expression. "I'll tell them about the baby. And I'll tell them not to come here to see you. In my opinion, you're not worth seeing. But I'm also going to tell them that one of these days you'll meet Dawn's needs and bring her back home."

Michael squared his shoulders. "I am meeting Dawn's needs. We're doing all right here. And why should I leave my boy with a woman who lied to me for over two years about something as important as the name of my own father? I can't trust her. You can either trust someone or you can't."

"You wear blinders, boy. You didn't hear how hard Wild Flowers had to struggle with himself and worse, that snob Eleanor, just so a mixed-blood could eat at their table. It's a hard and unjust world. Learn to live in it as a grown man."

Beartracks emptied his glass, took another swig, and turned away in disgust. Dawn heard the thump of Michael's glass as he put it down on the hall table. Michael's worn-at-the-heel boots stomped on the carpeted stairs as he descended.

Beartracks appeared in her doorway, plainly abashed to realize she'd heard them. "I'm sorry, Dawn."

"It's all right," she said. "The longer we're here, and the more I get to know my Blackfeet family, the more I understand how difficult their lives are. We're excited about the park while they still grieve the loss of their freedom and land, especially the special place, Chief Mountain." Her face crumpled from emotion still close to the surface in the aftermath of giving birth.

"I'm glad we came," she said, brushing away the few tears that fell. "At least for now so I can know and understand them, how they keep their dignity in the face of all they've lost. Mama and Papa Jim taught me well how important it is to have land that means home. Knowing my Blackfeet relatives makes that clearer than ever. Holding land gives freedom and… and people treat you with dignity. "I don't think Michael will stay angry forever. I don't know what will change him, but I just feel that something will."

Beartracks sighed. "It will have to be something earth shattering, my dear girl. Something I can't conceive of right now."

"Well, maybe our little son will be enough. I can't see Michael staying bitter and cold-hearted all his life. He isn't really like that. He'll grow to understand in time."

Beartracks nodded, and then waited while she wrote a note for him to carry back to Evening Star.

Dawn wouldn't tell Michael she'd written it. For now, in many ways she accepted that she would have to be the most adult half in her marriage.

Chapter Five

Dawn lay in the quiet of her employers' guest room after Beartracks left. Lace curtains billowed from the dry breeze entering through open windows. Men's voices and easy laughter along with the soft thud of hooves moving toward the barn sounded comforting and familiar. The best were the meadowlarks. She closed her eyes, then opened them again to go over all that had happened in such a short time. She wanted to remember every detail of her son's birth.

Eleanor reappeared to help the young mother settle into nursing Bird. The two women began feeling their way toward a new relationship, one almost but never quite beyond that of employer and servant. Eleanor's attitude toward Dawn, if not maternal, did reach that of a mentor.

The elegant woman spoke in tender tones of when her daughters had been infants. "Dan insisted I go into Helena for Isabelle's birth," she said, taking a chair next to the bed while Bird suckled in Dawn's arms. "When I came back, I had an Irish nanny to help with her for the first two years. We hired the woman back for another year when Patricia arrived.

"You won't have such assistance, of course. Quite the opposite. You'll still have the job of helping me if you can handle the laundry and cleaning along with this sweet babe. I won't mind if you take extra time to complete your work. You'll have to feed and change your little fellow." She smiled at Dawn as though bestowing a benefice.

Dawn sensed that having acted as midwife Eleanor would continue to assume a proprietary air about all things pertinent to Bird and his care. How long would this last? And how habitual might it become? There could be trouble if Dawn didn't assert herself from the start as the only woman in charge of her own son's well-being. If nothing else on the ranch belonged to her, Bird did. So did Michael. Her family was hers alone.

She took a deep breath and hazarded, "I want to breast-feed my son for at least the next three or four months. Molly Caldwell teaches me that's the way to keep him healthy according to Blackfeet elders."

Eleanor gave her an arch look and took a moment to consider. "The Blackfeet women may be right about this aspect of things. It might be easier for you to manage breastfeeding than preparing bottles. Just keep out of the men's sight when you're feeding little Bird. We are civilized here, at least within our house."

Dawn nodded, but wondered why a women's breast was such an improper sight. Molly and Marissa and she had bathed naked together, Mama at Evening Star might agree with Eleanor, of course. That Catholic God seemed more strict and punishing than the traditional elders' sacred Sun Creator. With that bit of success in asserting herself, Dawn ignored the implication about Blackfeet women. Shifting the baby, she added, "Molly and Marissa Caldwell are making me a cradleboard with beautiful porcupine quill work died red with blue and white beads. I want to put Bird in it sometimes when I'm working in the garden or hanging out laundry.

"I'll have them show me how to bundle my son into a moss bag and fasten it to the board. Then I can hook it to the cottonwood branches near where I'll be working. The wind will rock him for me. He'll listen to the meadowlarks or the cry of a hawk." She smiled.

Eleanor merely nodded with a neutral expression. When she stood to leave the room she said, "Try doing so if you like. Molly's been a good mother to Marissa. The Caldwells seem like decent people."

Bird finished nursing and fell asleep. Dawn slipped out of bed and placed him in his cradle. She walked to the window, then neatened the room. Later, she fed Bird again and slept. When she awoke she returned to the window. Soon the sky and the mountains would melt into rose and blue twilight. She supposed artists had better names for the exact colors of the world both here and at home.

She reflected, too, on the differences between her Blackfeet relatives and her white employers. The Flowers used nature to show a profit from the ranch. To Dawn taking the natural wealth of centuries to make you richer than you needed to be seemed senseless. The Blackfeet revered the earth and its natural generosity. They grieved for the loss of all that had been. They wanted to return to the old ways from before the whites arrived. Mama and Papa Jim seemed suspended somewhere in between both sides, stewards for the next generations, for Bird and any others to be born to her and Michael.

What world would their children inherit?

~ ~ ~

Once Bird survived life's first fragile months, he graduated to broth and mashed food. Soon he sat up and crawled along the carpet. Isabelle and Patricia Flowers treated him as their personal doll. They pulled him around the house and barn in a red wagon during summer or on a sled in winter. Sometimes the three children played patty cake seated on the Persian rug in the parlor until the sisters tired of the infant. Then they'd walk away chatting about what they'd do next as he sat in open-mouthed shock at their abandonment.

Dawn always hurried to swoop him up before he started in with howls of fury that she thought justified. Her beautiful son, tears dampening his angry red face, meant no more to these privileged girls than any other toy they could discard at will.

Ranch life and what she learned of her Blackfeet relatives left Dawn no illusions about differences between those confined in poverty and the white people who prospered around the reservation's borders. Willow Creek Boarding School still operated. Blackfeet children sickened and died while the Flowers girls played with Bird until he bored them.

Eleanor mentioned to Dawn that the sisters would be sent back East or even to Europe in a few years to attend private schools for future debutants. Those, Dawn bit her lip from observing, would be nothing like the brutal Indian boarding schools.

Would Isabelle and Patricia Flowers amuse classmates by telling how they played with a little Indian buck at their far away home? Or would they forget all about Bird? Most likely they wouldn't think to talk about him at all, and that suited his mother.

The guilty thought that Nora and Jim Li had not yet seen the grandson they would love gnawed at Dawn's conscience. Somehow she had to nudge Michael into the kind of maturity that allowed forgiveness. To deprive grandparents the right to see their grandson seemed heartless. They must not die without seeing him.

Watching Bird grow reminded Dawn of life's cycles. Time slipped into and out of the four seasons of each year with indifferent serenity. But family members remained precious. Dawn promised herself that she would somehow, someday, introduce Bird to his North Fork family

~ ~ ~

Father John, bent even farther with age, came out to speak with Dawn and Michael at the ranch several times through Bird's first winter concerning the matter of Bird's baptism. Eleanor, a Protestant, had no keen interest in this part of Bird's upbringing, but she finally had enough of the Father's unannounced appearances, often timed just as dinner would be served.

"Baptize Bird," she snapped at Dawn, "if just to get this old priest to stay away from the ranch. If you don't, he'll start trying to convert me or even worse Dan. We'd all live to regret that."

~ ~ ~

In late spring, Dawn and Michael bundled Bird up into his cradleboard and took him to Midvale for his christening. Strong sunlight poured in the church's windows as though the Blackfeet's great Creator Sun joined in taking pleasure in Bird's baptism. Molly and Virgil stood at the altar to serve as Bird Benjamin Larkin's godparents. Michael stood next to Dawn. Bird fussed, gasping as Father John spilled a little Holy Water over his dark hair. Dawn wondered if Michael thought how much it would mean to Mama Nora to know her grandson had been christened Catholic, especially by Father John.

After the ceremony, a beaming Molly Caldwell interrupted her own cooing baby talk with Bird to make the announcement, "It's time you showed this boy off to the rest of your mother's people. Time you take him to the reservation. Let the elders hold him and sing to him and later on tell him stories."

"You go ahead," Michael said with a smile. "I knew this would happen one of these days. I'll go stack wood with Virgil and see you and Bird at the ranch tonight."

Dawn kissed his cheek. "Thank you," she murmured.

Turning eagerly to Molly she said, "I want my son to hear the language, and I want to learn the language, too, so I can speak it with our Blackfeet relatives. Could an elder teach me while others are with Bird?"

"Yes. I'll take you to Lucy. Lucy is so old she remembers the days of warriors hunting the buffalo. The days when everything came to us from the earth, and we lived in freedom before the starving time. Those days we laid our heads on the mountains for our pillows." Molly sighed, "She remembers seeing the buffalo."

Molly handed Bird back to Dawn who bundled him into his clean moss bag wrapped in buckskin including a buckskin hood to protect his face from the fresh wind. She tied it to the cradleboard and secured that with heavy straps to the pommel of her saddle.

Molly nodded her approval. "You're good at being his mother, Dawn. And I think you will serve both yourself and us Blackfeet well by learning all you can about our ways. You walk in the white peoples' world and soon will be able to cross back and forth from there to our Blackfeet lives."

"I want that," Dawn said. "I took an oath to do it. I can help Sweet Grasses' people better when I understand Blackfeet and more of what went on before the reservations."

They rode the fourteen miles to Browning and north for two more, arriving at a squat log cabin. A large group of Sweet Grass's family members, old and young, had been waiting. They exclaimed in joy at seeing Bird. Wrinkled brown faces burst into grins, some toothless from age and malnutrition, some pocked from what they called the spotted disease. Dawn knew it as smallpox. Some of the faces had the beauty of youth and health. Hands, some small and smooth others scarred and crooked from lifetimes of hard use, reached out toward the newcomer.

After they settled on chairs or the floor, and everyone who wished to hold Bird had done so, Dawn spoke to her relatives. With Molly interpreting for the elders, Dawn told them all about Bird's being born on the same evening that his parents met George Bird Grinnell, the great man who'd been adopted into the Blackfeet tribe. She explained Bird's name. The smiles didn't turn to frowns until she told them that Eleanor Flowers had been Dawn's midwife. Then Dawn heard mutters of what Molly told her later meant, "What does that woman know? Married to a thief who trespassed on our land."

Male and female relatives and friends came into the small, dark rooms, entering and leaving all afternoon, letting cold air in and blasts of heat escape. A wood fire crackled background noise to their voices. Molly introduced Dawn to Stabbed-in-the-Water Woman, also called Lucy Drake. A skimmed milk-colored film of blindness coated the old woman's eyes, but Lucy Drake smiled with tender pleasure at Dawn's request that she teach her the old language.

They agreed to meet the next Sunday to begin Dawn's practical and spiritual education in the old ways. Dawn retrieved Bird who'd fallen asleep to the tune of a lullaby. Molly told her the words were funny: "Magpie, magpie, go before me and stab your bag by the door."

When the sun descended, an escort of men, each one Dawn's cousin or uncle, rode with her under a moonless night sky as far as the Flowers ranch boundaries. She thanked them and rode in alone as mute stars congregated into ancient pictures in the black sky.

Yellow lantern light flowed from the tall windows of the Flowers' home and also from her cozy bunkhouse. Dawn rode in eager to tell Michael what she'd learned. After all this time, her heart still quickened with anticipation when she knew she would soon be wrapped in his arms, gazing into his attentive eyes.

~ ~ ~

On the Sunday visits that followed, Dawn often left Bird with any of four different grandmothers in a three-room cabin near Lucy's. Dawn stayed with him until assured that he felt safe and happy. The time that took grew shorter and shorter.

Then she walked to Lucy's to learn the Blackfeet language, which had grown, she found out, from Algonquin roots. Seated at Lucy's scarred wood table across from Molly and the white-haired teacher, Dawn grimaced as the other two chortled in merriment at her first efforts to form Blackfeet words.

After a number of such Sundays, Dawn came to a slow understanding of how tribal language differed from English. As she tried to exchange words, listening for the tones and emphases that Lucy and Molly used, she realized why Blackfeet speech sounded so different from any she'd heard before.

"Why, there's no 'r' sound in any of these words! At least not so far," she said one Sunday to Molly as the two and Bird rode away from Browning while prairie outlines faded into red-brown and deep purple.

Molly nodded. "There are other sounds in English that we have no use for in our tongue. What are they? Listen for them. Three you haven't found yet."

~ ~ ~

Dawn began to listen and treat the tribe's language like a puzzle. What were the shapes and colors of missing pieces? After four more lessons, as she bundled Bird into his cradleboard and carried him outside, she declared to Molly, "When I listen, I don't hear b or f either."

Molly nodded. "That is good listening. I'll take pity on you for the last one. Do you ever hear l?"

Dawn thought for a moment then shook her head.

"You won't, I promise." Molly laughed at the other's exasperated groan.

But over time, Dawn started to hear the nuances and structures unique to the language of her mother's people. By late spring, she could use the additions placed at the beginnings and endings of words that allowed just one word to express a whole sentence. She could understand with a single word who was engaged in an action, what person or animal they were doing it to, and how and when they did it.

In time Lucy sent Dawn to White Bull, a tall, broad-shouldered elder with long snow-colored hair. In his cabin, with a daughter serving tea, he told stories of the Sun Creator, the Sun Creator's wife the Moon, and their son Morning Star. Dawn and Molly sat spellbound. Through White Bull's stories of these divinities and the animals and great chiefs of the past, Dawn learned the sacredness of the number 4, with its connection to the four seasons, and the four directions.

"One day White Bull announced, "I will now teach you of the winter count." He rose stiffly and beckoned them to enter the main room of his cabin. He left them seated together while he walked, limping from an old injury, to his room. Dawn heard him grunt as he lifted something that must have been heavy. He carried a buffalo robe when he returned to them. "This is a record of many things that happened to us."

As the old man unfolded his robe with reverence, she saw that its pale underside had been painted with a spiral of years. "It's a history," she breathed leaning over the table where he'd smoothed the tanned hide flat. "A history in pictures."

"It reminds us of what we must not forget."

Through the afternoon, he pointed with one bent finger to the pictographs in their spiral on the great robe. He talked of what had been important to the Blackfeet. There were scenes of sufferers ill and spotted with smallpox lying in lodges and attended by weeping loved ones. " This, he said, gesturing to a depiction of stars plummeting to earth. "The winter when the stars fell."

When she spoke to Molly about the star picture, she nodded. "Virgil says it was the winter of 1833. He says he read about it. Meteors filled the whole western sky."

On another Sunday afternoon when spring began to crack the ice in the creeks and snow melted into the prairie, White Bull showed Dawn the scars on his chest from taking part in the medicine lodge ceremony, as well as from wounds received during raids for horses, and in battles against the white soldiers. He spoke of the scalps he'd taken in battle.

"Did you keep them?" she asked, repulsed but also wanting to see.

He shook his head. "No. The women danced with them on big sticks. They took their time in that Scalp dance. They weren't laughing. It was solemn. Everyone remembered the many times sons and husbands did not return. We remembered that the pitiless owners of those scalps had killed those we lost. I gave my scalps to my son. He married a Blood woman and moved up north. He will hand them to his son one day."

White Bull went on to speak of the high value of bravery for a man and virtue for a woman. He told her stories about otters, bears, wolves, the under the water people, as well as birds: crows, owls, and eagles. He spoke of the dreary sand hills, that place where the dead lived on repeating the chores of the living, but with no joy to anticipate.

And he and his wife, a tiny bent-over woman who smiled but spoke little, initiated Dawn into the ways and ceremonies. More spirituality existed among tribal members than she'd imagined. She could hardly wait to go to the Medicine Lodge Ceremony that would take place in July.

~ ~ ~

But those visits to the reservation only took place on Sunday afternoons. Her daily labors during the week were exhausting and endless. Taking care of Bird and doing the menial tasks required by the Flowers meant long workdays and short nights. Mornings came all too soon.

Dawn kept many thoughts to herself as she cleaned and cooked for Eleanor. She understood that only politeness to her and Michael stopped Eleanor and Dan from expressing their scorn for Indians. Dawn also couldn't help overhearing cowboys talking. They often used such foul words about Blackfeet men and women that she trembled with anger.

Michael seemed happy, and that was a consolation to her. His shoulders broadened with the hard labor of the ranch as he matured into an experienced hand. Dan Flowers gave him more and more responsibility with horses and cattle. Michael also brought skills in building that he'd learned from Jim Li at Evening Star.

He only occasionally grumbled about Dawn's Sunday afternoons on the Blackfeet Reservation.

Chapter Six

May of 1910

Dawn picked up the *Great Falls Gazette* that Dan Flowers left beside his food-smeared plate after finishing lunch with his wife. The headline on page one caught Dawn's notice. The article described how after much debate by members of Congress about the law's wording, President Taft signed legislation creating Glacier National Park.

His signature reserved one million acres of the wilderness Michael and Dawn knew so well for posterity. Dawn felt happy for George Bird Grinnell, a little less so for Louis Hill, who had big plans to make the Park profitable for his Great Northern Railway.

~ ~ ~

Hill's enthusiastic conversation before, during, and after dinners with Dan and Eleanor Flowers throughout the next year and a half inevitably turned to promotion. He intended to develop Glacier National Park as America's new playground. Focused on luring the nation's tourists from their long focus on the European Alps, the railroad tycoon made the Great Northern Railway's motto 'See America First.' Dawn noticed that Hill planned to make his money off the well-to-do, those who could afford leisure and long train journeys. She hoped that somehow common people could enjoy the Park as well one day.

Dawn overheard these conversations as she served her employers and their guests, amazed they talked so freely in her presence. She felt as though she might as well have been invisible. But she listened and learned how entrepreneurs and ranchers held and influenced political power, enough to crush smaller landowners. Michael would tell her when she spoke of such things that, "A landless common man or woman has all the importance of a speck of dirt."

One December evening Dawn, beside Michael carrying a sleepy Bird, returned late to their bunkhouse. They'd had supper in the Flowers' kitchen. While Dawn bathed Bird and tucked him into bed, Michael brought in an armload of split logs to replenish the stack used for woodstove fires. They settled themselves in front of its comfortable heat, ready to chat about the day in private. Dawn picked up a sock to darn.

A knock sharp as the pecking of a large bird sounded on the door. With an annoyed grunt, Michael rose to answer it. Dawn peered from her chair. Louis Hill, bundled in his beaver coat against the cold spring night, stood outside alone. Michael invited him in as Dawn set aside her darning egg and needle.

"Dawn and Michael, what a cozy little place you have here. I take it the little boy is asleep?" Hill asked. He looked around the interior of the once impersonal bunkhouse, now made homey and comfortable. There were pictures on the walls, books, and a willow basket full of Bird's wooden and stuffed toys. "I was in here once when a couple of bachelor hands used it to sleep in. I wouldn't have thought even a woman's touch could save it, but I see I underestimated you, Dawn."

As he beamed at her, Dawn came alert. Where was Hill going with this flattery? It had never been a secret that her dark beauty charmed the man. But Michael hadn't been privy to all the dinners she'd help serve. Michael lacked Dawn's full awareness of Hill's many ways to charm and cajole others into doing as he wished.

Michael offered the tycoon the rocker he'd been sitting in and pulled out a table chair to sit near Dawn. He set it facing their unexpected guest. Hill paused a moment in open appreciation at how flickering gold-red firelight burnished Dawn's high cheekbones. Hill had a fondness for all things native to the Glacier region, including the Blackfeet whose history added to the romance of the West. When he called the tribe "Glacier Park Indians," Dawn felt the name for her friends and relatives veered toward insulting. Her mother's people were Blackfeet. At one time they dominated the Northern Plains.

She listened, not wanting to be distracted from Hill's words. Men like Hill were shrewd, interested in profit, not often passing time with flattering conversation among hired girls and cowboys. She waited for him to reveal the reason he'd come.

The rocker creaked as he leaned forward to speak across Dawn to her husband. "Michael, I judge you to be an intelligent and dependable young man with practical skills and leadership qualities. I have a proposition for both of you. I want you to work for me and my Great Northern Railway. There's no real future for you staying here drudging for Dan and dear Eleanor. You know that yourselves."

Michael and Dawn exchanged sidelong glances. What was Hill offering?

He continued, "Dawn, the agent in Browning has spoken of how you've worked to create a bridge between yourself and the Blackfeet. Learning the history and language of your mother's people shows you're wise beyond your years, young lady. Your tribal family and friends are fascinating survivors, or descendants of survivors, of an era lost and gone forever."

He pulled his luxurious coat off in the heat of the little cabin, laying it across the table gently as if it were a sleeping animal, not something reconstructed from sleek living things that would never wake again. "But we, and they, are able to recall it, at least in a limited way. I've been wanting someone with your skills, although I didn't expect that individual to have your beauty."

Dawn acknowledged that flattery with a small smile.

Over the next hour Hill wooed the young couple with promises of doubling their salary and providing opportunities for advancement for each. Dawn would start by cooking for the crews working to complete Hill's newest project, a hotel designed to be both rustic and luxurious in appearance. It would boast modern conveniences. It would be big enough to rival resorts of the Swiss Alps. Michael would be a foreman on one of the construction gangs under the Minneapolis builder contracted to build the great hotel near Midvale's west edge, a short walk from the train depot.

Hill surprised them as he continued. "Dawn would help fulfill my plan to send a group of Blackfeet to Minneapolis and points east to entice tourists to visit Glacier Park. I envision Blackfeet wearing full regalia, dancing before eastern audiences. You, Dawn, would serve as interpreter as needed. Of course, many of the Indians speak English, but not as well as you."

Dawn rankled at the display of it, as though her mother's people were exotic exhibits. She didn't say so though. The tour might never even happen. It seemed too fantastic.

Hill didn't stay long after he outlined his plans. After he left, Dawn checked on Bird, then sat back down in her rocker. "I need to think about that man's idea. Traveling East? Does that make any sense? He wants to show us off like displays in a zoo or a circus?"

Michael shrugged. "Take some time, but think of the opportunity to get off this place. You've never liked the way Dan and Eleanor lord it around." He sat down and took her hand. She could see how much he wanted to make the change. His yearning to accept Hill's offer softened her. She wanted Michael to be happy more than anything.

"I know you never wanted to cowboy forever," she said. "All right, let's make the move and decide about Hill's ideas involving train trips to Eastern cities later."

Michael took her in his arms. "Thank you, Sweetheart. You won't be sorry. It's going to lead to good things for us."

Dawn rejoiced in being able to leave the ranch with its thin veneer of tolerance for her being a mixed blood. Under the surface of their lives, where the foundation of her relationship with Eleanor might have flourished, Dawn sensed that her employer considered anyone with Indian blood unequal to any white person. The dinner invitation had never been repeated, even to Beartracks. He'd served his purpose when he'd provided information about Glacier Country to Grinnell and Hill.

Although Beartracks gave Dan Flowers an indifferent nod on occasions when he rode in to visit Dawn at the ranch, he didn't enter the ranch house again for any reason.

~ ~ ~

Something besides their change of employment occupied Dawn and Michael's attention in the summer of 1912. Lucy Drake and Molly explained to Dawn that the 4th of July as celebrated in Browning meant much more than the white Americans' patriotic holiday. It was a time of sacred ceremony for the Blackfeet. At the time of the annual Sun Dance the Sun God shows brightest and longest, coming closest to earth to bring life-giving warmth.

Lucy Drake had been the first to teach Dawn about the Sun God, the Creator's important representative. Seated in her cabin, Lucy, her white hair worn loose in mourning for a dead brother, leaned toward Dawn, seated on a stool before her. Lucy's white hair had no color, but pale blue like winter snow tinted the film over her eyes.

Lucy spoke, the words broken by wet sucking sounds as the grandmother inhaled from her pipe. The ember glowed in its bowl. "Long ago, the Sun God took certain of our ancestors up to visit him. He gave them blessings to bring back to give to the people." Lucy seemed to peer with her sightless eyes into Dawn's. Dawn focused on this woman who had known and loved Sweet Grass, her mother.

"There are holy women. I have been honored as one. We stand for those who returned with sacred blessings from their visits with the Sun God. Only a virtuous woman is allowed to sponsor a Sun Dance, a Sun Lodge some call it. I qualified because I swore before everyone that I never slept with any man except my husband. If I'd told a lie when I said it, I could never have lived to grow this old. And everyone knew how I nursed the sick people and prepared the dead, even those with the spots that whites call smallpox. I fed the starving, too, even when I grew tired and weak from my own hunger. I showed pity to all."

"What does it mean to sponsor a Sun Lodge?" Dawn asked.

Lucy pulled again on her lady's pipe. The scent of tobacco smoke joined the fragrance of burning pine coming from the stove. She puffed a moment and considered. "It means a lot of work and the responsibility to initiate others into sacred ceremonies. But that is also a great honor.

"The Sun Lodge woman must, with help, also build a holy lodge, and prepare food for the many who come to dance and receive blessings from the holy women in the lodge. This year you will receive a blessing from the Sun Lodge Woman. Her helper will paint your face in traditional ways."

Lucy coughed and set her small pipe aside. "The Sun Lodge woman will be tired and thin. She has to fast in her lodge for four days in preparation for the ceremonies. She and others will sing over a hundred songs during that time. Keep yourself a virtuous woman. Perhaps one day you will be initiated. Perhaps become a holy woman, too."

Lucy picked up the pipe again and blew a gray puff toward the already smoke-darkened ceiling. "Tell that husband of yours, that Michael, to come. You must come and bring your son. You'll see what we lost appear one more time. One more time…"

Lucy's voice trailed away. She coughed, set her pipe down, and did not pick it up again during the rest of their visit.

~ ~ ~

Molly and Dawn rode home over prairie covered with the soft green of returning life. Bird, a sleepy five-year-old, leaned back against Dawn. The little boy loved to explore the world of the reservation. He spoke Blackfeet. Days at the reservation were happy social occasions for him.

The riders smelled the soft earth full of spring's young arrivals, both plant and animal. Molly continued talking of the subject begun in Lucy Drake's cabin. "There will also be dancing. Our men are no longer allowed to torture themselves in sacrifice to the Sun God."

"Self-torture?" Dawn stared at Molly and shivered in the cooling air.

"Yes. A way of thanking the Sun God for having pity on them when they needed courage or speed to rescue themselves from danger during the past year. They used to pierce their chests twice and insert willow skewers with two ropes attached from them to a pole at the center of the dance. Then they danced with the ropes pulled tight until the skewers finally ripped out of the warrior's skin. The government says we can't do that now. They banned it over ten years back. But we still dance. Our relatives come from up north and other tribes come, too. And many others come to see us: white photographers and painters, other kinds of people like the ones who write books. Many come. Some from far away."

"Why do so many come?"

"Because they know it will be full of real true things: different dances, different parts, the actual regalia we wore and songs we sang and how we danced and what we ate. It won't be made up like those Wild West shows. The whites who come know, like we know, that the Catholic Church is pushing the government to stop the Sun Dance altogether. The whites who come to see us want to witness these last times while they still can."

She grimaced. "They want to wreck our lives and see into our past both at once. They'd better hurry from what Virgil tells me. That Bishop Carroll in Helena is making a big fuss about it." She made a face. "He calls our honored and sacred tradition barbaric. Virgil says this year or maybe next might be the end. Our last hurrah, or close to it."

"When it's closer to the time for the Sun Dance, I'll talk to Michael. If he agrees, our family will join you three at the camp." Dawn promised.

Molly smiled although the smile faded as she spoke. "We Montana Blackfeet, Southern Piegan we're known to some, will all take part. Our friends and relatives the Canadian Bloods, Northern Piegan, and other tribes from all directions will come together there. Like I said, homesteaders, ranchers, and other white people want to be there, too. It reminds all of us of the freedom we Plains Indians had. They keep us close, forced into one place. The game is free to go where it wants, but not us."

~ ~ ~

So, on the hottest day of July, Michael and Dawn rode with Bird a few miles beyond Browning. Dawn gasped as they crested a low ridge rough with dry, tawny grass. The circle camp appeared at the base below them, bigger than she'd expected and vibrant with hundreds of painted lodges encircling the big Sun lodge. A small lake within walking distance from the camp threw back the sun's reflection as its shining ripples supplied water to both people and horses.

They rode down to become part of the camp with the Caldwells. Molly and Virgil had already set up their lodge which would accommodate both families. Marissa almost hopped up and down, so excited for the opening procession to start. Drummers' throbbing beats issued what seemed invitations from their hearts. Dawn felt hers thump and pulse against her throat in unison with the drums. She felt a near compulsion to dance.

"You're just in time," Molly said with a smile. "We'll go watch the opening procession."

"I'll keep Bird here in the shade," Michael said. "He's too cranky from this front tooth coming in. You go on. See the sights."

Dawn smiled and kissed him.

"Wait. Marissa and I made something for you." Molly gestured for Dawn to follow into the lodge. There she pulled open a chest and lifted out a long pale buckskin dress with red quillwork on the blue shawl. Rows of elk teeth covered the shoulders and sleeves.

Dawn threw her arms around Molly and then Marissa. She took off her clothes and put the dress on. She imagined for a moment that she must look much as Sweet Grass had when she lived with her Blackfeet family before riding away with Beartracks. What had she felt that day? What would she think of Dawn being here now?

"We better hurry or we'll miss the procession," Marissa said, her eyes bright with anticipation. Dawn nodded, walking in pride with her auntie and cousin, the trio now a flawless part of the Blackfeet community.

Dawn thrilled at the sight of bedecked horses. Several white ones were painted with legendary scenes of bravery in battle. Everyone had dressed in the old ways. Gone were the everyday overalls and worn cotton dresses. These people appeared to have sprung from nature itself. Proud. Everyone looked so proud. Dawn would never forget the sight of them all seeming to share one feeling: that they were one united whole.

Eight riders, wearing feathered bonnets and carrying coup sticks, started the procession. They rode slowly at first, then gradually raised dust as they increased their speed. Behind the horsemen, tribal military societies, also called men's societies, walked with their shoulders back and their heads high.

Dawn noticed a tall blond artist flipping to a new page of his sketch book, intent on recording the whole procession as it passed before him. She watched him crouch for a new perspective, cock his head, and smile as he worked. No wonder he looked happy, she thought. An artist would want to capture all this.

"There's one of those artists you told me would come," she said to Molly.

"He's Heinrich Mann, a German painter Louis Hill talked into coming to paint scenes of us and the park for Railroad posters."

"He just paints advertisements?" Dawn felt let down. He looked like he loved what he sketched. He seemed fascinated.

"Heinrich likes to paint our portraits, too. He did one of me and Marissa. He's famous in Europe. Virgil says he's a serious artist, but he has to earn money. He paints for Louis Hill as well as himself. Virgil and Heinrich got acquainted because Virgil sends and receives telegraphs for Heinrich about his paintings. Heinrich doesn't speak either English or Blackfeet very well, being German. But he's been adopted into the tribe already. He paints all of us and wants to learn everything about our past. He listens and paints us the way we lived when the buffalo were here. He shows his respect for our ways."

The artist stood, brushed dust from his book, and glanced their way. He nodded to Molly and Marissa. His blue eyes rested on Dawn for a moment before he nodded to her as well. She felt he appraised her as a beautiful woman, but couldn't be sure. The man turned and resumed sketching the procession.

Before the Sun Dance ceremonies and dancing ended, Dawn had been allowed to enter the great Sun Lodge in the center of the camp. Inside, the Sun Lodge Woman's helper painted Dawn's face with red paint. Lucy was also there. Sun Woman herself imparted a blessing to Dawn. The woman wore a special headdress, the *Natoas,* with large plumes and feathers fixed to a rawhide band. For Dawn, that Sun Dance became a healing time, the first when her two selves, the white and the Blackfeet, came together. She felt changed. Complete.

~ ~ ~

Her sense of wholeness continued that night as she joined in the dancing and singing. The music carried her back to a lost time of freedom and bounty for her mother's people. She understood the depth and breadth of their loss. It wasn't just the land. They lost part of themselves when the great endless prairie shrank, when battles were lost, when treaties were broken, when powerful men sneered at their efforts to hold their culture together. Then others, like Louis Hill, urged them to act as though their lives hadn't changed, wanted them to keep the illusion he tried to create. It brought both pride and pain.

~ ~ ~

Michael spent most of his hours with the whites who'd come, including Louis Hill. On the day they packed to return to Midvale, Michael appeared with Heinrich Mann. The artist carried his sketchbook. When Michael introduced him to her, Heinrich bowed and smiled.

The long-limbed German stood a head taller than the other men. Although he spoke little, he carried himself with a relaxed assurance. Dawn noticed his dark blue eyes seemed to catch and store everything he saw. She wondered if it might be for a later sketch. Heinrich treated Molly, Marissa, and Dawn with the same respect as he gave the men. A white treating Blackfeet women with true respect was something rare in Dawn's experience. In fact, she noted a certain reserve in the German's manner toward her.

As she and Michael returned to Midvale, she spoke of Heinrich's difference from others.

Michael laughed. "Mann isn't just a painter; he's lived a big life. He speed-skated in competitions and became an important athlete in Germany.

He gained a reputation as a mountain climber and long-distance runner, too."

"A man of many talents," Dawn murmured.

After a few quiet moments, Michael spoke again. "We whites aren't all insulting to your people. It depends on our experiences. Growing up in Butte with my adopted parents, I heard nothing about Indians except that Indians were lazy, dishonest, and dirty. Same with Chinese. Then I found the three of you living together like you were, building up the ranch. I changed my mind. Besides, I'd fallen in love with you. I've never looked back from the first time I saw you."

Chapter Seven

Dawn and Michael settled into work in Midvale, its name soon changed to East Glacier Park. Louis Hill provided a cabin for their living quarters. This one had four small rooms, and Dawn loved having her own kitchen and a separate bedroom for Michael and her. They fit comfortably into their jobs of construction and cooking.

Then in the spring of 1913, Dawn picked up a letter at the East Glacier Post Office. Louis Hill had sent it along with a separate contract, a formal offer for her to travel east with the tribal members he'd hired. She read it as she walked home, and she kept on walking a mile out of town after she'd finished. She felt a flash of resentment so intense it startled her. She'd all but forgotten his earlier talk of her doing something like this. It would be another angle to attract tourists to Glacier National Park by exploiting the Blackfeet. Her inclination was to crumple and throw the offer into the prairie grass. *Let the wind carry it to the hawks. He turns us all into advertisements.*

According to the contract she'd be the interpreter for the other Blackfeet and would be paid well for that. Dawn knew that some tribal members who'd be with her could speak English, but not with her fluency in both languages. She'd also be expected to join the others in some of the dancing, help everyone during their hotel stays in various venues, and handle problems that might arise. Dawn smiled at how easy her achievement in languages sounded, how casually Hill assumed she could do this. In fact, it took months and years of practice for her to master the difficult Blackfeet language, and she still made mistakes at times.

She'd thought so often of Jim Li, her Papa Jim, when she'd been discouraged to the point of tears during her first months of learning. He'd come to America with some knowledge of English, but hadn't really become fluent until he'd lived among the white English-speaking Americans. Dawn learned the Blackfeet language because of her determination to know and communicate with Sweet Grass's family, to live close to her relatives, to understand them in part by knowing their words.

She'd awakened to the realization that the reservation Blackfeet had been placed in the most difficult situation imaginable. They'd lost so much of their way of living, their very culture. Yet white people wanted to see them as they'd been before the wars and the losses, as if they could keep and show only parts and all the rest didn't matter. The past had a romance that they were to reenact through dance, drumming, singing and costume even though it would never fully exist again. The shrinking land, the orders to stay in one place, to farm poor soil with inadequate tools, to speak English, and to lose the old spiritual ways, meant being part of a shadow culture, but without the great freedom and days of honor under the life-giving sun.

She told Michael she wouldn't consider going unless she could take Bird with her. He would be not quite seven years old by the time of the proposed journey, still too young to be without his mother's care. Michael surprised Dawn by agreeing. He'd seen the large payment figure on Hill's offer. He said it might be good for his wife and son both to see what else there was to America.

Still, even if Hill granted her condition that Bird be with her, she couldn't decide what to do. Those who were already committed to going would want her with them, but she didn't know if this were the right thing. Did it demean or did it elevate her native relatives? Would her doubts about the whole thing hurt those who'd decided on the journey?

~ ~ ~

She went to visit Lucy one day. "I don't know what to do," she told the blind elder. "I want to be a bridge between our cultures. Is this the best way?"

Lucy puffed on her ever-present pipe. "You have become one of us. We consider you so. But you need to be alone at times as we all know. Go into the mountains by yourself. See what signs you might find there. Give your attention to our animal families. They have much to show us."

Dawn decided to follow Lucy's wise advice and take time alone to decide what to do. On the morning of a rare day off, she left Bird with Molly and Marissa. They told her with excitement that they had agreed to go. When she expressed her doubts, Molly reminded her of her advice to Dawn about working for the Flowers. "We have to survive, not starve," she said. "We'll show the whites in the East our dances and come back with money for clothes and tools."

Dawn borrowed a pinto mare from the Caldwells and rode into the mountains near Two Medicine Lakes. Past the lower and upper lakes, she traversed up a trail the Great Northern Railway had built after contracting with the government. Louis Hill wanted such a trail because he planned not just hotels in Glacier National Park, but a series of chalets between them. Before long Dawn directed the mare to pick its way above the tree line into screed slopes that rose toward rocky peaks.

Scattered, unsheltered limber pines bent to near-horizontal angles from constant wind that made her eyes water. It tore through her hair as though with evil intent. She thought about turning back toward East Glacier, but feeling compelled, she proceeded on. Her shawl snapped hard. She dismounted and led her horse. Such a wind made all animals nervous. Their inability to hear above it made them helpless to danger. She leaned into the relentless rush and push of air.

At last she found rest behind a large boulder that offered protection from the turbulent onslaught.

She mounted again, but bent low to her mare's warm neck, urging the pinto on until they rounded into an area with more limber pine. Dawn turned the horse and onto switchbacks as she steadily gained elevation. She continued to climb on patchy ridges intermingled with shale. Finally, Dawn reached a ghost forest of long-dead white-bark pines. The mare picked her way between the vertebrae and skulls of winter-killed elk scattered among dry twigs and grass.

Horse and rider continued climbing up and up until they reached a jutting outcrop of rock that presented an endless view. Dawn gazed over Two Medicine Valley and perhaps one hundred miles away to the Sweet Grass Hills, sacred to the Blackfeet—visible white humps like apparitions in the sun-bleached distance. The three distinct rounded landforms rose up outlined in palest blue. The Blackfeet sold them only when under the unbearable duress of hunger and poverty. Dawn remembered how White Bull had explained that the time they sold the sacred hills was another sad chapter born of the whites' exploitation of her mother's people.

The whites had known full well that the Indians had no choice but to sell because they were starving. The chiefs and other leading men who'd hunted and raided as warriors couldn't accept their loved ones dying before their eyes. With bitter sadness the Blackfeet had no choice but to sell their Sweet Grass Hills.

Sweet Grass Hills. Dawn sat on her mount, scrutinizing the revered lands as they shone in the wind-billowed dusty haze. The Blackfeet had once been lords of all the endless sweep of prairie spread before her.

"Nothing prepared me for Hill's offer." she whispered into the gale. "I don't know what to do." She prayed for a sign that would show her how to answer the powerful, sophisticated tycoon.

Dawn tired but still felt drawn to ascend into higher country to the west. Finally horse and rider reached a plateau high enough that it let Dawn scan the Two Medicine River far below, a silver thread of twisting beauty. The Rockies rose purple-gray against the sky. She tied the mare to a bone-colored snag. Dawn still hadn't decided how to answer Louis Hill. She only felt she'd been drawn to this place as though she were powerless to do anything else.

She sensed some being's approach. Could it be danger, or would it be something to help her? She breathed hard, heart hammering in her throat. She startled when the pinto began to snort and pitch against the reins. Dawn turned to remount, but the mare resisted. Dawn spun to the ground when the horse snapped the branch off and galloped away.

She scrambled to her feet, looked back, and froze. Two long-legged gray shapes appeared not more than fifty feet away, paused, met, and studied her dark eyes with their own amber ones. Calm, watchful, the animals stood motionless. She should have been afraid, frightened witless, but she faced the creatures as if spellbound. "Wolves, are you spirits?" she whispered. "Are you sent to tell me what to do? To help me?"

The larger wolf turned its head then stared at her again while pack members walked out of the forest as if summoned. The pack, numbering eight, stopped. None moved. The biggest wolf's self-possessed gaze met Dawn's again without wavering. She spoke softly. "Wolf, are you here to hurt me or to pity me? Should I take my son and go to the cities so far away? Should I help Hill expose the people?"

The wolf's mate, or so Dawn assumed it to be, turned its head to look east, then swung it back. Its amber stare bore into hers again.

"Are you sure? I have been afraid."

Both wolves glanced east again and brought two sets of eyes back to her a third time. After an eternity they pivoted east in unison and loped away, their pack following.

Dizzy with relief, Dawn felt the ground tilt. She sat on a knee-high boulder and studied the pines behind the tree line that had absorbed the wolves. She inhaled breath in long gasps and considered how the wolves had appeared to guide her. Her Blackfeet teachers taught her that animals could show humans what to do. Dawn had seen how white men like Flowers reviled wolves—reviled them as Indians had been reviled. Many whites still hated and insulted them. But these wolves came to her with their pack, then traveled straight east.

She had her answer. She would show her Blackfeet friends and relatives in all their strength and beauty to the whites in those big cities. She would go east. She would present herself and the others with pride even if, like the wolf, they might be misunderstood by some of the city people they would meet.

Sitting there relishing her new clarity, Dawn breathed a prayer of thanks. She shivered with the new and powerful feeling, but also with the cold. Without her horse she could never be able to cover the long miles home. She'd be exposed to danger. She reproached herself. She should have been armed, but in her confusion had forgotten everything except her quest.

Dawn stood and straightened. The only thing to do was to press on. She started walking down the ridges moving toward the low country. She hadn't trekked far when she came upon her horse eating grass, as calm as though nothing had caused her to bolt. Dawn approached with care, then rested her face against the mare's soft muzzle.

Regaining her mount, she rode unhurried toward the plains. The day had left her somehow stronger, more confident. She would accept Hill's offer and she would take Bird with her. He should learn to take pride in his one-fourth Blackfeet blood. This would be an adventure to share with everyone.

As Dawn continued riding toward home in the fading light, she felt worry niggle again. Night would fall soon. She felt the evening cool.

Hunger attacked. She wished she could have started back earlier. Michael would be worried. Shadows lengthened and blended into indistinct dark patches on the forest floor. Then she saw Michael riding hard toward her in the gloom.

"What happened?" he called out.

When they'd reached each other, he swung a leg over the saddle and leaped down to pull her to him in rough relief. "Where the hell have you been?"

"The spirits gave me a gift." She pulled back just enough see his face. "It's for Bird, too. Let me tell you."

Michael held her face in his leather-gloved hands, breathing hard. "Come on home. You can tell me what happened as we ride. We need to warm you up."

Riding beside her husband, Dawn did her best to explain it all. He'd already agreed to her signing the contract. "I'll put in overtime while I'm alone," he said. "With both of us working, we'll eventually afford a place of our own."

~ ~ ~

And so it was that Dawn joined a troupe of twenty-one Blackfeet—twelve men, eight women and Bird—to ride the railway and spread enthusiasm for vacations in Glacier National Park. The group waited under the white-blue morning sky of August 1, 1914, to board their designated Great Northern passenger car with an accompanying dining car just behind it, and a baggage car after that. Before workers pushed its doors shut, Dawn had an unexpected glimpse of rolled up tipis with covers and poles. The call to board came before she could find anyone to ask about them. She kissed Michael goodbye. He hugged Bird, and then she took their excited little boy's hand. They climbed the steps and settled, Bird next to the window. He waved goodbye to his father, and the adventure started.

Dawn had been given an itinerary and the names of people assigned to meet the dancers at each city where they disembarked. She took the papers out to read so often she soon had both memorized. She prayed that all would go well, that they wouldn't be left standing confused and forlorn on station platforms. She hoped she could handle everything required of her. She hoped she'd been right to take Bird.

Dawn didn't understand until years later that taking Bird with her on the promotional tour for Glacier National Park did more than just introduce them both to America's great cities. It would instill a permanent love of travel in her son. He reveled in looking out train windows at the country rolling by. Enthralled, he watched the land roll out from mountains to prairies to cities.

Dawn often held him on her lap. They marveled to see the undulating prairie spread into eastern North Dakota flatlands that built into the gentle rise and fall of Minnesota farm country. They watched for milestones farther east. Even small towns seemed big to them. Yet as the train continued on, communities changed in everything from architecture to inhabitants' clothing. And then the cities! Metropolitan streets were so jammed with life and tall buildings that only the sky above appeared spacious.

Dawn felt nervous about her responsibilities. But she thrilled to be traveling east toward Boston where Mama Nora lived before coming to Montana. Dawn and Bird were seeing the same country. On her own, no longer hiding letters home from Michael's eyes, Dawn wrote back to Nora and Jim at Evening Star, describing everything she and Bird and the others saw and did. She posted correspondence at any stop along the way where she could hurry to a mailbox or post office and make it back on board before the train moved again.

She didn't feel as much on her own as she'd expected because Molly and Marissa traveled with her. The older woman might be overwhelmed by the crowds at times, but she served as a loyal confidante and counselor.

Marissa kept Bird company, almost as awed as the boy by the crowds, the buildings, the modernity of so much they saw.

Tribal members stayed together. Sometimes they slept on the train, but more often in hotels. Bird's uncles and aunties spoiled and entertained him. Well behaved by nature, he never lapsed into boredom or disruptive unruliness. The adults commented on how everything the little boy saw and heard seemed to thrill him. Nothing then or in later memories of the trip could ever dull his experiences.

Other Blackfeet told jokes and stories of tribal myth and history. The elders shared vivid early memories or events and myths their parents had related to them. Their fellow travelers' tales of legendary raids on other tribes and of brave acts by both men and women nurtured Dawn and Bird's already strong respect for traditional tribal ways. And they gossiped about everyone back home.

At Hill's insistence, the dancers wore regalia even as the train pulled into cities where they performed. Dawn wore soft white doeskin dresses with rows of elk teeth down their sleeves and fronts, quill work on their shawls, and blue and red bead work on her leggings and moccasins.

They performed their dances at the bigger cities. Many a society matron went home envious of a beadwork pattern or the way light played on Dawn's lithe curves as she danced draped in supple white doeskin. Bird dressed and danced like the others. He loved to whirl and weave in and out. He learned to stop when the audience didn't see his abrupt, still crouch coming. He was the eagle or the deer or the buffalo.

Dawn not only danced, but found the courage to answer the audience's questions. She let go of stage fright and spoke of her people and their home with pride. She interpreted and dealt with any problems faced by dancers. Thankfully, troubles were sparse. Blackfeet performances charmed and held audiences' interest. Many who spoke to the dancers after their performances announced the intent to vacation in Glacier National

Park. Dawn relaxed as the troupe progressed east. She felt proud of her fellow performers, who conveyed dignity and pleasure to their audiences.

Sadness invaded the group only when Marissa surprised everyone by becoming so homesick it appeared for a while she wouldn't be able to finish the tour. Molly, Dawn, and the rest wrapped the depressed girl in love, never leaving her alone in a room. They shared how they, too, sometimes felt about ugly, noisy cities. But they also talked of beauty in the way buildings and parks looked. She would never have a chance to see them again with this particular mix of elders and young people. They laughed about the sometimes arrogant, sometimes harried, and sometimes kind white people they met. And those who told Marissa of such things always reminded her, too, that the prairie and mountains would be waiting, that every day brought them closer to starting home.

Chapter Eight

Only once, just after they disembarked in New York City, did Dawn become truly angry. She'd maintained her quiet, even-tempered watchfulness. But in time so much responsibility wore at her nerves. She felt almost as ready to go home as Marissa did.

The troupe had gone by taxi from Grand Central Station to the McAlpin Hotel. A truck behind them carried lodge poles and the painted hides for traditional tipis.

They'd already been to Chicago and Philadelphia, but New York City had so many different kinds of people, crowds all moving with speed and purpose. Dawn clutched Bird's hand as they left the taxi. He almost walked into a streetlamp after he'd fixed his eyes on tops of the tall buildings around them. "Mama, I never imagined buildings so tall. It feels like I just walked into a big room and its walls go up to the sun! The room doesn't have a roof!"

Dawn laughed. "The buildings have roofs and ceilings in every room," she said.

An officious young white man met them at the hotel. He ignored Bird while he spoke in nasal tones to Dawn, informing her that he worked for Louis Hill.

"Mr. Hill has so many brilliant ideas." The young man smiled. His lips formed a thin line upturned to vertical at the corners. His eyes darted from her to the members of the group. "He says if you do something special, act on an idea he's had, there will be a bonus in it for each of you."

"What does Mr. Hill want us to do now?" Dawn sighed. She felt so weary from the day's train journey. Although her voice remained low as always, her grip tightened on Bird's hand.

She'd been traveling from Montana to strange cities and dealt with sophisticated people sometimes loud and always fast in their speech. They frightened or annoyed her at times. Some were arrogant like this tall man with his oily hair and reek of cologne. He smirked just a little as he looked down at them in every way a person could. Actually, he looked Dawn up and down. She'd seen this look before on the journey from other men. She glared at him with the level of cool disdain she'd shown the others.

Only decades later when she remembered such moments on the tour did Dawn feel a bit of resentment mixed with her gratitude. She'd appreciated the opportunity to travel, but Hill had required so much for a young and inexperienced woman to manage. It had been so tiring at times. Still, she'd grown into the job of being the group leader because of encounters like the one that involved her at the McAlpin. She'd show this white man that she could handle whatever he might be trying to hand her. She could move back and forth between the worlds. After all, that's why Hill hired her.

The young man straightened, rebuffed and ready to be businesslike. "Mr. Hill has decided you Blackfeet should show how you prefer to live at home on the prairie instead of sleeping inside hotel rooms. His plan is that you refuse to sleep anywhere but on the roof where you will be at ease and comfortable in the outdoors and in your tipis."

Dawn gave a mirthless laugh. "At Mr. Hill's direction and for the same reasons, I'm sure, as everything else we do. We're here to stir up publicity for Glacier National Park." She laughed a second time, but this held no mirth either, not the normal pleasure that bubbled up when she joked with Bird and their companions. She felt bitter and wanted all this to be over.

She excused herself to confer with the others, leaving Bird with the young man who reddened and frowned. "Speak to him in Blackfeet while I'm over there," she told Bird. "That will slow him down."

Bird did. His listener jumped a little at the sound of the piping voice, then peered down at Bird with suspicion. "You don't look like a little buck," he said.

Bird frowned. "I'm not a deer," he muttered in Blackfeet. But the man didn't hear him.

Dawn came back looking unhappy. "We will do this, but it's Mr. Hill's idea, not ours. It might interest you to know that I grew up in a home with a roof and walls. I'm as used to sleeping in a bed as you are. At least I imagine you are. Many of these people are as well. After all, they were taken from their families and placed in boarding schools as small children. Boarding schools with hard iron beds."

"The *New York Times* reporter or any of the others won't give a hoot about that. Just go on now and get set up on the roof. That will provide an angle for reporters covering the performances. We'll outdo what Wild Bill Cody used to pull off. Hill's a genius."

With that the man turned away to oversee workmen hauling cumbersome tipi poles up the stairs. People stared at the Blackfeet. Some shrank away as the tribal dancers walked through the lobby. Dawn reclaimed Bird's hand, and they stepped into an elevator that lurched in such a fast upward thrust that mother and son both jumped. Dawn felt uneasy to the point of disoriented. All their property had been transported to somewhere above them. To the roof, in fact.

~ ~ ~

In spite of the insulting implication in Hill's order that they couldn't sleep well indoors, the dancers had fun looking down from their high vantage point after their two performances at a nearby theater. Dawn lifted Bird and let him sit on the level, foot-wide concrete railing at the roof's edge while she kept her arms around him. He leaned back against her and they scanned the endless city lights. "Like upside down stars," Bird said.

"I'd like to fly over all this like a red-tailed hawk, but one with my human mind," his mother said.

Later, in their lodge, Dawn drifted toward slumber. Hill had provided hangings for tipi walls and sleeping couches complete with buffalo robes to keep the dreamers warm. The robes were necessary because the McAlpin manager did draw the line at fires in the lodges. Fire meant danger.

Unable to fall completely asleep with sounds of the city rising from below, Dawn imagined that in the shape of a hawk she did swoop through the magical city's canyons, looking into the windows of all who lived there, listening to their bouncing or elegant music, tasting their elaborate or simple dinners, flying inside to touch the soft or stiff fabrics of their curtains and their blankets.

None of those could be as warm and protecting as the buffalo robe she'd wrapped around her. Or as Michael beside her in their little cabin at home. She missed her husband.

Bird's voice surprised her. She'd thought he slept, but he spoke up. "Mama, Marissa still wants to go home, but I'd like to keep going. I'd like to see every big city in the world."

"Oh, tell Marissa you'll miss her too much if she doesn't stay with us, Bird. Tell her we'll go home soon. We'll all be filled with joy to be back home. We just have to stay now and do what we promised Mr. Hill we'd do. You can be a world traveler when you grow up."

~ ~ ~

One place would prove more memorable for the Blackfeet troupe than the lights, traffic, buildings, and multi-colored crowds of New York. When they arrived there, Dawn recognized Washington, D.C., as a place where marble and brick bespoke power that ran silent and strong as a deep river's current. Decisions that affected the entire world were made in that place. There were statues everywhere. Tribal members saw the White House and the imposing Capitol Building. They walked through the red castle of the Smithsonian Museum. For the rest of his life Bird would find joy in exploring new cities.

Dawn was invited to have coffee with a Smithsonian Museum administrator in his office. As it turned out the distinguished white-haired man was an anthropologist with a keen interest in all things indigenous. He was knowledgeable, and Dawn found herself telling him about both the joys and problems of native life as lived on the reservations. He told her of his dream that one day the Smithsonian would have a section devoted to American Indian and Eskimo history. Dawn left feeling optimistic and that she'd been of help to someone who respected tribal cultures.

They slept in regular guest rooms in the Hotel Washington. Bird and the others gaped at the waxy white blossoms and shiny dark leaves of magnolia trees. There were uniformed soldiers walking about the streets, and more dark people. According to one of his uncles, those dark peoples' grandparents had been slaves. Dawn explained to Bird what she thought he might understand about the Civil War. Bird was too young to grasp what being a slave entailed. "Why would one person even want to own another?" he asked with a baffled expression.

There would be time for all that. Dawn marveled at how fast Bird adapted to being in the nation's capitol. Everything fascinated him. Dawn knew with certainty she'd been right to bring her son with her. This trip changed and enlarged Bird's ability to understand the world.

On their second afternoon in Washington, the troupe gathered in the lobby to wait for one of Hill's employees to guide them through selected parts of the city. As instructed, they dressed in Blackfeet regalia, but the women wore calico dresses instead of deerskin.

Molly saw the painter first. "Look," she said, pulling Dawn's sleeve. "Isn't that Heinrich Mann?"

Dawn looked up from the book she'd been reading and straightened. She smiled.

"Why, it's Molly Caldwell and Marissa. And as I remember, you are Dawn Larkin." Heinrich Mann came toward her, his hand outstretched to take hers. He paused to give a wave to others who'd modeled for him in Montana. "What are my Blackfeet friends doing here?"

Dawn noted how firm but gentle the cultured artist's grasp felt.

"Mr. Mann, I hadn't thought to see you here. We're dancers bringing our performances to people Mr. Hill thinks will want to come to Montana on his trains after watching us. We're not introduced first as Blackfeet, but as the Glacier Indians." She gave a rueful little smile.

"Ah, yes. Well, I became a U.S. Citizen two years ago, but now I am on indefinite leave from Mr. Hill's employ. Mr. Hill understands that winds of change are twisting around us all. I suspect I am a political embarrassment because I'm German-born. Now I must register my address at the closest post office to my address. The trouble is, temporarily I don't have one. "

Dawn didn't understand his saying this, but noticed Mann didn't criticize even the man who laid him off— tact rare in her experience. He seemed so decent a human being.

"I thought you loved Glacier country and your Blackfeet friends. After all, the tribe adopted you," Molly broke in.

Heinrich leaned toward them and lowered his voice. "It's not popular to be German-born in America right now. There is a war in Europe, you know. The United States favors the English more than us of German heritage. I can't blame your government for feeling that way, but now nobody trusts or wants me or other Germans around. My paintings that were so sought after lean neglected against the walls of my room. They are unwanted and so am I, their creator."

"Will you return to Germany?" Dawn asked.

Heinrich frowned and shook his head. "No, I want to stay in America more than ever."

Dawn considered. "I come from a place more remote than Midvale, I mean than East Glacier Park as Mr. Hill calls the town now. It's almost a day's travel beyond Belton where the train depot is. My folks have a ranch called Evening Star near the North Fork of the Flathead River. They're about three miles north of a settlement called Polebridge, just a mercantile and post office and a few buildings. Mama's Irish and Papa Jim is Chinese. Believe me, Mama isn't fond of the English, and Papa Jim doesn't care where anyone is from. I could write to them to see if they could take you on as a helper for room and board. They couldn't afford to pay you. But you'd have privacy there. They don't get many visitors. You'd have a post office to register your address."

Heinrich said, "My God, you can't imagine what that would mean to me. I'm strong and I'll learn the ranch work. I would like so much to stay in the Rockies. And a remote place would be ideal for a German-born stuck in America. Our two countries are squaring off to fight each other."

Dawn pondered the possible war with Germany. Why would the United States want to fight a war so far away? How could such a war impact her life? It had changed everything for Heinrich Mann. The Indian wars had changed life for the Blackfeet, but had been fought where they lived. She didn't see how war in Europe could affect her much.

In years to come she'd marvel at how naïve her young mind had been.

~ ~ ~

When the promised group escort failed to appear, the German artist volunteered to be their impromptu tour guide. He took them out into the humid heat of a typical District of Columbia summer day. "The air just feels wet, and it's hard to breathe," a wilting Marissa declared.

Heinrich walked with them, no one hurrying under that enervating southern sun, to the Library of Congress. Bird gaped at its high ceilings. Many books, paintings, murals, and writings, along with quotes from great writers on the walls fascinated him. Heinrich Mann guided and explained what they saw, pointing out precious old books, some that even President Thomas Jefferson had owned.

Next, he took them to art galleries and explained the different styles of other artists. "Someday perhaps peace will return, and my own works will be shown here," he added.

But the troupe became most impressed when Heinrich took them to the Capitol Building with its big white dome. He ushered them into the offices of Senator Thomas J. Walsh, one of the congressmen from Montana. The hearty Democrat shook hands with each person and made a special fuss over Bird. After that the Senator stood with the visiting dancers on the Capitol steps and had one of his congressional aides take a photograph of them together. Heinrich lifted Bird to his shoulders, the child's hair bright in the sunshine, his smile even brighter.

~ ~ ~

Heinrich decided to ride back with the troupe on the Great Northern. Molly had invited him to stay with the Caldwells until they heard whether Nora and Jim could accommodate him at their ranch. He took out a sketch pad and drew every member of the troupe. He made several sketches of Dawn and Bird.

"If I am able to go to Evening Star, I'll take these to your folks," he said.

Dawn fought against tears that sprang from his thoughtfulness. The drawings would mean so much to the dear people at Evening Star who'd never seen their grandson. The Senator had promised to send each person a print from the photographer's finished group picture. She'd ask Heinrich to show his to them, too.

Heinrich also sketched scenery as the train rolled west. He gave Bird paper and pencil to do his own drawings along with him. He gave the boy suggestions in a gentle voice on how to put the eyes lower on a face. Halfway down looked more realistic. Children and beginners tended to put eyes too close to the hairline.

With a wry smile, he told Dawn, "The last time I rode this way I was Louis Hill's guest in his private car. My English and his German were so bad we could hardly understand each other."

~ ~ ~

The Blackfeet, except for Molly, Marissa, and Dawn, left the train when it stopped at the Browning Depot. All expressed joy at being home with loved ones. The three women, Bird, and Heinrich continued on to East Glacier where Virgil met them. He engulfed Molly and Marissa in a tight embrace. They clung to him in delight at being back.

"Michael is working. I'll see you and our Bird to your place on our way home," he told Dawn. He also held out a letter.

"It's from Mama," Dawn said, ripping the envelope open. After scanning it, she smiled at Heinrich. "She and Papa Jim say come ahead. And bring your art supplies. They'd be delighted to have you paint landscapes of the scenery around Evening Star. It's the most beautiful place in the world. You'll see."

Heinrich made arrangements at once to take the train to Belton. From there he would buy a horse to ride to Evening Star Dawn drew him a map showing the way. He elected to sleep on a bench at the depot that night.

After Virgil let Dawn and Bird off at the cabin, the Caldwells went on home. Dawn noted that Michael had made an effort to keep the cabin clean. She reveled in the peace and happiness of being in her own home with no one to keep track of and no one telling her what to do. She took a bath and dressed in a clean, soft, faded house dress.

When Michael arrived later that evening, the three ran to each other, arms opened wide.

"We slept on the roof of a big hotel," Bird announced over a stew one of the aunties from the reservation had left for them. He went on to tell his father a child's version of all they'd seen and done.

As soon as his stories had been told, Bird's eyes drooped. Michael picked him up and headed for the sleeping boy's bedroom. "I swear he's grown six inches taller," Michael declared, hoisting Bird as if to check his son's heft.

Dawn hung back at the bedroom doorway. She'd have to choose the right time to tell Michael about sending the German artist to Evening Star. But this night wasn't it. Bird had forgotten to mention the artist which seemed a mercy. Michael had become one of those who spoke with contempt about the barbaric "Hun."

This night she wanted no distractions from the reunion that followed in their own room. Michael's muscles felt harder than ever, his hands rough even as their touch against her body felt passionate and loving. But, oh, how good it felt to make love after such a long, lonely journey. She entwined her limbs with those of the man she'd loved since both were children.

And as Michael slept beside her during the starlit night, Dawn lay awake, knowing even before she could know that they had created new life once again.

Chapter Nine

East Glacier Park, Montana

April 6, 1917

Even three years after their journey performing in the eastern cities, Dawn and Bird often sifted through memories of all they'd seen and learned. The dance shows had drawn more tourists to Glacier National Park, and Hill had been delighted. As a result, Dawn participated in evening presentations at the big hotel, but otherwise stayed at home caring for Michael, Bird, and little Rose, Bird's sister.

Heinrich Mann still waited out the war at Evening Star. Mama Nora's letters expressed her admiration for his paintings and his helpfulness on the ranch. He even bought two goats and learned to make goat cheese. All three now considered it a delicacy. And it reassured Dawn to read that her friend did nothing to attract enmity or attention.

This afternoon, Dawn had thoughts only of the day's work as she washed, rinsed, and wrung out her family's linens, shirts, trousers, and dresses in the kitchen. That space did double duty as a laundry room in winter and early spring, when weather didn't permit taking tubs and washboards outside.

Rose, a black-haired, sturdy, ruddy-cheeked toddler, had fallen asleep on a rag rug under the table with a beloved birch doll Bird had carved for her. He'd taken the time this morning to tuck it in close beside her. Dawn smiled. Bird's protective attitude toward his stubborn, tempestuous little sister made both his mother and father proud. Dawn knew contentment in caring for her family.

Michael burst in the back door waving the Great Falls newspaper. "Have you heard? The U.S. has joined the war. We're in it!"

Dawn swung around to face him. "What does this mean, Michael? For us?" She already knew the answer.

"I'll enlist, Dawn. It's my duty."

Bird had been carving a small horse at the table. Pale cottonwood shavings curled on the floor around his feet. Startled by his father's loud jubilation, the boy let the blade slip and cut his hand. He dropped the knife, which clattered to the floor. Drops of blood from his wound left a red smear there.

Dawn stared at Bird's hand, then the floor, and reached into a drawer to pull out rags for cleaning and bandaging her son's hand. "It's all right," she assured him. "It isn't a deep cut. See? The bleeding's already stopping." She sighed, "Yours at least. The blood of others…" She ran water over another cloth and rubbed the bloodstain from the wooden floor. Some had soaked into the fresh wood on the arched neck of Bird's horse. She guessed it would make a dark stain forever, as if it were a war horse wounded in battle.

She would never forget that bright streak of her son's blood. In later years she'd think of it as an intimation of so much blood spilled with so much more to follow in a world awash in war.

Rose stirred and muttered a little protest at the noise, but slept on. Bird stood cradling his injured hand, his brown eyes wide. For brief seconds no one spoke. Then Dawn stood. She hadn't looked at Michael again after he burst in with his news and announced his outrageous plans. They'd spoken of the possibility of his enlisting if America joined the War, but treated the idea as only a possibility. His plans this morning sent fear and horror through her. A stab of anger swooped in, too. She lowered her head and studied the floral swirl of rose and green beads on her moccasins. The patterns seemed to twist by themselves.

Dawn didn't confront Michael often, but now she lifted her head to face her husband. He'd been close to sixteen when he arrived at Evening Star. She, at fourteen, fell in love without thought or hesitation. Headstrong, with the feisty nature of the Butte Irish, Michael usually led in all they did. Shy child of the wilderness, Dawn went along with his wishes and suggestions about everything from little decisions, like where the best berries could be found, to bigger ones, like when they'd tell Mama and Jim they wanted to marry.

But after seeing the hardships of her Blackfeet relatives, leading the troupe through Eastern cities, giving birth and caring for her children, she'd lost the tendency to be quite so pliant. This plan to enlist was too much. She had to stop her husband from joining the Army and going off to war.

"What does this mean?" Her voice trembled as she asked again, "What does this mean, Michael? Will you leave us to fight an enemy thousands of miles from here? I remember you mentioned you might enlist if America got involved, but you said it so lightly. I didn't think you were serious. I really believed you were too smart to be so careless with your life or ours."

Michael's eyebrows lifted, then dropped into a frown. "I haven't signed up yet, but I will. It's my duty. It's every American man's duty. I have to go. It isn't selfish or careless. How can you accuse me of that?"

Anger turned her tone scornful. "Your duty? That is selfish. Your duty is to me. To Bird and Rose. America is safe. Look around you. The Kaiser's troops aren't here. You'd leave us to throw your life away in Europe? For what? Michael, this is crazy. What will we do if you go to France?"

Michael blinked and frowned. "Do you think I want to leave you and our children? No. But they'll be conscripting men like me no matter if you and I talk it over or not."

Her voice began to rise. "Duty?" She balled her small hands into fists. "Look at me. I'm your wife, and I'm here. Look at our children right in front of you. We're your duty. What do we care about strangers killing strangers? Bird and Rose need their father, and I need my husband. Don't ride off and abandon us like you left Mama Nora and Papa Jim. Even I know a married man with children will be the last called. Do you think I've become stupid?"

Michael's face reddened. "It's not the same, and you know it."

Dawn drew a sharp breath. "I know you want to leave right away. Just like when you found out Mama Nora lied about your father. You'd have ridden off and left me there without a word of farewell if I hadn't caught you saddling up. I made you take me with you."

Michael's eyes narrowed as her words roused that long-nursed resentment. "I'd just killed a stranger who turned out to be my blood father. My Butte folks told me my mother's first husband was my father. She said the same. Instead that crazy man who tried to kill Jim was my dear old dad. I had to get away from her. My Butte parents lied. My mother lied. What else had she kept secret? Anyway, you know I meant to come back for you."

"At some point you probably would have," she muttered, her tone still accusing. "But when you decided to leave, you meant to go alone. Now you're going to go away again, way across the ocean, and this time I can't even follow. You're going to leave me and our children alone. What are we supposed to do?"

Michael's voice dropped to the soothing tone he used with frightened children and skittish horses. "It won't be long. Stay here and work for Louis Hill and the hotel. The Caldwells and your aunties will help with the kids.

Keep the home fires burning. Hill will give me back my job once we beat the Hun. What's that Blackfeet saying? I'll come home eating berries."

Dawn turned away. Michael's comforting approach wouldn't solve anything. She wheeled to face him. She repeated, "Don't enlist. We need you here. Your first duty is to us."

Michael grabbed her shoulders. "I will sign up to defend America so my family can be safe. Look at the Lusitania. How many Americans died? Look at Belgium. Those Germans are animals. They rape women and bayonet babies."

Dawn shook her head and glanced toward wide-eyed Bird, who was listening. Her voice rose. "We're not on an ocean liner, are we? We're not in Belgium. We're here. You belong where we are."

He released her. "I didn't expect you to be like this. It'll go easier for me if I enlist. I'll probably get picked for a sniper. I'm as good a shot as they'll ever get."

Dawn saw that part of him had left them already, and she struggled against tears. Her voice emerged as a despairing groan. "Oh, Michael! You know they'll call up the younger, single men first. The war will be over before you'd ever be taken. If you enlist and get sent to the fighting, you might be throwing away your life for nothing."

He let go of her shoulders and shook his head. "This is something I have to do. Too bad, though, that Big Pete Dumont is so long in the tooth. It would be good to have him with me. Two of us from the North Fork watching out for each other—"

Dawn cleared her throat and fought to control her voice. She felt sick and defeated. "You know you want to go. You think war is a great adventure. It's no adventure to kill other men, most of them just working men like you. It's no adventure to die. I'm begging you not to abandon your real duty to us."

Dawn saw how hopeless her chance of dissuading Michael was. *Would he ever grow up?*

She walked past her husband and outside. She continued to the edge of town where she could see the mountains. Evening Star lay beyond her sight. Her heart had fallen to the ground. Her tears fell to join it.

~ ~ ~

Three months later Dawn and the children found themselves standing on the East Glacier Depot platform. They were seeing Michael off on the first leg of the journey that would carry him all the way to France and the Great War. Bird and Rose hung back while their parents embraced in farewell.

"It will be fine." Michael tried to reassure a weeping Dawn. "I'll be fine. You just take care of yourself and our little ones. Do that and you'll be too busy to worry."

"I will. I love you so. Come home to me alive and in one piece." She melted into his arms. Coldness crept through her even though the sun shone on the world. *Would this be the end of the Michael she knew? Would all he was about to see and do make him come home different?*

Michael released her and walked to Bird. Dawn saw Michael's warm breath move their son's brown hair as he bent and kissed the top of the boy's head. She heard him say, "Take care of your mother and little Rose." She wished he hadn't put such responsibility on his nine-year-old son, who nodded, but whose lower lip trembled at his father's words.

Michael kissed and hugged Rose, who plastered kisses from her doll and then herself on his cheeks. Then he straightened, turned, and strode to board the Great Northern train that would take him away in minutes.

Dawn felt a twinge of the anger that clung to her since the day America joined the war. Michael wanted to go more than he wanted to stay with his family. Heavy resentment pushed its seeds deeper into her anxious heart.

She'd try to forgive Michael even as she tried to be brave for him and their children. How hard it proved to be.

Festering bitterness, like Michael's toward his mother, took hold. How could a mature man leave his wife and small children for a foolhardy adventure in France? She took a deep breath and let it go with a shudder. She had to cope because now her children depended on her for everything.

Michael didn't look back even once. It seemed as though the war consumed him the minute they parted. His eyes and energy were already focused on some imagined glory.

Dawn rested her hands on Bird's and Rose's shoulders as they watched Michael's train disappear. He'd go from Belton to Kalispell, then on to Helena, where he'd join up. After that it would be the Army training base in Tacoma, Washington, then France. She'd never felt so bereft or disappointed. The fears that women who love soldiers have harbored over the ages settled in her heart. Would a man who chose foreign adventure over domesticity with his wife and children truly return? He would if he could, but what if . . .? What if he couldn't?

She pictured Beartracks' cabin on Lake McDonald just a few miles from Belton. If she went there, she could hire a wagon and go on to Evening Star. At least she'd be with Mama and Papa Jim, the folks who reared her… who never failed her. She'd be home. Michael could have arranged transportation for her and the children, but of course he didn't want that.

Thoughts and worries whirled. She had to take care of Bird and Rose. And would this anger like hot lead in her heart ever go away?

She gripped the children's hands, turned and started toward the empty little cabin. They continued walking three abreast in a silence broken only by the wild cry of a hawk over their heads, its fierce eyes searching for prey.

~ ~ ~

Dawn dreaded facing the cabin with no one there. But when she returned with the children, they found it far from empty. Beartracks Benton and his old friend and fellow mountain man Big Pete Dumont had made themselves at home inside. They sat visiting at the table. Coffee boiled on the stove. The children rushed to Beartracks, then hung back, shy around Big Pete, almost a stranger to them.

Dawn went to Beartracks and embraced him. She fought back tears as she said, "Michael's joining up to go to France and fight the Hun. I argued with him. I begged him not to leave us. I didn't believe he would do such a foolish, heartless thing. But you know how stubborn he is. We just saw him off at the depot."

"So Michael's going. A good many others are following that path as well." Beartracks spoke in a firm tone but avoided looking into Dawn's stricken eyes. "Michael will be all right. He can handle himself with a weapon."

Dawn sank to a chair. "Why do the wars take so many? Our husbands and brothers should be here with us. I always thought Michael would forgive Mama by now and take us all back to Evening Star. Now my husband just goes off to a half-witted war halfway around the world. How could he leave us here? How could he go to war without a kind word of comfort to pass between him and Mama and Papa Jim?"

Neither Beartracks nor Big Pete had answers. In fact, the silence following Dawn's question drew out so long she straightened and studied the two men, then pinned them with a question. "You don't intend to go fight across the ocean, do you? You're in your fifties! Recruiters who aren't crazy will turn you away."

Pete, his black hair fanned over his broad shoulders, rose and paced the small kitchen, finally stopping to swallow from the dipper on the counter. He cleared his throat. "They won't know how old I am. Hell, I don't even know for sure. Michael will stand a better chance if we're fighting side by side."

"They might not care," Dawn protested. "They could separate you."

"We'll sign up for the same outfit. As I said, it can be done." Pete set down the dipper. "I'm not going to get lost, and neither is old Beartracks, although he intends to sign up in Canada."

Dawn gave Beartracks a sharp look. He nodded. "You keep on taking care of the little ones and yourself. The more of us who go, the sooner the carnage will be over. You'll have your husband back soon."

Pete spoke again. "I'll get your Michael straightened out. Hell, I'll get the whole war straightened out. We'll be back by summer's end, and I'll bring him to you. Straightened out." He saluted Dawn with a roguish grin.

Dawn stared at these old dreamers. All adventure-seeking fools chose using the Germans' aggression to justify risking their own precious lives. Without warning she felt a fearful premonition. She envisioned thousands of men dying in mud. Men torn apart and without limbs. Rivers of blood. She pulled away from such gory images. But she knew hundreds of thousands would die.

"Our neighbors to the north will never guess my age," Beartracks announced. "I'm going to ask Nora and Jim to keep an eye on my Apgar place. My inholding as they call it. And there's something else. I've heard of Canadian deserters, draft dodgers, hard cases coming down here from Alberta and British Columbia. Watch out for them. Start locking your door. Keep a gun where you can get at it fast, but the children can't. The country's changed."

~ ~ ~

The men stayed overnight. After Big Pete bedded down on the floor, Beartracks spoke with Dawn about what she would do now that Michael had gone to war.

"I'll stay here, I suppose," she said. "Unless…"

"We'll come back to you safe and sound. All three of us," Beartracks said in a tone of assurance. "But you're a sensible girl. If you need to go home to Nora and Jim, do it. It's not disloyal to Michael to take care of his family the best you can."

At daybreak he and Pete shook hands. Each kissed Dawn on the cheek and walked out carrying no gear or food; Beartracks mounted a big roan and rode north. Big Pete Dumont walked east toward the depot. A true outdoorsman, his long strides broke into the familiar half-jog of the mountain man. The sunrise streaked the sky in clouds like trailing red banners.

Clouds gilded the color of blood. Dawn shivered.

~ ~ ~

Later that day Virgil arrived with Marissa. "Molly said you'd need someone to help with the children," he said. "And Marissa needs to get herself used to town life at least a little. She'll stay with you and look after Bird and Rose."

Dawn gave Marissa a grateful hug and helped carry in her things. Dawn and her children weren't alone after all. She should have remembered that even if she didn't have Michael with her, she still had Sweet Grass's family, her family, too, after all this time.

But Marissa being the one next to her in bed that night made Dawn uncomfortable. She hadn't been without Michael since the trip east, and couldn't guess when he'd be beside her again.

~ ~ ~

Dawn went back to work in the East Glacier Hotel kitchens, cooking for employees and guests as well as dancing in performances with tribal members on the nights a second cook handled the kitchen. Nora had taught Dawn well, and now Dawn pored over recipe books to become a fine chef. She took an interest in foreign recipes and included Blackfeet fry bread with other Native foods for a special entrée.

Hill expressed satisfaction with her more than once. "When your soldier comes back, I'll have more than enough work for you both," he promised.

But adjusting to life without Michael proved hard. Marissa fell into the homesickness that had plagued her on the journey east. She missed her cousins and friends on the reservation and being with her mother and father. After hearing the girl struggle to stifle her sobs one night as they lay beside each other, Dawn made a decision. "Take the children home with you for a few days, Marissa," she said. "Spend time with your folks."

She hated seeing Marissa, Bird, and Rose wave goodbye to her as they rode off in Virgil's wagon. At least the children seemed to regard going to their auntie and uncle's as a fine adventure.

~ ~ ~

That same night Dawn stayed at work late. She could do some extra baking and give the kitchen a deep cleaning. She completed everything and turned off the lights. As she walked out through the big lobby, its Japanese lanterns dimmed, she nodded to the bored night clerk. The Blackfeet tipis gleamed in moonlight, stretching down the sloping flowered grounds toward the depot. She walked past a coastal tribe's painted totems that flanked the entrance doors.

Dawn took a deep inhalation of mountain air. A man, one of the hotel guests, stepped in front of her. She'd seen him before, but they'd never spoken, tucked away in the kitchen as she usually was. When he reached for her, she dodged to the side. "I'll scream," she said.

"Oh, want to start another Indian war, little squaw?" The man sneered. "You know what will happen to any buck who attacks a white man. It hasn't been that long, you know. Your kind isn't running things now and you never will. What's that motto your boss has, 'The white men are coming?' Well, we're here." He tightened his grip on her arm.

Dawn pushed against him while drawing one foot back. She kicked hard into her attacker's groin. Swearing, he folded in pain. She ran, kept running all the way to her cabin, unlocked it with shaking hands, and slammed and locked the door behind her. She slid to the floor with her back against the entrance. When she could stand, she walked to the armoire, lifted the rifle down from the top, loaded it, and kept it within reach. She would kill him if he tried to come for her.

When she'd regained her normal breathing, she listened. The man hadn't followed. Dawn moved catlike through the moonlit cabin without lighting a lantern. She looked out the window. The night hid so many predators. One of the worst had found her.

She watched the moon set, and the sun rise. In the full light of day, she made the decision to take her children and go home to Evening Star at last.

Chapter Ten

Dawn gave her notice at work, claiming Mama Nora and Papa Jim needed her at Evening Star. It felt true as she said it. She needed them, too. As a bonus to her as a departing serviceman's wife, Dawn received Louis Hill's gift of railway tickets to Belton. Dawn spent days giving away belongings and saying farewells to friends and family on the reservation. She caught a glimpse of her attacker once more, then not at all. She presumed he'd gone back to wherever he came from. She had the satisfying feeling she'd taught him a lesson that might benefit other women he'd meet in the future.

Then on a sunny morning in September, she hoisted Rose into her arms, reached down to take Bird's hand, and walked out of their little cabin for the last time. Virgil, Molly, and Marissa had taken her trunk and smaller luggage to the Great Northern Railway's baggage area. They waited there to say goodbye. Dawn walked through the town to the depot, fixing it all in her memory. Even if she couldn't stay, the hotel, the church, all of it formed part of her history with Michael and their children.

On the platform, she hugged the three Caldwells, and they all made promises to write often. Dawn and her children took the high step to board the same passenger car that had taken Michael off to war. But this was different, she told herself. Michael went to be a soldier. She sought peace for herself and her children. By returning to Evening Star they'd find love and security. For the children, of course, it meant leaving home and friends.

Bird, his expression solemn, held tight to his latest horse carving. Rose, equally unsmiling, gripped her doll.

For this occasion, Dawn wore what Blackfeet relatives called 'citizens clothes,' the style white women wore. She'd chosen a blue and white dress with a shawl collar, shoes with low heels, and a cloche hat. She'd twisted her hair into a low knot at the back of her neck, the way

Eleanor Flowers so often wore hers.

Fellow passengers sneaked curious glances at the three of them. Dawn whispered to Bird and Rose, "They wonder about me. Am I Oriental? Spanish? Indian? Watch what I do." She leveled a cool look, one eyebrow raised, at anyone who gawked long enough to be considered rude. The passengers looked sideways out the window or lowered their eyes to their books and newspapers. Bird and Rose gazed up at their mother, who winked at them.

For a while, Dawn reflected on how much she'd changed from that frontier girl who'd arrived in Midvale riding double with her handsome Michael. She'd been so shaken by the open, unprotecting nature of the prairie when they first saw it. But she'd learned how her Blackfeet tribe had made their home there, and did her best to bridge the abyss between white and Blackfeet worlds. She'd met a railroad tycoon, an international artist, and she'd impressed them both. Would Mama Nora and Papa Jim see the changes in their girl? They would, but she would also assure them that they'd always mean home to her.

~ ~ ~

Bird stirred and studied his sister and lovely, mysterious, dark-eyed mother seated facing forward across from him. "You always know what to do, don't you, Mama?" he asked. He knew too well by this time how some whites treated Blackfeet.

Dawn smiled. "No, not always, but it helps to watch the people around you and try to figure out what they'll do next. How they feel..."

Then she spoke to Rose and Bird about Grandma Nora and Grandpa Jim and what their new life would be like on the North Fork. Rose's eyes grew wide with excitement, but Bird looked uncertain.

~ ~ ~

When their train stopped at the Belton Depot that afternoon, the three stepped down from the passenger car. The high air was already turning cold. Dawn gazed at the nearby greenish-black mountains. She told her children the humped shapes were the Belton Hills.

A man's voice called out from the baggage area. "Dawn! Dawn Larkin! Is that really you? And who are these children? Surely not Bird and Rose."

Dawn set Rose down and rushed to the man, her voice high and excited. "Fred! Oh, it's so good to see you. Is Nan with you?"

"No, she's home in Polebridge. What brings you here?"

"Michael joined up. He'll be in France soon. I miss him, and I've missed Mama and Papa, so I decided to bring the children back where I know we'll be safe." She sighed. "I can't wait to see them. It's been too long."

"A wise decision, young Dawn. And your folks don't know you're coming?"

"No, I planned to surprise them. I need a way to get there though. What are you doing here?"

"I'm taking on supplies for the Polebridge Mercantile, our store. It wasn't here when you left. Just one of many changes. We sold out to the government after they included our place in the Park, and moved across the North Fork. It's good being close to Nora and Jim. Climb in. I can make room for you and your youngsters."

"That's a relief, Uncle Fred. And my trunk?"

"And your trunk. As you can see it's a big wagon. We'll just move a few boxes around. You'll have to hold this pretty little girl on your lap, but we'll manage."

On the long ride to Evening Star, Fred grew loquacious, holding forth about the store he and his wife Nan set up in the settlement called Polebridge. "Yes, indeed," Fred told his captive listeners. "In '14, we cast up a two-story frame building. You'll be impressed. Big white letters above the window of its false front proclaim our enterprise to be the Polebridge Mercantile."

Bird, used to the company of adults, fired the first of many questions. "What can we buy in your store, Uncle Fred?"

Fred's broad face lit up with pride. "Let me tell you, Bird, North Fork folks now have an honest to God link to civilization. Our Mercantile sells everything from 12-gauge shotguns, to tea, to upholstery tacks, to rat poison. Your Grandma Nora buys some items with cash, but she also trades eggs, butter, and handmade snowshoes for necessaries." He shifted to look at Dawn. "You'll soon see. Our store has changed life up on the North Fork. Before you know it, we'll have a road coming up from Columbia Falls on the west side. Right up to Polebridge."

Bird asked more questions. Did Big Pete Lamont kill many grizzly bears? When did Fred make friends with Grandma Nora and Grandpa Jim? Did Fred know other mountain men besides Big Pete Dumont and Beartracks? What wildlife did Fred see around Polebridge? Fred gave long answers with satisfyingly dramatic stories attached to each.

At last they neared Evening Star. Dawn began to exclaim over the new ranger station and the bridge. She expressed more happiness when the wagon passed trees and boulders that she remembered as old friends and resting places. And then finally, yellow lantern light poured from Evening Star's cabin windows. Familiar dark hulks of outbuildings met the travelers as well.

"Oh," Dawn cried, "It's too much joy."

The tired Larkins sniffed the scent of wood smoke and freshly baked bread along with pine and an earthy combination of greenery, manure, and hay. Rose stopped her travel-weary fussing. Her eyes widened with wonder.

"Home. I've missed this place so much." Dawn's voice caught in a sob. She stood, took a long breath, and hoisted Rose, now fully awake, into her arms.

When Hogan hallooed the cabin, a long-haired man's big frame blocked the light behind him as he opened the door.

"Papa!" Dawn, still carrying Rose, scrambled down from the wagon, and bounded up the porch steps into the silhouetted giant's embrace, leaving Bird with Fred.

His face obscured by darkness, the man enfolded Dawn in long arms and pulled her into the cabin, calling, "Nora! We have company! Come and see!"

Fred Hogan lifted Bird down, and the boy tore inside to join his mother and sister within the cabin's warmth.

Nora bustled into the combined kitchen and sitting room, caught her breath, and stood unmoving for a few seconds staring from Dawn and Rose to Bird. When she opened her arms Dawn flew into them. Mama Nora finally pulled back and perused Dawn, then drew Bird against her in a hug as she asked, "The children are well?"

Dawn nodded as her son ducked his head.

Nora continued, "Bird, I know you're called that, you see, although your name is really Jim. Welcome, dear boyo. And this must be Rose. Welcome to you, my little treasure." Then she spoke to Dawn of the absent one. "And where might these children's father be?"

Dawn explained that Michael had signed up. She left out the scene with her attacker. Perhaps she would speak of it another time. She did say,

"I'm afraid for Michael. He's gone to the war way across the ocean. Who will care about him over there?"

Jim Li came in again after unloading Dawn's baggage. He spoke as he fed split logs into the stove from a big box set beside it. "Michael shoots well. He had excellent aim when he saved me from the man who tried to end my life. He will be a skilled soldier."

Hogan took his departure, making Dawn promise to come and see Nan and their store.

Shortly after he left, a soft knock sounded on the door.

"Come in, Heinrich," Mama called.

The German artist entered, beaming with delight to see the little family from East Glacier. He removed his hat and stepped toward Dawn. She drew in a breath. Her happiness at seeing the artist surprised her. She'd forgotten how tall he was and how warm his smile.

"Dawn Larkin. It is a great delight to see you and your *kinder* here. I must be almost as pleased as their grandparents to see the three of you."

"Heinrich Mann. How are you? I'm so glad you've been able to stay here and help Mama Nora and Papa Jim."

"Not as much as they've helped me. And this North Fork setting… *Mein Gott*. I paint. When the work here permits me the time, I paint and paint. So much stunning beauty. My paintings are out in my studio and sleeping shed that Nora and Jim provide me. I'll show my work to you tomorrow if you'll allow me, *bitte*."

Nora announced that dinner was ready. They sat down to elk steaks, carrots, potatoes, and bread. She served warm rhubarb pie for dessert. After the meal Heinrich excused himself with quiet tact, as though he knew the reunion would go on most easily without him. Everyone wished him goodnight. He paused at the door, nodded in approval at the sight of the family together, and smiled again.

When he'd gone, Mama Nora said, "What a fine fellow Heinrich is. He's become like family. Mind you, not all in the community think we should have a German staying here. But most know his story, how he can't go back. And they're fine with it. If he were a spy, he'd hardly be here. Fred and Nan were a little huffy, but only at first. The few who still don't like us hiring him are the same ones who don't like to see a white woman and a Chinese man living like we're married."

"In our minds we are married," Jim said. "We call each other wife or husband when we talk."

Nora nodded, but looked troubled. "Dawn, let me tell you how I found out about them changing the law to void our marriage we believed was legal…

"That morning in the spring of '09 changed our lives even if we pretend it had no effect. I'd just stepped out of the hen house, the basket on my arm heavy with my best layers' lovely, big, white, speckled. and brown eggs. I planned to fry some with their thick yolks to have with bread and bacon for our lunch."

Dawn broke in. "I remember that Colleen laid the best eggs of them all."

"She did. Back to my story now, I saw Jim walking out of the barn after feeding the animals. I looked toward the North Fork, and wasn't it Big Pete Dumont I saw loping toward us on our side, the mountains across the river rising like sleeping Celtic giants behind him? That long hair of his flared like black wings over his shoulders."

"Mama, the way you tell it I can just see him," Dawn said. "I've missed your Irish lilt and your stories so much." Dawn lifted Rose from the old highchair next to her. The little girl had begun nodding over her plate. Dawn settled her on her lap where the exhausted child fought a brief losing battle with sleep.

Nora reached forward and slipped Rose's scuffed shoes off, set them on the floor, smoothed the little girl's skirt, and then continued. "Always the polite one, Pete swept off his hat. Then he wiped sweat from his long face with a buckskin sleeve. 'Nora! China Jim!' he said, seeing Jim join me there. 'Let me sit with you awhile. I warn you, though, I bring damned unwelcome news.'"

"That's when Pete told you?" Dawn asked.

"We went to the porch and sat together as we do so often. Pete just blurted it out. He said, 'If my folks had married in Montana, I'd be a bastard this year.' "

Nora frowned at the memory. "'What a thing to say' I scolded. You know I love Big Pete Dumont and Beartracks Benton, but sometimes those old mountain men go too far in their rough talk. Jim here only looked worried. I felt the day turn chill as if the sun had ducked behind clouds, ready to launch hail-stones."

Seeing Bird put his fork down while staring at his grandmother, Dawn gave him a reassuring smile.

Nora continued. "I'll never forget what Pete said next. Not a single word of it. 'There's a new law,' he said. 'A damned crazy one, but it affects the two of you. The state of Montana in all its wisdom has declared marriage between whites and other races illegal, be they red or black, and then he slid Jim a nervous look, 'or yellow. If you're married now, it's illegal—void—nullified by these what-they-call anti-miscegenation laws. Other states have gone and passed the same jeezely things.'"

"Oh, Mama," Dawn spoke again. "If the priest who married Michael and me hadn't taken for granted that I was white, we might have been included. His eyesight was bad, and I gave my name as Dawn Benton. Our marriage might be void, too, if he'd seen I'm a half-blood. But that's not how I'm recorded. He knows by now, but he doesn't care about it enough to change his entry. He's been priest there a long time. He does what he can for the tribe."

Bird gaped at Dawn. "It's all right, son. We're all fine," his mother reassured him.

Grandma Nora responded, "Then thank God for the old Father's poor vision. Void. When Pete said it the word thudded against my heart like a dead bird striking earth. Void means empty, you know. To me, void meant all our respectable married life cut down like a once-proud tree. 'It can't be, can it?' I cried. 'The priest in Midvale married us.' I thought the church would have a say in the matter, for certain.

"Then Jim said, 'The church makes rules for itself, Nora. But those only apply within itself, to itself alone.' How Jim's shoulders slumped when he said it. The state legislature, with passage of that unfair act, stole and trampled on all his resilience and serenity that I thought could never be shaken.

"So, I was a fallen woman again." Nora frowned. "People just can't stop telling us how to live, how to be in our lives. I'd thought things were getting better, that people accepted us. We worked so hard. Look at these calloused hands of mine." She raised her bumpy palms to show them. "They didn't come hard as pebbles from being idle."

"Remember, Mama," Dawn soothed, "most of your neighbors do accept you. It isn't just whites and Orientals they unmarried. It was whites and Indians, whites and Negroes. Like he said, Pete's own folks. His mother was Cree, isn't that right?"

Nora stood and started gathering up dishes. "So, I guess Jim and I have turned ourselves into a pair of criminals, living together like man and wife when the law says we're not."

She went to the stove and brought coffee back. The adults drank and talked on, catching up.

The conversation turned to other stories. Dawn told about her and Bird's trip east and life in East Glacier Park. When Rose started a purring snore, Dawn carried her into the bedroom just across a narrow hall from Nora and Jim's room. She and her children would share it while at Evening Star.

After his mother returned alone, Bird's head sank to his arm stretched out on the table. The adults smiled at his losing efforts to keep listening. Dawn saw that their voices must have blended into soft murmurs that put her tired boy to sleep. Grandpa Jim saw it, too. Without speaking, he gathered and carried Bird to the boy's cot as the sky lightened in the east.

~ ~ ~

Bird woke the next morning confused and still in his travel clothes. He stirred, finding himself on a cot beside his sleeping mother's bed. He got up and wandered out to the kitchen.

His Irish grandmother stood before the stove as Rose played with pots and pinecones on the floor. Both beamed when they saw him. Grandma Nora gestured with her stirring spoon for him to sit down. She hoisted Rose to the scarred old highchair and put a cut up buttered pancake in a dish before her, then set a plate of pancakes in front of Bird. She took her place across the table from him with her own breakfast.

Knowing something had turned his father against Grandma Nora made Bird feel wary in her company. The two eyed each other for self-conscious moments before studying their food. They ate in silence broken only by Rose holding pieces of pancake out and making appreciative smacking noises before eating them. "These taste good!" she announced at intervals.

In a few minutes, Dawn emerged from the bedroom, dressed and smiling. She heaped pancakes on a plate for herself and sat near Rose, helping the child with a glass of milk. Rose manipulated a fork and ate a second pancake, this one topped with huckleberry syrup.

When Grandma Nora finished breakfast, she took a sip of coffee. "Tell me, young Bird. Do you know how to milk a cow?'

He shook his head, dubious about where this might be headed, not sure he wanted to learn.

She stood up. "Well, you will by sundown. Follow me, boyo. Dawn, dear, I trust you remember how to do the dishes?"

Dawn laughed. "Nothing has changed in the cabin and that's just what I counted on."

Before noon Bird had learned how to milk a gigantic, but amiable cow. Then he helped clean stalls and spread hay. In the afternoon Jim took him fishing. By the time they returned to the family the boy felt drunk on the sight of red-tail hawks, bald as well as golden eagles, the clear, rushing North Fork, the green lushness of his new forest home, and the comfort of a big, gentle grandfather who seemed to know everything about everything in the whole wide world. In one day, Bird's favorite activities became herb picking or fishing with Jim Li.

Chapter Eleven

When family members went to Polebridge for mail or supplies they did occasionally meet transients. Some were the sort Beartracks had spoken about to Dawn. Hunched men in worn clothes, sometimes on horseback but more often walking, might tip their stained slouch hats and sometimes ask for food. Most walked with eyes fixed straight ahead or down at their boots. Grandpa Jim, Heinrich, and each woman carried a gun when leaving the house. Jim taught Bird how to use a .22 and allowed him to carry it. Bird learned fast and kept it with him everywhere when he went outside.

One late September morning Jim and Dawn took Rose along to Polebridge to pick up mail and supplies. Heinrich had gone deep into the forest. He'd seen three dead lodge pole pines and announced that he meant to chop them down and split the logs for firewood. Bird stayed behind in the barn, readying a fishing pole to take to the creek to try his luck.

His Grandma Nora had walked out to work in her two-acre garden. Bird glanced out to see her lean her rifle against a larch before she stooped to gather the season's last carrots. He gasped when he saw a big man carrying a revolver in his hand sneak up behind Grandma Nora before she started to turn.

Bird didn't hesitate. He picked up his .22 and, hunching low, moved out of the barn toward the man whose back remained toward him.

He heard the stranger speak to his grandma. "Don't move." The voice rasped as though the man hadn't spoken to anyone in some time. "My gun is pointed at your back."

Grandma Nora's voice as she responded sounded steady. "What do you want?"

"Money and food. I don't plan to harm you unless you cross me."

"Ah, yes. Beartracks Benton warned us that tramps like you might come around our place."

"I guess you run cattle for charity," the other sneered.

Grandma Nora turned around despite the intruder's orders. She said, "There's no cash on the place. The few dollars we make I spend on necessaries to keep going. You should know we have children here." The man stepped closer to her. Bird, edging around one pine to another, saw that the man towered over his grandmother. Grandma Nora froze when her glance slid over Bird. He, creeping behind the intruder, put a finger to his lips, the .22 in his other hand.

"There damn well better be money here—what?" The man stiffened as he felt the barrel poke his back.

"Drop your gun." Bird's voice sounded firm, but even to him it sounded too high to come from anybody but a kid. He stepped back, but kept his rifle pointed at the stranger.

"I can shoot Granny here before you shoot me," the man said, glancing over his shoulder. He had mean eyes and sported a bushy black beard that stuck way out at the sides.

Grandma Nora grabbed and hurled her hoe at the bearded head and darted for her rifle leaning against the nearby larch. She shouted, "Shoot him, Bird!"

Bird pulled the trigger. The intruder crumpled to the ground, clinging to his right thigh where a red streak soaked through his trousers. Shaken and close to tears, Bird struggled to keep his rifle aimed at the man. He glanced at Grandma Nora, darting to pick up and aim her firearm at the fallen man.

"You can lower your rifle now." Her tone to Bird was gentle, but then became sharp. "And you, you ruffian. Crawl away from your revolver.

"Boyo, retrieve this thief's weapon when he can't reach it or you. We'll be keeping it for the fright he gave us."

In the end, Grandma Nora slit the cursing man's pants to see the wound, then cleaned and bandaged it. She gave him a branch to use as a crutch, then ordered him at gunpoint to board an old raft pointed down the creek where it would join the river. "Remember," Grandma Nora told him, "I could keep you here and report you for trying to rob us."

"Why don't you?" the man groaned.

Grandma Nora put her hands on her hips. "Because I think you've learned your lesson. I know what it is to be hungry, you presumptuous *idjit*. You're lucky the bullet grazed you so light. Leave decent homesteaders alone from now on. I would have given you food. In fact, take a few carrots. They won't be so bad after you wash them in the river."

After the raft bearing six carrots and the profane drifter floated out of sight on the rippling water of the North Fork, Grandma Nora turned to Bird. "Nice bit of thinking, boyo. You saved us."

Bird grinned. His grandma rested a hand on his shoulder as they walked to the cabin. It would be more accurate to say she leaned on him, seeming to steady herself. "I was that scared, too, you know," she said. "Shaking like one of these aspen leaves."

"Grandma?" Bird whispered before they went in. He stopped.

"What is it?" she sighed, looking down at him.

"This was the best adventure I ever had. When Pop comes back, I'm going to tell him all about it. He's got to be friendlier to you after this."

She smiled. "Well, your papa might not see it that way. Anyhow, we won't have that adventure again. I'm finished with being as careless as I was today. Your grandmother made a bad mistake leaving the firearm out of reach."

"Do we tell Grandpa Jim?"

Nora laughed. "Oh yes. Your grandfather is a man we can always trust with our secrets. He's the world's most understanding fellow. Smartest, too, for certain."

"I know, but… Grandma Nora? I liked the way you decided so fast what we should do with the outlaw."

"What would I have done without your quick thinking as well, Bird? We make a good team, I'm thinking."

"A good team." Bird nodded and grinned up at Nora. "Let's go home and have cookies now."

His Grandma Nora's laughter pealed across the meadow and into the forest. "Home it is, boyo."

~ ~ ~

Dawn settled into life at Evening Star with a grateful sense of being home where she belonged. Life near the Blackfeet and in East Glacier had taught her a great deal about who she was and where she'd come from. Missing pieces of Sweet Grass's life had been filled in. Yet even back at Evening Star all ease slipped away when she went to bed at night without Michael, without even knowing where Michael was at that moment. She shivered in the cool sheets without his warmth to curl against. Was he safe? Would he come home to her?

Dawn visited Heinrich in his studio. He painted landscapes of the North Fork different from works she'd seen of the prairie with those ochres and browns. In these she recognized the soft, deep, pale, or metallic greens and the cerulean or gray-blues of sky and water. And he made almost unfinished-appearing depictions of wildflowers in degrees of red and buttery yellows. His skies, created in thick brush strokes, showed piling clouds settled on peaks that pierced or disappeared into mountainous thunderheads.

Sometimes she watched Heinrich paint outdoors. He called it *en plein air* painting. She saw with what quick, sometimes vague, brush strokes the artist created landscapes that included the people, meadows, buildings, and animals of Evening Star. He captured the shadows and sunlit meadows of the natural world that had been sacred to Dawn all her life.

Heinrich surprised her one day by murmuring, "Why would I paint a mere cathedral when all of this is so sacred?"

She hadn't articulated the artist's sentiment, but it put her own feelings into words.

Sometimes the two chatted as he worked. Heinrich missed the Blackfeet—their dignity in the face of devastating humiliations of forced reservation life, their stories, their colorful regalia, their dances and spiritual ceremonies.

"I miss them, too," Dawn said. "Remember Lucy Drake?"

"Of course. I painted her and Molly and Marissa, too. People wanted my work then."

Dawn rested her hand on his arm for a moment, then withdrew it. "I'm sorry," she murmured.

"No need," he said, looking at her with his alert eyes. "It has been very long since I've felt the touch of any living being other than one of the Evening Star animals. Or that any person has shaken hands with me or rested a consoling hand on my arm."

Flustered, she stood. "Well, I'd better go in. I want to write to Michael before the children need my attention."

She didn't know why she felt she'd done something wrong, but she took extra care with her letter and didn't mention Heinrich at all.

~ ~ ~

Dawn saw physical changes in Mama Nora and Papa Jim. The last years had aged them. Still, they'd prospered though and raised more cattle. Nora had made her vegetable garden bigger. Evening Star looked permanent. The settlement of Polebridge and the North Fork Bridge near the new Glacier National Park ranger station eased settlers' lives. Since she and Michael eloped at least twenty new homesteads had strung both north and south along the river.

Fred and Nan Hogan's Polebridge Mercantile had become the community center with a little U.S. Post Office tucked in the back. Dawn walked there every day in hopes of mail from Michael, or at least for the chance to read war news printed in Kalispell's *Daily Interlake*.

Michael wrote often. She read and reread every letter, sometimes spilling tears of loneliness on them for the man swallowed up into a strange and dangerous world of war. His first letters to her, Bird, and Rose were full of joking, anecdotes, and descriptions of everything Michael experienced after he left for Kalispell.

AUGUST 30, 1917

My Darling Dawn,

I've missed you every minute since I boarded the train alone. I even questioned myself all the way to Kalispell. Your tears and our children's sad, confused eyes haunt me.

You implied once that I only wanted some great adventure in the war. No, sweetheart. I was raised by two sets of immigrants. My Butte parents who adopted me worshiped America. So did Mother and Jim as I recall. I must serve my country. It needs me.

But if I'm honest, of course it's an adventure, too. Everybody wants a little glory. Remember your Blackfeet stories about proud warriors who came home from raids covered in it?

I have to admit it was a relief to see Big Pete Dumont pushing through the crowd in Helena, there to join up. He was looking for me. I couldn't miss the man. He was a whole head taller than the other enlistees. I won't be alone after all. Not that I could have been physically alone. The state capitol seemed full, shoulder to shoulder with enlistees, some goofy, some serious.

When Pete and I raised our hands to take the oath it hit me that I'd just given up any claim to the independence we Montanans take for granted. I felt such a final break from everything I knew, even from you and the children. When I shared that with Pete afterwards he said, "Now we serve as cogs in the machinery of war. We belong to Uncle Sam body and soul." Old Pete is quite the philosopher at times. Jim would call him my mentor, I guess.

~ ~ ~

In later letters, he wrote about life in the training camp at Fort Lewis near Tacoma. Most of what he wrote was about him and Pete being from the same district and proficient from the start in shooting. As fourth district men, they were assigned to the 362nd Infantry also known as the 2nd Montana, and to the 82nd Brigade, further narrowed to the 41st "Sunset" Division.

At training's end, the Division climbed aboard transport trains headed toward Hoboken, New Jersey. Michael wrote to Dawn:

At first, we kept to ourselves traveling east. Our troop car was crowded, noisy, and smelly. But by the time we disembarked at Allentown, Pennsylvania, everybody tired and needing baths worse than ever, someone who recognized Pete had spread word of his fame as a mountaineer and rifleman. After that recruits started conversations with him. Well, you know

Pete. The whole time we rode that train from then on Pete entertained the boys with tales of mountain lions, bears, Indians, citified dudes, and the legendary Beartracks Benton.

How are Bird and Rose? Are they settling in all right at Evening Star? I'm not angry that you're there. You must have been sure you had to go home. For now, stay there.

I can't wait to be back to see all three of you. Surely the war will be over soon.

I love you, dearest.

Michael

~ ~ ~

NOV. 5, 1917

Dear Pop,

The ranch is a good place. Grandpa Jim takes me fishing. I caught a rainbow trout. Grandma Nora says it tasted the best of any fish she ever ate. Grandma Nora and Mama talk to each other all the time. They say they have some catching up to do. Rose wants to be with Grandma. She helps with the chickens. Grandma likes that.

It's going to rain or maybe even snow today. Is it raining in France? Do you have good boots?

We miss you.

Love from your son,

Jim Bird Larkin

P.S. Grandpa Jim helped me write this letter.

~ ~ ~

Nov. 22, 1917

Dearest Michael,

I miss you. I'm so glad you and Pete are together. I already knew he and Beartracks were signing up. Those two stopped by the day you left.

It's so good to be home with Mama and Papa Jim. They're older, Michael. They miss you and worry about you almost as much as I do. Rose loves to help us in the garden and with any of the animals. She'll be a ranch woman, I believe.

Bird caught the itch to see new places on Mr. Hill's Great Northern promotional tour, and he's still scratching it. Besides exploring the North Fork he's always asking his grandparents about China and Ireland. They love to talk about their earlier years with him.

Soon I'll send Bird to the school at Red Meadow. The land's been donated for it by the couple who homestead there. They didn't want their children having to go too far so it's only a half mile from their house. The community went together to build the little schoolhouse. Bird could ride or walk on nice days. Still, I'm not sure Papa Jim wouldn't be the best teacher he could have. After all, he taught me. I can't help but think he knows more than the young woman hired for the position. What do you think?

I check for the mail every day. I'll post this tomorrow. Be safe, my love.

Dawn

~ ~ ~

Dec. 15, 1917

Dear Bird,

Well, all us new soldiers drilled for three months. Then we entrained for Hoboken, New Jersey, to be shipped out on board the USS Leviathan.

It used to be a German steamer called the Vaterland before our side captured it. Thousands of us slept in dark, stuffy places like the hold. That's a place below decks. Our beds are canvas stretched across iron pipes. Plenty of snoring at night, let me tell you. And some of the men are seasick. That makes for bad smells.

The food is nothing like your mother's, but it's good and we eat our fill. I hear we'll have turkey and all the trimmings for Christmas.

Take care of your mother and sister and yourself.

Love,

Your father

~ ~ ~

One early December day while Bird and Grandpa Jim sat outside the barn taking a break from cleaning stalls, Dawn brought a bucket of fresh drinking water. She sat down, ruffled her son's hair, then sighed. "I saw that new ranger, Ted Norman, at the Mercantile yesterday. He looks terrible. I smiled and he just looked away."

Jim nodded. "I have noticed him as well."

A young ranger with a ravaged expression, recently back from the war, had taken up residence after being assigned to the Glacier National Park Polebridge Station.

"People see him pacing back and forth across the bridge at night. Sometimes he lifts his hands as though he's shooting a rifle," Dawn added.

"Yes." Jim nodded, "Others see him walking the hills, too. Some around here suspect him of spying on all of us. The rumor goes that he just wants to catch folks poaching or running moonshine and report them to the government men."

After a few moments of silence, Dawn asked, "Do you think it's true?"

Grandpa Jim said he doubted the rumors. "He probably suffered through too much in the war," he surmised.

“Suffered how?” Bird asked eyes on a raven calling across the cloudless sky above. “Was he wounded?”

“In some way, I believe. Wounds aren’t always easily seen,” his grandfather replied.

Bird turned to his grandfather. “You mean under his clothes? Where they don’t show?”

“Perhaps. But perhaps in his mind, or his spirit. If he seems nervous and sad, it might be that sort of injury. Some soldiers go through things or see things that leave them with awful feelings. Painful memories.”

“Will Pop or Big Pete or Beartracks come back like that?”

“No,” Dawn said, her tone sharp. “Of course, they won’t.”

Grandpa Jim stood to go back to work. “We can’t know any man’s future,” he said. “Your father and our friends are strong. We’ll hope fate will return them to us as they were when they went away.”

~ ~ ~

Grandma Nora suggested that Dawn take Bird and carry a few jars of her huckleberry preserves to the ranger. Dawn wasn’t sure about her young son going there, but he’d already jumped up from his breakfast and hurried to join her. “Maybe we’ll learn where his wounds are, Mama. Maybe we’ll learn more about France.”

Dawn sighed, but nodded. They tucked the jars of preserves into a straw-lined basket, covered it with a flour sack, pulled on jackets and boots, and started out. They crossed the bridge to the ranger station in time to see three local boys, just under draft age, whooping and firing rifles while riding their horses in circles around the ranger’s cabin.

“Get off, you,” Dawn rushed forward, scolding the riders. “You hellions should be ashamed of yourselves. Stop that. Go away this minute!”

Knowing who Dawn was, and a little awed by her beauty, as men and boys always were, they ducked their heads and galloped back across the bridge. Dawn smoothed her jacket, nodded to Bird to follow, and they approached the cabin door. Dawn tapped on it. The two heard only the rasp of heavy breathing from inside.

"Should we go home?" Bird asked. Dawn shook her head and pushed the door open. They stepped into the cabin's messy, fetid interior. "A bachelor lives here all right," she muttered. She moved to open one of the windows.

Bird startled and took a step closer to Dawn. Ted Norman hunched on his cot in the shadowed corner, head in hands, body trembling so hard he created a rattling commotion in the bedsprings.

"I'll make coffee," Dawn said. "Stay there and catch your breath, Mr. Norman. They won't be back now we've recognized them. They looked ashamed to be caught out being so stupid and cruel. I'm Dawn Larkin, Nora and Jim Li's daughter. This is my son, Bird. I have a little daughter, too. We're staying at Evening Star. We're your neighbors, and we'd like to be friends."

Dawn gave Bird a little shove, and he took a tentative step forward and thrust his hand out. "How do you do?" he asked.

The man's tormented eyes as he glanced up silenced both Dawn and Bird, who withdrew his hand. The ranger shook his head. "I'm not fit company. I'll be right in awhile, but if you don't mind, I need to be alone. Please just—"

Dawn spoke again, "Bird's father, my husband Michael, is in France, where you were. I know it must be terrible in the fighting in Europe. I don't know if Michael is still training or in the fray."

The ranger, appearing desperate to be rid of his visitors, only shook his head and made an anguished gesture toward the door. Dawn set her preserves on the untidy shelf, noting mouse droppings on the counter besides dirty dishes. The ranger motioned again to the door. Dawn saw tears in his eyes as he struggled for control. She sighed and took Bird's hand, leading him outside.

Just after crossing the bridge and continuing nearer to home, they heard one shot from the cabin. Only one. Dawn froze. When the sound stopped reverberating, there was only the river's rush as it flowed fast beside them, and in moments a raven's caw.

"What's he doing, Mama? Going hunting?"

Dawn's knees threatened to give out, so she brushed away snow on a fallen tree and sank down to sit there. She forced herself to think of what must be done. "Bird, run home and fetch Heinrich or Grandpa Jim. Both, if you can. Tell them to bring the wagon or at least the toboggan. Go now."

Bird, still looking puzzled, nodded and took off.

Dawn controlled a wave of nausea until Bird ran out of sight, then she leaned to one side, retching. After being ill she cried in soft sobs of pity for Ted Norman and fear for Michael.

I know what that shot meant. The poor veteran survived the battles of war, but not the one he waged after coming here. Not war's aftermath. What it must be like. Our worst images of what goes on over there must not equal the horrors Michael and the others face.

Her tears subsided, and she sat, heart racing. Icy North Fork waters flowed past. When Heinrich and Papa Jim appeared in the ranch wagon, Dawn stood and walked to them. "I've been sitting here for a longer time than I should have. I think the ranger is past needing my help, or anyone else's, though. I—I'm sure he's taken his own life."

"Such heartache," Heinrich murmured.

Papa Jim said, "There's sad work to be done in our remaining daylight hours. Go home. We'll put the poor man's body in the shed behind the cabin and notify Park headquarters through the postman."

As Dawn walked back to Evening Star, she imagined the pale veteran who couldn't stop trembling now motionless as a hunter-felled deer. Would they find him lying on the cot where she and Bird left him? Had he fallen to the floor? Was there much blood? Were his wounds visible?

The ranger was the first shell-shocked man she'd met. What if Michael came back like that? Or what if he came back like the local boy who'd been such a mountaineer and now had only one leg? Or the other man who returned blind? That night she lay awake, in terror at the thought that she might lose Michael.

During that night's endless hours, their hush broken only by owl calls and rabbits' screams, Dawn made herself call up memories of happier times before they'd ever heard of this merciless Great War. As she did sometimes, she began to whisper to Michael as though he were with her.

"Dearest, do you remember that night in East Glacier? You surprised me. It was our anniversary. After the Blackfeet dancing you propelled me into the dining room of the great hotel instead of walking me home.

"You announced, 'We're staying here tonight. Bird and Rose are staying with Molly and Virgil.'

"After a late dinner we climbed the stairs to our assigned room. I remember how the tinkle of a piano playing *On Moonlight Bay* sounded so hopeful and carefree. In the room with its rustic furniture, you sank into a chair, pulled your boots off, and flopped onto the bed.

"I felt strange being there. I went to the window and pulled back the plaid curtains and studied the night outside. It was darkening bluish-purple over the peaks, stars trembling in the dusk as if not daring to emerge whole and shine in the darkness. I heard you rise from the bed, and I turned to you. All my life, I have turned to you.

"You nuzzled my throat. You said, 'I've never wanted any other woman in my life, and I never will. It was all over for me the first time I saw you.' Then you slowly undressed me.

"We kissed, and in that freedom of being away from our children, you lifted me and carried me to the bed. You removed your clothes, your eyes never leaving mine. You moved to lift me above you as you lay back, my thick straight hair a black curtain as I lowered myself onto you, and you still gazed on me. We were so passionate with each other. You showed me how grateful you were for your Dawn. We gave each other such great pleasure. After our lovemaking, we held each other close all that night. I remember how the pianist at some point changed to slow, silent strains of some song I'd never heard.

"I miss your strong body next to me. I miss making love to you. But you will come back to me. You have to. Our life together will start again. It must. I hope you will come home to me ready to stay at Evening Star. I don't want to leave again. Not ever.

"But I would if it were my only way to be with you."

Chapter Twelve

Dawn continued to write news of the ranch and how the children flourished to Michael. She didn't respond at all to Michael's contemptuous remarks about the German Heinrich Mann.

To her, Heinrich seemed the most gentle and sensitive of men. Even if saddened by the war that isolated him, he remained steady and helpful for Nora and Jim. Papa Jim had become friends with the artist, sharing discussions of books and art after dinner or as they worked together repairing fences, feeding stock, or repairing outbuildings.

At least Michael hadn't yet written any warnings about Heinrich to the children. Bird and Rose's friendship with the quiet painter continued to grow. He gave them paper and pencils for drawing when they visited his studio.

~ ~ ~

One day when Dawn arrived at the Mercantile with butter and eggs to trade for flour and thread, Nan Hogan stepped out from behind the window of the post office in the back and handed Dawn three packages wrapped in brown paper. "I didn't order anything, certainly not from New York," Dawn said. "Is it a mistake?"

"Doesn't appear to be," Nan said, taking a package back to study the address. "Maybe Michael managed to send something."

But it wasn't Michael. When Dawn and the children opened the parcels on Christmas Eve, they found that Heinrich had ordered each of them a pair of leather ice skates with gleaming blades.

Eyes shining, the children clamored to go out at once to try them in the dark. Heinrich laughed. "In the morning, *kinder*," he said. "I've found a place where the creek feeds into a nice little pond. It's good solid ice for keeping us safe. If your mother gives her permission, we'll go there tomorrow."

On Christmas morning, the four bundled up and hiked the short distance to the pond in a snowfall as fine as a bride's veil. Heinrich put his skates on and helped the others with theirs. He pulled his gloves off. His hand on Dawn's ankle sent a surge of heat even through her woolen stocking as he knelt to lace up one of her skates. She reddened, grateful that he'd bowed his head, focused on his task.

When all were ready Heinrich starting with Rose showed each beginner how to balance, push off, and stop. Frightened at first, Rose made her hands into fists, frustrated that she had trouble with her balance. Then she started to enjoy herself as long as Heinrich skated backwards, letting her cling to his index fingers. There were spills for Bird and Dawn and much laughter. By noon, they'd become confident skaters and even strung out in a line for a clumsy attempt at crack the whip. The little group started for home with each pair of skates tied and slung over its owner's shoulder. When Rose found the new drifts too high for her little legs, Heinrich lifted her to his shoulders.

Looking at the kind German laughing with her daughter, who tried to steer him by his ears while calling him "pony," Dawn regretted that Michael wasn't the one to share this holiday. But then she'd never known Michael to skate. And he wouldn't have let them come to Evening Star. She felt relieved to make it through Christmas and very grateful to Heinrich for making their fatherless holiday so much fun.

~ ~ ~

Nan and Fred were hosting a New Years Eve party for North Fork settlers at the Mercantile. Heinrich only shook his head when Nora and Jim asked if he'd like to come. "I'll stay and watch the children if you like," he said. "There will be drinking and toasts for the troops, and no doubt insults toward my countrymen and women."

"But I want to go with Grandma Nora and Grandpa Jim," Bird protested. "Other kids will be there, too."

"Oh, let the boy come with us," Nora urged Dawn. "It will be a community event."

"I don't feel good," Rose declared with downturned lips. "My tummy hurts."

Dawn checked the cookie jar. "And I know why," she scolded. "Four big cookies, Rose?" Dawn sighed and said, "I'll stay home, too. I'm not much in the party spirit anyway. I'll see the New Year in with Rose and Heinrich."

She caught a rare frown on Papa Jim's face. A few seconds later he seemed like his usual self, so she dismissed what she thought she'd seen.

After the others left, Rose threw up, then fell asleep after Dawn tucked her into the bed they shared, smoothed her hair and went out. She left the door open to let heat from the stove spread a little warmth into the cold bedroom.

Heinrich sat before the fire and gestured toward the chair next to him. "Tell me about your life here before you and Michael left," he said.

Dawn began to share her memories. He asked questions, and then she asked him about his German upbringing. He spoke of art school and studying in Paris before coming to the United States. He'd known some famous painters, but she didn't recognize their names: Renoir, Monet, Cezanne. He tried them out on her one by one, but she looked blank. "I have some of their prints in my cabin," he said. "Let me fetch them and show you." He grabbed his jacket, pulled it on and rushed out the door.

He returned in a few moments, and Dawn spent the last hours of 1917 learning for the first time about the Impressionist Art Movement. Sitting in the cabin surrounded by the white and black winter night, she fell in love with the prints. Their warm colors fairly glowed. They seemed so full of life depicted with such sensuous movement.

Heinrich had also brought two bottles of beer. "For midnight," he said. "We should celebrate the New Year. Let's pray that 1918 brings peace to this battered world with its hatreds and horrors."

At the stroke of midnight, they stood to click their bottles together and drink. As she gazed into the German's eyes, Dawn saw a yearning. "It is a custom to kiss the person nearest you to welcome in the New Year, is it not?" Heinrich asked.

"Yes," Dawn whispered, putting her beer next to his on the table.

He leaned to her and they kissed. That long moment brought warm relief from the loneliness and sorrow that both had felt during months of isolation and uncertainty. They wrapped their arms around each other, the kiss no longer a traditional nod to passing time. Dawn had never been kissed by any man other than Michael.

Michael.

Dawn broke the spell. "No," she said, lowering her arms and stepping away from Heinrich. "I love my husband. I can't…"

Heinrich turned away. "I am ashamed and sorry. You are so beautiful and have been so very kind and understanding. I cannot stay here. You know I am in love with you. That makes staying at Evening Star wrong and impossible."

"But where can you go?" Dawn didn't urge Heinrich to stay, but felt fear for his safety.

"I have a cousin who farms in North Dakota. He lives near a German immigrants' town called Strasburg. I was there once. I'll go work for him. He's a good man and we Germans stick together. I'll miss you. All of you. But this is best. I'll leave tomorrow for Belton if Jim will take me. Then I'll take the train east. May I write to you?"

"No, not to me. Write to Mama and Papa Jim. They'll tell me how you are. I hope you will be well, Heinrich. We'll all miss you. I'm sorry. If I hadn't come home…"

"You have nothing to regret. You gave me precious time in this haven while the world has gone mad. I will always be grateful."

And with that, Heinrich lifted her hand, kissed it, and left the cabin. Dawn sank to a chair and tried to sort out how she'd let such a thing happen. Was it only loneliness that overwhelmed her?

Next morning Papa Jim took Heinrich Mann to Belton in the wagon. They received only one letter from Strasburg, North Dakota, saying he'd arrived safely. He sent a painting of a red barn, but after that nothing more.

~ ~ ~

DECEMBER 31, 1917

Soulincourt, France

Dearest Dawn,

Happy New Year. We're still far from the fighting, my love. The days are cold here. We drill all the time. Hard. And we don't dress for the weather. My skin is chafed all over. Our barracks shoes are too thin, but then there are the canvas leggings, the puttees, and what they call blouses… shirts with hellishly high, tight collars.

We're learning what I call French Trench. It's what the officers call trench warfare. Pete and I have been having a great time with all the firearms. We knew about Springfields already, of course, right along with barbed wire and shovels. But we've learned how to handle Cauchet and

Hotchkiss guns, grenades, and bayonets, too. And guess what? As soon as marksmanship teaching started, the Army promoted old Pete and me to assistant instructors. It doesn't keep us from the endless drills and marching, but it is a step up and gives us some respect.

We live in long tarpaper barracks with oilskin windows and dirt floors. Our meals are salty affairs of bacon, hard tack, potatoes, and weak, always too weak, coffee. Pete yearns out loud for venison, elk, fresh bread, and huckleberry pie. I try not to think about such things.

I miss you. Let me know how you and the children are faring. Well, I hope.

Your loving husband,

Michael

JANUARY 15, 1918

Dear Bird and Rose,

Pete's become a favorite with everyone in the village, especially the ones your ages. The French children are so much like you except for the way they talk and dress. They wear caps and sabots which are wooden shoes. They don't have heels. The kids just slip their feet in and out of them. No shoelaces, but hard soles that don't bend. I don't think you'd like them.

The kids followed Pete around one day and he started talking to them in his French-Canadian lingo. They called him Le Sauvage, the savage. He gave them candy. Next thing he got them to find tallow for us to soak into our boots and wax to rub into the outsides for water proofing. It feels fine. We need it as the weather has turned not just cold, but rainy. We march in the rain until we're soaked.

Are you having fun at the ranch? What do you do with your mother? Do you ride horses? I miss you both. And I miss your mother.

Love,

Your father

~ ~ ~

JANUARY 30, 1918

My Darling Dawn,

How are you? Distance and time only make me miss you all the more. Do not worry about me, So far all the action I've seen is infestations of lice. They bring the delousing wagon, and we all have to strip and resign ourselves to a most unpleasant procedure that doesn't even help all that much. The creatures live on us in the darnedest places and in the seams of our clothes.

I miss our times together. Some of the men here go to line up outside a red lamp house. It's well established because there's been no action near here so far. Pete and I stay away from the women there. There's always been only you for me, my darling. Pete stays away because he says the very idea that a flower of manhood such as himself might have to pay a woman appalls him. In fact, the old rascal has found a bed to share with a lonely widow whose only son served at the front. They speak French together, so I don't understand what they talk about.

We've gotten friendly with the townspeople thanks to Pete's French. But these people aren't my people. I'm lonesome for you and the children.

I don't get your letters for weeks at a time. But keep writing to me. Hearing from you gives me hope that life won't always be like this. Mail call is the high point of any day.

All my love to you,

Michael

~ ~ ~

FEB. 15, 1918

Dearest wife,

I think of you at the ranch in winter. Christmas was a good time there in spite of the fact that we were snowed in so often. Pete and I are on the move all the time. So far, we've only been in inactive sectors, but they keep us in trenches all the time now. We wade through mud, we warm our hands over barrel fires, and we sleep crouched next to each other.

There will be a German offensive sooner or later. In the meantime, we fight lice and get sick. Some of the men have had the runs. Not good in our circumstances, believe me.

Your letters finally came, and Pete got some from Jim and her. Pete gets quite fancy when he writes. He draws little pictures to go at the tops of his pages. I'm glad all is well for you. I'm glad the Bosch moved on. I have to say, I didn't like him living on the ranch. He seemed all right when we met him, but you can't trust any Hun.

My love to you always,

Michael

~ ~ ~

The rest of that winter went by in a steady routine of ranch labor, housework, and caring for the children. Then a letter arrived from Michael with news Dawn had been dreading.

Chapter Thirteen

June 1, 1918

Near the Marne River

My Dearest Dawn,

The action has been light these past weeks. The Hun hit us with artillery but neither side engaged in frontal charges. Thank God because we have enough war battling rats and lice. Disease takes its daily toll in the filthy trenches. We're often up to our knees in mud, and trench foot is common causing feet to rot. They send bad cases to the rear.

Rumor is we'll soon see real action. This morning, loaded with packs and guns, we marched several miles to board camions. They're trucks for carrying troops and supplies. Crammed in so tight we had to stand all the way to the railhead at Maux, we rode through white chalk dust that rises off the roads around here. We didn't get there until almost dusk. Pete looked at me, serious for once, and said, "This will be it. The real thing."

Chaos met us at the station. Confused refugees crowded into boxcars to be taken off to supposedly safe camps. They had to leave their shops, and looters broke windows and doors to get into them. Thieves took everything.

Our camion turned up the road toward the town of Chateau-Thierry. We met more refugees, women with aprons over their dresses, tired old people, and kids with the saddest eyes I've ever seen. Some rode on wagons.

Some were driving bony cattle beside little carts. They walked without talking. Those that glanced at us appeared to pity us. I pitied them. They looked like ghosts, even the children. Our camion finally stopped. We got down and marched through the darkness for miles. We got the hang of marching and sleeping at the same time, useful for any soldier. Finally, we made it to an abandoned town somewhere behind Chateau-Thierry where we could take a break. We lowered our packs, just dropped down on the cobbles of the town square, and slept.

Next thing I knew Pete shook me awake and pointed. French soldiers, poilus they're called, were shambling past. I've never seen men so exhausted. Some were bandaged. Pete went up to one and asked him a few questions. When he came back, he said, "He says we'll never stop the Hun. We have his pity for what's to come .We got up to march in darkness again. We got our first faint whiffs of mustard gas. Nasty stuff. Our officers gave us salty rations as usual, but no water. Some fell out sick. We marched past the thinning French until we were alone on the road.

At the abandoned town of Montruiel-aux-Lions, our officers ordered us to forage at will. We helped ourselves to cider, wine, brandy, anything in the abandoned shops. Pete and I found wine. Some of the boys went a little crazy, dancing around in corsets and French lacy items. I caught a pink hat as it spun through the air. I thought how beautiful your face would be under its brim.

We marched again. God knows how long. We marched here and then we marched there. We rested here and waited there. At times it seemed we marched in large circles. All I know is we were bone-tired and somewhere below Chateau-Thierry. We're in country with woods and fields. Rumor says U.S. Marines are to our right.

A man's here to gather mail. I don't know when I'll be able to write again. I love you and our children.

Michael

~ ~ ~

How did I end up here? Toying with that question, Michael grimaced. Neither Michael nor Big Pete had been made a sniper. The army came up short on plain old infantry so they became soldiers in the front line.

Any taste for glory slipped away. No glory here, only death. Killing that twisted, tore, and disemboweled. Thousands of bodies lay alone without a trace of dignity. Michael and Pete grit their teeth and shook their heads. They spoke less and less.

They learned their division's new objective would be heavily fortified Torcy Ridge, above Chateau-Thierry. Michael and Pete's division had orders to roll up the German left flank to help Marines on their right who'd been instructed to retake a forested area, Belleau Wood. The North Fork men joined a forced march of nearly twelve miles to reach the new position.

Finally, they arrived at a line of dilapidated trenches. If they could take Torcy Ridge which appeared as a deep shadow, the Germans would be trapped between the Second Division and the Marines.

But the Americans needed to cross a flat soft plain, once no doubt a rich and promising wheat field, reduced by war to a swamp of mud and craters. Only a few tufts of remaining weeds showed. *How could anyone cross that field?* Michael shivered. Pete rested a hand on his shoulder.

Yet thousands of good men would try… under fire on rising ground. Germans would be in those woods, waiting. *How many of us will die taking that gentle slope?*

The company's Captain spread his men in long lines. Michael saw with a sinking heart the men were placed very close together. That meant Germans had a strong hold and American officers expected heavy losses.

The Captain assigned Michael to his jump-off point. Pete waited about sixty feet to his right. *Will any of us make it?* Michael brushed such fear away. Only God knew men's fates, he reminded himself, rechecking his rifle.

German cannons started firing… heavy, deadly, accurate. Men fell, some buried alive in collapsing trenches. Air bursts and shell impacts shook Michael's body to its core. The sharp, arid stink of burnt powder drifted over the countryside along with the stench of dead horses and rotting corpses still there after battles of the last weeks.

Are we, like them, doomed in the thousands for the gain of a handful of yards?

Then the Germans hit with poison gas. Nevertheless, an American officer bounded out of his hole and blew the whistle that ordered his men to charge. Michael struggled with his gas mask as he rose from his trench and tried to run forward on rain-soaked, sodden ground. He might as well have weighed half a ton. Adrenalin-powered strength pushed him to stagger forward. Looking to his right he felt relief amounting to joy. Big Pete Dumont, still alive, ran ahead of him.

Where does that old man find the strength?

Thousands of Americans ran through the muddy field. Massive numbers fell to Michael's left and right, victims of German machine guns on higher land. As Michael lurched forward, the thousands of soldiers who'd started with him were reduced to hundreds. In the last three hundred yards of the assault, waves of maddened Germans left their lines. The enemy fired from only feet away, their rifles tipped with bright bayonets. Americans closed with the enemy in hand-to-hand fights to the death.

A dark square helmet loomed in front of Michael, and he plunged his own bayonet through the man's throat. It stuck there. He pulled the trigger of his Springfield. Blood and brains splattered his own face and torso. He took no time to ponder the horror. He shot two Germans less than ten yards in front of him, then turned to find Pete, expert and dispassionate, bayoneting another of the enemy.

A German sprang on Pete's back. Pete threw him off. During the hand-to-hand combat that followed, the German pulled off Pete's gas mask and the two rolled in the tainted air and leaves until Pete knifed the other, who grunted and fell back, eyes rolling.

Michael wrestled a bear of a man. They gripped each other's throats. Michael forced his fingers up into the giant's eye socket, his thumb behind the man's eyeball. With all his strength he ripped it out. The German screamed and fell. Michael grabbed his fallen rifle and sank his bayonet into the man's skull. He readjusted his gas mask.

Without warning the Germans disengaged, retreating. Michael shot two in the back as they fled. Each reached to the sky as if for God's hands. No American would have to fight them again, he thought.

Michael became aware of Pete retching and choking. In this maelstrom of violence Pete was on his knees screaming. "Gas! We rolled in the damn leaves. I can't see! I can't see!"

Michael had never seen Big Pete Dumont lose control. He pulled his friend up, and they moved in a stumbling, crouching run toward the rear. They'd never make it, the gunfire just too heavy. "I'll get you back, Pete," he grunted. But when he looked up, he saw two stretcher bearers coming to pick Pete up and rush him back over that dangerous ground to safety.

Michael watched as bullets struck around Pete and his saviors. The filthy Hun would even shoot unarmed stretcher bearers. Berserk with rage, he turned back to the battle. He wanted to kill them all: every man, woman, and child in the German nation. He joined prone soldiers giving as much suppression fire as possible while stretcher bearers saved those they could.

~ ~ ~

An officer stood and shouted the order to move forward. A hundred enemy machine guns seemed to commence firing at the same moment. Relentless German cannon hit the torn field. Michael tried to keep running forward through that rain of steel. A bullet struck his rifle stock, knocking it to the mud. He snatched it up. One glance told him it should still function. But after he took two more steps his helmet took a glancing hit and spun off his head. When he saw the line of soldiers to his left being mowed down, Michael dropped to the ground, hoping he wouldn't drown in the watery mud as others had. If he hadn't noticed the ranks falling to his left, he'd have been cut in two. He heard the sharp cracks of bullets fly inches overhead.

He and thousands of his comrades hadn't made it far into the ravaged field. Despite the Allies' three-hour pre-assault barrage and in spite of hundreds of thousands of bullets, the still intact German lines remained over three hundred yards away. During the shelling on his new position Michael struggled to hold his rifle with hands that trembled in spasms. Ringing in his ears affected any clear thinking.

Hundreds of wounded and dead Americans surrounded him. He stretched out, positioning himself like a dead man in a shallow grave, his face so low he tasted, inhaled, and choked on the cold soggy ground.

The world moved in slow motion. He called up a trick that had worked before. He shut his eyes, seeing an image of Dawn, Bird, and Rose walking beside the cabin at Evening Star. It calmed him and brought renewed determination to make it home alive. His capacity to reason returned by mental inches.

The killing fire, at least most of it, came from hidden machine gun nests to his distant right. The machine guns' ability to end thousands of lives in minutes seemed beyond the comprehension of those who sent men into battle on foot. If he could find those guns, he could save himself and others. He chose to resist fear and nurture hate. Hate of the Hun gave the ability to endure anything and fight against all odds. And God knew he hated them.

Michael raised his face, surrounded by a thick, endless ocean of mud. Still exposed to a storm of bullets and shrapnel, he slithered over to one of the many shell craters, this hole full of slimy water and corpses. Floating canteens showed that men had perished here. No living soldier would leave his canteen whether empty or full. Michael kept his head and rifle above water, the rest of him encased in mud and that bloody stinking slime.

He shivered in a uniform rendered unrecognizable. He didn't even know what this battle might be called. *Thousands of us die in places that are completely unmarked and unknown.* He stopped himself. He couldn't indulge in such thoughts. To reflect too long could be worse than pointless to a soldier. He charged to a deeper crater.

An American officer pushed up and whistled his men forward. Michael lurched with the others about eighty yards before he spotted rolls of barbed wire. He understood and felt sick. The American attack would be futile. Planning officers hadn't known about the shallow depression hiding barbed wire that formed a barrier twelve to fourteen feet wide.

Beyond this and even worse, two hundred yards of wire in small squares stretched ten inches above ground. The cunning enemy had created a tangle of barbed wire too low to crawl under and too high to run over. Caught by German fire, hundreds had tried to pierce the wire only to wind up hanging on those cruel barbs.

He took in the horror before hitting the earth again—good Mother Mud. His heart broke for brave Americans who gave all for what he now knew was no good reason.

The enemy poured thousands of rounds across the gently ascending land. The fire turned so heavy that the few tufts of weeds he'd seen were gone. The very ground trembled under this huge bombardment. Broken pieces of barbed wire twisted, shook, and bobbed under waves of lead coursing through the field.

Maddened German gunners shot into bodies that danced like marionettes controlled by insane puppeteers. Those who didn't move hung in an endless row of crucified martyrs on crosses made of barbed wire.

The Germans left some Americans screaming for help as bait. They slaughtered those who tried to free them. Michael's rage boiled. *What idiot general ordered this attack in this sector?* Michael cursed that man to hell. How could the architect of such a disaster ever sleep again? Hell, probably like a baby. Michael had heard the stories of luxury for high-ranking officers far behind these lines. He cursed again.

His only chance of survival would be to stay down until after dark and then try to make it back to his lines, if dreaded friendly fire didn't kill him. Thousands of others must be trapped in shell holes, the newest filling with water. Fast.

Was Pete still alive? Oh, God, Michael hoped so.

Silence arrived like a giant holding his breath. The ringing in Michael's ears stopped. He made out screams of wounded men begging for help, for water, for their mothers, or for God. Agonized moaning floated over the cursed place in low waves washing in from all directions.

Michael also groaned. *Will the sun never go down?* Then clouds gathered with foreboding darkness. In one instant, rain teemed in cold gray sheets while lightning ripped a sky the color of dried blood. It went on and on. *What God inflicted this on mortal men?*

With the forlorn land already saturated, relentless rain had nowhere to run except into the craters. Those wounded unable to move cried out for help but lay beyond reach. The enemy cut down anyone trying to make it to them. Michael clapped his hands over his ears to block the pleas. He gripped his head so hard it seemed he'd crush his own skull. Entreaties of the doomed reached a crescendo.

But then, one by one, dying men fell silent as if the merciful angel of death had come, smothering the flames of an endless field of candles. Rising water covered the faces of the immobile wounded. They died by drowning. They died of their wounds, American youth banished from life's warmth, never to see their loved ones again.

~ ~ ~

Michael rested until dark on that longest day of his life. Finally, the hour arrived to start toward the safety of his line. He guessed he had about 400 yards to cover. He crawled on his belly for an hour. He'd made about 200 yards, he thought. He froze in place whenever illumination lit the ground from huge balls of bright gray-white light. He waited as lights from floating parachutes wafted down to the battlefield.

After that he rose to his hands and knees and crawled, stopping often to listen, letting his jaw hang open a little to better hear his surroundings. Those in the line would be trying to catch sounds of returning survivors.

He began calling, just above a whisper. No answer for a long while. At last, he heard a strained voice call, "Who goes there?"

"I'm an American. I want to come in."

"What state are you from?"

"Montana."

"Come on then but stay on your belly. Snipers have been giving us hell."

Michael finally reached the sandbags. Friendly hands pulled him over the lip of the trench. A burly soldier asked how many of the troops were lost.

"Thousands died for no gain at all." Michael replied. Then he slid to the filthy duckboards and fell asleep.

Chapter Fourteen

June 21, 1918

The losses were horrific. Michael decided an individual soldier never knew the big picture. Yet the war continued. Combat had stretched on several weeks. Michael's exhausted outfit regrouped with what was left of their division. Pete rejoined them showing no ill effects of the gassing, or at least complaining of none. He refused to speak of it except once. He shook his head and muttered, "Blindness," like a curse. "It's better for a man like me to die."

Michael felt waves of relief at having Pete beside him again. Nothing could be certain, though. Weak and strong had equal chances to die. Far better to be lucky than anything else, he concluded. The Battle of Belleau Wood, considered an Allied victory, ended.

~ ~ ~

The next battle would be for the village of Vaux.

"I swear it shines prettier than Polebridge in this late afternoon light Take a good look," Pete told Michael. They glassed the streets for their objectives until the sun lowered and the town, which had no streetlights, shaded to dark gray. "Tomorrow we blast the morning shine right off." Pete added, "Us and the Hun."

They did take Vaux, fighting across treeless hills, patchy woods, and then the streets of the town itself. They'd been gaining ground, moving from building to building, when a German stepped out of a doorway and fired. The bullet drove into Michael's thigh. The German, a little man this time, ran at Michael, who ducked away, protecting his stomach from the Hun's bayonet, but the blade sliced his arm.

The German gave a surprised "Huh!" as Pete shot him in the back. Pete swept Michael up before their dying enemy landed on the cobblestones. He carried Michael to a stretcher bearer, then turned back, shouting over his shoulder, "Don't die, boy! Nora and Dawn would never let me hear the end of it."

~ ~ ~

Stretcher bearers carried Michael and lifted him into an ambulance. A body had just been removed from a lower birth and they replaced the dead man with Michael. Blood dripped from the bunk above him to the floor. The man overhead groaned with every breath. The vehicle's jolting, the moans of his wounded companions, along with Michael's second separation from Pete finally took its toll. Michael shivered. By the time they reached the field hospital at Coulommiers, he'd gone into shock.

When he came to on a field hospital cot, his arm had been stitched and his bullet wound cleaned and dressed. But he lay unable to stop painful, trembling spasms. He grew aware of a murmuring voice coming nearer. A young, deer-eyed priest, dark, with a long, aesthetic face, moved down the aisle, speaking to each stricken man, pausing longer at the cots of those Michael guessed must be Catholic. Michael closed his eyes, uncertain as to whether he could or even wanted to talk to any priest. He opened them when the footsteps paused beside him.

A pallid face with a thin-lipped mouth hovered over Michael. The boyish impression decreased as fine lines around the priest's eyes showed him to be at least in his late thirties. "I'm Father Laurence. How do you feel?"

That the Priest could sound sincerely interested baffled Michael. His trembling quieted a little, though. "You must ask that a thousand times a day, Father. Lucky to be alive is my answer. Embarrassed I can't stop this shaking, though."

They spoke, their tones muted as befit a sick room, murmuring about Michael's wounds and how he'd received them. He included the part about Pete shooting the German who'd hurt him.

The priest only nodded. "I've witnessed daily the loss of limbs, sight, and life. I'm beyond remonstrating about the horrors of war to battered young soldiers like you, caught up in its realities. I pray that you forgive all you can. The world will need to heal for a return to sanity when this is over. Where's your family?"

"Montana. Up in Montana—North Fork of the Flathead River—just across from Glacier Park." For the first time, the shaking stopped.

"Ah. The Crown Jewel of the Continent, our Lord's finest scenery."

"Yes, it is all of that." Michael shifted. "Do you think I could get a letter off to my wife? Just a note?" He winced.

"Of course, I'll help you write it. Sleep a little, and I'll be back with paper when I have the chance."

After the priest walked away, Michael slept. He awoke hours later to see that more wounded had arrived. They never seemed to cease coming. He smelled unwashed bodies, the spoiled meat odor of gangrene, and the awful stench of gas. There were groans, and farther away in the operating section, screams. Prone figures on nearby cots made little noise. Like him, these wounded lay exhausted, craving elusive, dreamless sleep.

~ ~ ~

At dawn, a weary-looking blonde nurse took Michael's temperature and changed his dressings. After she left, a large-boned Red Cross volunteer arrived. Buck teeth didn't spoil her smile's warmth. She spoke with a flat, Midwestern accent. "Oh, Father told me you asked for someone to help you write a note. He's been too busy, but I'll take down your words and get it in the mail."

Feeling awkward and inhibited at the idea of dictating to a stranger instead of writing his own letter, Michael tried to give the general idea of what he wanted to tell his wife.

The woman raised her eyebrows slightly at the greeting. "Dawn? It sounds poetic."

"Blackfeet," Michael explained.

The woman from Minnesota only nodded, her pen poised above the paper.

Michael asked her to write that he'd been wounded, but not badly, only enough to justify a rest. A priest who'd come in hadn't even seen fit to perform last rites. Michael wished he was with Dawn. After the nurse left, he considered whether he should have written to his mother, too. What the priest had mentioned about forgiveness kept entering his thoughts as he lay alone among the rows of wounded and dying.

~ ~ ~

He woke later when a tired doctor with thinning hair came to examine him. The physician appeared satisfied with what he saw. He rested a hand for a moment on Michael's shoulder, then moved on.

Father Laurence came through two days later. "I didn't ask before," the priest began. "Are you Catholic?"

"Yes."

"Do you wish to make a confession?"

"No. I want to talk to you, though. What you said about forgiveness. I have a story to tell you." He glanced around them. "I think I could walk a little if I had canes or something."

Father Laurence gave him a curious glance but disappeared and returned with crutches.

Shaky, still weak, Michael hobbled out of the tent as the priest steadied him. The day warmed, and a linden tree glowed in sunlight. Michael drew appreciative breaths of unadulterated air that fluttered the linden's leaves. "I thought every tree in France might be blasted by now," he said.

He heard occasional explosive thumps, but from such a distance the sound carried no true threat. He did think of Pete, but still shared the general belief among the men that Big Pete Dumont could be slowed down at times, but never stopped—not that invincible mountain man.

Michael and the priest moved to a table and wrought iron chairs a ways from the tents. "Now, Michael," Father Laurence said in a smooth, practiced tone, "How might I help you?"

Michael looked at the ground. "These Germans. They aren't the first men I've killed."

The priest had been relaxing against the back of his chair. He sat forward at hearing Michael's opening words. "Did you commit murder, my son?"

"No. I defended a good man, Jim Li. He's married to my mother, at least in the eyes of the church, but not the state of Montana. Anyway, the man I killed tried to murder Jim for revenge for something he didn't even do. I found out after the shooting that I'd actually shot my natural father. I killed my father to save my mother's half-Chinese husband." Michael rubbed his face, then dragged his fingers through his shaggy hair.

Alert, Father Laurence's eyes bored into Michael's. "Start at the beginning."

And so Michael told his story from the shooting to the present moment. He chose the words with hesitant care, and the telling took a long time. The priest focused all attention on what the troubled young soldier related. When Michael finished, his listener sat in thoughtful silence.

Then he spoke in tones of a wise counselor when he voiced his conclusion. "Your mother erred, but think how desperately she must have wanted to keep your high opinion of her. In her mind you must have seemed a miracle appearing after she'd given you up fifteen years before. She wanted to protect you from the sordid truth, and herself from you ever knowing it.

"She wouldn't be the first lonely soul to stray and then try to make it right by hiding what she'd done. She atoned as best she could. She gave you to decent married people. She married her Chinese companion in the church. She took in another child who's now your beloved wife. Your mother committed sins, but atoned with all in her poor mortal power. She's led an upright life for many years."

"But I had a right to know who fathered me. She didn't have the right not to tell me. I can't ever trust her again."

The priest gave a low, sardonic laugh and shook his head. "Now you sound like a boy. Your mother chose a wrong direction twice in her life, but if you truly believe that made her evil, you'd be more distraught that your wife and children, your dearest beings, are in her and her husband's care. One or even two mistakes don't make a human soul who is remorseful over such lapses of judgment eternally bad or untrustworthy."

"You're saying I should just forgive her and forget about it?" Michael's words sounded angry, but hope hovered behind them.

"The Bible tells us to forgive seventy times seven. It never commands us to forget. Forgive and be glad you've became wise and strong enough to be merciful. Forgiving your mother who's been strong enough to ask you to do so will make you a moral father for your children. A man of good character. Give yourself and your long-suffering mother hope for fruitful lives after this carnage."

"All this death does tend to put things in perspective, I guess." Michael stretched out his good leg and tipped his head back to watch leaves play and shine above him in the breeze. He flashed to an image of the aspen at home.

"Life demands that we be forgiving of our fellow flawed human beings. You'll need forgiveness yourself one day. We all will since we're all flawed."

"I'll try. I want to move on with life at home after this hell. I'll go see her and Jim when I go back. I will forgive her." Michael sat a little straighter, sighed, and tipped his face to the sun. When he opened his eyes, Father Lawrence had moved off to speak to a man missing one foot who'd been sitting alone nearby, tears drenching his face.

In a little while a nurse came for the man who no longer wept. The priest returned and helped Michael back to bed, then excused himself to say Mass. Michael participated from his bed, the first time he'd taken part in the ritual by himself since leaving Butte as an orphaned adolescent determined to find the woman who'd given him life.

After Mass Michael slept again, the first peaceful sleep he'd known since being wounded. He awakened at dawn. Orderlies loaded him and other wounded into an ambulance and transported them to Paris to a hospital near the Bois de Boulogne. He didn't see Father Laurence before leaving the field hospital.

~ ~ ~

In Paris, he convalesced in an austere ward with white walls and beds. He spoke little, but thought about his mother, remembering her gardening and cooking for them all at Evening Star. The priest's last remarks to him after saying Mass referred to her as "a decent woman who suffered much."

Restless, irritable with those who worked to help him heal, Michael knew what he wanted. He wanted to be back with the men. He felt more and more anxious for word of Pete and others back in the trenches. Cries of men in physical or mental pain pierced the hospital's hush. The air, redolent with a heavy antiseptic odor veiling the smells of infection and worse grew intolerable to him. The trenches held the only reality he wanted, called on the deepest loyalty he knew. The promise of one day walking out to see Paris's Eiffel Tower, outdoor cafes, the Louvre … meant nothing. He belonged with Big Pete and their platoon.

Thinking of his mother seemed like thinking of someone in a story that concluded with a moral. His sense of her as a real person blurred as if she'd become someone he'd made up. And it frightened him. What if he came to think of Dawn that way, too? He thought of his young wife's touch, their past together, and remembered her scent, her taste, her laugh, her eyes. No, Dawn existed as his woman, his love. She embodied his only vital reality back in America.

~ ~ ~

Troops were needed badly on the front lines. After three weeks his doctor pronounced the young patient from Montana fit to return to the front. Still limping and sore from his wounds, Michael boarded a camion with two fellow soldiers, each tense and quiet. They rode toward a village called Saint-Mihiel. Their truck stopped and started, caught in a massive, chaotic traffic jam of other trucks, vehicles, weary horses, and men. Michael saw bloated cattle and horses lying in ditches, maggots feasting in their open bellies.

He could tell from the harried bustle of supply officers that he and his companions journeyed to something big. Tense and impatient, he ground his teeth. He had to get to whatever it would be in time to fight beside Pete. Since Pete had been gassed, Michael felt as protective of the older man as Pete did of him. It pressed the breath from him, this compulsion to protect the man who'd been one of his boyhood mentors. Big Pete Dumont was part of the war, but he was also part of life on the North Fork, the only part Michael could see and feel beside him. He yearned to hear his old friend joking and cussing.

At last the three climbed down from the camion in darkness. Michael marched eight miles from a deserted village to rejoin his company. His leg ached. After a search that threatened to turn frantic, he found Pete trying to sleep in a shallow trench. They embraced. Michael heard a catch in Pete's voice as the older man said, "I thought they might have kept you out of this one."

Michael gave a wry laugh. "Hell, it's safer here. A sickness they call the Spanish flu is hitting Paris. People catch it fast and die from it pretty quick, too. What's up?" Michael asked.

"Don't know, but I know it's big."

~ ~ ~

JULY 14, 1918

German divisions broke through the French lines near the Marne, threatening to take Paris only 60 miles away. If the Germans seized Paris all the Allied losses would have been in vain. The Germans would stand across western and eastern Europe, masters of the land.

The enemy struck along the line in desperate assaults. The Allies made counter assaults. During a lull, commanders gave each soldier a new written order from General Pershing himself. It said the Allies had their back against the wall. Each doughboy would attack on command and when ordered to stand must not retreat a foot but die in place if necessary. Paris had to survive.

With no reserves available to block a German attack, the city would be open for the enemy to ravage. The Second and other weak divisions remained the last vital defense. There were rumors that the fierce Marine regiments would fight with them.

Many rumors flew. Some claimed Germany had fifty fresh divisions from the Eastern Front who'd soon mount a major offense. Others claimed the Hun had already taken Paris. Some announced the war close to over.

Michael didn't know what to believe. Officers who made the big decisions didn't confide in low-ranking soldiers like him. But something different drifted in the tension among the troops, a sense of bewilderment.

The slog of marching seemed endless. They were shifted from sector to sector. They had to shore up the weak spots in the lines. Soft soil morphed into mud. Pershing's order had been clear enough. March, fight, and probably die. Michael marveled how each soldier faced death with such fatalistic calm, inured to its constant presence.

Michael never knew the exact details in this maelstrom of combat. It went on for weeks. Finally, news spread that Paris had been saved. The remaining Army soldiers had gone on defense and stopped the Germans. The counterattack forced the Germans to retreat. The Second Battle of the Marne was an Allied victory. It was the last great German offensive of the war.

But the war went on. There was no doubt the Allies continued pushing the Germans back. The German offense to seize Paris had failed. It seemed their last bolt had been shot.

Pete explained the recent rumors they were to follow a familiar plan, fighting their way through shrubby, crowded woods the Montanans called shin-tangles. They were to proceed north to the town of Jaulny, part of what Pete guessed would be "a jeezely big offensive" to drive the Hun back from ground they'd long held. The doughboys would set out over land treacherous with rusty barbed wire and deep trenches. This time they carried huge clippers and rolls of chicken wire to throw over the barbed wire in advance of walking over it. The mention of clippers and chicken wire reminded both Michael and Pete of life at Evening Star. They didn't speak of it, only exchanged half smiles of recognition.

Once in heavy timber, they waited out the relentless artillery bombardment that fell on the German lines. It seemed that the Germans shot fewer shells back toward them. Michael hadn't forgotten the sound of thumps, thunder, barks, and pops. "A familiar tune," Pete muttered with a weary grimace.

"Yeah, you can't get it out of your head." Michael willed himself not to tremble any more than he could help. He feared he might never be able to stop this time.

They moved again under cover of a smoke screen. They chucked grenades and took angry, frightened prisoners who scrambled out of dugouts, hands raised, eyes either resigned or filled with hate.

At Jaulny, the two Montanans followed orders to load German wounded onto a captured German hospital train. Neither the Germans they'd captured nor the bloody, groaning enemy injured looked so different from themselves. Pete gave one moaning boy a drink of water from his own canteen. When Michael shot him a questioning look, he shrugged. Pete still recognized common humanity. Even here. Michael only nodded.

They celebrated their victory in mid-September, then moved on for the next offensive in the Meuse-Argonne area sixty miles from Saint-Mihiel. They traveled at night through spectral walls of rain, their camions bogging down over and over in deep mud.

Orders changed and they found themselves diverted to Reims, the city known for its cathedral towers. They prepared for an engagement at "Blanc Mont," a promontory of chalky cliffs and wooded ridges fifteen miles northeast.

At dawn on October 2, the French Corps Artillery bombarded the Germans until late morning, followed by a barrage from American cannoneers. The company maneuvered around a high ridge to capture its objective, the Medeah Farm. Without warning, they encountered the enemy, who'd overthrown some French lines during the night.

The work of bayonets and bullets became bloodier and more desperate. This time they took no prisoners. The Americans drove the

Germans ahead of them without mercy, stopping for brief rests at night, then pushing forward, the astonished French following.

Filthy, so bone-tired they felt like chronic illness victims, they fought across ridges north toward the town of Sedan. By November 1, in smoke and twilight, Michael, Pete, and the rest engaged in hand-to-hand fighting again. They covered each other as best they could. Michael and Pete fought back to back during one whole fearful hour. At last, they broke through to the banks of the Meuse River, and then joined soldiers from other divisions in a barbaric race to be the first to enter Sedan.

~ ~ ~

Abruptly on the eleventh hour of the eleventh day of the eleventh month of 1918, word of the Armistice arrived. Pete and Michael heard the news of peace from a drunken farmer who shouted his message and waved a newspaper verifying what he said.

Michael climbed out of their trench, threw his rifle to the cold clods of dirt, and sank beside it.

"Listen," Pete said.

"I don't hear anything."

"That's it."

They lay on their backs in the stubble of that cold field and watched clouds bulge in the pale sky. Bird song began. They waited awhile, not quite trusting the news. Then they shook the passed-out farmer awake. All three trudged to the nearest village where they drank full-bodied French wine and listened to the songs of celebration all around them until long after dark. They tried not to be afraid of letting themselves be unafraid at last.

Michael sat half-drunk and half-asleep. His head rested back against the rough stone wall of the crammed café when someone called his name. A soldier he'd befriended at the field hospital waved an opened bottle and sat down, his scarred face sweaty and flushed.

"It's a day I never thought we'd see." The former patient refilled their glasses, his grin lopsided. "But we've seen a lot we never thought we'd see, haven't we, boys?"

"How long did they keep you?" Michael asked.

"Only two weeks. I wasn't bad once they stitched my cheek. Say, did you hear about that priest?" The soldier shouted his question as the men behind him bellowed a bawdy version of *Mademoiselle from Armentieres*.

Michael hugged his arms to his body and shivered in spite of the heat from so many others crammed into the low-ceilinged room. "Father Laurence?" he asked, already knowing.

"Yeah. Father Laurence he was. Got killed in the Argonne. They'd moved up to say a Mass and then couldn't get back. In the night he went out to help pick up wounded. A sniper got him. Hey, where're you off to?"

Michael half-turned and held up a hand to silence the swaying doughboy who shrugged and staggered back into the crowd, singing along with the ribald lyrics. Michael pushed his way outside.

Pete found him on a bench under an ancient chestnut tree in the village square. He sat down, too.

"I only spoke to that priest but the one time," Michael said. "All we talked about was how I should forgive my mother. I told him I'd try."

"Honor the good Father's memory. Don't just try. Show some respect for Nora and do it. Nora never meant to hurt a living soul. She's been as good to you as she could. China Jim, too. They raised your Dawn from a baby."

"I know. I have forgiven her. I'll tell her when we go home."

~ ~ ~

Nov. 8, 1918

Dearest Michael,

I wish I knew where you are. I haven't had a letter for weeks. I hope for one tomorrow.

In the meantime, I lie awake at night and remember happier days. Last night I thought back to the anniversary we had when Bird was two. It made me smile, but long for you and miss you at the same time.

I've met a friend here. Her name is Celia Van Eick. It's all strange in a way. She's a widow who moved into a big lodge built, we all thought, as some sort of hunting lodge, on the ridge west of Polebridge. It's solid and impressive, but only she and an older couple who are some kind of servants live there. She's going to have a baby. Nobody knows much about Celia, but we met the other day at the Mercantile. I liked her.

Mama Nora and I invited her to visit someday. She seems lonely, and some of the gossip around here can be mean. Some say she's a rich girl who got herself in trouble. I'm going to be her friend anyway. Mama and I can teach her to make snowshoes. Not that she will use them soon. I'm tucking Bird's letter in with this one.

I love you. Write to me.

Dawn

~ ~ ~

Dear Pop,

I hope you are well. We miss you. Kill the Germans and come home. Mama misses you. Rose and I miss you, too. Come home all in one piece.

I suppose it's not fun to travel in a war. When we beat the Hun and I'm older I want to go to China. And Ireland. That would be fun. Grandpa Jim is teaching me Chinese words. And he's shown me his Chinese writing. I like how it looks, but I can't read it yet.

I'm getting better at shooting and trapping. Grandpa teaches me something new every day.

Love,

James Bird Larkin

CHAPTER FIFTEEN

The Great Influenza pandemic that devastated countries, cities, and whole armies, made its first hungry foray into the North Fork early in 1918. During the initial round that threatened North Fork homesteaders Jim, Nora, and Dawn protected themselves and the children by isolating at Evening Star. When the threat appeared to have spent itself, when that menacing beast had slunk away, they'd been relieved to the point of giddiness. They were free to leave the ranch and mingle with neighbors.

But while buying supplies at the Mercantile in November, 1918, Jim heard about a second outbreak of the disease, more potent and deadly than the first. The Great Influenza wasn't finished with them. No. It had just been flexing its muscles. Its first victim this time had been Ambrose Hutch, an old friend and one of the elderly settlers. Within a week, three people new to the community followed the frail frontiersman to the grave.

"Well, it's a tougher damned epidemic this time," Fred told Jim as the two conversed in the back of the store. "People are being struck down in Kalispell, Columbia Falls, even Belton. A ranger's wife at Apgar died within a day of feeling poorly. You don't know who's bringing it in. Anybody who shows up after being in another community can carry it to us. There's at least fifty cabins scattered around here these days."

Other customers spoke in wary voices about this new menace. "Worst of all," Nan Hogan spoke up from behind the postal window, "it's hit our troops overseas."

Jim thought of Michael, Pete, and Beartracks , all still in Europe, and shuddered. He noticed that the newcomer Celia Van Eick turned from perusing canned food on a shelf to listen to their conversation. She had her baby daughter with her. Locals with sharp tongues whispered about Celia's absence of letters from a husband even though her left hand bore a gold ring.

Locals had assumed the newly built two-story rustic mansion Celia had moved into was to be for hunting by wealthy East Coast sportsmen, but the only resident remained Celia, her needs seen to by an unsmiling housekeeper and her chauffeur husband who snubbed all social overtures.

Nan had introduced the Evening Star family to Celia during one of their earlier visits to the Mercantile. Returning to Evening Star, Nora, Jim, and Dawn agreed that they'd each known enough of loneliness to recognize it in the constrained young woman. They considered that she might well be a widow carrying the child of her deceased husband. In any event they'd be welcoming.

Dawn and Nora chatted with Celia every time they met at the Mercantile. She let them know she'd been widowed by the war and had no living family. Celia expressed real interest in all of them, but seemed especially drawn to Dawn, of her own generation. She didn't explain nor did they press her on the matter of her caretakers, who sometimes seemed like guards. In due time Celia produced a baby daughter. Bonnie Van Eick's heart-shaped face promised to become an echo of her mother's.

Celia had Bonnie along that November day of Jim's talk with Fred at the Merc. She cooed to her baby while others traded news of the sinister pandemic. As Jim carried his purchases to the door, he stopped to admire the infant.

Celia asked about Nora, Dawn, and the children, her wistful look a testament to loneliness. Jim passed on an invitation from Nora and Dawn that the young mother come with her baby and stay for a visit at Evening Star. He hadn't accepted that the influenza did not present so serious a danger this time. He didn't want to believe that it could once again pose a threat to his family.

Celia beamed as she accepted. "My keepers can't stop me."

Jim raised his eyebrows in an unspoken question.

"My housekeepers, I mean," Celia amended, fiddling with Bonnie's satin ribbon.

~ ~ ~

Celia arrived at Evening Star the next morning in her Pierce Arrow, still an exotic sight in the remote North Fork. Bonnie lay in a basket beside Celia, who beamed and climbed out swathed in a long fox fur coat.

"I feel so free," she crowed, hugging Dawn and then Nora, who'd hurried out to welcome her. "Thank you for inviting us." The coat swirled as Celia pivoted to lift Bonnie's basket. Her dour driver unloaded a leather suitcase and bestowed a stiff bow before starting the eight-mile drive to Celia's grand home south of Polebridge. He hadn't acknowledged the others.

"He's like Scrooge," Dawn laughed, taking the suitcase.

The women and Rose spent the day chatting and cuddling Bonnie. Nora and Dawn demonstrated how to make snowshoes, and promised to let her do it the next day. Feminine laughter and low confidences filled the house until Jim and Bird escaped to spend their day repairing outbuildings.

Disaster struck that evening. Midway through Mama Nora's feast of elk steaks, potatoes, carrots, and rhubarb pie, Celia complained of a sore throat and headache, then asked to be excused. By bedtime Nora reported to the others that their guest's fever had spiked.

Jim could hear Celia groan. Peering through the opened door when Nora went to check on the sick girl, he saw that her teeth were chattering. She shivered under her quilt in the cot they'd set up for her next to Dawn's bed. Celia's cool beauty had vanished, replaced by pallor, miserable groans, and a grimace that conveyed desperation.

Dawn paced with Bonnie, who'd turned fussy, while Nora prepared Rose for bed and tucked her in. Bird and his grandfather read to each other by the stove. Each member of the family tried not to be upset by moans from the sick room and wails from the mother-deprived baby.

Nora emerged from the bedroom, concern evident in her eyes. She addressed Dawn. "She was nursing Bonnie. That's stopped now. We'll heat a bottle of cow's milk. I still have one of the bottles I used for you when I took you home with me. You were so tiny and motherless."

Dawn nodded and smiled. "I'm so glad we came back home to you, Mama. You have such a sure way of knowing what to do."

"I'm glad, too," Bird declared.

The two women, so focused on the baby, jumped, and looked at Bird as though they'd forgotten he existed. Jim wrapped an arm around the boy's shoulders and squeezed. The two returned to the adventures of *Treasure Island.*

~ ~ ~

In the morning, Bird came into the kitchen to an ominous sight. Grandma Nora had come down with the awful sickness, too. She shivered as though a blizzard instead of warmth from the fire enveloped her. Grandma Nora groaned and slumped to a chair. "I let the others sleep while I tended the fire and nursed our suffering guest. I also fed her sweet babe. Your grandpa is milking the cows."

Bird stared at her, then toward his mother as she came into the room shivering and sank down next to Grandma Nora. Then Dawn rested her head on the table.

In a panic, Bird jerked the door open and shouted for his grandfather. "Grandpa Jim?" There had to be some adult who wasn't stricken.

"I'm here, Bird." Jim rushed in from outside, carrying a load of split logs. He dumped them into the wood box by the stove, stood, and for a long moment studied the two women as they tried to hold themselves up by gripping the table.

He turned to Bird. "I have something very, very important for you to do. It's much to ask of any young man of your age."

Bird had a bad feeling, but he borrowed courage from Grandpa Jim's steady voice. "What, Grandpa?"

Jim spoke as he bundled up Bonnie and pulled a protesting Rose's arms into the sleeves of her winter coat. Then he slipped his granddaughter's hands into mittens and pulled up her hood. He kissed the top of her head and handed her the old birch doll.

"I don't want to go today. I want to stay home," she said, her lower lip quivering. "I want to stay here." She sank down to the floor, and cried, leaning against a table leg.

Jim wiped her cheeks, picked her up and turned to Bird. "I'm not sick. Not yet, but all three women are. As long as I can, I'll nurse them and keep things going. But you children must be safe. Take the baby and Rose to Polebridge."

"What should I do when we get there?" Bird sounded incredulous.

Grandpa Jim put a reassuring hand on the boy's shoulder. "Nan Hogan will take you and your little sister in. She'll know what to do."

"But what about Bonnie?"

"Celia's servants can see to Bonnie. Nan will get a message to them. They must not come here and be exposed, but they can care for Bonnie. That's their job."

Bird nodded, relieved that Grandpa had it all planned.

Grandpa Jim continued. "Nan and Fred are like aunt and uncle to you and Rose. If you can't be with us—and you cannot—you'll be as safe as you can be with them. Perhaps Doctor McBride will come by. If so, tell him we need him at Evening Star.

"You can't carry both little ones the whole way. I fixed the toboggan for you. I meant to save it as a surprise for sliding downhill in the snow, but now you'll have to pull it on the roadway with both girls on it." He sighed before continuing. "We have new snow and that will help. The girls have been fed. Don't stop to change Bonnie's nappies even if she smells bad and cries. Just get the three of you to Polebridge."

Bird's eyes widened at this whole morning's turn of events. The grownups didn't even let him walk to Polebridge by himself and now Grandpa Jim wanted him to take a baby and little Rose with no help? But he glanced at his mother and Grandma Nora. Grandpa Jim was right. They couldn't be left alone. Grandma Nora was holding her head in her hands while his mother rested hers pillowed on her crossed arms at the table.

Grandpa Jim directed Bird to bundle up. Jim put Rose down and told her she had to go now, but could come home soon. "Bird can't do everything. Can you be a big girl and help with Bonnie? Sing to her? Pat her?" Rose nodded.

Carrying Bonnie, Jim opened the door and beckoned for his grandchildren to follow. Outside Jim laid Bonnie down, wrapped blankets around her in her basket on the toboggan, and secured it to the curved front. He sat Rose, with a pillow behind and a fur robe around her shoulders, close to the baby.

He spoke to Bird. "You won't need the gun. You have enough to manage without it. Go as fast as you can. All of you children seem healthy, but..."

Bird threw his arms around his grandpa. "I'll sing to them," he said. "Rose always likes that."

"I'll sing for the baby, too." Rose's little voice piped. "Don't worry, Grandpa."

~ ~ ~

Jim would long remember how Bird strode away, the toboggan leaving a faint depression in the snow-filled road. Bonnie had awakened and cried, but Bird's and Rose's high sweet voices singing *Mollie Malone*, a song Nora taught them, carried louder in the cold air than the baby's wails.

Jim went back into the cabin and put Nora and Dawn to bed. Dawn lay on hers beside Celia's cot. Nora tossed fitfully in the room Jim and she had shared for many years. He paused and brushed her hair aside, then kissed her forehead. They'd seen each other through illnesses and injuries. Fear that this might be the last time darted through him. What if he couldn't see her through? He banished panic and raised his jaw in defiance.

Jim located his notebook and pen. In his meticulous hand, he kept the first of what would become pages of notes on each victim's symptoms and his efforts to care for them.

He bathed the women's foreheads with cool cloths. When they did speak, he heard nonsense. Spiking fevers brought delirium. He brought in more wood, built up the fire, and heated water. That, along with washing clothes and bedding, brewing tea and broth, taking short trips to the barn for minimal care of the animals became a haze of work and worry without end.

He dozed when all three invalids quieted sometime before dawn. He woke to see a late November sunrise showing salmon pink against skeletal larch, green-black fir, and lodge pole. He'd never felt so alone. This differed from when he'd wandered in the West, a transient responsible only for himself. Now three women teetered between life and death, each depending on his ability to nurse her through. He loved two of them more than his own life. Why had he been careless enough to invite the melancholy widow?

On the third day he stepped outside to breathe in fresh air, think, and peer down the road as if help might be on the way. It was not.

Jim continued to wash soiled bedding and nightclothes, spreading them around the room to dry. He mixed willow bark tea with other plant medicines he'd learned to use from Sweet Grass so long ago. He held each patient half sitting in his arms and attempted to have them sip the tea. He murmured in soft tones, searching for encouraging words to soothe the women's delirious wretchedness.

But this time the medicines did no good. Temperatures stayed high, breathing and pulses remained far too rapid while incoherent murmurings spoke of merciless pain. Jim bathed Nora's brow, then hurried to the other room to the young women. "Do not die," he implored each of them. "You must be strong for your daughters and your son Bird."

To Nora he murmured, "My beloved, you must live for me and to see Michael return to us."

Back to Dawn and Celia, "Bonnie and Rose need you. You must be strong for your little ones. Bird is so young, your daughters are younger still. Stay with your son, Dawn. Stay with your little girls."

During lulls in meeting the sufferer's physical needs, Jim made his notes. He also worked in the barn and made more broth. The stricken women's relentless moans and coughs sounded so pitiful.

For five days and nights Jim struggled. He only dozed in a chair for brief moments of relief, always alert for sounds that led him to leap up and help the others. Nora moved very little, which frightened Jim more than the others' fevered tossing. He worried about Bird. Did Bird make it to the Mercantile? Had he been wrong to send the boy? Had Bird and the girls succumbed to this flu as well? He shouldn't have sent them away. But what else could he do?

On the sixth day, back in the cabin after milking cows and pitching hay to horses, Jim sat down at the table and found himself weeping. After a few minutes, when he wiped away his tears and stood to go to Nora, the room spun. He stumbled. For a fearful moment he thought he might be ill, too. He splashed water over his eyes, then built up the fire. *Only embers. How could I have let it come so close to dying? I am not sick, only weak from forgetting to eat and having so little sleep.*

He made himself toast and fried eggs. Then he fed, or tried to feed, broth to his patients. He covered them, banked the fire, checked the sick women again, pulled on his winter clothes, and went outside. He gulped the air, so fresh after the fetid sick rooms. His head cleared, and he snow skied through the frigid morning toward Polebridge, exerting himself with desperate speed, taking sobbing breaths that made it hard to hear the whispery patting of a light snow.

He arrived at Hogan's store to find a pale Nan Hogan dressed, but recovering from a light case of influenza herself. She conversed with the doctor from Columbia Falls.

Bird hurtled from the back of the store to throw his arms around his grandpa.

"Rose?" Jim asked, panting from pushing himself beyond his limits.

"We're all fine, Grandpa Jim. She's just taking a nap. I got those girls here just fine. Is everybody better?"

"I had not one doubt." Unsteady again, Jim felt on the brink of weeping. Glancing at the doctor, he said, "But I see help has come to Polebridge."

Jim approached Doctor McBride, a beefy man known to be an avid hunter. Beartracks Benton had guided him on occasion, always with success. Nan introduced Jim to the Doctor.

"Everybody is so sick," Jim said. "Nora, Dawn, and Celia. I don't know what more to do for them."

"Celia Van Eick? I delivered her baby. Don't tell me that young woman has been under your care. How bad is she?"

If Jim had been more alert, he might have bristled at the doctor's overriding concern for Celia over Nora and Dawn, but he only answered that he thought she might be approaching death. When the doctor asked what he'd been doing, Jim described the willow bark tea, the feverfew, broth, sponge baths, and trying to keep the bed linen clean. The physician nodded. "You're doing well."

"Please, will you come?" Jim's voice cracked. "Hoping to find help, I had to leave them alone. It's my wife Nora whose condition concerns me most."

Dr. McBride gave a weary sigh, but signaled acquiescence when he buttoned his coat to prepare for the ride to Evening Star. "You're the Chinese I've heard of? Living with the Irish woman? The early homesteader?"

"Yes, Irish. My wife. She—you will come?" Jim broke off and faced the doctor, leveling his gaze as he had always done in the face of prejudice.

Nan rested a hand on Jim's arm. "Jim, I'm on the mend and we're managing well with the children. Let me keep them," Her expression and the touch on his arm showed Jim more friendship than he'd ever seen there. Had her prejudice turned to tolerance after all these years?

Relief washed through him, as though sunshine had reached a man frozen in mountain water. He could have put his arms around Nan, but he hesitated, still not certain how she, or her husband, might react to an embrace from a Chinese man, even one with a right to claim friendship.

"It's a great deal to ask when you're still weak, but I can care for the others more easily— be good, Bird."

The doctor interrupted. "There was a young man, wasn't there, serving in the Army?" He turned to the door.

Jim followed as he answered. "Yes, Michael. In France with Big Pete Dumont and Beartracks Benton. Well, Beartracks is in Canada. They should be home soon."

"The pandemic is everywhere. In France. Spain. All over America. No one on earth is safe."

"I did hear something of this," Jim said, new fear striking him for his friends. "But I preferred to believe that with the Armistice the boys would be safe at last."

~ ~ ~

Jim stashed his skis in the back of the doctor's horse-drawn sleigh, then climbed into the passenger seat. As they skimmed over the snow, the physician looked at the river and skeletal aspen, cottonwood, and larch layering on the ridge of the far bank. "It's great country," he muttered. "For nature, for hunting, for finding peace. Your Irish woman owns a piece of paradise."

Once in the cabin, the doctor listened to the sick women's chests and examined them. Afterwards he looked over Jim's notes. "A fine record. Meticulous. Detailed. It tells me a great deal.

"Watch for the skin, the lips, and the nail beds turning light blue. If they do, your patient will be slipping away. I'm a blunt man. I must add that if I hear a bubbling in the patient's chest, it's next to hopeless. They taught us in medical school to listen for a sound like bacon in a skillet. The saying is cruel, but apt. 'If they fry, they die.' "

"A heartless rhyme," Jim agreed. "But you didn't hear it? The frying?"

"No. The one to watch is Nora. She's not a young woman. If she starts to cough harder, there's trouble. I have something to give you. It's a new drug called aspirin, very effective for lowering fevers. Medicine is making amazing progress in our young century."

When he left, the physician extended a hand to Jim as he would to any man he respected. Jim watched him climb back into his sleigh and drive off into late afternoon shadows. Alone, Jim turned back to his patients. He remembered to eat something himself.

He found that he'd passed through a wall of fatigue and could keep bathing, feeding, washing, giving aspirin and tea to the women. He could also tend enough to the stock to keep all the living creatures in his care breathing.

~ ~ ~

On the eighth morning, when he entered Nora's room, the green eyes that assessed him from the paper-white face registered recognition. "You look done in," she said in a hoarse whisper. "Sleep all right?"

"Not badly," Jim said, lifting his wife's hand, kissing it, and laughing in relief. "Just not at all to speak of. Everyone but the children and I came down with the flu."

"Where are Bird and Rose? Bonnie?"

Jim told Nora about Nan and the doctor before he left her sipping tea and went to nurse the younger women. Nora slept peacefully, her bedding soon soaked from sweat. Later when he stroked her face, she felt blessedly cool.

Jim went to the barn and sat at the milking stool. Leaning against the cow's warm side, he allowed himself a few tears of gratitude as he milked the placid beast.

He couldn't rest, and so he started a venison stew and bread. Setting the dough to rise, he sank to his chair by the stove. Then he felt Nora's familiar hand slip through his hair. Drawn, hollow-cheeked, and lank-haired, she faced him, moving her hand to rest on his shoulder. He stood and they embraced.

"You must go back to bed, he whispered. "You must not get pneumonia. The doctor warned me of that."

They went to check on Dawn. Her fever had broken, and she recognized them both. On edge and missing Rose and Bird, she admitted, after a weak argument, that she couldn't care for her children for some days yet.

And there remained Celia.

Celia began to cough harder that night. Jim wrapped her in heavy blankets, fed her aspirin and hot willow bark tea. He rubbed her chest and applied a hot mustard plaster. He pleaded with the young mother to think of her infant daughter, not to leave Bonnie alone.

The physician returned next day, pleased with Nora and Dawn's progress, but worried about Celia. He read Jim's notes with concentration and left more aspirin. "This is an important young woman," he announced in mysterious tones. "We can't lose her."

By evening both Dawn and Nora could sit up and walk short distances. They insisted that Jim go to bed, but first all three went to check on Celia. The girl's fever had broken. She would live.

"Now," Nora ordered, leading Jim out of Dawn and Celia's room, "you sleep."

The cabin looked as though a grizzly had invaded it, but they had some water, some wood. Stew simmered. Jim nodded and walked to their bedroom, crawled into bed, still in the malodorous clothes he'd worn when the influenza struck. In the next three days, drugged by fatigue, he woke briefly to swig water, stumble through snow to the outhouse, return and fall back into a sleep as bottomless and dreamless as death.

Chapter Sixteen

One sunlit morning in late March, 1919, Jim returned from taking hay to Evening Star's bull and nine Jersey cows. They were fenced in a meadow a half mile up the creek. The cows weren't calving yet, but a few looked as though it wouldn't be long.

He dismounted from the skittish buckskin mare he'd bought from a war widow desperate to sell and move back east. Nora emerged from the cabin to join him. Dabbing her eyes with a kerchief, she squeezed his hand. "Michael and Pete are home."

A large, white-haired figure caught Jim's attention. Big Pete Dumont filled their doorway, but coughed then wheezed and leaned against the doorframe. Jim strode toward him.

"Don't worry, China Jim. It ain't the flu. Mustard gas instead," Pete assured him as he brushed aside Jim's proffered hand, enveloping him in a bear hug instead. "A German knocked my gas mask off when we were rolling around on the ground like we were doing the deed. Gas rolled in thick. Burned like hell. Nearly killed me. But I kept my word. I brought Michael back to you. Straightened out. We're both of us a lot older and a little wiser."

"You straightened him out?" Jim grinned.

"Not me by my lonesome, China Jim. The war gave me a hand. Michael got wounded, but he's all right. A priest at the field hospital helped him see how he needed to forgive his mama."

"Any word of Beartracks ?"

Pete turned somber and looked away. "Old Beartracks was an ace sniper, but the Germans had a few of their own. Jeezely ironic." He looked into Jim's eyes again with tears in his own. "Our old friend took a bullet to his forehead. He'd become a legend, though. We learned about his untimely perishing from a Canadian troop newspaper that passed from hand to hand even to us American doughboys."

"Beartracks seemed invincible," Jim muttered sinking to a chair on the porch.

Nora had taken Jim's mare to the barn before trudging back. She wiped away renewed tears with her shawl. "Woeful waste," she said. "I can't get my arms around it. Our dear old friend. The first one to befriend us when we arrived so ignorant of wilderness ways." She sniffled. "I'm not sure we'd have made it without him. Beartracks placed Dawn into our safekeeping. To think he lost his life in this terrible war. He should have been like Ireland and stayed out of it."

"How we will miss him," Jim said, standing to put an arm around her. "Is Michael here now?"

"He's with Dawn and the children," Nora said. "Oh, he's changed for certain. He's not the hotheaded boy who took himself and Dawn away to the East Side. He's quiet." She looked up at Jim, both relief and sorrow in her expression. "He's forgiven me it seems, but he grieves for Beartracks and suffers from the war."

"There's something else." Pete pushed his hat back. "Beartracks wrote a will before he left. He told me he filed it at the courthouse in Kalispell. He left his Apgar inholding to Nora. 'Would have left it to both of you if not for the laws. He knows Dawn and Michael will have it in time, and then their children."

Jim and Nora gripped each other's hands. Fresh tears fell.

"Let's go in and find the others. I haven't greeted Michael," Jim said.

The three joined Michael, a glowing Dawn, adoring Rose, and entranced Bird. Dawn showed signs of having wept at the news of Beartracks, but her joy at being with her husband again was a thing incandescent, outshining sorrow.

~ ~ ~

Jim and Nora offered to take the children into their room that night so the reunited young couple could have privacy. Soon their grandchildren breathed in sleep; Bird's cot three feet from his grandparents' bed, Rose's even closer. Nora and Jim lay down next to them and all grew quiet.

Michael and Dawn began making quiet, urgent love. After a time, they slowed into gentle rediscovery. They touched in wonder and compassion. Their bodies had been through so much since they parted: war wounds for one and the gauntness left by influenza for the other. Yet Michael still seemed to find Dawn beautiful. His scars and the faint lines around her eyes only made fresh paths on maps known by heart.

Afterwards they whispered together. Dawn told all the news of Polebridge that hadn't been shared at supper, and they discussed Rose and Bird.

Michael refused to recount his battle experiences. "I mean to forget them." He turned haunted eyes away from hers, which remained full of anxious questions.

~ ~ ~

Hours later Michael's dreams plunged into a wartime nightmare. He crouched in a fetid trench with dead men, rats swarming over their bodies. Climbing out of the foul-smelling trench in a panic, he stepped into thick soupy fog. Shells exploded around him. He tripped on a corpse, but instead of hitting the ground, his body torpedoed through space. His arms flailed. He woke with a jerk, terrified, drenched in sweat, just before he'd have shattered on rock-strewn earth. Every night for months it had been the same thing.

He gazed at Dawn's night-shadowed face and touched her dark hair. It seemed miraculous that he could. Then he slipped from the covers, pulled on his clothes, and tiptoed out. He didn't see Dawn's eyes open or hear her breath catch at his leaving their bed.

~ ~ ~

Nora sat in her blue wrapper, in a circle of light from the kerosene lantern on the table. A low fire glowed from the wood stove. Michael smelled coffee.

She gave him a rueful smile. "I can't sleep for sorrowing over Beartracks, and at the same time feeling joy that you and Pete are with us. You're a hero and so is Pete. He and Jim are out in the barn catching up on the war's end."

After giving his hands time to stop shaking from the nightmare, Michael poured himself black coffee. He settled across from her. "Jim's the best man any of us can ever know. He's the real hero. He pulled all of you through the flu. *Saved* you."

Nora stood and refilled her cup from the heavy pot, not remarking on its handle still being wet from her son's sweaty grip. "Family is everything. The ranch—the land—once it was only for Jim and me, but now it's for all of us and those to come after. It means our life, this land. You know I came into the world not so long after the hunger in Ireland. The way I heard it, landlords forced barefoot tenants like skeletons wrapped in scabby skin right out of their little cabins. With neither food nor shelter they died barefoot with grass-stained mouths from grazing in the ditches like beasts." She shuddered. "Buried in mass graves, too many of them. It's land and family. The land is for the family and the family for the land. That's how to survive."

Michael leaned toward her. "The saddest sights I saw were French refugees. They walked the roads dirty, hungry, their feet bleeding through their shoes if they wore any. They looked like their souls had been emptied out of their still-living bodies. I'll do whatever it takes to keep us safe at Evening Star with this roof over our heads. Our own roof. And food on our own table."

"I know you will, Michael. Jim and I will do the job right along with you as we're able. I'm so thankful you've come home to us."

Michael shifted and swirled the dregs in his mug. "Well, you can see I'm finally ready to leave off hard feelings. I know you kept the story about the man who tried to kill Jim from me because you thought it for the best. I think I would have shot him to save Jim Li no matter if I'd known he was my father."

Nora refilled his cup, sat down again, and sighed. "It was a terrible thing, and I should have told you long before. I'll always be sorry. But as you say, it's in the past. You and Dawn and your children are home. It's grand to be together again."

They lifted their coffee cups in a silent gesture and drank, set them down, and reached across the table to clasp each other's hands, holding on as though sealing a vow.

~ ~ ~

Big Pete Dumont and Jim Li talked all that night in the barn where Pete had spread his bedroll. When false dawn hovered, they walked outside. Pete gestured toward the Canadian Rockies and his beloved Belly River Country. "I might go on up there and never leave it, China Jim. I believe I'll see out my days alone in that peaceful place." They walked to the cabin. After breakfast Pete clasped Jim's hand, then left, his tracks pointed north.

Still half-asleep, Bird stumbled out to his Grandpa and the two watched Pete leave under leaden first light.

"He's going so soon?" Bird asked.

"Yes, he intends to stay away a long time." Jim pulled Bird against him for a moment and murmured as if speaking to himself. "Evening Star exists because Big Pete Dumont and Beartracks Benton helped us in those first years. I wonder if they ever guessed how often I feared I'd made a mistake bringing your grandmother to this wilderness of the North Fork of the Flathead River. I didn't know the stubborn will to survive it would take to stay. Those two knew and saved us, so generous with their knowledge."

~ ~ ~

The family reestablished the routines of a peacetime working ranch. Michael took up handling the horses, cattle, and with Jim, setting the winter trap lines for martin and fisher.

The last heavy snow fell in late March. By April winter warmed into spring melt, and Jim repaired fences, or cleaned stables. He also fished and hunted, accompanied by an adoring Bird and sometimes Rose. Nora and Dawn planned their expanding garden. They hoped to raise more of everything including rhubarb to have for food and some rhubarb wine. They churned butter, dressed furs, gathered eggs, baked, and sewed. Rose helped them, but spent as much time as she could with Jim or Michael in outdoor work.

Bird pestered his grandfather for more stories of life in China. "Tell me about the ghosts, Grandpa, the ones in the mountains who scare travelers."

"You've heard so much about those ghosts. You know the stories as well as I do. Instead, let me show you how to do a Chinese way of writing. All children in my country are taught this at an early age. You are late to start, but we can catch you up. It's calligraphy, the picture writing you sometimes ask to see in my old books."

Just as Jim had taught Dawn her basic reading, writing, math, and history, he sat Bird down at the kitchen table, then disappeared into the bedroom and emerged with a few objects in a silk bundle.

"I have not used these for such a long time," Jim said, sitting beside Bird. He remained silent for a moment, eyes far away. "They bring back memories of my home and our lessons there. I was as eager then to learn about America as you are to learn of China."

Bird grabbed the chance to learn more about his grandfather's mysterious past. "Why were you? Why did you come here?"

Jim smiled. "I knew that my father was in this country. I had never met him."

Bird gaped. "You never met your own father? Why not?"

"He came from America to be a missionary in China. He went back to work here before my birth. He left China without knowing my mother was to have me."

"I don't know anybody in China or Ireland, but I want to because those places are where you and Grandma came from. China. It sounds like a magic place." Bird grinned at his grandfather and began chanting, "Dragons and spirits and devils and writing in pictures. Princesses and emperors and warriors…"

"I can show you the picture writing. It will be even harder, though, than your carving. It requires much practice. As children, we spent long, long hours trying to succeed at it. My cousins sometimes cried in frustration, but I, only a poor nephew in that fine house, wanted to do everything better than they could, so I worked and concentrated. I can teach the four treasures and the strokes, but I warn you, you might want to quit. You are an American boy."

"Yeah, but with a Chinese grandpa, don't forget." Bird grinned, eyeing the objects as Jim unwrapped his bundle.

Inside rested ink sticks and an ink stone, a small, shallow basin in its surface, along with sheaves of paper and a brush. "I brought these from another life." Jim's voice broke a little. "I kept them, perhaps to show to you, my grandson. This is how we mix the special ink. You can work with me. Make your wrist and fingers strong and flexible when it is time to hold the brush."

Jim went to the kindling box, pulled out an old newspaper, and spread it on the table. He set the ink stone on it, poured a little water into the stone and began to grind the ink stick into the stone's depression using smooth clockwise motions.

Bird grinned, his eyes bright. "Grandpa, you're making ink!"

"Now you do what I did for two minutes."

Bird began to work, his face puckered from the effort of keeping the stick upright.

Michael entered just as they began and leaned against the door, watching. "Bird has Red Meadow School soon, and his chores. Even if we let him have the old mare, it will take time just to ride there and back. He doesn't have hours to spend making Chinese ink when we can buy ink at the Mercantile. He needs to learn about ranching to survive around here."

Jim smiled and shook his head. "So American. When Nora and I came here, the wilderness only allowed us to labor to survive. We had to create our own food, clothing, and shelter. But now our children and their children can spare a little time for the better life we wanted for each of you. This special ink will allow Bird to write calligraphy, picture writing in smooth, perfect strokes. It will teach him patience and self-discipline, integrity about his endeavors. In China, writing is an art. Dawn says Bird has shown talent for art."

Bird lost his smile when his father shrugged and said, "Bird did some good enough whittling. The deaf Blackfeet carver in East Glacier gave him lessons for free, but—"

"But what?" Dawn stood in the doorway, arms crossed, staring at the three in the kitchen. "Bird has real talent, Michael. People can make their living painting, carving, or even writing. After all, don't you remember Heinrich? I know you weren't happy that he came here, but he's written Mama and Papa Jim to say he sold some of his paintings again now that the war is over. He'll make good money because people love beauty."

Dawn set her jaw and the others stared at her. Michael appeared dumbfounded. She swallowed and spoke again, still defiant. "If our son has talent, we should encourage that. My Blackfeet family value art. People don't survive just by making money, do they? There's more to life, like Papa Jim just said."

Bird, Jim, and Michael continued to stare at Dawn, who so seldom contradicted Michael or anyone else. After a silence Michael shrugged, apparently choosing to ignore Dawn's mention of the German artist. "Just so Bird takes care of what needs doing around here. Evening Star comes first. It always will. He can whittle and doodle as long as he keeps up with his chores and learning."

"I will, Pop. I promise." Bird looked into his father's eyes, and then returned to grinding the ink stick.

Michael went outside again. Dawn sat at the table. "Show me what you've learned, son," she said.

Bird worked at the grinding in two-minute intervals for an hour, amazed at the rich black of the Chinese ink, and at how soon his wrist and fingers ached from grinding. His grandfather assured him that in time his wrists and fingers would be strong, perhaps stronger than those of any of the local boys they knew. He'd be able to pitch a ball the best, too, because of his strength. They'd look up to him.

~ ~ ~

On Christmas Eve, the community gathered at Hogan's Mercantile to dance, feast on elk and venison steaks, biscuits, and canned corn. There were apple, serviceberry, and the favored huckleberry pies and cobblers, too. Neighbors played cards, and when tired of sitting, went moonlit cross country skiing or took sleigh rides. A forgotten zest for carefree fun seized the North Fork.

Still the living remembered those faces of young and old who'd passed during the influenza outbreak or the war. Those who'd known Beartracks Benton and Big Pete Dumont commented with regret on the mountain men's absence. Those who returned from France, including taciturn Michael, looked wary.

"Pete and Beartracks left us with no farewells," Nan complained. "When they went, they took away more than a little of our old North Fork's romantic history."

Nora agreed. "They took away something we don't have a proper name for, didn't they? We just knew it when those two walked among us. Like giants they were. Jim comes near to them, but his daily presence as such a family man at Evening Star dulls the glamour a bit now, doesn't it?"

"They had more freedom, that's a fact," Nan said. "But they were rascals, too. Your Chinese Jim is one we can count on. I should have recognized it years ago."

Pete had indeed disappeared into the Belly River country he loved. Although they didn't know it yet, Nora and Jim would never see him again. After making that last visit to leave word they'd lost Beartracks and to say his farewells, Big Pete Dumont walked into Canada for good. All that he left was his legend.

On a spring day years later, his body would be found in a remote trap line cabin. Their old friend had likely sustained some illness or injury and died from it or from malnutrition when he couldn't hunt food. Nora would always wonder whether the war caused Pete to withdraw so far from human society. If so, she hoped the wilderness had been a comfort to him as it had been for her years before when she'd been through a sort of war of her own.

~ ~ ~

Hogan's Mercantile also saw the Li and Larkin families and their North Fork neighbors celebrate New Year's Eve as the old decade gave way to 1920. At midnight, some celebrants had the notion to set off dynamite in the meadow in front of the store. As chunks of ice, dirt, and rocks erupted in the resulting explosions, Nora turned to see Michael, white-faced, hunched, and trembling. Fred Hogan saw him, too, then scrambled into his wagon bed and stood bellowing, his breath shooting out in white puffs at the guffawing homesteaders. "Stop all that damned crazy noise. Now!"

The admonished revelers fell silent. Bird turned to Nora. "Why did he tell them to stop, Grandma?"

"Look at your father. He can't abide loud noise since France. It's too much like sounds of battle. He's got what's called shell shock. All these people know what that means. It means your father went through too much. See how they feel properly ashamed for their thoughtlessness."

Bird frowned. "He won't do what Ted Norman…"

His grandmother pulled him to her. "No. Never worry about a thing like that. Ted Norman was so terribly alone. Your father has us around him. People understand better, too, after so many have come back with bad nerves. Most of the time, they understand. He's had enough of the party, though. We'll all go home to Evening Star. Evening Star means peace to him and to us."

She squeezed his shoulders and gave him a gentle push back from her. "Your parents are gathering Rose and looking for you. Your grandpa and I are ready, as well. We have work to do tomorrow at Evening Star. A new year doesn't change that."

"Always ranch work," Bird muttered. "It's almost always the same thing." He saw his grandmother's eyebrows rise, but his complaint hung unrebuked in the night chill.

~ ~ ~

Even after spring snowmelt Michael still jerked awake drenched and disoriented from recurring nightmares of crouching in the same trench with silent dead men and foraging rats. Every time he'd race up the same ladder and out of the trench only to step into fog. He always plummeted, shells whistling, shrieking, and exploding around him. He tumbled and hurtled and jerked awake a moment before boulder-strewn ground sped up to strike him.

Sleep meant merciless terror.

After each waking, he turned to look at Dawn but didn't disturb her, not realizing he'd already cried out as he slept. He stroked her hair, and then reached for his clothes. He checked on their daughter sleeping spread-eagled in her cot, her rosebud mouth slightly open. Next, he stopped by Bird dreaming on his bed. Reassured, Michael threw on his clothes and tiptoed from the room.

Outside, he'd saddle his appaloosa stallion and ride it deep into old growth forest. Wary night creatures scurried away or peered, their eyes aglow with calculating hunger as the grim man and his spirited mount passed by.

Chapter Seventeen

Bird, Rose, and Dawn enjoyed a late spring morning walk to Polebridge, admiring the bright Glacier lilies with petals turned back as though in an imaginary breeze. White trillium glowed against the fresh green foliage. They entered the comparatively dark interior of the Mercantile, planning to pick up the mail and purchase flour, yeast, and other sundries.

Nan greeted them from the post office window with the satisfaction of a gossip with fresh news to share. "That Celia and her little one and the snooty old couple have gone, practically overnight. Locked and shuttered their place and that's that."

"I'll miss Celia. I wish we'd had a chance to say goodbye, at least. I wonder how she and Bonnie are faring so far away back east," Dawn said as she picked a container of Bon Ami off the shelf for spring cleaning. "I remember the great cities were exciting, but they frightened me, too. I can't imagine living in one."

"I can!" Bird piped up from where he was gazing at a collection of knives in the glassed counter, from small pen knives to adults' tools for skinning bears. "There's always something new going on there."

"Here, too!" Rose replied.

Nan shrugged. "Well, in the end the rumors were probably right. I doubt there was ever a husband. Your Jim saved the life of a society girl from back east who'd gotten herself in trouble and came west to hide her disgrace from her friends."

"Mama and Papa Jim won't talk about Celia much," Dawn said. "They say her life's her own."

Nan narrowed her eyes at the possible reprimand, but held out an embossed envelope. "Well, to change the subject, here's a letter for Jim. It's from Doctor McBride. I hope he's not sending you a bill."

"A bill?" Bird piped up, staring at the envelope. "He wouldn't send Grandpa a bill, would he? Grandpa took care of Celia besides Grandma and Mama. That would mean you could send us one since you took care of me and Rose when everybody got sick." Bird gave the woman who formed part of his circle of beloved adults a mischievous grin. She caught and hugged him to her generous bosom as he squirmed and snickered. Then she scooped Rose up for a big hug.

~ ~ ~

Nora slid bread into the oven and Jim brought in extra logs for the stove just as Dawn and Bird arrived back from Polebridge. Dawn thumped her sack of purchases on the table, then pulled the letter from her pocket and held it out to Jim.

"It's from Doctor McBride!" Bird danced in impatience for his grandparents to open the envelope and read its contents. Rose joined in, hopping around the kitchen.

Jim and Nora exchanged apprehensive looks before he took it, as if afraid to think why the Doctor would write to them. The two sat side by side at the oilcloth-covered table, staring at the letter as if a snake had slithered into the cabin. In contrast, the comforting, normal scent of baking dough spread through the golden light of late afternoon slanting in from the window. "It could be a bill," Nora said.

"Read it to all of us, Grandpa," Bird said. "Mama and I can't wait to find out what the Doc wrote."

Jim slid his carved letter opener under the envelope's crease, pulled the cream-colored paper out, and smoothed it. He read in tones of increasing amazement.

Dear Mr. Li,

I hope this finds you and your wife well. I write to let you know that Celia Van Eick is at home again with her father, U.S. Senator Hammond Dale of New York. Both Celia and Bonnie are well and thriving at home.

I took the liberty of writing to Senator Dale regarding your estimable care of Celia and your wife and daughter when all three fell ill at Evening Star. I told him quite truthfully that without your care and detailed notes on the patients, their temperatures, coughs, even bodily functions, I would have been much more challenged in my visits to assess and prescribe for their recoveries. Stretched thin as I was, as attending physician I depended on you and you saved all three women. Your care for each proved exemplary and equal, one to the other. Celia has said you encouraged her not to give in to her illness. She heard through the haze of fever your pleas that she live for her child.

The Senator has taken an interest in rewarding you by means of his considerable political influence. He has long had the ear of our President Wilson. Senator Dale successfully requested an Executive Order which bestows United States citizenship on you. No history or documentation was required. The Order only lists your history as a productive member of your community and your extraordinary service in saving American lives during the recent pandemic.

I expect you will want to meet with me soon. I have the documentation to prove all that I've written you is true. Your naturalization papers rest in my safe.

Sincerely,

Andrew McBride, M.D.

The awed family erupted in cheers of "yeehaw!" and "Yay!" as Jim lay the letter on the table and smoothed it like the precious gift it was. He caught Nora's hands in his. Even Michael, who'd come in while they were reading, grinned and thumped Jim on the back.

For once, Jim looked thunderstruck. "Good will, compassion, joy, detachment," he murmured. "I once thought they were their own rewards. Look what has happened to us."

"You deserve this, Jim. You did save all three of us." Nora rubbed happy tears away with a handy dish towel. "You did the impossible. You've become a United States citizen. I never thought such a thing could happen to a man born in China, even one as fine as yourself."

"Yaaaay, for Grandpa!" Rose cheered.

"Beartracks must have told someone about me," Jim mused, looking out the window.

"No. He never would. I'm sure Nan had it figured out long ago," Nora said. "She must have told the good doctor."

Jim read the letter to himself. "I wish Beartracks could have known of this, of what he started when he smuggled me into the country. I am an American." Jim's face crumpled and he, too, shed joyful tears.

"Read it to us again, Grandpa Jim," Bird urged.

Jim did, and when he stopped, he turned to Nora. "A United States citizen. I thought it enough to be here, but now I have no fear of discovery and deportation. Such a fear has haunted me like ghosts emerging out of a disastrous future." Jim rose and walked to the window.

The others sat silenced by his words, but Nora went to him, resting a hand on his arm. "I didn't realize," she said. "You seldom spoke of your fears. I thought us safe enough from government men here in the wilderness."

"Perhaps we were, but we aren't in the wilderness any longer. It's still wild, but never again as isolated as it was. The bridge and the road from Columbia Falls on our side of the River have changed all that."

Grandma Nora rested her head on Jim's shoulder. "No matter now. We're both United States citizens, and we have our piece of the best part of America. We're as good as any of those here or who'll come in time to be our neighbors."

Jim turned to the others. "I'm free from those worries that followed me like hungry wolves. I am here to stay."

"You made it so. No one could ever do more, my treasure, my American husband," Nora said.

~ ~ ~

After returning from the Polebridge Mercantile one day a few weeks later, Michael announced that three neighboring households had relinquished their homesteads, giving up their independent, hardscrabble lives on the North Fork. "Park rangers have doubled crack-downs on poachers across the river," he added. "They can't earn money selling hides from there now."

Jim shook his head. "Most of our longtime neighbors have hunted and trapped on both sides of the North Fork for years. We used to do it, too. Old timers don't like being told they can't legally hunt or even trap for meat and fur across the North Fork. They know so many deer, grizzlies, and wolves roam there for the taking."

Dawn joined in. "Government men have become much more aggressive about catching moonshiners, too. They can't sell from their stills now."

Michael smiled. "The Hogans were complaining today how they can't keep sugar in stock. Just about all the homesteaders except us purchase hundred-pound sacks of sugar at the Merc to mix with the grains and ferment the stuff in their root cellars."

Nora frowned. "That outlaw practice works to supplement their meager incomes. I know about such things all too well. But I'll never agree to this family having any truck with making the poteen that killed Paddy Flanagan."

The others fell silent, respecting Nora's insistence on this point. They knew the story of her father being struck and killed by a thief wanting what was left of Paddy's pay while he staggered home drunk on a dark street, oblivious to danger. The image of the act came to symbolize both human frailty and evil to the family.

Over dinner of fried chicken, fresh biscuits, and beans, Michael brought up the failed homesteaders again. "Their bad luck means more available land, you know," he said, returning to the forced sales by creditors as well as the simple property abandonment going on in the homesteads around the ranch. "Our family is growing. If we want to stay and have our children stay, too, Bird and Rose will need room to ranch, run cattle, and raise their families."

Nora looked up from spreading her biscuit with butter she'd churned herself. She eyed Michael with interest. "That's true, but do you think we can afford to stretch ourselves so thin as that?"

He gave a little shrug of impatience, put down his fork, and gave her a steady look. "It's as cheap as it's ever going to be."

"It would mean more taxes," Papa Jim said. His tone registered misgivings.

"But if I hire out and Dawn works summers as a cook for Hill or the Park, we can buy more land and manage to pay it off along with tax costs," Michael answered.

"Land," Nora murmured. She touched Jim's arm. "Remember Jim, we wanted it so badly we left everything we knew to come here. Michael has that same desire in his blood, not to be denied. Seeing all those poor wretches on the roads of Europe only deepened it."

Dawn stood and started lifting plates as she protested, "Michael, the children and I need you here. I don't want you or me working away from Evening Star. We'd have to leave our children. I don't want us to live separate again. We've had enough of that in our lives. I thought when the war ended—"

"More land will keep us together except for when we work to have a stake for it," Michael argued. "This is America. We're supposed to prosper, every generation better off than the last. I want to leave something for our children the way Mama and Jim will for us. Life is too short to wait for good things to happen in their own sweet time. I learned that in France. Better than I ever wanted to."

He leaned back and looked around the table. "I saw exhausted, dirty, hungry refugees who didn't have anything because they didn't own enough to begin with. If we're going to get ahead, we don't have time to wait. Nothing is certain. Not even tomorrow. Especially not tomorrow. Tomorrow never came for Beartracks, did it? Not for all those others either."

In the end Michael cajoled a still reluctant Dawn into the purchase of one-hundred-and-sixty acres bordering Evening Star Ranch. During the next months Michael only grew more single-minded. With fierce determination he added stock, hunted, harvested timber, and plowed so Dawn could make a garden full of spreading rhubarb, raspberries climbing up poles, carrots and potatoes swelling in the acquired land. Dawn worked as hard as he did, satisfied because he'd agreed to stay on the North Fork, at least for the time being.

~ ~ ~

Nora and Jim settled into the life they'd wanted with their children and grandchildren. Nora felt more at peace than she'd ever been. Jim made her a beaver coat as beautiful as any worn by tourists who traveled to the Park.

They bought an old Ford truck so untrustworthy the family sometimes had to drive it uphill in reverse to keep it from stalling. Still, Nora felt that at last they had achieved security. They had two home places and the skills to survive and prosper. The younger members of the family flourished. She who'd known so much poverty and prejudice rode in the old truck swathed in flawless fur, her chin high, her glance proud.

~ ~ ~

In early summer of 1921, after picking up some parts for the truck in Belton, Michael and Dawn decided to spend a night at Beartracks's old Apgar cabin. They picked up a copy of the *Daily Inter Lake*. Sitting on a log on the beach, they listened to lapping waves, a sound that always seemed to end in a questioning little high note. They read that Glacier Park Superintendent Logan had obtained an appropriation from congress to construct a macadamized road from Belton to Apgar. And serious work could finally start on a route around Lake McDonald.

Michael folded the paper. "I'll sign on next year to work on road crews."

Dawn repeated her earlier objection. "I thought it was settled that you'd stay at Evening Star. The children and I need you at home."

He argued that taxes and the need to make more improvements on the new land made it necessary. In the end she accepted his going.

~ ~ ~

Dawn, Bird, Rose, and Michael moved into the home Jim had helped Michael build. It sat just fifty feet from the property line dividing the two ranches. Jim and Nora's cabin sat the same distance from the line going the other way.

More log house than cabin, the younger family's home stood two stories high with a gable roof. Next to Celia's, theirs was the most handsome structure on the North Fork. But sometimes Dawn missed the warmth and intimacy of the Blackfeet lodges she'd visited so often. She'd never felt lonely when she visited Sweet Grass's family or other friends in their homes.

She wrote often to Molly, who sent short letters back. The Caldwells were well, but both Lucy and White Bull had gone to the Sand Hills from which none returned. Dawn had been among the last young people to learn from those beloved elders. She began to write down what they'd taught her, including the Blackfeet language.

She thought both Sweet Grass and Beartracks Benton would have liked that. She wrote for them as well as for her strong, dark-eyed, proud children, and those like them.

~ ~ ~

Within months, three-and-a-half miles of road existed around Lake McDonald. On Nora and Jim's frequent stays at the Apgar cabin, Jim complained about so much change. Lewis's steamboat, carrying passengers from the foot of Lake McDonald to his hotel at its head became a memory belonging to nostalgic old timers. Jim said the road ran like a surgical scar through the trees above the lake. But early automobile drivers loved it, and soon more motorists enjoyed it with them.

Autos traveled from Belton to Lewis's Hotel in numbers that left both Jim and Nora wondering how to feel about these changes. After all, such matters had been determined by unknown businessmen and bureaucrats. Rumors trickled to them about a Transmountain Highway to run from east to west over the Continental Divide in the Park. Neither of them believed it could be done. Nor would they have believed how it would, in the end, affect their family's lives.

Nora sympathized with Jim's complaints about the increased noise of human voices, automobiles, and general activity around Apgar. Visitors approached her on the beach to ask for directions or what she knew of the history of the place. Sometimes she wanted to curse the road that interfered with the old life that had brought only forest creatures and sounds.

But she happily used the checks Michael handed her for depositing ahead on paying off his and Dawn's ranch. When Michael and Dawn's land was theirs free and clear, he'd feel pride in his accomplishment. Nora hoped her son would lose the guarded, hard-eyed look he'd turned on the world since France.

~ ~ ~

The Kalispell Daily Inter Lake soon carried news that affirmed the National Park Service planned to build a road through Glacier National Park over a pass above Trapper Creek at the Continental Divide.

Jim and Michael shook their heads. Workers would have to excavate thousands of tons of the Rocky Mountains which had been formed over millennia. The road would be a sort of ledge along the series of precipitous cliffs known as the Garden Wall. Men laboring by hand or with minimal machinery on limited space would have to accomplish the blasting. Eventually the Transmountain Highway should reach Logan Pass dividing the west side of the park from the east.

The Seattle contractor needed men to whack out tote roads and trails for horses carrying equipment and supplies to blasting sites. Pack strings would bring such essentials to the work camps. Blasters who lived in the camps would be lowered by strands of rope over sheer cliff faces to lay dynamite. Explosions meant the danger of rockslides from above the workers. But one dollar and fifteen cents an hour for such excavation labor pulled Michael to sign on as if he were steel and the money a magnet.

~ ~ ~

Jim and Michael both signed on.

Dawn approached Papa Jim in the barn one afternoon as he shoveled out stalls. "Why have you decided to go, Papa?" she asked. "It's bad enough that Michael won't stay with us."

He set down his shovel and straightened his back before he answered. "I want to stay near Michael to keep him safe. I know well how to handle both horses and dynamite. I've proved my ability on the ranch, blasting tree stumps and creating our root cellar in rocky ground. Working on the road won't be so different. And now I'm a U.S. citizen, I fit with the hiring policies. First, of course, they're hiring war veterans. But then they want men familiar with road building, and next men with families. Fred Hogan wrote me a good reference telling of my work on the Polebridge structures and roads."

Dawn nodded. "I understand. I'm so glad you'll be there to watch over Michael." She gave Papa Jim a quick hug. "Promise me you'll be careful."

~ ~ ~

Michael, a married veteran and rancher, fit into each favored category and was hired on as a "powder monkey," to do the blasting job he wanted. Jim hired on to control a pack string of thirty mules and horses from Evening Star. He would handle transport of blasting powder and other supplies to the crews and camps. He received $5.00 a day plus a dollar for each animal used, usually ten at a time.

Although he'd miss Nora and the children, Jim liked the idea of being alone with his horses. It crossed his mind that in a year Bird could join him. They'd continue the lessons in Chinese that Bird had taken to so well.

~ ~ ~

Rose loved nothing more than the peace of life at Evening Star. But fifteen-year-old Bird had yearned to go for the adventure of the building of the road and several times expressed disgust at being left behind.

Grandma Nora approached Bird one day as he sat pouting on the porch. "You're too young. They're only starting boys at sixteen. Besides, we need you here, Bird," she soothed, patting his shoulder. "It's our home that Jim and Michael are working so hard for. Let's show them we appreciate their efforts by taking care to keep it running while they're away. What they're doing is worth our hard work even if some of it isn't so exciting."

Bird gave a glum nod and turned away. His grandmother and his father always brought up the land as though nothing else mattered. He loved both families' halves of Evening Star, but his studies with Grandpa Jim made him crave adventures of the mind as well as the physical exhilarations of hunting, ranching, and mountaineering. He trod the mental waters of a rising sea of curiosity. He hungered to know more of what stretched beyond Montana.

Perhaps more than those putting their muscles into creating the road through Glacier National Park, the boy intuited how it would show people the wonder of the Rockies. Evening Star would always be home, but the world held so many wonders. The Transmountain Highway would be one of them right along with the Great Wall of China, or distant cities like New York, where a fellow could learn—*anything*. Bird wanted knowledge without limits.

So he wallowed in futile longing to be part of the adventure. In one year he'd be old enough to work with his father and grandfather. But he'd need his parents' permission to do it, and his father might continue to insist that Bird stay with the women on the North Fork.

Bird would miss his grandfather and the horses. He hated to admit even to himself that he wouldn't miss his angry father and his demands.

~ ~ ~

Before Michael left he gave his son a curt set of orders and the admonition, "Stop spending so much time with your nose in books. Your job is to work for your family, and that means our ranch."

Bird thought his father flat out wrong to tell him not to read so much. His grandfather read every evening and still did his share of work around the place.

And besides, Bird had a dream he hadn't mentioned to anyone, not even Grandpa Jim. He'd begun to imagine himself enrolled at a college.

~ ~ ~

Jim and Michael worked from a tent camp at Apgar. The North Fork road made travel to Apgar much easier than it had ever been. Nora and Dawn alternated weekends, each joining her husband for two nights before returning to the North Fork.

Nora found Jim gradually more accepting of the changes the road would bring. One evening as they sat on the beach watching points of starlight quiver on Lake McDonald, he said, "This road is a great undertaking. I've not seen anything designed to fit more like nature herself into our mountains than this road. There are engineers, landscape architects, stone masons, many men from Butte brought in for the work. I'm the only Chinese, though."

"It will bring people in more numbers than we're used to since coming here. Have you accepted that?" Nora brushed a finger along his cheekbone.

Jim smiled and captured her hand, rubbing his thumb along hers. "It is such magnificent land. I think I must practice good will and compassion and be pleased that those who live in less stirring places can come to see it."

"Come they will," Nora said. "Come they will."

Chapter Eighteen

By 1923, the road extended over five more miles from the head of Lake McDonald to rippling Avalanche Creek. Its clear mountain water roared down over red and blue-green river rocks from Avalanche Lake, creating a deep, narrow gorge whose waters straightened out to eventually flow into Lake McDonald.

But Jim, Michael, and the others didn't have much time for gazing at the sights during daylight hours. Demanding bosses supervised brutal and dangerous digging, hauling, blasting, and masonry. The men's morale stayed high thanks to their sense that they were part of creating an engineering wonder in those wondrous mountains. But Jim and Michael, so long immersed in the natural world, were loath to see too much change take place.

Among those who shared their hope that nature not be too disturbed stood pudgy little Thomas Vint. One day Michael happened to be taking a break within earshot when Vint, face to face with one of the engineers, stood firm.

"You want too many 360-degree turns on the ascent. Efficient, I suppose, but it will make it look like they've been mining up there. Surely that's not the purpose of a road through the Crown Jewel of the Continent. We're to treat people on vacation to the natural, unspoiled beauty of the

Park." Vint argued for a plan that meant mostly one long graceful ascending sweep of road rather than a number of switchbacks.

The two men walked away, lowering their voices. Michael nodded. Before he started back to work, he looked up at the clean slopes of the mountains, cleft only by avalanche chutes full of tumbled trees. He remembered the generally despoiled earth of copper-rich Butte, Montana. He took in a breath of pleasure, catching only a scent of pine. It differed so from the choking smoke and gritty dirt of the mining city. The profit grubbers who polluted Butte could never despoil this place.

But then, no one in France could have conceived of No Man's Land on their beloved pastoral fields. He turned away from the mountains, resolved anew to keep Evening Star safe from the greed, brutality, and selfishness of humanity.

The hardened laborers, their hands callused and their faces weathered, found building the road tough work even before they reached Logan Creek. But in 1925 they were tested to their limits. The most taxing part of the road's construction ascended in front of them. From relocated Camp 1, they hammered, drilled, and blasted east, eventually to form one necessary switchback loop in the road. It would allow thrilled travelers that long extension of highway to be carved out from the series of towering peaks and cliffs, The Garden Wall.

The road would enable travelers driving east to reach Logan Pass at the Continental Divide. Near the road, bears lived in forested mountainsides that plunged down to McDonald Creek, which curved like a silver snake at ease among green drainages and clearings. The precipitous or soaring views from the highway were destined to tighten the throats of humbled humans.

"You and Dawn have traveled beyond the Garden Wall," Jim remarked to Michael one night as they ate their dinner. "We couldn't just shelter you at Evening Star as we thought, could we?"

Michael only shook his head. He spoke less and less to Jim and never to the other men unless the conversation related to work.

"Heinrich Mann should paint it someday," Jim added as though talking to himself. "He painted the mountains in ways that make you see them with fresh eyes."

Michael stood and muttered, "That Hun had no business staying at Evening Star." He stalked off to return his dirty dishes to the cook's helper and turn in.

Jim only shook his head. "We were privileged to shelter such an artist," he murmured to Michael's retreating back. "You're fortunate he was also a man of honor."

~ ~ ~

Camp 1 housed sixty men in tents. It bustled with the throaty rumble of truck engines, the rattling of horse-drawn wagons, and the shouts of workers loading crates and barrels of supplies and equipment. The daytime din proved constant. Six separate camps finally ranged from Logan Creek up toward Logan Pass, the workers' breathtaking Holy Grail.

Prejudice against Asians stayed strong. Jim remained the only Chinese-born employee. There were plenty of Swedes and Irish though. To Jim and Michael's surprise, immigrant Russian and Italian stonemasons arrived from Seattle. The two North Fork men learned that the newcomers were skilled in building retaining walls and bridges that fit into the natural look so desired by landscape architects like Vint. The Italians mostly endeavored to craft stone guardrails. These artisans placed their material with calculated uneven patterns, as close to nature's appearance as possible.

Despite his expertise with dynamite, Jim's age, along with the fact that he owned and knew how to load and manage up to twenty strong horses, led to his permanent assignment as a packer. He guided his string of animals over narrow trails cut on ledges above the laborers. He brought supplies including dynamite that he lowered to those below. And he told no one how much the elevation and strenuous work wore on him. More than once he struggled for breath, and at other times an aching pain gripped his left arm.

He joined the rest of the road workers headed to their homes every October, glad to rest before spring thaws melted heavy snow and ice from the high country. Then letters from their employers summoning them to start in again arrived.

~ ~ ~

Accidents happened, varied in their seriousness. In midsummer 1925, Jim Li rode a seasoned bay leading a strung-out group of pack animals that included a favorite of Nora's, the big white gelding named Cotton Two. The mild-mannered horse had been named after one of the draft animals that pulled his and Nora's wagon when they made their long-ago journey to settle in the North Fork wilderness

A young man from Coram sat his mount in the center of the string while a jocular boy from Martin City rode in last place. Jim didn't dare pigtail the animals, which would mean one horse being tied to another throughout the line. On this steep, narrow trail heading to Camp 4, if one horse stumbled over the edge it would pull the whole line down to their doom.

Cotton Two carried four 50-pound boxes of dynamite. Jim heard the Coram boy's shout of "Damnation and hell fire!" A horse's scream drowned out the rest. Jim turned to see Nora's favorite slip over the side and roll down and down, disappearing among the trees almost at once.

The boys calmed their mounts, then stopped and took off their hats. They waited for Jim to say something as they gazed woefully toward where Cotton Two must have landed. Jim's one word, "Detachment," seemed to puzzle them. They shrugged, replaced their battered hats, nodded with troubled expressions, and proceeded.

At Camp 4 Jim spoke briefly to Michael and helped unload supplies before he rode back to Camp 1 headquarters. He ate a thick ham sandwich for an early supper, then picked out the horse they'd named for the original Cotton's teammate, Wink. As the sun slipped toward the western peaks, he rode Wink Two along a darkening trail.

Jim wanted to be able to tell Nora exactly how Cotton Two died. He wanted it to be true that the animal perished on impact with a broken neck. He dreaded finding it still suffering and in need of shooting.

Jim's breath came hard. He gasped air that felt cold in the back of his throat as he approached where he calculated Cotton Two's carcass should be. He planned to bring home the horse's pack saddle and halter, and hoped he could handle the job alone in the dark. His heart sounded in his ears as ragged as his breath.

A familiar whinny broke the night stillness. Jim got down and tethered Wink Two to a branch. He walked toward the sound, not daring to imagine what he'd find. He stepped into a clearing full of high grass. Cotton Two stood before him in the last light of the day, the sky like a wall of ice lit from the other side. Cotton Two grazed with the solemn mien of a stoic accepting whatever fate intended for him. Except for a torn, bloody ear, and a few long scratches, the gelding appeared able to stand without pain. After running his hands over the horse, Jim felt sure it had sustained bruises, but no broken bones or life-threatening injuries.

"Cotton Two, Nora will be so pleased." Jim, astonished, paraphrased a line from the WWI poem, *Invictus.* "Your head is bloody, but unbowed." Then he stroked the animal he'd given up for dead and rested his forehead against its white muzzle. For a long while neither of them moved.

Jim finally raised his head and breathed in the cold night air. Nora's horse seemed a miracle that called for some act of gratitude, some bloodless sacrifice. "We want to go home, don't we, white horse? We don't do so well away from Nora and Evening Star. We should give these jobs of ours to ambitious youngsters. The two of us have earned our rest."

Cotton Two nickered in full agreement.

~ ~ ~

Cotton Two's fall and unlikely survival made the gelding famous in all the camps. But on an afternoon three weeks later, Jim rode into Evening Star's yard on the horse with the well-known torn ear. He dismounted and leaned against the barn in a spasm of coughing. Nora ran to him from the cabin.

"I fell ill," Jim said without giving her a direct look. "It got so I couldn't breathe."

Nora put her arms around him. "Our Bird's been so discontented. We'll send him to work with Michael. You stay here with me. I've missed you too much anyway. You look so drawn and haggard."

Jim's eyes turned to hers. He stepped out of her embrace saying, "I don't know if we want to send Bird, Nora. The pay is good, but if men want to get the highest wages they do the dangerous work. Michael wishes Bird to be with him on the blasting, and he's convinced the foreman to let our grandson do it."

Nora lifted her chin. "We've none of us ever stepped aside from taking risks to achieve what we feel is necessary. What do they have to do?"

"First the men drill holes in the stone while hanging off cliffs on manila rope. Then they use dynamite for blasting. Any spark can set off an explosion."

Nora ran a hand across her forehead. "You say our Michael does this work?"

"Yes, he does what the rest do. He lets himself down and dangles with stockings covering his hobnail boots to keep them from striking a spark. The only difference between Michael and the others is that he refuses to wear the tin Army hat they issue for protection. He says it's because it reminds him of France, and he wants to forget everything about the war."

They stood in the barn, its late afternoon air pungent with smells of hay and manure. Jim coughed hard again while unsaddling Cotton Two.

Nora began currying the gelding in its stall. She was careful of its scarred ear. When finished, she put the brush away, fed the weary animal, and stroked her favorite's soft nose before she left.

Coming out again to Jim, she leaned against the rough wood stanchion and said, "It makes me fear for Michael. Tade went in an explosion, as you know. The memory of his death comes back now like a cold wind. So sudden . . ." She shivered.

Rubbing his chest, Jim lowered himself to sit on a three-legged stool. "I know. But Michael won't quit no matter the danger. All he speaks of is how we can build up and expand Evening Star. The war left him wound tight as a clock." Jim rose to start toward the cabin.

Nora frowned. "Is that all such a bad thing? Is it my fault? You're not saying it's wrong to want to prosper when we have the means?"

Jim faced her. "Nora, it's a good enough life now. Perhaps it is time to pull back. This American economy is an unstable thing. Let us stay out of debt."

"What about our old age? What about the children? Anyway, he's chosen to be a blaster, and he'll want Bird doing the work with him. I don't see us changing his mind."

As they walked Jim leaned on Nora, one arm around her shoulders. In the cabin she gave him two tablets of the miraculous aspirin that lowered high temperatures and eased pain. Then she sent him to rest until supper.

~ ~ ~

Bird had grown into a gangly youth whose long-fingered hands pushed out of his shirt sleeves to expose an expanse of forearms above knobby wrists. His feet lengthened so fast they outgrew the boots he'd worn for only months.

When he walked in from school and mucking stalls, his face lit up at the sight of his grandfather emerging from the bedroom. He hugged him. "Hi, Grandpa. I saw Cotton Two in the barn. Isn't he something? Did you bring him home to rest his bones for awhile?"

After Jim explained why he'd quit working on the road, Bird insisted that he should leave at once to take Jim's place beside Michael. Bird turned pleading eyes to Nora, who'd joined them. "Grandma Nora, we need the money a second worker brings home. If they take me on blasting with Pop, I'll make top dollar. With Grandpa Jim back the rest of you can run the cattle and keep up the gardens and horses. I want to go. It's my turn."

Jim sank down at the trestle table and looked up at the handsome boy, so eager to take on the responsibilities of a man. "Now that I'm back we could continue your studies, Bird. We've only grazed the top of China's history. I come from an ancient land."

"I know, Grandpa Jim, and I want to learn more about it. But history is happening just over in Glacier with that road." Bird paced. "I'm missing out on being part of it. You know you don't really need me here. I'll turn eighteen my next birthday. I can help Pop. You don't need me at your part of Evening Star as much as we need money for the new house and land. And, Grandma, you said yesterday we need a dependable truck. There are taxes coming, too, you know. And everybody needs clothes for winter."

Nora nodded. "Taxes are always a fearful thought. But Jim says it's dangerous work, boyo. If you go, you'll have to be careful."

Dawn had come in from fetching jars of canned rhubarb from the root cellar behind the cabin. She shook her head at Bird. "It's bad enough Michael's dangling off a cliff on a rope after all our worry over him when he went to France. I thought I was finished with wondering if he might be hurt or worse. I won't have it that way with you."

"But, Mama, the money's too good to pass up. I'm way ahead with school now anyway."

They argued until Dawn relented, knowing all too well that Michael wanted Bird with him. But she made a surprise announcement of her own. She turned to Nora and Jim. "I hear they're hiring experienced cooks at the work camps. And I need to be with Michael. I've been having awful dreams about him falling or getting blown up. They scare me. If both my husband and son mean to be there doing that dangerous work, then I have to go, too. I have to know every day what's happening with them. I need to know every night that they're safe."

Rose came in from playing outside with the barn cats after coming home from school and doing her chores. She pulled off her coat, then rested her head against her seated grandfather's. She moved next to put one arm around Grandma Nora's shoulders.

Nora and Dawn had spoken of how Rose had grown used to her father's sorties into the greater world. They concluded that Evening Star remained the child's haven. Her grandparents, especially Nora, always made time for long talks about North Fork plants. Nora told Rose stories about animals and even of the little people back in Ireland.

"This road," Dawn mused. "It must look like a big gash slashed on the mountainsides."

"It does," Jim conceded. "Nothing will be the same with autos crossing from one end of the Park to the other. Still, it will be something for the tourists to see all of it if only once in their lives."

Nora had fallen silent, looking more and more unnerved after Jim's description of the perils of blasting. Finally, she turned to Dawn and Bird. "Maybe you shouldn't do it," she said. "Maybe we should convince Michael to come back. After all, it's not worth such mortal danger and the family being apart again."

But she came to that too late. Dawn and Bird left three days later.

~ ~ ~

Reunited at Michael's assigned work camp, Michael and Dawn kept mainly to themselves. Bird mingled with others whenever he could. He visited among immigrant men of various nations. He approached strangers to learn as much as he could of their life stories, how they came to be working on the road, what their homelands were like. Bird found the Irish and Swedes usually spoke English. They were approachable, especially if the boy accepted a drop of the whiskey some workers packed in at their own expense. Its shared effect enlivened conversation around evening campfires.

The Russians at tent Camp 6 stuck to themselves. Few spoke English, but Bird felt drawn to the rugged, tireless, bearded giants. Everybody knew about the Russian Revolution, about the communists and what they'd done to the Tsar and his wife and children. Bird had seen pictures in the *Daily Inter Lake*. He wondered if these stonemasons escaped Russia as threatened aristocrats or poor immigrants. Maybe they were even communists.

By the time the Transmountain Highway reached past the Loop beyond Haystack Creek, he'd become accustomed to marveling at the Russian artisans' skills. During their own breaks, Bird and his father watched them, fascinated by how the Russians labored to complete the first of the arch bridges. Father and son marveled at the eighteen-foot arch. It had an almost seven-foot rise built to support the road in a section between the Loop and another creek. Bird learned what a keystone meant and what effort and knowledge it took to fit the great stones together for the arch.

"Poor men," Dawn said one evening as the three rested after her shift on the food line outside the cook tent ended. "The Russians, I mean. Cookie told me some are well-educated fellows who had to leave their family homes and all their valuables behind to escape the Revolution."

"Aristocrats?" Bird leaned toward her. The photographic images of the Tsar's daughters showed they remained beautiful and charismatic even when imprisoned. The gigantic, unkempt Russian stonemasons gained a kind of glamour by association. Bird hated that the cool, remote, vulnerable princesses had been murdered.

"I heard a few of the men talking about the boys in Camp 6. Some might be what you call aristocrats. Some Jews high up in Russian arts and business," Michael said. "One published poems over there. You don't hear them speaking English, just their lingo among themselves. They work like machines no matter how rich they used to be, harder and later than our crews, and that's the gods' own truth."

"A poet? I've never met a real poet. I wonder which one he is." Bird thought of poetry he'd read in school and with his grandfather: Keats and Shelley and Whittier. He never thought of such creative souls working with their hands, just assumed they wrote in book-lined rooms or seaside flower gardens always in bloom. His Grandpa Jim had taught him some translated Asian poetry, too, and he pictured it being written by delicate women in luxurious palaces. He grinned at this different reality.

"I think I know who he is," Dawn said. "Tall and burly like the rest, with curly black hair. He came down one morning to the cook tent. He wanted to thank us for the raisin pie Camp 6 found so delicious. He spoke English with such a heavy accent we had trouble understanding him. But he left a book. The lines look like poetry, but they're in Russian."

"Could I see it?" Bird asked.

"Here we go," Michael growled. "I thought we got you away from books, at least for the summer."

Dawn stood up and began removing dishes from their camp table. "Books could get our son away from having to do dangerous work to earn his living. He could get a real education."

Michael leaned back and stretched. "It hasn't helped that Russian much, the way I see it."

~ ~ ~

Bird slept with other men in a long tent near his parents' small one. That night he tossed on his cot in frustration. Curiosity about the Russian poet nettled. What does Russian writing look like? How much English does the poet know? Would it be too brash to approach those big, standoffish Russian giants, the stonemasons?

He finally threw off his blankets and left the fusty tent with its smells and noises of unwashed men sleeping the sleep of exhaustion. One or two veterans made sounds born of night terrors left over from the war. Bird knew those moans and cries. They echoed his father's.

Moving through the cold alpine air, Bird passed his parents' shelter. The scooped canvas sides of each structure reflected blue-white from the waxing moon's brilliance. The cook tent poles stretched up twenty feet to keep bears from reaching the all-important meat supplies hanging from them. Bird stepped inside with an excruciating awareness of how furious Cookie would be if he found Bird there uninvited, especially in deep silent hours meant for sleep.

Bird searched the cookbook shelf. A small volume bound in elegant leather appeared among the stained recipe books. It looked magical, as exotic and foreign as a poetic stonemason among the rough laborers. He took the book down, its binding smooth and soft in his hands, and carried it to the work counter, where he lit the lantern. He traced gold lettering with his right index finger. He couldn't read the title, but sounded out the poet's name, Kresimir Karpov. The K's swirled in dramatic, sensual loops.

He opened the book and gazed on the script. It was like American printed material only blockier, not like the Chinese calligraphy he and Grandpa Jim loved. But he could see the language must sound very different. Consonants together, dashes—he tried sounding it out in a whisper.

"What the hell is your business in my kitchen?" Ever territorial, Cookie stood, eyes glittering in the lamplight.

Bird jumped. "Sorry, Cookie. I came thinking my mother might be here. She told me about this book. I thought she might want to show it to me."

"Your mother doesn't have to be here for another four hours. You'll have to do better than that. What's in your hand there? Stealing my recipes?" The bald man took a step toward Bird.

"No, I swear, no. I'm looking at this Russian poetry. I've never seen anything like it."

Cookie snorted and put down a cleaver Bird hadn't noticed in the dim light. "Take the damn thing and get out of here. If it weren't for your ma I'd have you fired. Don't let me catch you here again in the dead of night or any other time. Tell your mother to keep the book. Useless thing takes up shelf space, such as it is."

Bird grinned. "You mean we can have it? Thanks, Cookie. You'll never see me in here again unless my mother wants me."

Cook grunted and stood aside at the tent flap in an obvious invitation for Bird to leave.

Bird raised the book in a wordless gesture of gratitude as he went.

Back on his cot, he stroked the leather, running his fingers over its velvet feel. He'd never seen such a book. He wished he could show it to Grandpa Jim. A need to know what the poems said overwhelmed him. Somehow, he'd find a way to meet Kresimir Karpov.

The Russians struggled to construct the Triple Arches, three arch bridges built to span deep crevices in the mountainsides. Bird watched them labor to set the keystones. As much as he wanted to talk to Karpov the poet, he knew better than to interrupt Karpov the stonemason with uninvited questions.

Chapter Nineteen

Unstoppable winter shut down progress on the road. Weary men went home. By the time they returned to work in the summer of 1926, Michael expressed open pride in Bird's ability to learn and master the work. His bookish son took to blasting without fear, performing it with the competence of more experienced men.

"Grandpa Jim showed me a lot, you know," Bird reminded his father in casual tones, relieved to win Michael's approval at last. The boy's only concession to the danger of falling rock was to put on one of the tin WWI Army hats the foreman handed out.

Michael continued obstinate in refusing to wear his. "I wore one just like it for too long as it was," he growled. No superior insisted.

In August, foremen insisted on laborers accelerating their pace. The onset of early autumn threatened in the sharp mountain wind and occasional yellow leaves that twirled from the aspen. The bright summer sky paled to the color of a faded blue work shirt. One morning in early September, they awoke to a fine dusting of snow. Although it melted away by noon, it meant the Garden Wall reared up to meet the brink of winter.

~ ~ ~

The day it all came apart, Michael and Bird dangled a few yards from each other, drilling and loading dynamite into holes in the granite facing them. Bird wore his helmet. Michael worked bareheaded, his tawny hair riffled by cold squalls blowing swirls of white mist. The sun showed weak and dim, as though it would prefer to shine on some tropical place.

Michael shivered but not just from the dropping temperatures. The damned falling dream—he'd had it over and over the night before. Every time he drifted off it intruded again, dreadful and disruptive. Dawn thought he might be coming down sick and pleaded with him not to go to work that day. He'd shrugged away her hands on his shoulders. The aftermath of his nightmares affected each of them.

~ ~ ~

Michael didn't see the rockslide start above him, kicked off by a workman's heavy boot. The plummeting granite rocks weren't large at first, some not even the size of a man's fist. But they hurtled vertically, bouncing off the cliff in fast momentum. When a bigger rock struck Michael's temple with stunning force, he let go of the rope and fell from his makeshift seat.

He was living his nightmare. His body wheeled and tumbled. He went dizzy. Blurred rocks, trees, clouds, and sky swirled past. Bird's frantic shouts didn't reach him. Michael heard the old terrifying sounds of shells exploding. Then something differed from the night terror. Instead of waking at the last moment, Michael knew a second's excruciating physical awareness of crashing to cold earth hard as a headstone. After that no pain existed nor fear of pain nor any sound nor any sight at all.

The Great War and all its horror no longer existed for Michael Larkin.

~ ~ ~

Dawn knew what had happened the minute she saw Bird's agonized grimace as he jumped from the truck bed and ran toward her. She dropped her wooden spoon and bowl full of sugar, cinnamon, and sliced apples. She pulled her heavy sweater across her chest and made a clenched fist over her heart as if to stop it from bursting. She froze in front of the cook tent, dark eyes on her son. He raced past the men's tents, slowing as he approached her.

She held her breath, then gasped like a woman suffocating. "Your father has had a bad accident." She announced it as though she and not Bird were the messenger. She closed her eyes and sank to her knees holding her head in both hands. She continued in a voice thick with tears, "He fell. Michael fell from a rope. My husband fell a long way. Too far to wake up and come back to me. Oh, God!"

Bird's hoarse breathing slowed as he bent toward her, his hands on his thighs. "Yes, Mama, Pop fell so far he died right away when he landed where the rocks..."

Dawn locked his eyes with hers. They ignored Cookie and the other men. "Can they bring his body up? I want to take him home to Evening Star. We need to take him home. Oh, this will kill Mama Nora and Papa Jim. They love him so."

Bird coughed, but his voice sounded firm. "I'll go down and bring my father up. They'll lower me with extra ropes."

Dawn's head jerked up and she gripped his arm. "Not you, Bird. No! I won't lose you, too. No. Impossible."

Bird had anticipated her objections as he rode back to the camp. "I'm the one who can do it best. He's—he was—my father. He worked beside me all the time. He showed me what I didn't know. He was proud of me. I want to do this for him."

"You're only nineteen."

"Mama," he leaned down and lifted her to a standing position, then walked her back toward her tent. "I'm as big as any man here. I've already said I'd do it. There's something else. You know Pop refused to wear our head protection—the tin helmet. It might have saved him. Nobody wants to risk their own lives because he was so stubborn. They might just leave him there..."

"I want to see where he is. Take me there. We'll see about this." Although her voice trembled, she glared up at him with determined eyes.

"We're wasting time arguing. We can take a truck back. I'll take you to see, but I have to do this in daylight."

They rode to the site in silence. When they arrived, the crew, hats in hands, parted for the devastated widow and son to walk to the cliff's edge. Dawn knelt and leaned on her hands, peering over. She saw Michael's broken body, small so far below, on a mossy boulder surrounded by bracken. He could have been sleeping. But, of course, Michael had never slept so still, not since the war.

"Mama?" Bird crouched beside her, one arm around her slumped shoulders. His arm felt muscular, his voice firm.

She straightened and studied her son. They were entering a new life where they had to do everything themselves without Michael's energy and tenacity. "Can you really do this? Bring your father's body back to us?"

"I know I can, but I have to do it now."

Dawn looked over her shoulder at the foreman and nodded.

~ ~ ~

Fog hovered over the mountains across the gorge where Michael had fallen. At intervals, tendrils and white vapors obscured Michael's body from Bird.

The men lowered him by inches until he disappeared into those curling mists. Bird clung to the rope. He could almost hear his father's voice directing him as he searched below. He would spend many future hours trying to analyze what had been between them, father and son… what of conflict and what of love. But for now, he had to retrieve his father's body. His mother and grandparents would need Michael Larkin's final resting place to be at Evening Star where they could sit and grieve near to their lost loved one. It wouldn't be decent for them to picture him left to the wild creatures. Bears and ravens would find him soon.

Drenched in sweat and freezing by the time he reached the broken body, Bird made the necessary knots to keep them both secure on the ascent. Finally ready, he called to the men high above. "Take us up!" The extra rope pulled taut with their weight. Bird had affixed it in a loop under his father's arms. Still secured by his own rope, he clung to Michael's neck, legs around the lifeless waist. He hadn't embraced his father this way since childhood in East Glacier.

The team assigned to bring up Bird with Michael's corpse pulled hand-over-hand on the ropes. Snow started to fall, first as a few stinging pellets, then in a thick white shawl covering the heads and shoulders of both men and mountains. Dawn wept as indifferent flakes dissolved and mingled with her tears.

They hoisted Bird up over the final lip of the cliff, freeing Michael's body and laying it on the ground. One man murmured, "You did well, boy," and wrapped wool blankets around Bird after he'd unfettered himself from his rope. Dawn knelt over Michael, brushing and smoothing the snow from his colorless lips and bloodstained face. He'd smashed one side of his forehead and broken other bones in his body. Rivulets of blood had already dried and flecked off at the touch of her hand. She closed his vacant eyes.

"Your husband should have worn his helmet," the foreman said, looming over her. "I guess Michael figured he'd worn one more than enough in the war, but he should have put it on all the same."

"The war never ended for him. Not until today," Dawn murmured without looking up. She smoothed back the shock of tawny hair, stiff with frozen blood.

The foreman cleared his throat. "Mrs. Larkin, I'm sorry, but we need to move out of here. You can see the weather's blowing in."

"Yes, we'll take Michael home now," Dawn said, pulling the blanket they'd placed across her shoulders over Michael, covering his face. She rose and waited while they lifted him.

One of the workers drove as Dawn and Bird rode in the pickup's bed, Michael's body between them. They sat that way to Belton with no words being spoken. Snow turned to heavy slush. Fred Hogan happened to be there, picking up supplies.

"You always seem to be here in time to help us," Dawn said, hugging him and sobbing. After expressing his own shock as well as grief for the man he'd known so long, Fred took the sad little party home in his truck.

~ ~ ~

Jim Li was filling feed troughs in the barn. He saw Fred's truck and its passengers approach, framed by the open door. "Rose," he said, turning to the girl as she laid aside the shovel she'd been using to help muck out stalls. "Go and tell your grandmother her family is here."

"Who's here?" Rose peered around her grandfather.

"The ones we have left," he answered. "Go."

Rose ran to the cabin. Nora emerged before the girl reached the porch.

"Grandpa says the ones who are left are back!" Rose called in a high voice.

Nora grasped her granddaughter's small hand, so cold and wet from the snow. "I can't see if Michael's come, too," she said. "That was a strange way for your grandfather to put it."

Soon enough, she knew. "Twice!" she cried. "I lost him twice!" Nora's keening rose to a pitch that threatened to rip her into fragments. Jim held her together while Dawn and Bird soothed a sobbing Rose.

~ ~ ~

Later, Nora lay on her bed while Jim dug the grave on a knoll above the river near Michael's Evening Star home. They'd bury Michael in the morning, but wait until spring to hold a service. None had the heart to observe that there'd been no opportunity for a priest to administer Last Rites.

Nora couldn't sleep. She rose and went to the shed where they'd laid Michael's body. She felt no sense of his presence. She wept alone in the cold darkness.

Before returning to bed, she stopped to look in on Bird in Heinrich's old studio. Nora had asked Dawn and Rose to stay at the cabin and Bird in Heinrich's old studio that night. The lanky youth lay sleeping the hard sleep of exhaustion. Standing for long minutes in front of the low fire, Nora watched the embers' glow diminish, and all but die out. She felt herself dying piece by piece as well. Nora shook herself into action and added kindling to bring back the flames. She pulled the quilt up to Bird's shoulders. Such a handsome man he would be—had already become.

Michael had seemed to her like a young god the day he reappeared in her life at age fifteen. Like a miracle. She sat on the chair beside Bird's bed, remembering.

She gazed out the window seeing the dim spires of pine, black against the charcoal sky.

Was it my fault? The question haunted her. *Was it my fault?* But what else was there? She and Jim had given the boy shelter in the wilderness. Like her, Michael thought the home ranch worth any sacrifice. How she had loved her son.

"Ah well," she whispered. "It's the fattest calf we kill. The one it hurts most to lose."

She studied Michael and Dawn's boy, her grandson. His sensuous mouth, dark lashes. She'd urged Jim to wait until morning to start digging, but he seemed driven to do it at once. Perhaps it gave him an excuse to weep alone. She sighed and spoke as though Jim were with her instead of chopping and digging in the cold-hardened earth. "Oh, we thought coming to this beautiful wilderness would keep us and our loved ones safe. Well, there are still our children's children, and the land will be theirs. Michael's death won't be for nothing. The rest will know what's worth taking a risk for."

But even as Nora said it, she wasn't certain.

She wasn't certain at all.

~ ~ ~

When Nora returned to her own bed she still couldn't sleep. She heard Jim come in, take off his boots, and drop them on the kitchen floor. She heard the soft splash of water, Jim washing away sweat and dirt from the sad task he'd just performed. She shuddered, thinking of the rectangle he'd created, a black hole waiting to hold Michael's body.

Jim slipped under the covers, sighing as though bone weary, and then lay quiet beside her.

Dawn appeared hovering in the doorway, not venturing into their bedroom, but not leaving either.

Nora sat up and spoke to her. "I can't help but think I had a hand in his taking on the job of blasting. Maybe the earth is resisting our hands upon it? Others should think of this."

"It was the war, too," Jim told Nora. "You didn't make the war."

"No, but I let him go into danger."

"Oh, Mama," Dawn said, coming to sit on the edge of the bed, "you said yourself he wouldn't stop."

"Do you blame me? Does Bird?"

"We're only full of sorrow. Anger finds no targets here. Michael chose to be where death could find him. We all grieve. Molly would say Bird was a fine warrior to bring his father back up from the mist. Michael is finally at peace." Dawn wiped away tears with her palms.

Nora took her hand. "Bird and Rose will help us keep going now."

Dawn gave her a long look, but in her grief, Nora didn't try to read it.

"I'll go in to Rose. Is there anything you need?" Dawn asked. Without their daughter making the conscious decision, it seemed to Nora that Dawn had picked up the reins of leadership that Michael had grasped so tight by himself. His young widow, carrying the dignity of grief, had become the only adult of her generation left to the family.

"No, see to yourself and your daughter," Nora murmured, closing her eyes. "She will need you."

~ ~ ~

An hour later Nora sat up, pulled on boots and a coat, and walked out into the night air so laden with the promise of snow. She stopped beside Michael's prepared gravesite. Jim would make a simple coffin in the morning. Neighbors would arrive with food. They'd have help with the stock for a day or two, and then the routines of ranch life would go on. But their lives would always and forever be without Michael.

Was his death her fault? The question still haunted her. But what else had there been to do? She'd given them a home in a wild land. Michael, too, had believed it worth great sacrifice. Land made harsh demands on those who claimed it for their own. This day had extracted its price in the struggle between nature and humans who had the arrogance to think they could subdue it.

She turned as the cabin door opened and Jim approached, stooped with this new sorrow. She opened her arms. He walked to her and they held each other.

"Ah, Jim," she sighed. "We thought the wilderness would keep us and our family safe."

"There are our children's children. The land will be theirs." Jim's voice, so low and sad, belied the optimism of his words.

"For certain, Jim, Michael's death won't be for nothing. His children will have what their father worked to give them."

Jim took her hand and led her back into the cabin. In the dark, in their bed again, he gathered her close. She rested her head on his chest which still had a slight wheeze from that lingering cough. But in the intimate comfort of his close warmth, Nora drifted into a deep sleep at last.

~ ~ ~

Although none of them had realized how much Rose idolized her undemonstrative father, her desolation at his loss mirrored Dawn's. Devastated by grief and recognizing it in her daughter, Dawn wrestled with whether to go back to cooking for the men.

She had no desire to try to function in the world of working men's camps without Michael as her protector. In the end Dawn said she couldn't face being alone in the tent she'd shared with Michael. No, she must go on, but not by rejoining the work on the road in spring. She explained to Jim and Nora, "I'll be of more use helping at the ranch through the winter and spending time with Rose, then finding work somewhere else next summer. Hill or the Park Service will rehire me in due time. He's always praised the work I did for him."

She had to be the true head of her little family and honor Michael who held the worth of land to be above life itself. She would find her own way to contribute and make sure they kept the ranch prospering. Mama and Papa Jim would need her and her children. For all their sakes she had to stand in the gap left by Michael's death. It seemed a law decreed by life.

~ ~ ~

Those first treacherous squalls in the year of Michael's death in Glacier's higher elevations retreated at Evening Star into a golden Indian summer. Butterscotch-yellow aspen and scarlet, magenta, and russet mountain maple seemed to mock the grief that weighed on Michael's young widow. She went about gathering herbs, setting traps, digging and planting with stoic resolution.

Dawn agreed to Bird going back to labor on the road when work started again next summer, but only if he'd take up Jim's old job of packing in supplies with the horses. She didn't want him to return to the blasting that had cost the family so dearly and left her empty-eyed and empty-hearted.

Frowning at his grieving mother, whom he could almost always overcome in an argument, Bird drew breath to challenge her. He hesitated when Jim stepped forward and shook his head. Bird nodded and went to the barn to gather tack. He paused to stroke Cotton Two's neck. He'd never take the horse with the scarred ear back to the Transmountain road work. Perhaps his mother had a point about tempting fate.

Men doffed their caps and held out their hands to shake his when he returned. These hardened workers had, after all, witnessed Bird's act of love and courage when he gathered his father's body and brought it up from that valley of death.

Chapter Twenty

Rose helped Dawn and her grandparents with ranch work, but when school started the sad child rode her pony off to the donation school every day. She lacked Bird's old enthusiasm but went with a dutiful resolve to make life as trouble-free as possible for her mother and grandparents.

Nora and Jim Li's hearts ached, but they drew solace from each other. They'd always done so in painful times. After the first shock, Jim seemed the least altered by Michael's death. Nora wondered whether Jim had grown inured to loss. Her husband drew from some source that allowed him to work, observe, read, and love her. Only his mouth turned down further at the corners, and his hair began to turn white.

As dry leaves clattered and fell, elk bugled in the meadows and hard blows of clashing antlers sounded ancient battles and rhythms. Wolves howled in the lengthening nights. Coyotes and deer in rut ran themselves to vulnerable exhaustion. Inevitable cycles kept the rhythms of Nature's dependable old authority, her reliable indifference comforting to those sorrowing at Evening Star.

Both Nora and Jim felt the cold more this year than in any other. Jim spent hours chopping wood to try to keep the cabin warm. Rose seemed indifferent to the cold. She seemed equally comfortable with all seasons even before this period of grief. The girl seemed to find solace in the beauty and peace of nature, and her grief became less severe. She grew from strength to strength as her loving mother and grandparents watched. Rose seemed an indivisible part of every aspect of life at Evening Star.

~ ~ ~

When Bird returned to work the spring following Michael's death his new assignment as a packer took him back and forth from headquarters to various camps. He took horses on narrow trails well above the blasters. Riding in front of the pack string gave him the quiet he needed to ponder his relationship with his father and grieve his loss. That abrupt tragedy had left Bird more adrift than anyone realized.

Michael's nerves had sometimes been so taut Bird expected his father to snap, to lose his temper and strike him. That never happened, but neither had he voiced any pleasure in Bird's artistic tendencies or quick mind. He'd been proud of his son's ability to set the dynamite. Bird's lack of fear on the risky job had matched Michael's and given them a sense of comradeship cut so short by Michael's fall. But there'd never been any recognition of the things Bird cherished.

While Bird remembered and pondered, he carried the Russian's poetry. The book seemed a sort of talisman. It rested in his inside pocket the day of the tragedy. Could it have protected him as he went down to retrieve his father's body? But that made no sense. He couldn't even read the poetry, so how could it have helped him?

He observed the Russians when he could. Their work staggered him. How could they create such perfect, complementary results that appeared a precise match to the mountain cliffs and boulders? It seemed as if nature alone placed each setting of stone. This effect awed him.

A day came at last when he prepared to leave Camp 1 now at Logan Creek with ten horses carrying supplies for Camp 6, the Russian camp.

"You won't understand the Russky's lingo," one of the loaders said. "They only talk to each other. They sing sometimes, too. They work like they're not even human. Half the night, I hear."

~ ~ ~

Bird rode on, higher and higher after Oberlin Bend. The Russian camp appeared as though suspended in air. Its shelters rested on stilts that kept them level and created the illusion that they levitated. He stopped short of his destination and camped with his horses on a grassy gentle slope in between the steeper ascents. Still suffering the sharpness of loss, he gazed at the vaulting roof of constellations. He hadn't abandoned himself to grief yet, but wrapped in vast and beautiful solitude he wept, dozed, then wept and mourned until he felt the simple comfort of giving way to grief at last.

Michael had reduced Bird's self-confidence at times, but while his father lived, there existed that brass ring of impressing the man. Whatever the reason, the last weeks together had been their best in a long time. It would never happen again. Bird would never know what Michael might have said or thought about anything Bird might accomplish in the years ahead. He cast off a bit of immaturity with each tear. He understood and accepted that loss is a part of living.

The stars blurred, and he finally slept.

He slept all day. He'd tell the boss he'd gotten sick on something he ate so had stopped short of the Russian camp. That evening he rode into Camp 6 just as the weary stonemasons tramped back to it from where they'd worked on the road. Bird sought out their camp cook, also Russian as it turned out. The two of them communicated with gestures. At one point the cook held up his hand for Bird to stop unloading. He gave him a drink of water and Bird had a chance to gaze around the camp, finding this site not much different from any of the others.

He noticed a giant of a man staring at him. Bird nodded and looked away from the attention. Grief and the long hours alone on the trail hadn't prepared him to be social. Not yet. But the man took long strides toward him, and then stopped and extended a calloused hand the size of a dinner plate, speaking in English with a heavy Russian accent. "You are that boy who went down into the clouds to bring his father's body back to your mother. I should not say boy. It was the act of a man. Strong man. Strong and brave."

"It was my place to do it, that's all." Bird tried to match the pressure in the giant's grip. The Russian's calluses felt like stones pushed into his own palm.

"Modest. Speaking like hero," the man declared. A delighted smile lit his lined, weathered face. "But even hero must eat. Come."

Bird followed his new Russian friend to the cook tent for a plate of beef and potatoes and a second plate with raisin pie. They walked to a campfire surrounded by more reclining Goliaths. He had the impression he'd stumbled into a camp of giants or gods.

Had he dismounted into a Russian fairy tale? The fact that one of the men strummed an instrument Bird had never seen finished the impression. Only later would he know the instrument was a balalaika.

Taking a stool and offering another to Bird, his host picked up a coffee cup and drank. "I should introduce myself," he announced. "I am Kresimir Karpov. I know you are the one they call Bird. Bird Larkin. A name like poetry. Your beautiful mother and your father, may he rest in peace, named you well."

Bird nodded and reached inside his jacket. "Cook let me have this. You're the poet."

The man laughed. "Yes, my poems. Don't they look good like that? But no one in America can read them."

"I've been curious about them. My grandfather is from China. He taught me some Chinese. I wish I knew Russian so I could read your poetry.

You're the only man I ever met who writes it. You speak English. Can you translate one for me?"

"First, I read in my own language, my mother tongue, so you hear the sounds I meant you to hear."

Kresimir began to read and the others fell silent. A few wept, and the musician played on, slow and soft, each note floating toward the stars. One poem expanded to others, but Bird didn't mind. Kresimir's voice swelled and sank like waves.

The boy from Polebridge had never heard the likes of it.

~ ~ ~

In her house at Evening Star, a dream about Michael's death settled into the depths of Dawn's sleep. She shuddered awake, her nightgown soaked in cold sweat. In a reflexive gesture, she reached for Michael after becoming conscious of her cheek wet against the soaked pillow. Her husband was gone. Dead. There could be no snuggling into his shoulder, arm resting across his rising and falling rib cage. He wasn't there, would never be there again.

She sat up, rested her arms on her drawn up knees, and considered. The constant repetition of his dreams had become her nightmares. "Is this how you choose to haunt me?" She whispered into the moonlit room.

She rose, stripped off the nightgown, pulled a flannel robe around herself and walked barefoot across the wood floor, her hair spread like a black shawl over her shoulders. She'd comfort herself with tea in the kitchen of the house Michael had built for her and their children. She and Rose had moved back, but before they did, they pulled down the section of fence that separated the original cabin from their new home. They both needed to feel close to Mama Nora and Papa Jim. She lit a fire in the wood stove, set the kettle on to boil, and sat at the table. She lifted her head and inhaled. The walls around her still exuded the sweet scent of fresh, unvarnished wood.

She released her breath in a long sigh. It smelled new as a beginning, but the start of a story that couldn't conclude as she'd wished.

The scent would fade away like Michael's dreams of their future. She stood and pulled herself back from such thoughts. Her children looked toward long futures. She'd be strong in order to show them how they should live. She had to raise them well. She had to support their dreams. They'd learn that every future held promise as well as pain.

Dawn filled the teapot and watched the leaves settle and the water darken. She poured herself a cup, held her lips against its warmth and smelled the fragrance of rose hip tea, an ancient smell that comforted and healed generations before her. She didn't fear the future. She was at home on the North Fork. She feared only loneliness.

The Army had returned her husband damaged by war's brutality—a Michael reduced to a shell of his old exuberant self. Her veteran husband had lived a humorless, hard, even bitter life. And then, what the world called an astounding feat of engineering had robbed her of him.

With him gone, rearing their children and keeping the ranch functioning were her only goals. To hold the land for their inheritance would be her greatest act of love in memory of Michael. Dawn knew he would agree. After all, he died trying to leave them enough land to guarantee their financial security. She intended to do whatever it took to deserve the land that had carried their family dreams.

She glanced toward the open door of her sleeping daughter's room. She couldn't imagine Rose being happy anywhere but the ranch where she'd thrived since she was a little girl gathering eggs, helping in the garden, then with the milk cows and the horses. Dawn turned to the window with her tea and looked out at the fading darkness. She pondered the growing mystery of Bird, such a deep, intelligent boy. What would make him happy?

A high-resting owl made questioning sounds. Harbinger of wisdom, some said. Others said it meant an imminent death. Life with its fearful storms would come to her children. She had some inner certainty though that Bird's future would include brilliant calms with dazzling vistas. But she had to teach him to be ready for both joy and sorrow.

Bird had proven his skill and strength when he retrieved Michael's body. Their son could keep working on the road without family to watch over him. He'd make his own decisions. That admitted, she'd been right to insist he return as a packer and never again as a blaster. Mama and Papa Jim always spoke as though Bird would come back to do ranch work when the road building came to an end. But were they right?

Her thoughts returned to the image of Michael dead, bloodied, and shattered. It visited her at such unexpected moments. She missed him most during this early spring when life burst into song and color and the North Fork swelled with spring melt. That's when grief used its weighty club to force her to her knees more than once.

Papa Jim had acquired Booster, a sensitive blue heeler that licked Dawn's tears on days when she slumped by the riverside. The swelling water's ragged white ripples drowned out sounds of her soft weeping and Booster's sympathetic whines.

She heard Booster's toenails as he emerged from Rose's room to investigate why Dawn had left her bed for the kitchen. He sat beside her and nuzzled her hand.

"OK, boy," she said, waggling his nose. "Let's get more sleep if we can."

~ ~ ~

Dawn applied to work for the hotel system again, but this time at one of the Great Northern Chalets built for the entertainment and pleasures of well-heeled, adventure-seeking Midwestern and Eastern tourists.

She'd be head cook at the Going-to-the-Sun Chalet complex. She'd never been there and didn't particularly look forward to it. But the family needed the money she'd send home. She would labor anywhere but the Going-to-the-Sun-Road to earn it.

In late May Dawn traveled the familiar journey on the Great Northern from Belton to East Glacier Park. She wrote to Virgil and Molly that she'd arrive and stay just one night in Glacier Park Hotel before leaving to begin the tourist season at Going-to-the-Sun Chalet.

She'd never made the trip from Belton alone. She looked out the window at scenery that hadn't changed at all when so much in her life had. She found it soothing that the earth itself—peaks, boulders, clear waters—remained. Her Blackfeet relatives understood the circle of life. How many generations had been born and buried within earth's cycles?

Molly and Virgil Caldwell met her train. Her auntie and uncle looked older, both with thinner faces and graying hair. Molly had written Dawn with news they'd lost Marissa to the Great Influenza. At the depot she introduced Dawn to the cheerful, stocky grandson their daughter had given them before falling ill. Marissa's husband, a mixed blood like she was, had been killed at Belleau Wood after going across to do his part in that bewildering war. The three old friends talked over dinner in the hotel, their eyes filling for lost loved ones, before shared old memories brought laughter along with sadness.

Dawn had been pleased to see that Blackfeet in full regalia still met each Great Northern train. Dancers also performed that evening as they'd done in years past, their shadows against the walls rising and falling to the drum beat. Dawn spent hours catching up on tribal deaths, marriages, and births, talking with the Caldwells and several Blackfeet she'd known who stopped to greet her after their performance. Lucy Drake's old enemy, Dan Flowers had died.

"Eleanor sold the ranch and moved back east," Virgil said. Molly reported that the greatest loss to the Blackfeet was that the Sun Dance had passed into history, at least for the time being. The Catholic Church and its influence with white politicians stopped that ancient ceremony. Whites could kill on a gigantic scale and then deprive the Blackfeet their ancient celebration of life.

"It will return someday," Molly insisted. Dawn didn't doubt her aunt's words. The great circle of life never stopped.

The best advance for the Caldwells and the tribe was that Blackfeet born in the United States became United States citizens as of 1924. Molly and Virgil credited the valor of enlisted warriors like Marissa's husband for swaying the government in favor of citizenship for tribal members. "Of course, it didn't hurt that women in different tribes organized a good Red Cross Chapter like ours in Browning to help our boys over in France," Molly added, lifting her chin in pride.

They moved from the table to sit in the lounge area before the fireplace. Virgil turned to Dawn during a conversational pause to ask, "Have you seen or heard from Heinrich Mann? Since the war, I mean."

She could read nothing but innocent curiosity in his question. "I can only tell you that he left Evening Star to be with his cousin in North Dakota before the Armistice. He wrote one letter from there to all of us at Evening Star. I don't know if he returned to Germany after the war finally ended or not."

Molly said, "Heinrich wrote just last week from St. Paul to let us know he's coming back to paint our people and the landscapes of Glacier Park again."

"I'm so glad," Dawn said. And she did feel happy at the news. "Heinrich loves this place so much."

~ ~ ~

Dawn stayed the night in the Glacier Park Hotel. She was tired, but the stimulation of seeing old friends chased sleep away. She felt sad and unnerved returning to where she and Michael had spent their early married life. Their children had been born and spent their first happy years here.

When the first hues of gray showed through east-facing windows, she rose, weary and irritable, missing Michael and everyone at the North Fork. Hearing news of Heinrich had made her feel again as if they'd done something wrong that New Year's Eve at Evening Star. She couldn't say just why. After all, she had sent him away with a promise not even to write to her. Perhaps her guilt was born of the fact that at some deep level she'd wanted him to stay.

Chapter Twenty-One

That morning Dawn and others, mostly young people assigned as staff to the Going-to-the-Sun Chalets, stuffed themselves with pancakes and bacon and downed strong coffee. After eating they climbed into the eleven-seat open motor buses that would carry them to Going to the Sun Chalet.

"Don't mind the bumps and lumps," the jovial, pot-bellied driver advised as they pulled away from the great hotel. "You'll be seeing one of the prettiest spots you could ever imagine when you catch your first glimpse of Sun Point."

Bone-rattling hours of riding on the rough dirt road followed. The balding driver would have been accurate had he described it as a cart trail, Dawn thought. The next hours involved lurching into holes water-filled from recent rains. Both men and women climbed down to help push the bus out. Mud-spattered and hungry, they reached the St. Mary at last. There they ate another filling meal before boarding the steamboat that carried them across St. Mary Lake to their home for the summer season.

The boat ride on the blue-green lake's sun-spangled waves and frothy riffles made up in spectacular beauty for the jolts on the way there. Dawn forgot her jostled bones and aching muscles when she lifted her eyes to see the log and stone structures on the rocky peninsula that was known locally as Sun Point. The outcropping jutted out at least one hundred feet above the lake. Snow-daubed peaks towered to the west.

But heartening as the glorious scenery was, she reminded herself that her immediate future would mean days filled with scouring, scrubbing, rinsing, and airing. All had to be done before the Chalet could open for the first pleasure-seeking summer guests.

Dawn and the high-spirited young waitresses and porters disembarked and climbed the steps to the chalet complex. Both the view and steep ascent subdued even the giddiest, panting from exertion, they paused to take in the lake, deep green forests, and gold, gray, reds, and greens of limestone cliffs soaring toward the rugged, thrusting summits of the Rockies around them.

Dawn's uplifted mood at the inspiring sight plummeted when she accompanied the head porter as he unlocked the big building that contained the dining room and kitchen. The promising model of rustic elegance had been closed during the harsh winter. Small creatures, including pack rats, mice, squirrels, and even a fox, had sheltered there, at home and saturating the fusty air with rank animal smells.

When Dawn opened the shutters, she recoiled at both the sight and the strong musk stench of pack rat nests in the windowsills. Sighing, she took off her cloche hat, and rolled up her sleeves. She knew from learning at Nora Li's knee what she had to do. Two grimacing young porters drew the duty of helping her evict the 'critters' and sweep up chinks of mortar fallen from between the log walls during the freezes and thaws of frigid months.

Dawn continued by scrubbing and polishing her kitchen, scouring the big wood-burning stove and all pots and pans with Bon Ami. She rinsed the cleanser away with boiling water. Too tired to miss her loved ones, she fell into bed in her allotted dormitory room. Her reward for the exhausting day Sun Point had demanded was the gift of her first dreamless sleep since Michael's death.

~ ~ ~

In one week the first tourists arrived, awed by scenery, and catered to by eager-to-please staff. Visitors wrote home on post cards of St. Mary Lake and its surrounding waterfalls and mountains. The happy descriptions left for mail pick up conveyed no disappointment about the place.

The young women who'd arrived with Dawn now waited tables in uniforms consisting of dirndl skirts, white stockings, and kerchiefs intended to continue the Great Northern Railway's theme of Glacier Park as the American Alps. The motto, 'See America First' drew growing numbers to 'The Crown Jewel of the Continent.'

It took a while for anything like friendship to grow between Dawn and the young women who'd come from as far away as Minneapolis. The girls weren't sure what to make of her. They'd seen her arrive by train in East Glacier and heard about how close she was to the Blackfeet. They guessed she must be an Indian, but not exactly like tribal members they saw living in tipis in front of the big Lodge or coming and going from the Reservation. She wore clothes in the latest styles, as the tourists did. And once settled at the Chalet, the dark beauty ran her kitchen with efficient authority, speaking to waitresses, infatuated porters, and even guests, without a hint of deference. No dirndl skirts for Dawn Larkin.

~ ~ ~

Dawn stood on Sun Point Cliff as wind blew in strong and clean off the shivering lake. It whipped her black hair loose and to one side like an unfurled banner, as she watched the steamboat, Red Eagle, dock below. A tall, tanned figure with white-blond hair disembarked ahead of the other passengers. He carried an easel and large canvas rucksack.

When Heinrich had almost reached the top of the steep climb to the Chalet, he glanced up and Dawn felt a jolt on looking into his familiar gray-blue eyes. How could they seem so warm when they were the color of ice? She pulled her heavy sweater tight against the wind and waited. One of the waitresses called from behind the man, "Mrs. Larkin, someone's here who says he knows you."

Heinrich scrambled up the last steps, lowered his burdens, held out both hands and smiled. "Dawn. I am so very happy to see you. At last, I've returned to these mountains and people that I so want to paint again. With the war's end, I'm reestablished in Louis Hill's good graces. I'm his guest in one of the little private cabins above us here." He hesitated. "You've grown even more beautiful. I didn't suppose that could be possible. I am—I was, so sorry to hear of Michael's tragedy. Grief has given you the gravitas of melancholy. As though you belong in a pieta."

Dawn looked beyond him. She watched a wave shudder and pass over the lake—a little frisson of warning? But what could be wrong with this artist's friendship now that she had no husband? Perhaps she wanted none of Heinrich's, or any man's, eagerness. It was too soon. Far too soon. She pulled back the hands he'd grasped in both of his. His had grown rougher than she remembered. She supposed hers had, too.

"It's kind of you to say so, Heinrich. It's good to see you, but I have to get back to work now." She thought she heard him speak as she walked off, but the wind muffled and rushed away his words.

~ ~ ~

Dawn had a ritual of bringing out coffee and cookies to relaxed but weary guests who gathered in the lobby in the evenings. A young man bartended for those who preferred something stronger. Refreshments raised their flagging energy and made them feel pampered even after a day spent hiking or riding. When their pep surged back, music and dancing followed. That evening when she entered, Heinrich Mann rose from his chair. Flames filled the oversized hearth behind him, almost turning the man into a silhouette.

After she passed around the treats, he asked her to dance to music from the Victrola. Having no excuse to turn her old friend down, Dawn accepted. She felt awkward to be so close to a man who wasn't Michael. Especially this man who'd hurried away from Evening Star because of a New Year's Eve indiscretion.

When the dancing ended and she'd put the kitchen in order, he walked her to her room. She dreaded his asking to enter it when they'd reached the door, but he didn't. Instead he asked her to model for him. He named a sum for payment that seemed too high. When she protested, he assured her that his finances were in order again. His paintings were selling, and he wanted to pay her a fair wage for her time.

"Being my model can be hard work." He gazed at her with the gentle smile she remembered. And she accepted.

~ ~ ~

Dawn sat for Heinrich Mann three days later during the daily lull between putting the kitchen in order after lunch and preparing dinner. Posed within an elongated rectangle of afternoon light slanting through dining room windowpanes, Dawn wore a red blanket dress, elk teeth running down the sleeves, with a blue shawl glowing in the light with red quill work. Her hair lay in two unbraided plaits each tied beside her collarbone with ermine strips. A beaded band adorned with one feather encircled her head.

The artist had lost some of his eager youth but showed himself confident and more mature. He wasn't quite as she remembered from before the war and during the time he spent at Evening Star. Noting new lines in his face, Dawn considered how hard wartime life had been in America for German aliens, some insulted or driven from towns—even American-born people who carried German names.

To fill the silences as he painted, she told him about life after the war at Evening Star. And, on the fourth day of posing, she described Michael's death. When she wept, Heinrich put down his brushes, hurried to her, and held her in silence. Only that until he said, "We've done all we can for today, my dear."

~ ~ ~

Something appeared different about her in this finished portrait from the ones Heinrich had painted before, although she could still recognize herself. She looked like a full blood with her dark eyes larger than in life, their expression pleasant but watchful. She didn't know then, as she would learn later, the artist painting her had developed a personal style of portraying tribal members. He made her appearance, and that of others, authentic while adding a suggestion of art deco to his stylized work.

Dawn took his pay and mailed it to Nora to apply toward the land debt. She had all but forgotten her first panic when Heinrich asked her to pose. They'd become friends again, sharing hours of silence and hours of conversation. By his questions, he showed a genuine interest in her life.

~ ~ ~

Heinrich told her little of his sojourn in North Dakota. "Did you paint very much there?" she asked, as she posed for a second picture, this time in a white buckskin dress with a blue beaded shawl.

Heinrich stayed silent for a moment. "I did a painting of my cousin's red barn and house, all glowing in sunlight. I made pictures of his cows and draft horses. I followed with more of his dun-colored sheep. We worked so hard I had little time to paint as I wished. My cousin certainly didn't see any need for it."

"Didn't he know of your reputation?"

Heinrich laughed, but there was no happiness in it. "He only wanted us to produce food and more food to show our loyalty to America, to contribute to the war effort. My thoughts were always of my mother and sister in Berlin. They were the ones going hungry in the British blockade. We were just ostracized."

"Are they all right?" Dawn asked. She couldn't see Heinrich's face as he worked behind his easel. She heard him inhale a shaky breath.

"No," he said at last. "My mother died of pneumonia during the war. My sister, well, my sister killed herself three months after it ended. I think she may have become a suicide out of loneliness. There was a fiancé who died on the front lines. I wish I'd been there to comfort her."

"Do you have family left in Germany?"

"No. No one."

Dawn paused. "You still have friends here, Heinrich. You have the mountains. You have your talent. You create beauty."

Heinrich nodded. "I hope to stay for a long while. I could go to Germany, a war-weary, impoverished land. But I have nothing there."

"Mama and Michael, and in a way the Blackfeet, taught me that the land means everything. Our land keeps us secure."

"But if everyone feels that way and there is not enough… Look what has happened to the Blackfeet, to your mother's people. They have lost their lands because others chose to take them. Even the tribes fought over lands in their own history."

Dawn stared at him. "This was to be the war to end all wars. Surely those who would just take what they want have learned better."

"We shall see," Heinrich said, putting his brushes down. "What do you know of colors?" Dawn thought for a moment before saying, "I know blue, green, yellow, red. Wait there must be more. Purple. Brown!" She laughed and almost startled herself. Her hand went to her mouth. Laughter had been rare for her since Michael's fall.

"There are many colors. Let's stop for now. Tomorrow we won't work at all on this portrait. It's your day off from the kitchen, is it not? We'll use your free time for a study in color and a new painting challenge for me. We need to expand our appreciation of all this incredible land and water, and the sky above us."

Heinrich drew a deep breath and smiled at Dawn. "Thank God, we don't have to own it to be in awe of it. And we can take great joy in that its colors are no other's sole possession."

CHAPTER TWENTY-TWO

On the morning of their planned hike along the lake, Dawn stepped out to watch for the artist. She'd worn a khaki skirt and white blouse with a shawl fastened Blackfeet-style inside her belt. The breeze came cool and fresh from the Continental Divide sweeping down and toward her from the far end of the Lake.

Heinrich descended from his little summer home. He focused on not sliding out of control on loose trail gravel. He wore boots laced to the knee, light wool pants and a jacket, a brimmed hat, and a kerchief over his shirt collar. She noted that he wore glasses, which he hadn't before, but the usual unlit pipe rested in his pocket. The corner of a sketchbook stuck up at an angle from the flap of his bulging backpack. When he saw Dawn, his smile included his mouth, his eyes, even his mustache.

Dawn carried their lunch and a Hudson Bay blanket in her pack. She'd tied her wide-brimmed straw hat under her chin.

"Where should we go?" she asked, feeling the need to start at once. Ever since Michael's return from the war he'd instilled the need to always be accomplishing something in her, almost as strong as in him.

"Well, there's really no direction that could be wrong. What about a hike around our beautiful St. Mary Lake to see her three famous waterfalls? I know I'll want to paint each one someday. I have to observe St. Mary in different lights to conceive how to do her justice."

Dawn nodded. “I’ve wanted to see the falls, but I’ve been so busy. Which one is first?”

Heinrich pointed to the Lake. “We’ll take a path down to the beach and follow it until we come to a little trail that goes up rather steeply to Baring Falls. It’s the first. Each one is beautiful, but different from the others. Like children. Like Mother Nature’s children, yes?”

“I suppose. I hadn’t thought of it that way. Do you want to be in front?”

“No. You lead, my little friend. I will be going this way often, you not as much. You don’t want to be having to peer around my old bones all the way.”

Dawn started off walking as though in a hurry, casting only glances at the sunlit water shivering to her left side. She glanced at the scarlet paintbrush and the white yarrow on the right. She felt conscious of Heinrich walking behind her. After they’d hiked about half a mile he spoke. “Dawn, slow down. There is so much to take in, yes? We must take the time to look. To look and really see.”

She turned to him, surprised. No one had told her to slow down for so long. She faced the water again. “Oh, yes,” she breathed. “Water the color of trees.”

“Yes. Now look up. I remember the first color you mentioned yesterday. Do you remember what it was?”

“No, and don’t tell me you do. I won’t believe it.”

“I take colors very seriously, as you can imagine. Color and form provide me with my subjects in a way. I remember that you mentioned blue. I felt happy for you when you did. It is the color of the sky, what people consider a heavenly, peaceful, spiritual color. Can we look up and not feel it?” He tipped his face to the blue expanse and stopped speaking.

Dawn looked up, too. "It doesn't ever end," she murmured. "It's not alive."

"No. The sky changes, but in time it always restores itself to depthless blue. Certainly we humans cannot rush it, though, can we? We have sunsets, dark nights, sunrises, and on clear days—and there are always some clear days—the blue again. But we must look up to know that."

Dawn lowered her head and sat down on a rock beside the trail, her gaze on the lake. "You'd think the water would be blue, too, but it has so much green."

"Today it does. Much more green than even that little touch of gray in the blue of the sky. That was your second color, you know, green. This is so green it might be called emerald. Blue and green, we are surrounded by restful colors."

Dawn drew in a breath, and then stood. In a short while they turned off the trail and climbed to Baring Falls. It plunged, its power noisy and mysterious in a tall rock grotto. a big, constant, plummeting of white water onto rocks and fallen tree trunks at its foot, it would descend into the lake below.

Heinrich took out his sketch book. Dawn sat on a flat rock and listened to the water's steady rush. It was such a clean place, so removed from anything near it. It holds its own, she thought. No matter what, it holds its own.

Heinrich put away his sketch pad. They sat without speaking for a few moments, then started down the rock-strewn path to the lake.

They hiked on for half an hour, then Dawn turned back to Heinrich. "What was the third?"

"What?" He'd been studying wildflowers along the trail. Most of the Glacier Lilies had already bloomed, but they saw a few, then Eggs and Butter, and Brown-eyed-Susans.

"What color did I mention third?"

"Yellow. That is a great favorite of mine. Remember all the ochres, and golds, and buttery yellows of the prairie? They are here as well, sometimes so bright and clear in the flowers. Sometimes in the sky..."

"And the sunrises."

"And the sunsets. You do take time to look after all. Have you ever noticed how the sun can outline things in yellow? This is especially true if trees or hills are backlit by its rays."

They took long steps on rocks rising above the water in small streams. The trail turned and they weren't in the open anymore, but back in forest. Deer raised their heads from a meadow rimmed by cattails. They studied the humans, then turned back to browsing, indifferent and safe. Squirrels scolded and songbirds flitted.

The path descended a little at the lake's end. Dawn and Heinrich had arrived at St. Mary Falls. Its waters fell in stages from high above them to pool among boulders. Then it continued into St. Mary Creek, and under the little wooden Park Service Bridge and on into St. Mary Lake itself.

Mist rose from the Falls. Looking one way Dawn faced the clear, plunging water. She turned around and watched the peaceful little creek, its current always to the lake and mountains beyond. Trees, including willows, graced the banks, pushed in light rhythms by the breeze, bounced back, were pushed again, but did not resist. They danced instead.

Dawn sat watching busy brown ouzel birds fly and duck under the clear water, then come to air again, fly a few feet, only to repeat the process until ready to swoop away.

They hiked on around to the far side of the lake from Sun Point. There were more little streams to cross, stepping on rocks again so that only their boot soles were soaked. They came out of the woods to a flat terrace of rocks above the creek below. Dawn spread the blanket out and unwrapped their roast beef sandwiches and sugar cookies from cloth tea towels. They sat, eating and drinking long swallows from their canteens.

They had a luxurious view over a chain of mountains from their terrace perch. Dawn studied it. Heinrich spoke in a low voice and pointed to the flat rocks well below them. "Look at that big fellow."

A grizzly, so far beneath that he didn't smell them, padded in the creek, drank and walked out flat-footed in the other direction.

"Let's go to our last wonder." Heinrich helped her repack their things.

Virginia Falls was the biggest, the highest, and the most commanding of all three cataracts. Dawn and Heinrich stood in billowing mist from its waters crashing to the flat rocks in front. They didn't speak—the din prevented that—but they smiled. Heinrich moved back and sketched before they started the long trek home. He touched Dawn's shoulder for a brief moment when he finished. She'd been lost in watching the plunging water, but his touch didn't startle her. She'd known he would do it. His hand felt warm.

They reached the trail's end and plodded weary and wind-burned back to the Dining Hall.

"I'll paint a sunrise tomorrow morning," he said, when they reached the door.

"I'll be sure to look at the sky, and then see if your work has all the right colors," Dawn said.

He touched the brim of his hat, turned and bounded up the path toward the cabin he didn't own. He turned part way up. "You know, we owned everything today. We owned all the colors we could see!"

Dawn lifted her hand and stepped into the Dining Hall, which was closed for the evening. "Yes, Heinrich," she murmured. "But we only owned them today." Then the thought came to her, *that was perhaps all anyone could say about anything… or anyone.*

~ ~ ~

Heinrich didn't ask Dawn to pose for him during the month after their hike. He was out painting waterfalls. He returned just before late afternoon sun dipped behind the mountains. He'd come back walking with long, slow steps, his arms and pack loaded with easel and canvas.

But he appeared for Dining Hall gatherings without fail. He lit his Meerschaum pipe and puffed as he watched the kitchen door. When Dawn emerged with her tray, he stood, bowed with a quick half stoop, and accepted her offerings of cookies and coffee. Some evenings he asked her to dance to music from the Victrola. At other times he only visited a bit, then said good night. But she grew used to how he acknowledged her entrance with that warm smile and slight bow.

A night came when she entered to see a stranger in Heinrich's usual chair. It seemed at once that night air invaded to chill the room. Even with the great stone fireplace burning she felt a drop in her body's temperature. She wondered about this as the evening drifted on.

When the guests grew tired of dancing and left, she locked the kitchen and dining hall and started for her dorm. She looked up toward Heinrich's cabin and noted that lights shone from there and from Louis Hill's private cabin next to it. The two men emerged from Heinrich's. Hill's voice sounded as though he'd found something to be enthusiastic over. She heard them laugh. They shook hands and Hill retired.

Heinrich glanced toward the Dining Hall. "Dawn?" he called.

Before she could move on, he'd scrambled down the path and stood in front of her. He stopped a few feet away on his descent. She had to tip her head back more than usual to see his face. "Did you show Mr. Hill your waterfalls?" she asked.

"My waterfalls, yes. Isn't it strange that we call them our own? We don't create or possess beauty, but I have created my own version of how I see the falls in my art. Well, I don't own the subjects. That was only a fancy.

But I have created my own version of them, haven't I? My art is all I really own, and I must share it. Otherwise, why create it?"

"I don't know. You haven't shown them to me." She pulled her shawl tight around her shoulders. She hadn't been able to shake the drop in temperature she'd felt when Heinrich wasn't there to stand and bow when she entered the dining room.

"I wanted to be certain they were truly completed before you'd see them. Hill is only a buyer, but you, you were part of my inspiration. My muse."

"A muse whose hands smell of kitchen work," she said.

He took a step closer. "You carry the scent of cinnamon and yeast dough baking, scents of my childhood home. Remember how Blackfeet women perfumed their hair with the scent of pine? You kept doing it at Evening Star. You carry reminders of sweet times. Dear lost places."

She stepped back, wanting to avoid talk of Evening Star and memories of that New Year's Eve. She changed the subject. "The paintings must be finished if you've showed them to Hill. When can I see them?"

"I'll show them to you tomorrow if you can escape the demands of your fragrant kitchen. Perhaps you'll come in that lull after luncheon has been served?"

"Yes. I'll be happy to see them. I'm no critic, though."

"Thank *Gott* for that. I'll see you then."

Dawn nodded. She walked back to her chilly sleeping quarters. Michael's presence seemed to haunt her in the shadowy silence of the room. How he would disapprove of her growing friendship with Heinrich. Could a ghost be jealous?

Dawn washed her face and body, then drew on her flannel nightgown. She brushed her hair and slid into the cold sheets of her narrow bed. She never got used to being away from the children. Sleeping alone still felt strange and lonely. Would grief ever yield to renewed life? Could the shift be happening? Would memories of her first passionate love allow it?

She wasn't bowed down by those attacks of grief she'd endured on the North Fork. She'd been right not to go back to the camps on Going-to-the-Sun Road. The Sun Chalet had felt like a place to make a new life. Although the ashes of her life with Michael lay cold at her feet, she could feel life stir in her pulse. Could new love come from the wasteland left to her by war and fatal misfortune?

Heinrich had hovered on the fringes of her life even before the war. Dawn's loving loyalty to Michael hadn't allowed attraction to be anything else. Even now, bereft of Michael but feeling an insect's wing of lessening grief, she saw differences between herself and Heinrich. She'd been raised in a remote place to a simple life. Heinrich had been educated in a big city, in Berlin. He'd been raised in an upper-class home and thrived on competition.

Perhaps he didn't consider land so vital to own because he came from a family that owned other precious things. Bank accounts, securities, valuable possessions. Of course, much of that had disappeared in the war.

But Heinrich had an ability no one else she'd ever known possessed. He could create beauty; he could show nature in ways that made you see it brand new. Tomorrow he'd show her how he'd painted the waterfalls. His visions. No mortal enemy or bank or government could take away what he owned. Would his work speak to her?

She'd never talked of such things with Michael. Michael saw the world as a big place to delve into to see what his hands could do with it, what it could do for him in terms of fun, provisions, profit. He'd been too much a part of the world to see it for its beauty alone. It would be like looking at the beauty of your own hands. His hands were there for what they could do to give her pleasure when they made love, or to serve him when he needed to subdue a horse or plant a field. Or shoot a gun. He had never seen his hands as sublime beauty. Heinrich saw the world as providing subjects for his art in abundance. Michael used the world. What a great difference.

Would she always be condemned to compare the two men? Should she just accept a solitary life of widowhood? She pushed such thoughts away and considered tomorrow's menu. The heavy blankets warmed from her body heat. She rolled to her side, facing away from the window and slept, a woman who'd pondered the ways of men until such long thoughts benumbed her mind. But the dreamless sleep that followed began to knit together something in her that had come unraveled. She'd resigned herself to the belief that it could never again be made whole.

But when she awoke, she felt excited. She felt excited to see the artist who said she was his muse.

~ ~ ~

Heinrich arrived at the hour he'd come weeks ago to paint her portraits. As they set out to his cabin he said, "I feel a bit nervous. Why not? I am showing my pictures to my muse."

"Louis Hill doesn't count as a muse, I suppose?" She gave him a sidelong glance.

Heinrich didn't laugh. "Louis Hill is a patron. A somewhat erratic benefactor. If our two countries can keep from going to war again, he'll be a great help to me. If, God forbid, we ever do go to war again, I believe I could be Gustav Klimt and it wouldn't matter. He'd turn his back. Ah, well. He's a critic, too. And an astute one. He's a landscape painter himself, you know."

"There's no chance of another war, so you're safe," Dawn said with no doubt whatsoever. Michael fought in the War to End All Wars. President Wilson had said so.

"Well, just to make sure my personal history won't repeat itself, I'm going to apply to be a United States citizen."

"You plan to stay in this country? Here?"

"Here and other places. I think this is my spiritual home." He gave her a gentle smile. "You and other people I care for are here. But I've met a photographer named Ansel Adams. He told me about a place called Yosemite Park in California. I feel drawn to see it. And there's another man, a Scot named John Muir. They and some others are working to preserve wilderness areas in the United States."

A red-tail hawk flew over them and screamed: half-hungry, half-triumphant. Dawn watched it soar and vanish into treetops and beyond. Would he come back? There was no telling. She lowered her gaze and noted the cobalt blue of the lake as they neared Heinrich's door.

"I remember when George Bird Grinnell came to dinner at the Flowers'. He would have approved of preserving wilderness. I was so shy that night I couldn't speak to him. But I listened. He was right about Glacier National Park, wasn't he?"

Heinrich nodded, as he opened the door and gestured for her to step inside.

Rows of windows without curtains stretched along the walls. The series of waterfall paintings leaned on easels before her. She studied the first, the painting of Baring Falls, the water white and gray, falling in shadow above trees and rocks. The sky showed a pale gray, too, with a few gold-rimmed clouds. "I almost feel the mist, but you've made it a little different from how it was. It's as though the roaring noise we heard is in the power of the plunging water that we see."

Heinrich said nothing. She moved to a painting of St. Mary Falls. Heinrich had captured it at sunrise, with the mist rainbow sparkling. "Oh, Heinrich. The water, it seems so…"

"Louis called it incandescent," Heinrich said. "And now this for last."

The last painting was of Virginia Falls. He'd painted it almost from the side and as though he were at eye level with the explosion of water crashing to earth and dancing back up in drops that looked like shining heads of water sprites. White needles of light shone over the slightly glacial-blue tinted waters as they plummeted. Heinrich had used only shades of blue and white, the sky brilliant with the color depicted like the waterfall itself in heavy brush strokes.

"How powerful," Dawn murmured. She turned to Heinrich. "How powerful," she said again. "You must have had a different muse."

"No," Heinrich said. "You are in every color, every form, and every brushstroke. You have only begun to know your power."

Dawn hesitated. "I'm honored."

Heinrich started to speak, then caught his breath. "We must get you back or the guests will go hungry tonight." He turned and this time went through the studio's doorway ahead of her.

On the way back to the dining hall Dawn moved forward and her hand brushed against the artist's long fingers. Without hesitation he claimed it, his fingers warm on her skin. She didn't pull away.

Chapter Twenty-Three

Bird once again packed supplies into Camp 6. After seeing to his horse and mules, he ate with the Russians, and then joined them around the communal fire. Clouds obscured the gibbous moon except for brief intervals. The other men, who spoke their own language and knew little English, remained silent with respect as the poet read in new translations of his Russian works. He read the poems a second time in Russian to keep all his listeners content.

One of the poems celebrated Glacier National Park's eagle-inhabited rocky heights and steep-sided green depths. He wrote lines about the granite and limestone the stonemasons converted from the eternal mountains into the inevitably temporary bridges and walls. He wrote of treetops as towers pointing into the night sky, and tattered clouds blending into rumpled moon glow.

The second poem touched Bird most. It spoke of loss. Kresimir had loved a woman who died or had become separated from him in some irredeemable way. Bird wondered as he listened if he would ever find a woman to love so much. Kresimir's eyes filled with tears as his deep voice thickened. Perhaps it would be better not to lose yourself to another person. He thought of his mother and how his father's death grieved her.

When the poet finished, Bird just shook his head. "I can't think of words to say how that makes me feel."

Kresimir said, "I have poem about my own father, but it needs much work. The translation, I mean."

"Your father?"

"He died in Russia. He was an educated man, a man of commerce. But the new Revolutionaries, the Bolsheviks, they had no place for a man with friends among the aristocracy. My mother died after they shot him. She had a weak heart and losing him broke it. My love, my Anna, died in 1917 at the hands of the Bolsheviks. She refused to be a prostitute for the Reds. She died proud and with unbelievable courage, shining scorn on her captors. With no one left, I fled the country like my father had wanted me to do."

"How did you come to be a stonemason if your father was so well off?"

"Ah, I am a Russian Jew. In our culture it is believed that besides being a learned person, a man should know how to work with his hands. A wise precaution against times like those we experienced in Russia. I apprenticed to a stonemason in St. Petersburg before the Revolution. What he taught me has kept me from going hungry or being thought useless. Who knows? Maybe it's why I can still write poetry."

The poet sighed. "All these things that happen to us… They rob us of our loved ones, our families, but they don't last. Look up at these massive mountains, Bird. Time and nature have sculpted them. They don't care about us, and they are right to be indifferent. They have eternity in the minerals that form them. They will be here when you and I are gone just like our poor fathers." His eyes held a far-off look. "We have great mountains in Russia as well, you know."

"The Urals, you mean? Grandpa Jim has shown me where they are on one of his maps." Bird lifted his chin, feeling relief at being able to say something that might sound halfway intelligent. He also liked to show off his Chinese grandfather's knowledge.

"Yes. The Urals. They don't concern themselves with war and revolution. Lost love. Such matters don't concern them. The boulders, the peaks, they endure. Our small politics and maneuvering for power on the world's stage aren't even remembered so much in the end. Why should they be?"

Bird said, "But we blasted away the sides of these mountains for the road." This had been bothering him for awhile. His mother's Blackfeet dislike of tearing at the earth had driven its influence deep into him.

"Just a light scratch on these big shoulders. Look at what is left. And if someday it went away, long after we do, would even that matter so much?"

"But you lost property, didn't you? My father, he thought only keeping the land mattered. Keeping it in the family."

"We had a house in Moscow. A big house, but just a house. Your father saw too much suffering and death in the war. Maybe he cared so much about keeping the land because he had you and your little sister, and your mother. He wanted you to stay strong and well fed. Free from the fear of people who would control and hurt you.

"My father wanted me to be in America even if I came with almost nothing but my skin, and it covered by one shabby set of clothes. And so, I did. He said I could build a new life in this country. And so, I am building.

"I still have my poetry, my knowledge of the serenity in these massive stones. I miss my parents, the woman I loved, the children we will never have. The only woman I will ever love was murdered. I don't believe life will take anything more from me than that, but to make sure, I won't give my mind and my soul to anyone again. I like working with rock, being a stone mason. Rocks don't ask much, not even the boulders. They don't ask because they don't feel. At least I don't think so. I'd be disappointed in them if they did."

Bird studied the man's profile with its fine features ruffed by shaggy hair. The Russian caught him looking and shrugged, lying back to stare at the night sky. "Look how the stars fit in their places, like an army in formation carrying torches. I wonder what they search for. Certainly not me. No light is bright enough to illuminate this human fragment lying beside you."

"My grandma says they're a spangled map of the night sky," Bird said, tilting his head back to look."

"Ha! Your grandma is poet."

"No, but she's a tough immigrant like you, I guess. She thinks a lot like my father did. About the land, I mean. My Grandpa Jim is from China. He reads everything he can get his hands on up on the North Fork. He might agree with you about the mountains being so calm. He believes in detachment."

"Detachment. Is that the same as not loving anyone? It is right to be that way."

Bird laughed, made uncomfortable as his companion had begun to drink from a bottle of vodka. "No, Grandpa loves our family. He doesn't seem to care as much about owning a lot of things, but he loves the beauty up at the North Fork. He just wants a place of his own, doesn't care about the size as long as he can grow food and make enough to hang on."

"The beggar can whistle as he walks by the highwayman. The old Roman Juvenile said that."

"Grandma would say any beggar would be too hungry to whistle. Ever hear of the Potato Famine in Ireland?"

The Russian laughed and drank again. "Of course. Give me my book. I'll sign for you."

They made their way back to the campfire. Bird declined the opportunity to share the men's quarters. He felt uncomfortable when they talked their language. He couldn't tell when they might be talking about him and of his father's fall.

He added wood to the fire and spread his bedroll next to it. Then he stretched out on his back, alone with the stars. Like an army carrying lanterns. If they were to show the watchers below anything, would it be to wear armor of the sort Kresimir wore around his feelings? The constellations seemed perfect in their detachment. Bird shivered a little. He preferred the sun's warm company to the night's cold, and his grandfather's concern for people to Kresimir's distance. Even if you lose people, Bird thought, they leave you with something.

And you carry that something with you forever.

In the morning he rode back to Camp 1 as the sun brought the green slopes to life. He thought about Kresimir the stone mason/poet and the rocks he physically hefted and hewed, as well as the lines of words he mentally hefted and hewed with even more effort. The man could seem warm and welcoming one minute, then turn as cold and brilliant as stars on a clear mountain night. Bird had never known such a complicated person. He wanted to know him better but doubted the poet would allow Bird to become any closer to him.

~ ~ ~

Bird took one more string of four mules loaded with supplies to Camp 6 before the close of road construction season. This time the Russian and the boy from Polebridge spoke together all night, feeding logs into the fire as they talked.

"Are you excited to go back to Seattle?" Bird asked. "Are you in a hurry to do something there?"

Kresimir laughed. "I can write here as well as there. But I'll get a room somewhere and maybe find enough work to keep from starving."

"If you're not in a hurry, maybe you could come back to Evening Star with me and stay awhile. I'd like you to meet my grandparents and my sister. You already know my mother."

"Write and ask them first," the poet said. "They might not want a big hairy poet on their Evening Star Ranch. I'm moody. Bad influence on you, maybe, with my vodka. But tell them I'll help around the place for a month or two if they like, and then I'll leave. It must be beautiful for a man to see."

"A lot like here," Bird said, "only not so high. We have forests and meadows. We're near the North Fork of the Flathead River. Three miles away there's a little settlement called Polebridge. I love it there, but…"

"Ah, there's a but in your love. Always bad for future relations."

"No. It's just that there's so much more. Grandpa Jim knows all about China, Grandma has all her memories of Ireland and Boston. My father knew about Butte and then France. I've only been to a few big cities on one trip when I was little. I'm curious. Restless, I guess. Maybe I can finally understand why my dad wanted to get sent to France so badly."

"Ah, your patriotic father carried torch of idealism for his country. That mixed with thoughts of adventure can drive men mad. Your poor father paid a high price as did many of my fellow Russian countrymen in our Revolution."

~ ~ ~

Snows blew in early to the high country where shivering road workers in ice-crusted wool clothes labored until they sweat, and the perspiration turned clammy on cold skin. Slushy gray flakes splattered and darkened against the Garden Wall. Mists like burial sheets promised difficult journeys down to the lower elevations. The men broke camp and rode in trucks and on horseback down to Headquarters at Apgar, then on to Belton.

Bird had continued to urge Kresimir to the point of nagging the poet to visit Evening Star before going to Seattle. Kresimir finally agreed and the two traveled together. The snow hadn't yet gripped Apgar and Beartracks' cabin at the head of the Lake. Bird wanted the poet to see it before he saw anything else. "It will inspire you," he said, knowing he sounded proud, but it wasn't that. It was more a sense of privilege to show such magnificent scenery to the Russian.

The two had dinner at the Belton Chalet in West Glacier. Afterwards they rode two of Bird's horses, the rest and some mules strung behind them. They went over the new Middle Fork bridge and then on the road through old growth fir, hemlock, and cedars to Apgar. A bright, outsized hunter's moon washed light over the trees and bracken. Bird pulled up at the livery and saw his animals fed and settled for the night.

When he finished, he walked toward the cabin. Kresimir had gone ahead, standing transfixed on Lake McDonald's beach. Then he heard the poet speaking in Russian as though summoning someone, punctuating his words with desolate sobs. The water held a trail of moonlight.

Bird cleared his throat and called, "Kresimir? Are you all right?"

He expected the man to hide his tears, but instead Kresimir sank to his knees and reached toward the lapping waves. "I weep and kneel before this," he said. He wiped his face with his jacket sleeve, then his scarred hands. "A man should never be ashamed to weep before what is divine."

"Divine? My grandma would agree with you. She always says this is how she pictures paradise. Well, let's go in. We're right in front of Beartracks' cabin. He left it to Grandma, and she'll leave it to Mama."

Grandma Nora and Dawn had made quilts for the two beds and hung pictures on the walls. A shelf held pots and pans. Bird started a fire in the wood-burning stove and the room warmed in no time. Bird showed Kresimir where the privy stood and where the outdoor washbasin sat on a rustic table, both a few steps behind the structure.

They went to bed, grateful to be in a warm place. But at first light, Bird saw Kresimir had risen and gone outside, the quilt from his bed wrapped around his shoulders. The Russian sat under the salmon-pink sky on a fallen fir. He held his pen suspended over an opened notebook for long moments, then wrote, then scratched out what he'd written. He blew on his hands before repeating the process, all concentration, like a condemned man composing a petition for someone to spare his life.

Bird went back to bed for an hour, then he slipped out to wash his face. Kresimir soon returned to the cabin and tucked his notebook in his rucksack. They straightened up the room and went to organize the horses and mules.

They reached Evening Star late, with the bright moon again lighting their way. Grandpa Jim greeted them and Bird introduced the two men. Jim explained that Dawn was still working to close the Sun Chalet for the season. Nora and Rose had gone to bed. He added that Rose was sleeping alone in Dawn's house except for the blue heeler and a scruffy cat she insisted on letting into the house.

Grandpa Jim and Kresimir seemed to Bird to understand each other right from the beginning. The poet studied Jim with interest. "You look like the Mongolians of Russia. Big, strong Asians. Bird tells me you came to America from China. Me, I had to sneak out of Russia ahead of the Bolsheviks."

Jim nodded. "I had to sneak into America." While Bird listened, the two talked in low voices for an hour or so. Kresimir finally stretched and admitted being weary from the long ride. Jim said he'd guide him to the studio that the artist Heinrich Mann had occupied on his visit.

"Kresimir, you'll feel at home in the old studio Heinrich used to stay in. We count ourselves blessed with good fortune to have creative artists come to Evening Star. There's a bed made up, a wood burning stove, and a table should you wish to write at it. Sleep as long as you like."

Bird said, "I'm off, too, Grandpa. I'll go over and stay with Rose. We've got a lot to catch up on."

Bird walked on a path to the home where Rose slept. Inside, Booster's toenails clattered across the floor accompanied by a soft, wary, woof. "It's me, boy," Bird said, kneeling and putting his arms around the dog, ducking as it licked his face, and noting Booster's graying muzzle. "I'm home." He looked around the neat kitchen. Rose's muddy work boots sat by the door. Bird remembered when there would have been four pair of different sizes. He sighed. "Well," he muttered, "I'm home for now."

He added wood to the fire and carried his rucksack into his bedroom. The air in the room seemed stale and cold. Bird pulled off his outer clothes and dove under the bedcovers. The cat, who scarcely knew him, leapt, landed on his chest, curled up, and purred. An hour later, the harmony of wolves sounded to the North. Bird had always liked the wild sound. He'd have to ask Kresimir about Russian wolves. He wondered if the Russian lay awake listening to the pack, too.

Did Kresimir, alone in the studio, weep to hear such communal, harmonious strains?

Bird turned away from the window and slept.

~ ~ ~

In the morning he woke to see Rose, dressed in a plaid flannel shirt and coveralls, sitting on his bed, grinning. Her brown eyes sparkled. He realized his black-haired little sister had become a pretty girl, almost a woman. He sat up and she leaned forward to hug him.

"It's about time you got here." She ruffled his disheveled hair. "You brought somebody else, too. Grandpa says he's a Russian poet. Will he pitch in?"

Bird realized she sounded like their father in those no-nonsense sentiments. "Some. He's not just a Russian. He's a poet and a stone mason here as a guest. He's educated like Grandpa Jim. He'll be going back to Seattle before too long."

"Well, get dressed and we'll go over to Grandma's so I can meet your poet."

"Bossy as ever," Bird said, but he grinned.

~ ~ ~

They entered the cabin to find Grandma Nora, Grandpa Jim, and Kresimir deep in conversation. Grandma rose at the sight of them and threw her arms around Bird. "Oh, my treasure, I'm so glad to have you home with us safe and sound."

She turned and kissed Rose on the cheek. Bird introduced Rose to the Russian, who rose and bowed a little.

Rose smiled a welcome, then went to the stove to crack eggs into the skillet for Bird and herself. Bacon was already waiting on the table. She cast sidelong glances at Kresimir. Grandpa Jim and the big man spoke together of the literature of their countries and of the United States, a conversation the others listened to, but didn't attempt to join, except that Grandma Nora had a few complimentary words to say about the Irish poet, Yeats. Kresimir agreed with her and quoted a few lines from *The Wild Swans at Coole.*

After breakfast, Grandpa Jim, Bird, and Kresimir went to the far meadow to harvest the last of the timothy that would be feed for the horses that winter. Rose and Grandma Nora packed mason jars of canned fruit and vegetables into wooden boxes to carry down to the root cellar and place on shelves. As they worked, the women discussed the Russian.

"I don't know…" Grandma Nora said. "I think this Russian might be a bad influence on our Bird."

Rose put the last jar of huckleberry jam in a wooden box on the table. "A bad influence?"

"That's it. He sees the beauty, perhaps he'll write lines about it, but he has no passion for this place of ours nor ever could. He's a city man, as I see it. And I expect he fills Bird's head with ideas of faraway places… countries and cities. Our boy has always been curious about the world beyond Evening Star."

Rose turned to stare at her grandmother. "Bird would never leave here for good, would he? He promised he's here for the winter and then he'll go back to the road. Pop died for this place. Mama's working all the time to make money to pay off our land. Bird knows he's needed to work it. He loves Evening Star, too."

She pushed the full box to one end of the table and started filling another box with jars of canned carrots and corn. She frowned at Grandma Nora's silence. Surely, she wasn't the only one who would object to Bird leaving. "What would Bird do, anyway? Where would he go?"

"I hope he doesn't go anywhere, for certain. Jim is getting older. When it comes down to it, so am I. Thank heaven for your devotion to our Evening Star, dear girl. I hope no handsome fellow ever comes along to tempt you away."

"Never," Rose gave her grandma a quick hug. "I'm like you and Pop. I know where I belong and where I'll be safe. I'll never leave. This is home. Home forever." She opened the door and hoisted up one of the boxes. Before turning to carry it to its winter home, she grinned. "I'll get Bird to see what's right for him. He'll listen to me before that poet can fill his head with wild ideas."

When the girl had gone out the door, Nora sighed and sat down. She'd never considered that either of the grandchildren would not treasure the land as she did. Jim did, too. She must remind Bird that the family had worked and bled and even died to keep this, the one place they called theirs. Evening Star meant refuge in an uncertain world.

For the rest of his visit, both women watched Kresimir with narrowed eyes. He shared in the work, and he also spent time alone tramping in the woods or along the North Fork, stopping at times to write. In the evenings, he gave some readings to them, but he also talked to Bird and Jim about the aftermath of World War One in the rest of the world. And he spoke of places of learning in Europe. He and Jim spoke of Asian countries and of the end of the Ottoman Empire. Bird listened to them wide-eyed and asked questions.

One night as the brother and sister walked home together, Rose stopped and faced him. "You are going to stay at Evening Star, aren't you?"

"Of course, until winter's over. Then I'll go back to the road work like always. Don't worry, one of these days it will be done."

"Is Kresimir going back, too?"

"I think so. What's it to you? You aren't friendly to him, you know. It's embarrassing when you act so distant. Why be like that?"

"All his talk about the world. I think he's trying to lure you away somehow."

"Lure me away? He's like a window open to what's beyond. The future shouldn't be a bolted door. But don't worry, he's struggling himself, and I have no money. I'll come right home when the season's over next year, too. I don't have any choice."

"It's what Pop wanted and what Mama still wants. Grandma Nora and Grandpa Jim are counting on you and me. They made all this for us. So we'd have something. Evening Star is like no other place and you know it. Everyone who comes feels better just being here. Don't lose sight of what we have. Don't let everything slip away."

Bird shrugged. "I'll be here all winter. Mama will be home, too. You've just been alone so much your imagination is running away with you."

"You and Mama keep bringing people who are so artistic they scare me. She's bringing Heinrich back for a visit. He's been up at the Sun Chalet painting landscapes and portraits of Blackfeet tribal members as Louis Hill's guest. She wrote that she posed for two portraits."

"Well, well. Maybe you're worried about the wrong one of us."

Rose's head shot up. "What do you mean by that?"

Chapter Twenty-Four

All that summer Dawn and Heinrich had hiked trails along and above St. Mary Lake as often as she could slip from her chef's duties to go with him. A day together usually meant trekking to destinations where Heinrich saw a view worth setting up his easel and painting while Dawn either posed for him in traditional Blackfeet dress or explored on her own. She took Mondays off, turning lunch and dinner preparations and service over to her assistant, Christina Larsen. A blonde Norwegian by heritage, Christina Larsen came from Minneapolis by way of North Dakota.

Dawn liked the earnest girl and took extra trouble to teach her how a hotel kitchen should be run. As the season drew to its close there were also fewer guests, so fewer workers needed to be on duty to cook for them. Dawn found that teaching the girl made her miss Rose. Not that Rose wouldn't prefer working with stock, planting in the fields and garden, or tackling anything she could do outdoors to cooking inside all day. Rose sometimes said that if she could, if they ever agreed to hire women for the jobs, she would become a Park Ranger on a fire lookout. But Evening Star would always come first.

Heinrich also made pencil drawings of Dawn as she waded in St. Mary Lake, her skirts lifted above little waves that lapped at her bare calves, or sat by waterfalls, or canoed along the shore. She stroked her paddle into the water with her back straight, alert and listening to the sounds of water, birds, and the occasional moose or bear stepping or padding down to the water.

He made a trip to East Glacier to see Molly and Virgil and returned with more Blackfeet robes, dresses, and shawls. Dawn modeled for him until the two became completely natural and at ease. She came to sense how he wanted her to sit or stand, where to put her hands, what to look toward.

Heinrich, both landscape and portrait painter taught her about different European and American artists. She taught him about her mother's people, even though he'd already learned a great deal from Blackfeet friends after being adopted into the tribe. He hadn't been able to make the jump from German to Blackfeet completely though. They tried to speak it together.

The occasional brush of a hand often turned to a lacing of fingers. Dawn found an occasional bright paint smear on her palm. She liked to run her finger across such transferred colors. She felt Heinrich shared what he held most important in his life. This sweep of yellow was from a sunset. The white from waterfalls.

One day when they stood close enough to the mists created by Virginia Falls to feel the spray cool their hot faces, Heinrich took Dawn's hands in his and kissed her. The mist felt cold, his lips soft and warm. He kissed her for a long time. She put her arms around his neck and looked up at him. They smiled and started back.

~ ~ ~

Heinrich sat in his accustomed chair by the great fireplace feeding in bigger logs as it took a good blaze these nights to warm the room. Dawn sat in a rocker, her eyes half closed, watching the flames leap to their task. There was only one night to go before Dawn would help shut and lock the buildings. Every piece of furniture was covered in muslin. In the morning, they would strip their beds and pack the bedding to be taken to East Glacier.

"I suppose by next spring the packrats and other creatures will have taken my beautiful Dining Hall back as theirs," Dawn said with a rueful grimace.

"Well, they were here first, as far as we know," Heinrich responded. Then he stood, but not to leave just yet. "Dawn, there is time even after you lock up tomorrow for us to go to a place over by Many Glacier where I have stayed before. It's a cabin on Lake Josephine. I've dreamed up a painting I want to do with you as my subject. The colors will be perfect now. I think I could express something there that has eluded me, certainly the words to say it have."

"Aren't we good enough friends for you to tell me anything you want to say?" She watched the last red embers flare and turn to gray.

"Ah, perhaps, but I must say this so well that neither of us will ever regret my saying it. Besides, I need you to model for me one more time before you leave for Evening Star and your family."

Dawn smiled. "I can send word to them that I won't be home until the last week of September. After all, a little more money from posing for you will make them accept a short delay. We could go there together rather than you coming along sometime after." She hesitated. "Heinrich, I don't want you to be hurt. I don't know what I have to offer you. Michael was my love since I could feel and know such an emotion. And he wouldn't understand. He had such a resentment of you."

"Was he jealous? He should have seen us packing me off from Evening Star. One kiss and that was on New Year's Eve."

Dawn frowned. "Don't try to change what it really was, Heinrich. And I've scolded myself about what it was and why I shouldn't have let it happen."

Heinrich stood. "We can't live in the past which has been so cruel to you and your family. But nothing we did was cruel. Our honor and your love of your husband didn't permit anything we need be ashamed of. We are a woman and a man. We have emotions and sensations and we're more than friends. I'll say no more if you don't wish it. But come with me. I've dreamed up a painting that only you can model for me. No one else will do."

Dawn remained seated after he left and the room turned cold as she considered his invitation. His art came first always. Perhaps all he wanted was for her to model in regalia amidst the late fall colors. She liked to pose for him. No one need know they were in a cabin alone together. She hadn't told the family a date when she'd be back. They would expect to see her when she had no duties left.

She stood to lock up and make her way to her room. The thought came that surely this man who held her hand and kissed her might believe her coming meant consent to more than that. Was she ready? And what if that led to a marriage proposal? She felt haunted by Michael. Would he wish her well or be jealous or angry that she'd taken a German as a second husband?

The thought of being with Heinrich brought its own heat. His tall frame, his muscular limbs, his intense eyes on her. His touch… She could let the sensuality of her life with Michael dim until only ashes remained. Or she could ignite something new. Could she do it? Could she fully reawaken that fire within every healthy woman or man? Could she?

~ ~ ~

Sleep came fitful and dream-ridden. She dreamed of both men. Michael fell to earth over and over. Sometimes it was she who fell. But when she did, Heinrich stood on a ledge, held out his arms, and caught her.

In the morning she walked up the path and met him coming down, loaded with his easel and art supplies. "Louis loaned me a Great Northern auto to take us to Many Glacier," he said. "I have loaded my things into it and locked up my studio. All I need now is your answer."

"All right," she said. "I'll go with you. For two weeks. Then you must promise to go back with me to Evening Star. I don't know what will come of all this. I won't know until we're there together."

Heinrich cupped her chin and smiled. "Good. I agree."

They closed the Dining Hall and loaded Dawn's baggage into the car. The few remaining employees were waiting for the last boat to take them to St. Mary's and back to East Glacier. Everyone had received their pay for the season. Dawn waved to the others as they stared curiously at the artist and his model.

The porters and waitresses had long ago decided Heinrich and Dawn were the most mysterious and romantic couple they knew outside the movies. Dawn felt only exhilaration to be sitting beside Heinrich Mann and going to an unfamiliar place that her mother's people had known for so many generations.

After several hours of bumping along on the road to Many Glacier Camp, they reached the chalet assigned to Heinrich. Louis Hill didn't have to know that Dawn Larkin would be his guest as well. The chalet sat high on Mount Alton, above the big log cabin that was the camp clubroom and dining hall during tourist season. Now Many Glacier Camp seemed big and empty. Their chalet was of two stories with an outside stairway and balcony along the front. Inside it was the coziest place Dawn had ever entered. Heinrich began building fires in both the large fireplace and the cook stove. There were two tables, chairs, and a writing desk. And there was one large bed.

Heinrich moved in a flurry of activity. He brought in boxes of food, bottles of water, their bags and his art supplies. Dawn, compelled to activity as well, unpacked and shelved beans and canned goods, flour and bread, and canned chicken. She found cooking utensils and dishes for the table. She also found bottles of wine and beer.

Finally, they looked at each other and laughed. "I feel like an awkward boy," Heinrich said. "Are we doing something we shouldn't do? Two grown people like us?"

Dawn turned to the stove and her stew. "Sit down and we'll eat," she said. "There's nothing wrong with a good meal."

"First, the good German wine." He took two wine glasses from a cupboard and filled them.

When they were seated, with bread and stew steaming in front of them, he proposed a toast. "To artists and their models."

"To artists and their models," Dawn agreed, and took a sip. It tasted cool and smooth.

Before she had her glass lowered to the table, Heinrich lifted his again and proposed a second toast. "To love."

"To love," she repeated.

When they'd cleaned up after dinner, gone to the outhouse and come back in to stay, Heinrich opened a second bottle of wine. They drank and talked of the summer just ended. At last, he stood and went to her, lifted her hand and kissed it. Then he turned it over and kissed the inside of her wrist.

She stood, still not certain of what she wanted to happen next. "You are so new to me. You've studied me from all angles hiding behind your easel. What do I really know of you? Michael and I grew up together."

"And you and I? I am the man you may grow old with after years and years of love and beauty. If you will. Is it a matter of your honor? Do you want me to sleep on the floor? I can do that, but I had hoped to hold you for hours and hours."

"I want you to hold me," Dawn said. "I made love to Michael before we married. The honor comes with love."

"So, you do love me. There is room in your heart for this German artist, so desperately in love with everything about you?"

Dawn moved into his arms. They undressed as they moved to the bed. They made love as though they were the last man and woman on earth, full of loss and passion. The wind blew against their chalet until it rocked, but neither noticed. The firelight showed them a new place of tenderness and warmth, in a country innocent of war.

~ ~ ~

In the morning they washed and dressed, then toasted bread and boiled coffee on the stove. They ate in front of the fireplace before making love again. Heinrich arched over Dawn, his eyes open and intense. He murmured words of love in both English and German. Dawn stroked his face then ran her hands along his long body. Making love, and she was in love, felt as if she'd been living with her throat parched and he'd come to give her clear mountain water.

Later Heinrich turned to his easel. His first love, Dawn thought, watching how eagerly he picked it up.

"I'm going up to the balcony," he said. "Pull on your coat and come up for the view. Don't worry, I won't ask you to model today, but you must see the splendid view set before us."

The panorama from the balcony displayed wilderness in its truest sense, indifferent to Dawn's reverent admiration. All was out of reach, but familiar, too. Swift Current River plunged out of Lake McDermott and down into its deep old channel. Grinnell and Gould mountains and even part of the Garden Wall, along with the green gem of Grinnell Lake, spread out like an undeserved gift.

Heinrich, immersed in work, painted and sketched for the first week. He went back to the jewel colors he'd often used to follow his vision of the bright world of the prairie. Then he turned to dark moods of the mountains with lowering skies and odd colors that didn't really belong there, but showed a world that might have existed before humanity's entrance. Fallen pine needles without number and endless rain had made that rock-solid world soft enough in places for flowers, shrubs, and graceful trees.

As she watched Heinrich's progress, she realized he would complete some of the best landscapes of his career alone in this place with her. He was lost to her during daylight hours, but at night they laughed and talked, then reached for the pleasures each had been denied for so long.

Heinrich painted Dawn, sometimes from only feet away, sometimes at a distance, a lone woman in traditional dress walking by a lake or sitting in the sun amidst the bright foliage of autumn.

The day came when temperatures dropped and the damp, bright smell of snow filled the air. They packed and drove toward East Glacier with the first scant flakes coming like scouts sent to check the terrain. They must have found it hospitable as a vast white army followed. Dawn and Heinrich made arrangements to go on to Belton by train next day. From there they'd hire a wagon to take them on to Polebridge and Evening Star.

The lovers spent that night with the Caldwells and their grandson. Molly and Virgil exchanged questioning looks, but then made separate beds up for their guests. There was little sleeping anyway as the old friends talked almost through the night.

Before their arrival, Dawn had asked Heinrich not to speak of being in love with her. "It's just that I need to see how things go at home. Glacier was so romantic it didn't feel real. Evening Star means my children and Mama and Papa Jim and a lot of unromantic work. We won't have privacy, much less this whole wilderness to shelter us. I need to see how things are there."

"Or how we are there?"

Dawn turned away from the unhappiness in his eyes. Yet he hadn't asked her to marry him. Perhaps he'd always sensed that if he did, her answer would be far from certain.

Chapter Twenty-Five

When they drove into Evening Star with the man Heinrich hired to deliver them from Belton, the family and, to Dawn's surprise, Kresimir Karpov all rushed out of the cabin with embraces and happy exclamations. Everyone's welcome was high-spirited, although Dawn noted that Rose, fiddling with two long braids, appeared less enthusiastic about seeing Heinrich than others did. Dawn reminded herself that the girl in her teens hadn't seen the German artist almost since he'd carried her home on his shoulders from skating on the pond that Christmas so long ago.

Rose had changed from a giggling little girl to this watchful beauty edging into womanhood. She studied her mother and Heinrich as if something about them bothered her.

"Where should we take his art supplies and everything?" she asked. "Kresimir is already using the studio."

Dawn had taken Rose in her arms for a quick hug and felt the unmistakable bosom that hadn't been there when she'd hugged her daughter goodbye. She felt quick self-reproach that she'd been away during so much of Rose's childhood years. Her daughter's early years had moved into memory. Rose reminded Dawn of herself at fourteen, except for her daughter possessing a skeptic's way of eyeing everything around her that Dawn never had.

"Carry the bags and other things into the cabin, my girl, and we'll sort it all out," Grandma Nora said.

Dawn took a breath. She'd been in charge of the kitchen of the Dining Hall at the Sun Chalet. In a way, it was a relief to have Mama Nora so sure of what to do. In another way, it wasn't.

When they were inside and seated around the table, Kresimir surprised everyone by solving the problem of where guests should sleep. "Please, let the artist have his studio," he said to the others. My friends have been looking for me already for a month. I also have translated a collection of my poems with Jim Li's help. I need to send that work to publishers. It's like fishing. Perhaps one of them will nibble and decide to bite. Then I'll become known in America. I promise you, I can sleep on blankets on the floor before your stove for one night with no damage. I've done much worse. Let this fine artist have his studio."

Dawn glanced at Rose, who gave the Russian a cool smile and said, "Promise to leave Bird with us when you go."

Bird scowled and elbowed his sister. "I'm an adult, Rose. I make my own decisions. I know what's expected for at least a couple more years."

An awkward silence followed. Heinrich broke it by saying, "I appreciate your kindness. Being here again feels like coming home, although better than before. I'm not in that shadowland I inhabited during the war."

Dinner conversation over elk roast and fried potatoes, corn, and apple pie was a lively mix of viewpoints about progress on the road and the state of the economy, the arts, and the problems and successes they'd experienced at Evening Star. Money was a concern, but they'd been able to pay property taxes on time. Dawn's and Bird's paychecks and the efforts of those at home kept the ranch afloat, the animals healthy.

Rose had inherited Michael's way with animals. She could break horses and assist her Grandpa Jim at calving time. She spoke with almost defiant authority about how the ranch was doing in every aspect: gardens, building maintenance, animals, and egg prices at the Polebridge Mercantile. When Dawn asked questions about ranch profits and losses, Rose gave long, detailed answers. When Heinrich asked about the pond where they'd skated on that Christmas years before, the girl only looked blank. "I don't remember that," she said. "If you mean that puddle back in the woods, it dried up."

After dinner Kresimir excused himself to pack his things. The others remained at the table, sipping coffee, all but Rose clearly saddened by Kresimir's departure.

"I'll miss the Russian poet," Jim said. "He's kind and sensitive. A brilliant man, he's taken an interest in you, Bird."

"Not too much, though," Rose said. "Nothing is more important than all those hours at his poetry. That's what he really cares about. He doesn't pay much attention to anything else unless he has to."

"Ah, yes," Heinrich said with a rueful smile. "We artists are a selfish lot. Those around us have to suffer our absence at times, either our emotional absence or our actual physical absence if we're off pursuing our muse." He glanced toward Dawn.

Rose said, "Maybe you should be where there aren't other people around you, at least not those who have important work of their own."

"Heinrich needs to protect his creative time," Dawn replied. "His art has done wonders for preserving our Blackfeet heritage. It shows our old ways, our clothes, our lives, all with the dignity that we deserve. It's a way of making everybody see what we value, what we lost."

"Not to mention the work he's given you as a model," Mama Nora broke in. "Professional artists lift us up in our spirits, Rose, my treasure. I remember the harpists of Ireland, and the poets, and the storytellers."

"Nature and art," Jim murmured. "We cannot live without the first, but we cannot live well without the second. We should treasure our artists, Granddaughter. But I think it takes time to learn how true that is."

"You are so like Pop," Bird said, looking at Rose. "Everything with you is about making our Evening Star bigger and better."

Kresimir broke the uncomfortable silence that followed as he came in carrying one bag packed with clothes and a satchel stuffed with notebooks and papers. He studied the group for a moment, lingering over Rose and Bird's angry faces, then the adults' troubled expressions. "What's this, my dear friends? It is a beautiful night. The Northern Lights are flashing over the North Fork, putting on a lovely display to welcome you and bid me farewell. They are eternal, as is my fondness for all of you."

"We'll see you in the spring, Kresimir," Nora said. "And I'll fix you a good breakfast before you go tomorrow morning. Everyone has had such an exciting day. Rose, please help me with the dishes. Dawn, perhaps you can help Heinrich to the studio with all his easels and so on. Then we should ready ourselves for bed."

"I'll take you to the train in the morning," Bird said to Kresimir.

"I'll see to the animals and bring in more wood for the stove," Jim offered.

They all seemed relieved to be up and moving away from Rose's barbed comments about art and artists.

~ ~ ~

Dawn and Heinrich, loaded with the artist's supplies and easel, as well as his duffel, made their way to the studio. Flames sprang up in the hearth when Heinrich opened the door and the two stepped inside. Being there with him brought memories of the war years to Dawn, so strong that she caught her breath.

"It hasn't changed at all," Heinrich said with a smile as he lowered his bags and took supplies from Dawn's arms.

"Rose has," Dawn said, sitting down on the fireside chair with a troubled sigh. "I apologize for her behavior."

"She barely remembers me," Heinrich said. "And she hasn't seen much of you for some time. Perhaps she wants you to herself for a while." He pulled a stool close to her and took her hand.

"The truth is, she's much closer to Mama Nora and Papa Jim than to me. I've been away too much. I've been working for her and Bird, and for this ranch she loves so much. But I wasn't *here*."

"She is also clinging to her father's values and to what she believes he would have wanted. That is, of course, that you all stay on and keep Evening Star Ranch for the family for generations to come."

"It's what her Grandma Nora and Grandpa Jim have wanted, too. I'm not so sure about Bird, though."

"Ah, Bird has a curious mind. That boy wants to see the world, travel, and taste its wonders. Do you think he is wrong? Would you ever want to see the countries of Europe? See the coasts of America?"

Dawn shrugged. "I don't know. We just arrived. I don't know what will be asked of me by anyone—or really, what I want. Except that I want Rose to be polite to you."

He leaned forward and kissed her forehead. "She's trying to sort out her place with strangers coming and going. I think she feels me as a threat. Perhaps she is right to feel so if what she really wants is for nothing more to change."

Dawn kissed Heinrich's lips, drew a hand along his cheek, and whispered her good night.

She reached the cabin to find Rose pulling on a jacket to go back to the house she shared with Bird and now her mother.

As they walked together snow started to drift down. Dawn turned to Rose. "Thank you for being such a help to your grandparents while Bird and I have been away."

Rose faced her. "They need all the help they can get. They work as hard as they can, but it takes all of us to keep the ranch going. It's worth every second, though. Grandpa Jim says we live in paradise."

"I loved the Chalet, too, and having Heinrich there gave me a chance to earn extra money as his model. We might continue that while he's here."

"How long will he be here?" Rose's voice sounded sharp.

"As long as he wants to be. Don't worry, he'll help all he can, and I think he will go to California at some point to paint the ocean and hills in the Big Sur area."

Rose sighed. "Good. I'd like it to be just us again. Don't you still miss Pop?"

They reached the house and went in. Bird had gotten there first and lit the lanterns and started a fire in the stove before going to his room.

Dawn sat at the table and gestured for Rose to do the same. "What are you really asking me? If there's nothing more to your question than the words, the easy answer is that I miss Michael every day and every night. I loved my husband enough to leave here with him when I was sixteen, you know. My home was always with him first and anywhere else including Evening Star second. Don't think I wasn't homesick for this place though. I always am when I'm away.

"And in a way, Michael is here, and he always will be. He'd set his heart on making Evening Star a haven for us. As long as we care for it, we're caring for his dream. I understand that. And it's your dream, too, just as it is Mama Nora's."

Rose nodded, but her face twisted in worry. "But I'm not always so sure about you and Bird. You're always bringing strangers here. Bird's forever asking Grandpa and Kresimir all kinds of questions. And tonight he started in doing the same with Heinrich. What's it like in Germany? What about Norway? And Vienna? It's like everyplace else is more interesting than home."

Dawn stood and went to the stove to put the teakettle on to boil. She stayed standing as she turned to her daughter. "First of all, we've always had visitors from time to time at Evening Star. If we hadn't, Grandpa Jim wouldn't have saved Celia Van Eick. If he hadn't done that, he never would have become a citizen. We don't help ourselves or anyone else by sealing out the world. Michael only turned his back on other people and places after the horrors of the war. He was wounded over there in every way a man can be wounded. The only good thing was that he did come home ready to forgive your grandma."

The teakettle whistled. Dawn poured them each a steaming cup of rose hip tea. She set one on the table for Rose, then sat across from her again. "It's where he felt he could keep us safe. "There are many places to be safe, but by the time of the Armistice, he felt this was the only one. We love Evening Star because it's home. Of course, we want to keep it. But, Rose, Bird and I don't 'always' bring strangers here. Kresimir and Heinrich are dear friends to us, and if you let them, they could be to you, too. They bring us knowledge, and both are so very creative."

Rose looked suspicious. "Is that all you see in Heinrich? That he's smart and a big artist? Are you sure that's all? I don't know how Pop would feel about this."

Dawn stood again. "You forget yourself, Rose. I'm not going to talk to you any more of this. Just be polite to our guests. They wish you no harm."

"I'm sorry," Rose muttered. "But people cause harm even if they don't mean to, you know. They bring problems."

That night, Dawn lay in her cold room, wondering what she should have said. The Chalet had been like a dream. She'd felt such happiness there. Now her daughter brought her back to the old ache for the life that had been so intertwined with Michael's. Rose resented anyone who threatened to alter their lives here in any way.

Dawn pondered what she owed the family, and what would eventually come of this new love. Heinrich did speak to her of places they might go. His reputation as an artist was international. Where would this lead them?

~ ~ ~

Rose studied with her Grandpa Jim during the winter months, then regular school in summer. Bird worked with Jim to feed stock, repair buildings, bring in wood, hunt, and trap. Kresimir wrote letters to Bird, clearly intended to be shared with Jim and the rest of the family. Kresimir was teaching Russian lessons and had begun working on an advanced degree in Russian Literature. With a doctorate and the publication of his poems in English, he felt he would be able to make a living as an academic in some American University.

One letter contained a page that Bird didn't share with his family. Kresimir suggested that if eventually hired by a good university, he might make a condition of his employment that Bird be allowed to enroll and would be given a full scholarship if he met all requirements and passed exams and interviews. Bird tucked that page away. But he began to wonder: Could such a thing come about? And if it did, would he accept such an offer to become educated, even at the cost to his family of his leaving Evening Star?

He tried to shrug off thoughts of such a decision, but he also began to study in the evenings with Grandpa Jim: geography, world history, literature, and a field he hadn't realized Jim Li knew so well, mathematics.

~ ~ ~

If Jim suspected that this renewed zeal for knowledge meant imminent change and departure for his grandson, he said nothing of the matter to anyone. He'd left home as a young man to wander in search of his own identity. Perhaps Bird would do some version of that as well. Perhaps all young people felt compelled to do so if they could.

He didn't mention such thoughts to Nora. Like Rose, she believed the family owed it to Michael to stay and keep Evening Star growing and the family secure and prosperous. They all felt a need to preserve the beauty of their homestead on the North Fork. It had served as a haven for Nora and Jim, and later Dawn and her children. The wilderness had sheltered them. As more activity grew across the North Fork and in Glacier Park, Jim felt the first stirrings of unease that the North Fork itself might one day need to be sheltered.

Chapter Twenty-Six

The stock market crash of October 29, 1929, changed everything. Work on the Transmountain Highway stopped. As a result, motorists could only drive to Logan Pass, use it as a turn around, and return to Apgar. The completion of Highway 2, the Roosevelt Highway, lessened any urgency to finish the East portion of the spectacular highway in the Park. Because of it, people could drive the scenic, but less spectacular distance between West Glacier and East Glacier.

The Great Depression didn't affect Heinrich in a negative way. He became a U.S. citizen in 1930, then went to work for the WPA creating murals wherever the government sent him. He returned to Evening Star when he could, not nearly often enough for him. He asked Dawn more than once to visit him where he worked, but she declined each time.

They were alone in his studio late one winter night when he invited Dawn for the last time to come with him to California.

"No," she said, stroking the light hair on his chest. "I can't. Mama needs my help and Rose is in her last year before she'll take exams and graduate. I've missed so much of her childhood because I had to be away. I want to be together with my family this whole year."

He caught her hand and held it still. "And do memories of Michael keep you here as well? Has it all come back to you? Is widowhood enough?"

She kissed him. "Memories are dear, but no, they aren't enough. Still, Rose isn't ready for me to openly be with you. Try to understand. You're gone so much, and I can't be spared."

"And our marriage?"

"I don't think it would do anything but harm. Life here is all work just to survive. I want to be your wife in time, but for now this has to be enough."

Heinrich stood and began to pull on his clothes. "For now. How long is 'for now?' It's always now, my beloved. I want you with me forever."

When they parted, he seemed distant. His letters came less often although they did come, full of news about his teaching and murals, but with almost no words of love. Dawn's letters to him seemed dull even to her. She wrote of gardening and making clothes out of flour sacks.

~ ~ ~

Bird studied with his grandfather and took on the greatest share of hard physical ranch work. Jim hunted, and cared for the horses. Nora and Dawn saw to food production, butchering wild game, and selling eggs, butter, and produce when they could. Nora continued to make snowshoes to be sold at the Polebridge Mercantile.

The women sewed clothes and made candles. Rose continued with studies, eager to graduate. Brown and strong, she'd inherited dimples and a small, sturdy stature from Sweet Grass, the Blackfeet grandmother she never knew. She didn't have Bird's sharp and curious mind, but she had a passion for learning what would best serve livestock and crop production, and for the natural world of Evening Star and its surroundings. Although she didn't realize it, she knew as much as many naturalists about the identity and uses for wildflowers, mushrooms, trees, and animals.

Also in 1931, Horace Albright, the National Park Service Director, fearful of losing all Federal funding for the Transmountain Highway opened bids for two contractors to finish the job. They were to do so by 1933. Work on the road opened up again in 1932.

Enough time had passed since Michael's death that Dawn felt able to hire on as a cook at the Logan Pass work camp. Bird qualified to run heavy equipment.

Kresimir had come back in 1928 to work on the triple arches, part of a retaining wall considered an engineering marvel for any who saw it. The roadbed carved from the steep face of the Garden Wall needed shoring up. Retaining walls had to fit the landscape architects' vision of what blended in with the natural environment. Huge native stones were either mortared or dry stacked to create this. In some precarious places the stonemasons created half-arches to provide outlets for culverts or small bridges. Kresimir and the others worked even into the dark of night to set the arches' keystones. They used chisels and hammers to ensure that each rock used was a perfect fit.

Such labor kept both Bird and Kresimir busy, but they managed to meet for some visits. One had taken place at the 1929 season's end. They met at Logan Pass at the recently built turn-round. Its stone-walled rest area in the center was surrounded by 360 degrees of soaring mountain scenery. As they talked, they watched a massive grizzly forage across a long grassy slope, too far away to fear.

Watching the bear, Kresimir said, "It will snow soon, and he will sleep in his den until spring. Then he'll come out thin and hungry. He'll be cranky, too."

"I hope we won't all be that way come spring," Bird replied. Out of habit he scanned the higher areas for mountain goats and bighorn sheep.

Kresimir paced a few paces then stopped and turned to Bird. "Ah, my poems have found a publisher. And I finish my Ph. D. work in two years. Then I'll find a place to teach. How would you like to put in for a scholarship like I wrote to you about and be at the college or university where I teach?"

Bird rubbed his face in frustration. "That's a kind thought. I'd like to, but I don't know, Kresimir. You're just you. You're not responsible to anyone else and I'm sorry for that. But I have grandparents and a widowed mother and a foolish kid sister to think of. They need me at Evening Star. At least that's what my sister keeps insisting. Pop wanted us all there. I know that. We're to think of it as his legacy."

The poet nodded. "Don't wish for the kind of freedom I have, young Bird. But think long and hard. Think what you owe yourself. And you might do more for the family as a well-educated man. Keep the offer in your thoughts, but not for too long after I'm hired as a professor at some good school. Others want and deserve a chance to attend college as well."

~ ~ ~

Nora welcomed Dawn and Bird home in the late fall of 1932. They reported, more tired than jubilant, that work on the Transmountain Highway was over except for a few finishing touches. The great engineering feat would bring tourists in droves. Before that, there would be a great ceremony for the dedication of the historic accomplishment sometime in mid-summer.

"Finally," Rose crowed, "you'll be able to stay at home afterwards. Like Pop always wanted."

"Yes," Dawn murmured. "Now and always, I believe."

Nora gave Dawn a quick look. The woman she had raised looked thin and weary. Lines had formed around her eyes that looked almost as sad as they had during the year after Michael's death.

"Are you well, my treasure?" she asked Dawn.

"Just tired. I'll go to the house and lie down for a while."

Jim asked, "What do you hear from Heinrich? Will he be with us soon?"

Dawn shrugged without turning to face him. "I don't think so, Papa. His work for the government keeps him far away and so busy. I don't hear from him much anymore."

A moment of silence followed. "Well," Rose said, "he must be happy painting all the time and getting paid for it."

"I don't hear about it," Dawn repeated and left the cabin to go to the house built by her lost husband.

"Nice, Rose," Bird said, glaring at his sister. He picked up his duffel and headed after his mother.

Left with her grandparents, Rose stared at them. "What did I do?" she asked.

Nora addressed her directly: "Come for a walk with me, my girl. We've talked about what men and women do to make babies, but we've never talked so much about the love and loss parts of such things."

The two went out together. Left alone, Jim sighed. He hoped Nora could reach the girl using her hard-won wisdom about men and women. As for himself, he had only desired the Irish girl he'd loved since he'd come upon her when both were young, so long ago.

~ ~ ~

Nora steered Rose away from the cabin and onto the empty road toward Polebridge. They walked past golden aspen and red mountain maples and knee-high yellow dogbane. "I never spoke to you much about my husband who died in the mines."

Rose kicked a clod of earth out of their path. "He seems like someone from a different life you had a thousand years ago. I don't see much reason for you to tell me about him."

Nora flared a little with irritation. "You have yet to meet your first love, my girl. You never forget that person no matter whether he's a young boy or a man full grown. Mine was that last and he knew well what he wanted. There were no barriers for us. No one to be selfish about not wanting us to marry or keep us from finding happiness no matter what we'd suffered before we met. He was the father of my daughter who died so young." Her voice wavered as she turned her face away from Rose.

"But you fell in love again. Wasn't Grandpa Jim the love of your life?"

"Jim Li was the second true love of my life. He redeemed me as only someone who loved me could do. But if Tade Larkin had lived, I'd have spent my entire life with him. No man was ever more loved by a woman than Tade was loved by me. But he died. I was young. And I grieved for my lost husband as any woman would.

"Obstacles existed between Jim and me, him being Chinese and myself Irish. I'd been hurt by the world, by Tade's death and the mistakes I made when I was so confused and lonely. I kept Jim Li waiting a long time for an answer when he let me know he wanted me to be his beloved. Of course, by then I was as in love with him as he with me. I would have been so unhappy if I hadn't married him. I've been blessed by his devotion and courage. But at first I did think of how Tade would feel about my decision to marry a Chinese man."

"Well, but wouldn't your first husband have wanted you to be safe and happy?"

"I believed he would have. I like to think any man who loved his wife would want her cared for if he passed with her still a young woman such as I was."

"But Mama and Pop were so perfect together. Heinrich was just a friend. He'd stay here with her no matter what I think about it if it was real love." Rose stopped and studied the river and the bright, fluttering aspen on its banks. "Wouldn't he?"

"Heinrich is a gifted man, and he has his dreams. One is to be with your mother. But his art is to him a necessary thing. Perhaps even bigger than what Evening Star meant to your father. And your mother feels guilt about how Michael would feel about her remarrying, especially to a German. She also feels she neglected you, even while she had to be away working for all of us."

"But Pop was your son. Don't you want Mama to keep his memory sort of sacred?"

Nora took Rose by her shoulders. "Think about this, my girl. Your mother is a beautiful woman, still young enough to find a loving companion. Not the companionship of grown children turning toward lives of their own. Young enough to love a man and all that means. I was never so lonely as after Tade died and before I gave my heart to Jim Li. Think carefully before you contribute to the guilt she feels. It's a grave thing you're doing. Don't try to fit a human woman into the mold of a guilt-ridden, self-sacrificing saint."

"But, Pop—"

"Your father is dead. He cannot speak to us or hold us or contribute anything except old memories. Your mother and Heinrich are alive with all their futures before them. Perhaps they'll spend it here together or perhaps elsewhere. What I want most of all is Dawn's happiness."

They turned back to the cabin and walked all the way in silence as the temperature dropped.

~ ~ ~

Bird recognized Kresimir's distinctive handwriting with its big loops and flourishes. The envelope addressed to him felt thick. His mother had left it on the kitchen table. Bird lifted and hefted it in his hand. Kresimir had either written a long letter or had included some poems. That would certainly be a first. Bird smiled thinking of his friend.

He stood by the window. Late spring snow fell outside as it had since early morning. The sky cast a blush-tinted glow. The days had grown longer. He opened the envelope. No poems… it conveyed only news. But what news.

Kresimir had completed the work for his Ph.D. in Russian Literature earlier than expected. It certainly hadn't been difficult for the poet. That step out of the way, Kresimir applied to various universities and colleges. He'd negotiated with several of them, and had settled on taking a professorship at Georgetown University in Washington, D.C.

Alone in the room, Bird whooped. That brought Booster, thinking they were about to go outside for an adventure. "Not right now, boy," Bird said, moving from the window to sit by the table as he continued to read. Booster groaned and settled on the floor between Bird and the warmth coming from the wood stove. His old eyes remained on the reader.

Kresimir wrote that true to his word, he'd requested that if Bird performed well on entrance exams he should be admitted to the school and given work as Kresimir's student assistant. Kresimir had no wish to give up his poetry, so would need someone to help him with office and other work. "You have to come, my friend. I know how you dream of studying at a fine university. And I know you would be happy exploring and living in Washington, D.C."

Bird took a deep breath when he'd finished reading. This was exactly what he'd dreamed of. But could he leave the four people he loved so much to cope without him?

He'd give himself time to consider it. He slipped the letter into a drawer in his bureau. He wrote a quick note of thanks to Kresimir, saying he knew the risks of delay, but needed time to decide whether he could leave the others at Evening Star. He asked for six weeks.

He'd watched his mother after Heinrich stopped coming for visits and all but stopped writing. She'd lost the vital spark she had when she and

Heinrich arrived together after they'd closed the Sun Chalet. She seemed listless now. Had she sent Heinrich away because of her sense of duty to the ranch, because of Rose's objections to their mother's fondness for the artist?

~ ~ ~

Bird shared the news of Kresimir's success with the family, but didn't include his offer to Bird to come along to the nation's capitol. He didn't actually show them the letter. He explained that Kresimir had included some thoughts that seemed quite personal.

Bird turned irritable and restless as melting snow, stronger light, and the return of geese, ducks, songbirds, and new life appeared with deer, elk, and bears in the form of fawns, calves and cubs. The cattle dropped their contributions to the Evening Star herd. Bird kept to himself as much as he could except for continuing to study with his grandfather.

Rose and he finally tangled one day. She taunted him about not being happy he couldn't leave again to work on the Transmountain Highway. "You're being such a grouch because you have to stay here and you're sooooo bored. Poor Bird."

"None of us will be here all summer without a break," he said. The Park Service is calling some of us back to help get everything set for a big dedication ceremony in July. Everybody we know will be there. Well, I don't know about Heinrich. It depends on his job, I guess."

"I guess you'll be happy if Kresimir shows up," Rose said. "Who cares about Heinrich?"

"If you had eyes, you'd know that Mama does," Bird responded.

"Not as much as she cares about Evening Star," Rose shot back.

"Thanks to you and your childish jealousy, it's all she has left."

Rose threw a dish towel at him and slammed the back door as she stomped out.

Bird shrugged. He remembered Heinrich from the winter he stayed with them during the war. The man had seemed kind. Bird remembered the skates and how the artist had helped them learn to create their early attempts at pictures. If Dawn wanted to marry the German, Bird had no objections. He'd mourned his father after bringing his cold body up from the rocks. Bird had seen the destroyed, lifeless corpse. His father simply was no more. If his mother could move ahead with her life and find happiness in middle age, then she should.

He went to the cabin to visit with Grandpa Jim. Perhaps they could study together. Chinese was such a difficult language, but his grandfather wanted him to learn it so badly. And it might help Bird someday, although he wasn't sure how.

But Grandpa Jim talked to Bird instead about his future. They hadn't spoken of it so much before. He suggested they go back to Bird's house to speak in private.

When they arrived at the house, they built up the fire and sat together. "You are struggling with something, Bird. If it is what I suspect, you have been offered help toward an education by our friend Kresimir. Does he want you to study where he will be teaching?"

Bird's tense shoulders relaxed in his relief at being found out. "That's it, Grandpa. I've tried not to let it show how much I want to join him. I know I'd be making your lives harder if you don't have my help."

"Grandson, the world is complicated and varied. It will become more so. I feel the day will come when all of us at Evening Star will need help from a man with a fine education. Perhaps the world will need you. Go on our account as well as your own. We will find help with ranch work. We have before. Thanks to all your care of the cattle and horses we have some savings. There are so many boys coming with the CCC. Perhaps one will fall in love with the North Fork and be willing to hire on while you are studying."

They talked on until dinner. Bird still wasn't sure, though. There was Grandma Nora. And Rose. Could he betray them? They believed so firmly in Michael Larkin's dream of a secure life together on the North Fork of the Flathead River.

Chapter Twenty-Seven

July 7, 1933

Jim, Nora, and Rose arranged for the oldest son of a North Fork ranger to stay at Evening Star for ten days while they went by truck down the North Fork Road to Apgar. They planned to stay at their Lake McDonald cabin for a few days' fishing, then go up to see the dedication of the Transmountain Highway, to be officially named Going-to-the-Sun Highway on July 15.

When they arrived at Apgar, they found preparations in full swing for an outdoor dance that night. They'd heard that such dances took place every Saturday. CCC boys and road workers came down to Camp 1 headquarters from the farther camps to dance with local girls, and summer help arrived from as far away as Minneapolis to work in the Park as waitresses and shop clerks. The family knew of these dances, but Rose had never expressed any interest in going to one of them.

"Rose, I brought a couple of your good dresses. Why don't you wander on over to take part in the festivities?" Nora asked. "We'll follow behind you after a bit and find chairs along the edges to see that there's no trouble for you young girls. Make some new friends or meet up with some you know who have summer jobs. Isn't Patricia Reed working at Belton Hotel this summer?"

By the time strains of music drifted down to the beach, Rose took no more convincing. She put on a navy-blue dress that Nora had sewn for her, and a pair of pumps with low heels. Her black hair tumbled to her shoulders. She tied a navy-blue ribbon in a bow at the crown. Her natural high color and thick dark eyelashes showed her vibrant enough without make up. Nora and Jim both straightened with pride when she asked them how she looked.

Nora felt a catch in her throat. "I wish Sweet Grass and Beartracks, not to mention your father, could see what a beauty you are, my treasure. Some young CCC boy will try to carry you off."

Rose threw her arms around her grandmother. "Not a chance, Grandma Nora. I'll give anyone the brush off who'd try to take me away from you two and Evening Star."

Rose met Bird walking toward her as she walked from the beach cabin to the pavilion where dancing would take place. "Well, well." He gave her a brief hug and then stood back and whistled. "You've turned into a beauty. Be careful. The guys will be lined up to dance with you. Don't let it go to your head."

"Don't be goofy. Is Mama here?"

He reversed direction and fell into step beside her. "She will be in about an hour. We just finished cleaning after supper at Camp 1. Mama is helping with some last meetings about the ceremony. It's only a week away, you know."

They reached the dance platform. A band already played *Stormy Weather*. Young men and women moved together, with many more milling around the edges or standing still, their eyes following the dancers or checking new arrivals. Young men, in shirts and denim or khaki pants, hair slicked back, faces smoothly shaved, radiated restless energy.

When Bird stepped away to greet a friend, Rose noticed one of the CCC boys who scrutinized the girls clustered together in little groups was smiling at her. The young man's eyes were large and intense. She smiled back as a reflex. A friend nudged the handsome boy's arm and made a comment.

Without taking his eyes off Rose, the stranger shook off his companion and walked across the distance to her. He had a muscular build, was taller than she, but not by much. And he swaggered with a cocky, rolling gait. *Like he owns the place,* she thought.

By the time he reached her, she halfway regretted her encouraging smile. Too late. He already held out his hand. "Would you dance with me, Rose Larkin?"

She nodded and they climbed up the platform steps and started. She hadn't danced with anyone but local boys before. He smelled clean. She rested her left hand on his shoulder as he captured her right. The muscles of his shoulder felt tight and hard.

"How do you know my name?" she asked.

"From the CCC camp at Red Meadow up on the North Fork last year. Everybody knew who you were. You never even glanced at us slum guys. Never mind we're as American as you. Anyway, I've decided…"

"Decided what?"

"Everything. That I love you. That we'll get married. Everything."

She laughed. "You're pretty darned sure of yourself. I don't even know your name."

"Enrico Rossini. My friends call me Rick."

"Rossini? I can't be Rose Rossini. The whole thing's off."

They danced again and again. Rick established that she was Catholic. He told her about his family. "Everybody's from Italy. All from the same little town or close to it. We live in Little Italy now, in New York City. You'd swear some of my folks never left the old country. My mother, she's the tough one. Even my big brothers toe the line or they get smacked."

"She hits them?"

"If Papa's home she complains to him and he does it."

"Nobody smacks anybody at our house," Rose laughed, but she shuddered a little, too.

They talked and danced. At midnight, Bird appeared and tossed his head in the direction of the cabin, then glared at Rick. Rose bade her dancing partner a quick goodnight. "We'll probably see each other at the Dedication," she said.

"Count on it," was the self-assured reply.

Rose joined Bird who stood by with a half-grin. "You look stunned, kid," he said. "Do you like that character?"

"Well, I've never met anybody from New York before, have I?" she muttered, flouncing down to the beach ahead of her smirking brother.

~ ~ ~

The dedication ceremony was to be an impressive event according to Dawn and Bird. Both of them were assigned food preparation and the transporting of all that went with the lunch for dignitaries and visitors. Dawn would assist Head Cook Glenn Montgomery in organizing and readying food. They planned on twenty food lines to feed about 2500 people for a Fireman's Lunch. It would be served at noon before the scheduled dedication ceremony that would commence with a flag raising at 2:00 p.m.

Montgomery needed 500 pounds of red beans, 125 pounds of hamburger, 36 gallons of tomatoes, 100 pounds of onions, and 15 pounds of chili powder. The resulting chili simmered on four woodstoves in nine copper-bottomed washtubs for hours. Dawn and Bird, along with others assigned to assist, used long handled spoons and spatulas to keep stirring the aromatic food. It was hot work during the day, but cool night air made the workers more comfortable.

At midnight, Bird as truck driver, with Dawn as his weary passenger, carried the first batch of hot chili to Logan Pass. They unloaded it with help from workers brought up ahead of time and hung it over cook fires that would continue heating it through the night.

Head Cook Montgomery stayed below and put together a second batch that bubbled in more copper-bottomed wash tubs hanging over all four woodstoves for the rest of the night. As almost an afterthought he laid in additional hot dogs and more coffee than he'd first anticipated they'd need. Lunch would be served on paper plates.

During the week of preparations Dawn had reunited with Blackfeet friends from her earlier life near the Reservation. She visited with eighty-year-old honored guest Duncan McDonald, after whom Lake McDonald was named. Like her, Duncan was the offspring of a mountain man and an Indian woman. Others who came included Blackfeet interpreters Dick Sanderville and Pete Flint.

At their suggestion, Dawn was designated to stand by as a substitute interpreter if needed. She would wear her precious white buckskin dress. The thought of wearing that was a sharp reminder of happier days modeling for Heinrich Mann. As if on cue, one of the men mentioned Heinrich would be at the ceremony, arriving with his easel and other supplies in one of the trucks coming from St. Mary to the east. The Blackfeet would come at the same time, bringing their tipis, tipi poles, costumes, saddles, and tack for the horses. They would be transported to the ceremony by CCC drivers.

The Park Saddle Horse Company would supply over fifty horses for the pageant planned by the tribes. The Blackfeet had chosen this occasion to enter into a traditional peace ceremony with their ancient enemies, the Salish and Kootenai.

~ ~ ~

On Friday, July 14, Park Naturalists arranged a big flower stand showing flora in Glacier as it would appear to a driver starting at Belton and moving up the highway to Logan Pass. Cedar boughs added to the stand's soft look. No other decorations would be used in any part of the ceremony, except for two mounted white goats that would flank the speakers' platform.

Dawn took an afternoon break from endless preparations to walk over and study the flower stand. Banks of wildflowers rose up, including Glacier Lilies, the cheerful yellow flowers that spread in meadows and slopes all around the Pass. It had been a slow spring so they, too, had bloomed later than usual. Their petals swept back as if in an Alpine breeze. Glacier Lilies had been her favorites at Evening Star Ranch and the Sun Chalet.

Other flowers were arranged in the order of those seen from Belton: Arnica, Snow Cup Lilies, and Indian Paint Brush on up to the Pass. They mirrored the variety that spread like hanging gardens on the slopes and cliffs. As she admired the stand, a long line of trucks and cars pulled in from the St. Mary's.

Dawn watched as Blackfeet, some with familiar faces, some new to her, parked nearby and piled out to begin unloading the poles and coverings of their lodges. They'd brought everything needed, even firewood, and carried it to their camp on a slope of Pollock Mountain above the separate camps of the Blackfeet, Salish, and Kootenai. The Caldwells were among others who climbed out of the trucks. Heinrich, his tall, lanky frame unmistakable, stood looking over the Pass with them.

He straightened when he saw Dawn, and walked toward her as she waited. It suddenly struck her how often Heinrich had walked toward her: at the Sun Dance; in the hotel lobby in Washington, D.C., at the Sun Chalet; and so often at Evening Star. He came within two feet and stopped.

"I was told you would be here," he said. "How good it is to see you. I've missed you. I just couldn't—"

"I know. My letters must have seemed so dull compared to your art and seeing the Coast." She couldn't look into his eyes, instead gazed across the plunging slopes and soaring mountains.

"No, they weren't dull at all. But I couldn't be there with you. I've stopped painting murals for the government, but there are other opportunities in the offing. I should help the Caldwells, but could we talk later? Perhaps tomorrow after the ceremony? I know both of us will be occupied until it's over."

"Yes, I'd like that." Her eyes held his. He set down his ever-present sketch pad and took a step closer.

This time she walked the last steps to him. "I've missed you, too," she whispered as they reached out to each other and embraced.

Heinrich broke away first. "We have so much to talk about. I love you still." He picked up his things and walked away to join the Caldwells set up camp.

~ ~ ~

After Heinrich had gone, Dawn noticed that something had agitated both tribal members and the others across from her including the rangers, cooks, and assistants. She couldn't make out words but noted raised voices. She left the flowers and their peace and went down to join the others.

"There was an accident," Bird told her coming up from the kitchen to meet her. "One of the trucks carrying the Salish tipped over. Two men were killed. It's terrible, but the rest of the tribe talked it over and decided the Peace Ceremony must be honored. They're still coming. All of them. Even the family mourners. They plan to participate because it's so important."

"More death," Dawn murmured.

"It didn't happen anywhere near here, Mama," Bird said. "Not on this road. Accidents happen no matter where we are."

~ ~ ~

Dawn worked late into the evening helping to feed Blackfeet and Flathead tribal members as well as others who would be working next day. She oversaw the evening cleanup and finally had time to herself. She washed in the private tent assigned to her and tried to sleep but found she couldn't. She rose from her cot and walked out into the black night. Everyone had exhausted themselves and almost all had fallen quiet. She walked east across the area made ready for tomorrow's ceremony and passed the plaque that would be unveiled as a memorial to Stephen T. Mather, the founder of the National Park Service.

Dawn hadn't seen Heinrich since their meeting before the flower stand. As he predicted, both had been busy. She stopped to close her eyes and breathe in the cool air. All wasn't quiet under the great canopy of stars. She heard the breeze sighing, then from the camp on Mount Pollack a woman's keening, wailing in her sudden widowhood. Her husband had been one of those killed in the accident. Dawn felt the woman's sharp sorrow, the despair of fresh grief. She'd felt such fathomless grief at the loss of Michael.

But she understood at last that widowhood meant being left alone, but alive. Life. She'd known its best and its worst. She hadn't died with Michael. And now she had to think of how she could best spend the years left with her heart able to love again and her body still ready to respond to passion.

She heard the groans of another woman, one who'd hurt her back in the accident. Would healing occur and leave her whole again? Could Dawn function in the world that Heinrich offered her? Those wounded, but still alive, lived in a world of grandeur and beauty if able to recognize it.

A third sound drifted down from the camps. An infant crying for comfort. A baby. The circle of life continuing, eternal.

Bird had told Dawn how Rose flirted with one of the CCC boys at the dance last week. Had Rose grown into a woman? What might that change about her headstrong girl, so loyal to her dead father? She'd discovered that young men admired her. Would that lead Rose to more understanding of Dawn's love for Heinrich? Would it be possible for Rose to love something or someone more deeply than her devotion to Evening Star?

Bird might find love as well out in that big world he wanted to explore. His yearning would soon take him away to gain knowledge beyond what any of the rest except Jim Li could realize for themselves.

"Mama?" She turned away from the ragged peaks of the Garden Wall silhouetted against the sky. Bird appeared beside her. "I'm working all night. We'll be ready to feed the multitudes tomorrow."

"I couldn't sleep, but I think I can now."

Her son put his arm around her shoulder and squeezed a little. "I saw you talking to Heinrich. You know, you were a great wife to our father. If you want to be with the artist, it's fine with me. He's a good man. Anyone can see he loves you. And he cares about the Blackfeet and the mountains as much as you do."

"Thank you, son. But what about you? What decisions have you settled for yourself?"

"You know me well, Mama. I'm going to go to college next year where Kresimir is teaching. Washington, D.C. It's a dream come true."

"You have my blessing. I hope our paths don't take us too far from Evening Star."

"They might from time to time, but never so far that we can't come home if they need us."

Dawn reached to pat the firm young hand on her shoulder. What a young man's conviction he had. She knew that it is possible to go so far away that you can't return to your origins. It had happened to Heinrich. She hoped it would never happen to her or Bird.

She only answered, "No, of course, we'll always come when they need us."

~ ~ ~

On the 15th, rising at 5:00 a.m., Dawn paused to stroke the soft white buckskin of her dress. A memory struck her of the day she received the gift of it from Molly and Marissa. Images of that Sun Dance Ceremony followed, tumbling like a waterfall. She remembered it as the first time she'd felt complete: a true combination of white and Blackfeet in one whole woman. And she remembered her first sight of Heinrich, his long body hunched over his sketch pad while his hands flew over the paper, preserving it all before it vanished like the buffalo. He'd been so intent in his admiration of the pageantry, the procession of riders and people in regalia walking behind them. He'd been respectful to everyone there. He understood and loved it all with his artist's instinct for what speaks to the human spirit.

But for now there was much to do. She'd been freed from kitchen and food work to participate with the tribe. Their leaders had scheduled a general council for 7:30. Before the meeting, Dawn accompanied George C. Ruhle, the Park Naturalist, and Dick Sanderville to see the three tribes' campsites. The camps had been set up in separate areas with Alpine fir creating a natural hedge between the Blackfeet Camp and the others. Pointed sticks had been planted that separated the Blackfeet from those below. No peace had been made yet.

Dawn's heart lurched at the sight of the Blackfeet camp with its colorful lodges stretched in a long line, their traditional doorways facing the rising sun. Molly Caldwell embraced Dawn and beckoned the visitors inside to see the cooking fire and seating for family and guests. Drying meat hung across the center of the lodge.

All members of the three tribes, and several hundred early visitors, came to the great, solemn council. To her relief, Dawn didn't have to interpret since all three of the selected interpreters were present and able to carry out their assignments. But the others asked her to stay as her grace and beauty added to the solemn joy of the occasion. Everyone sat on benches with their tribes while the council began. The naturalist gave each leader a gift of Bull Durham tobacco. He addressed them all with the interpreters translating for the tribal members.

Ruhle began with words of welcome and sympathy for those who'd lost loved ones in the accident. He went on to describe the relationship of the Park Service to the Blackfeet, Salish, and Kootenai, and explained the ceremony and rehearsal to follow. Dawn felt the pre-pageant excitement running like a current through the tribal members. This would be a celebration of the wild freedom and spirit of the plainsmen such as had not been seen for decades. Dawn was again carried back to the Sun Dance; her heart thumped the drum beat of lost days.

When the council ended, Dawn rode with Ruhle to a hillside above the Pass to help him direct the peace ceremony rehearsals. She found herself thrilled by the traditional spectacle that was so much more exciting than she'd imagined.

As she rode back to the Pass, she saw busses and cars arriving at the parking area. She found Nora, Jim, and Rose. Bird arrived where they stood and there were happy embraces all around. Bird had to excuse himself to help with the food lines. As there were twice as many crowding into them than the 2500 expected visitors, he and the other workers were sorely needed. They were also grateful for the last-minute addition of hot dogs as the chili alone wouldn't have fed the multitudes.

After they ate, Nora and Jim wandered with Dawn and Rose, admiring the flowers and plunging St. Mary and McDonald valleys, and the peaks of the Garden Wall. "I had no idea," Nora murmured. "So, it all came to this. Was it worth it, I wonder…?"

Dawn knew what she was thinking. Michael seemed to be with them especially today. To them, the answer was a simple, firm, 'No.' Nothing would have been worth their loved one's life.

"Let's find places. The general seating area will fill up soon. Where's Rose?" Dawn asked as they found chairs as near the speakers' platform as they could.

"Flirting with that CCC boy she danced with Saturday night. His group will be singing this afternoon." Nora stood and waved to Rose, who came, turning back twice to speak to the CCC fellow with curly black hair.

The Dedicatory Ceremony started with the raising of the flag. It had taken twenty-two years to complete Going-to-the-Sun-Road. Dignitaries from the United States and Canada, senators and House members, state officials, representatives of the National Park Service and Bureau of Public Roads, all gave congratulatory speeches.

One moment that caused the Larkin and Li family members to reach for one another's hands came as the Glacier Park Superintendent read a letter from Harold Ickes, Secretary of the Interior. It read in part, "It is a magnificent job perfectly accomplished. Workmen who risked their lives daily on the faces of the steep cliffs that had to be conquered to make this modern trail deserve special honor for their share in the great undertaking."

The Blackfeet Tribal band played after the unveiling of a plaque to the memory of Stephen Mather. The CCC chorus sang two songs. There were more speeches, then at last, the pageantry of the three tribes making peace.

Dawn had slipped away from Nora, Jim, and Rose to stand with first Park Naturalist Ruhle, and then the leaders of the three tribes. Each introduced himself and his people in sign language, which the interpreters translated into English. During the ceremony Dick Sanderville, known to the Blackfeet as Chief Bull, interpreted more sign talk to the crowd who were spellbound by the first important peace made between the three tribes of hereditary enemies since 1868.

The ceremony began, and she felt the drumbeat of her heart quicken. Scouts in advance of a Blackfeet war party approached the Pass from the east. With excitement, the scouts sighted a party of Flatheads in the west,

The Blackfeet continued forward and placed a bent stick decorated with tobacco and horsehair at the very top of the Pass. Sanderville explained that had the stick been straight, undecorated, and pointed, it would have sent a message of war.

The scouts went back to the larger body of mounted Blackfeet, leaving the approaching Flathead, scouts to examine the stick, talk its significance over with each other, then go back to report what they'd seen to their leaders. Next the Salish and Kootenai approached on foot, the Blackfeet on their horses, all chanting. The chiefs communicated in sign, the Blackfeet dismounted, and the tribes formed two parallel lines. The ancient enemies knelt to face each other. The pipe was produced and passed from right to left down the line, each man smoking.

When the pipe smoking concluded, the Blackfeet rose and passed on the highway into the land of their former enemies. The Salish and Kootenai passed to the east into the land of the Blackfeet. As all this happened, the women and children stood on the slopes of Pollock Mountain, echoing the yells of the warriors. All returned to the Pass and began the joyous celebration of peace, beginning with the Grass Dance.

Although the dancing would continue on into the night, there was a pause while the dedicatory ceremony concluded with the singing of "America" and "Montana."

Photographers, both professional and amateur, and Heinrich with his ever-present sketch pad memorialized the event. Afterwards he would be especially proud of the sketch he turned into a painting of the Blackfeet Two-Guns-White-Calf whose profile would later appear as the Indian on the Buffalo Nickel.

Dawn intended to hang back, but Molly and other grandmothers and aunties urged her to dance with them. The spectators drifted away; Mama Nora, Papa Jim, and Rose waved farewell. Only Bird on clean-up duty and Dawn were left.

And Heinrich.

Dawn kept dancing, gliding then moving so straight, with such dignity. Her white buckskin dress glowed in the golden hour of late afternoon sun not quite ready to give way to twilight. Still the artist sketched, his eyes finally singling her out. A sense of her own power filled her. Not power over her grown children, or over Heinrich. Heinrich had his own power when he held his brush. But she felt herself his equal. She'd loved Michael, but he'd always made the decisions. Even when she'd been right, he'd made the decisions. She'd been a girl and young woman with him. Now she was a woman of strength and virtue.

She stopped dancing and stood before Heinrich. He lowered his sketch pad.

"Walk with me," she said.

They moved away from the fires and people moving to clean and restore order to the Pass. They walked to the dark plunge of St. Mary Valley.

"I want to marry you," Heinrich said. "And to live most of our time at Evening Star… but at times I'd like you to travel with me."

"As your muse?" Dawn smiled.

"Not just that. You are a woman of strength. I want you to love me, accompany me when you wish, miss me when you can't. I want you to tell me when I'm painting well and when you feel something should be better. I want to help at the ranch, but I'm not a rancher."

"I know. You're an artist. I want to be beside you whenever I can. I've missed you so much. You put bright color into my life. It's felt so gray without you. Even at Evening Star."

"And Rose?"

"Oh, I think Rose is learning how a woman's heart may surprise her."

"So, I will ask again. My beloved woman, will you share your life with me?"

Dawn took a deep breath. "Yes. I want to be with you. I can't imagine another who would understand the things I honor and treasure as much as you do. And most of all, I honor and treasure you."

"How far I have traveled to hear you say that."

Dawn reached up to embrace her future, and the man who would be by her side to share it.

~ ~ ~

That night she lay in her tent, considering her life since the night she'd watched stars become constellations outside her bunkhouse window, and vowed to be a bridge between the white and Blackfeet worlds. But she realized she'd know many others who became bridges: her natural parents, Beartracks Benton and Sweet Grass Braider; her foster parents Irish Nora and Chinese Jim Li; Kresimir Karpov, the Russian poet who escaped a revolution to add to America's culture. And, perhaps most important, her beloved Heinrich Mann who made others aware of the beauty of the Blackfeet, her mother's people and their ancient culture. She felt happy that her loved ones were safe in America. They'd won the War to End All Wars. At peace, she closed her eyes and slept.

-THE END-